C000068125

Auntie-Uncle Moon is everyone's confessor: controlling tides, and ovulation, waxing and waning over space and time while the tectonic plates of people's lives shift and collide. A new writer with an absorbing tale, Paula Coston gives us a wonderfully contemporary book with a very contemporary voice.

Jamila Gavin, Whitbread award-winning author of *Coram Boy*, novel and show in London and on Broadway

Paula Coston addresses what will, in time, be seen as one of the central themes of our time: what becomes of the woman who wanted to be a mother but it didn't work out? Considering that 1:5 women born in the 60s hasn't had children, and that it may rise to 1:4 for those born in the 70s, this is a question on which our culture is in collective denial. Not everyone facing middle age without a child chose that outcome and indeed, some of the choosing and not-choosing is rarely clearcut. So it is for Martine, the novel's protagonist. *On the Far Side, There's a Boy* is an important novel which finally fleshes out the interior world of the 'nomo' (not-mother) and shows how the themes of motherhood-or-not surface in unusual ways in the lives of modern women. She has set a high benchmark, but I hope it encourages other nomos to write their novels too – we need our stories to be heard!

Jody Day, Founder, Gateway Women;
www.gateway-women.com

On the Far Side, There's a Boy

To Angie Angus

With all warm wishes,
Paula (Coin)

On the Far Side,
There's a Boy

On the Far Side, There's a Boy

Paula Coston

Winchester, UK
Washington, USA

First published by Roundfire Books, 2014
Roundfire Books is an imprint of John Hunt Publishing Ltd., Laurel House, Station Approach,
Alresford, Hants, SO24 9JH, UK
office1@jhpbooks.net
www.johnhuntpublishing.com
www.roundfire-books.com

For distributor details and how to order please visit the 'Ordering' section on our website.

Text copyright: Paula Coston 2013

ISBN: 978 1 78279 574 2

A CIP catalogue record for this book is available from the British Library.

Design: Stuart Davies

Printed and bound by CPI Group (UK) Ltd, Croydon, CR0 4YY

We operate a distinctive and ethical publishing philosophy in all
areas of our business, from our global network of authors to
production and worldwide distribution.

Dedication:

To the many I've loved, the few I've lost and the one
I never found.

'There is nothing you can think that is not the moon.'
Matsuo Basho, 17th-century Japanese poet

1 Martine

Martine Haslett stoops, hands on knees, her salt and chilli-brown hair any old which way, watching the chameleon she bought recently. She's thinking for both of them, *We're cornered in a landscape. We shouldn't be where we are.* More words rise up, from a fund of feeble cracks. *Once they made a joke about a chameleon but nobody could see it.* Her lined brow crimps, narrowing her eyes down to black dots.

She sprinkles brown crickets under the heat lamps, into Sancho's cage. He clambers through the foliage, they jump pointlessly about and he shoots his tongue and whisks them in. He sees the water gun in her hand, creeps forward along a branch and averts his grey-green head in anticipation, shutting his limpet sockets and opening his mouth. The warm jet hits it at the corner. It closes, opens, closes on the stream. His cage is wedged into the railway-carriage squeeze of the kitchen. He was a momentary indulgence to delay important changes.

On 15 November last, her mother said her usual 'Love you,' as if ending one of their phone calls, and turned over in bed, away from her. A statement of closeness, then one of separation. She was eighty-seven. With her gone, Martine has been shuffled up to eldest in the family. It's a promontory, further from some people than she'd like.

She activates her smartphone on the square of kitchen table, pushing on her varifocals.

An email rebukes her. 'Martine, I need a decision. Jocelyn Teague.'

There are new texts, too.

Friend Leanne says, 'Going into the rush hour grind. Talk about it at Stew n Pickle tomorrow night?'

Matthias says, 'IM ON THE TRAIN!!! Retreat OK. Have prayed over peanut fudge and posted.'

Pearl says, 'Remember what my feminine side did to me. Dont rush in.'

Ali says, 'Moored by a pub, drinkin & thinkin that u shd take yr time.'

The texts take Martine back to the email from Jocelyn Teague and the decision she hasn't made.

She murmurs, 'All thanks but let me be.'

Her eyes turn to the window, to the waning moon above the city. *Years ago,* she reminisces, *I was Martine the scientist and it was just a turning rock, scientifically explicable; now it seems like a strip torn from a message, fluttered my way.* She's discovered now that life is one part fact and one part fantasy, like the moon.

The correspondence that also hangs over her is in the guest room. It's in a large, grey-lidded carton, somewhere among her mother's barely used golf clubs, two cases of her mother's redundant clothes, the dog bed holding the pointless dog toys, bowls and lead and all her mother's secret trophies, wrapped up in paper in their box.

She re-read the letters only last year. Most envelopes are empty, the contents unfolded, their crinkles spread. The letterhead announces 'InterRelate' and under it, there's that jumpy English typing. The Sinhala script is filigree, the foreign paper slight; staples, not even rusted, join the pages in one language to the pages in the other. There's a blue manila wallet full of sheets; also, three unfoldered letter bundles, labelled. There are other documents and messages as well. She sometimes wonders why she's kept them, chiding herself with, *As if the past, like them, is solid.*

Of course she doesn't have the emails from the crisis of last spring, the pinged-off words whose sting will never leave her: 'How dare you neglect me, fail me, lose me? Just when I thought I'd got you, why weren't you there – not least to help me with the fact that you weren't there?'

If she says yes to Jocelyn Teague she'll have to clear the carton, find it a new place out of her eyeline. She moves to her bedroom. She leaves the door ajar and switches on a lamp. She climbs on to the white IKEA four-poster, swinging her legs up, sinking her head back on the pillows. So much to recover from back then, let alone since. Among the papers in the box she recalls that there's a postcard somewhere, an ordinary view of an English country market, and on the back her mother's round hand, unhurried, as if the two of them had all the days in the world. But it's Mum's real voice she needs, a warm hand between the shoulder-blades, a steer to some new way.

The city glows between the undrawn curtains. Their pattern of stems and leaves writhe in the moonlight over their folds: paper-chase creeper; *Mussaenda frondosa*, to a tropical botanist. She turns her head, staring at her wardrobe with its tall white doors to nowhere, and thinks of its high shelf. If she agrees to Jocelyn Teague, she could stow the carton there.

* * *

1982–1983

In 1982, Martine felt fine: happy and fine.

An ordinary day back then found her dotting about in a seminar room, ignoring the rubbing of her left high heel and resigned to the little comedy of her stubby darting body, she and assistant Pippa arranging chairs and putting out dry-wipe pens at the whiteboard, notepaper for the students on the tables. Her disobedient, mud-toned hair caught inside her shirt collar as she wrote up 'Welcome to "Identify, Analyse, Create"', adding her name with the expected naff-but-disarming smiley face. Teachers sleepwalked in from their London working days and sat with their friends as close to the back as they could. From the sidelines she kept up an intent, unwavering smile, welcoming them with rum jokes about school life. Her voice alto with a hint of lisp, fluid with saliva, a thing men seemed to like.

She gave them a paired exercise, then pinballed between the tables registering the raised voices of the baffled and the belligerent and the mutters of the lazy. Some had been sent by their senior managers, some really wanted new skills.

'The secret,' as Martine would remind her team, 'is to ration your speech, to let the students talk.'

She cajoled the argumentative with teasing or a question. Each student she had down as a different challenge.

Soon she announced a movie. Popcorn went round, to some giggling. She flipped off lights and the group slumped, relieved to be passive for a while.

'You'll see a total lunar eclipse,' she explained. 'Afterwards, we'll talk about two or three things about it that you could ask children to identify; one that they could analyse; and one that you could ask them to create. Remembering,' she added, 'that "creation" can mean hypothesis.'

She switched on the film. The captured eclipse would turn from penumbral, then partial, to total, then maximum, stages that a class of teenagers could break down. On the screen a silver-rimmed moon flicked on, stamping the darkness, and the time-lapse sequence started.

In Martine's early decades, like everyone she'd got scars. She'd lost her father to America as a child; coped with her mother coping; was kept prisoner by someone for five whole days in her mid-twenties; and said goodbye to several lovers, one someone more special. These were her seas and craters, over time giving her her smile nearly as unchangeable as the moon's.

On the screen now, shadow overtook the 2D lunar circle, progressing. Then the player rattled and chewed to a halt. Martine tried to fix it; two teachers rallied to her, but failed to help.

She used the phone in the room to contact assistant Pippa.

The voice grumbled, 'Tell me how much you need me.'

Martine said patiently, 'Please, Pipsqueak, get one of the

technicians.'

'I'm your flipping saviour, aren't I?' Pippa said.

'Meanwhile, bring me overhead transparencies and pens.'

'"Thanks, Pipsqueak," I hear you say,' said the remorseless Pippa. '"And thank you, God, that Pipsqueak can multi-task."'

Martine grinned. Pippa was needy; she'd give her flowers or something after a few more incidents like that.

This was Martine at the work she loved: people who were problems, and smoothing them out.

But in 1982, something new started.

One Sunday in March, after a three-bottle lunch at her best friend Ali's, Martine shuffled the Sunday papers. 'Where's the *Observer* supplement?'

Ali, a statuesque blonde who alternately pestered or stung her friends out of love, pestered, 'Tell me who your latest man is.'

Martine said, 'There's something I want to cut out,' but Ali said, 'Answer the question,' and she said, 'Nobody you know. Nobody *I* know, come to that.'

Ali frowned.

Sprawled on the floor still searching Martine said, 'Men are my colour supplement: I'm not really fussed if there isn't one, although of course I'd prefer ... And where the bloody hell's the colour supp?'

Weeks later, on Friday 6 April, Martine had finished work. Gusts of wind tangled her hair the colour of leaf mould as she rushed to Harry her newsagent's booth and bought the *Evening Standard* news of the Falklands War Cabinet, *He's a Tease!* and her regular *Time Out*.

She fluttered *Time Out* with a sideways look. 'If you read this, you'd get out more.'

Harry laughed. She hurried off for Bernard Street and down into Russell Square tube.

At 27 Aldebert Terrace, Stockwell, a tall, Victorian house in a row of others, she scaled the stairs to her maisonette, unlocked the door and hung her coat. She tucked the heels of her ankle boots round a Habitat stool at the red Corian breakfast bar, with Joe Cocker rasping from her new CD system and the telephone pulled towards her, and a Cinzano and soda and her Neville Brody calendar and Filofax to hand. With *Time Out* open, she made a spate of phone calls, 'When? OK,' 'We'll meet there, shall we, loverboy?', bantering, agreeing dates with friends and scribbling them in her diary. The full moon was at her window when she got up to clean a smudge from one of her mirrored kitchen cabinets on the loosened cuff of her power shirt.

But that night in *Time Out*, she also read the Lonely Hearts pages. 6 April marked the peak of her ovulation. She was indifferent to the moon back then; all the same, like a woman from an unlit tribe her body responded to it. Its complete, ovoid light dragged at her left ovum and floated it into her peritoneal space, urging her cells towards something her mind wasn't even aware of. Her fingers were drawn to even more slippery pages than just the Things to Do, Places to Go. The Lonely Hearts pages, there to be stroked and turned.

She limited herself to one ad, responding with a letter. In the photo she sent, a hand was pulling her up onto a stage. She wore a lace blouse with puff sleeves over the broadness of her shoulders; a low bodice beneath it enclosed a boyish bust. Her skirt was full and gauzy, one arm hoicking up a handful, hurrying as usual, exposing a dimpled knee. There were balloons onstage, daubed with male nudes, and in the background a line of sequined figures of some gender or other. She was scrunching up her near-black flakes of eyes and smiling, as she so often does.

She chose only one ad to reply to because she worked, at the London College of Education, more than full-time. Monday evenings were filled with late meetings, followed by swimming at the nearby public pool. Tuesdays, she usually visited friends in

Pimlico. Wednesdays were often a work friends' night out. Thursdays, swimming again. Fridays and Saturdays meant a party or a club. Sundays, a social lunch or an outing. Thursday was the only dating slot left.

The man from the ad wrote back. On meeting him, she thought, *He sniggers too much*. But after that she saw others. Brian talked dirty, tasting of lychees; Ben sanded her like timber; when Oliver undressed, she ejaculated violently; there were bruises on Faruq's thighs that had an intriguing texture; Si made her orgasm with a sinuous big toe. Each time she took her watch off, but not her precious armlet. This secret token marked the fact that sex was the one thing she was lyrical about.

À Bordeaux, off St Martin's Lane. Lautrec prints and wine racks, guttering candles stuck on oak barrels. It was a rainy day in August. People criss-crossed shaking out umbrellas, carrying filled glasses. Her work friends Claire, Leanne, Lesley and Pippa surrounded her table, gabbling mock-advice. Beneath a jade-green satin sleeve, her armlet circled her bicep. Her hair was tightly permed, taming its scattered life.

'You've given me the benefit of your piss-dom. Now bugger off,' she growled.

They reeled off with laughed goodbyes.

Waiting, she kept turning her eyes on the doorway, and suddenly her half-brother banged through it. He cradled a box: he made deliveries back then. He loomed there turning his long, rain-shedding muzzle, then side-stepped behind the bar: he'd seen her, not seeing she'd seen him.

He leaned towards the bar boy, mouthing 'Sister'.

She distracted herself by lining up each new male arrival with mental portraits of Lucho from university, Angus from the drug squad, diamond broker Patrick, and Fred, Freddy to her, the one of them who'd been significant enough to infantilise his name.

The date with his red book came. She stayed with him, and

7

Jonas left instead.

She invited Jonas to Stockwell.

He'd set foot in England fourteen months before, thirty he was then. His excuse for leaving Chicago and their shared father was finding his roots; things hadn't worked out with some girl he'd met on the plane; he'd contacted Martine almost straight away; but it was her mother who'd managed to overlook Verdon Haslett's abandonment, taken in Jonas and let him stay. These days, when Martine saw them together she'd catch Jonas frowning protectively at her mother's fragile-looking kneecaps in the slacks she'd taken to wearing and think afresh, *He's become Mum's son.*

The moon was piercing a window again. Whiffing of sweat and cheap deodorant, Jonas shambled about her flat startled by the mirrors multiplying his image. Martine plundered the fridge for wine, uncorked it.

She said, 'New jacket. Members Only. All that shine!'

Her mother had bought it. Jonas's gaze took off.

She'd looked forward to seeing him. On the kitchen counter she'd laid out chicken pieces, garlic, lemons and the other raw ingredients, and now she was trying not to look as Ali said she often did, already wanting to clear the table and wash up.

'Dinner was at seven, right?' said Jonas.

'You want to cook for Mum,' she said.

'You're giving me a lesson?'

Martine said, 'I saw you in À Bordeaux,' and Jonas said 'Mom has a cold' at the same time.

'When?'

'Wine bar, last Thursday.' She ducked into the peppers charring under the grill. Her message, why he was there, was, 'There's no need to say more.'

He sniffed, 'You brought it up.'

She said, 'I'll tell Mum when I find someone.' Smiling, she

passed him the wooden spoon and a decoy question. 'How about your love life?'

On a reflex, he blurted some dating details. They sounded thin to her ear.

The letters that haunt her were spawned by Jonas, she used to think.

One night she was in The Wellington, in a booth.

'What's your house like?' the man was asking.

It was a dull question, but his jacket sleeves, turned back to an orange lining, showed a forearm with a promising thicket of black hair.

She was rambling, '*Boudoir*... bed. Painted and gilded it myself... It's...'

His eyes rested on her mouth. 'Madame, are you making me a proposition?'

Suddenly she took in a gust of sweat, and smelt Jonas, definitely Jonas, arriving behind her with another boxed delivery.

Catching her half-brother at the corner of her eye, she tipped forward and away. 'Let's go.'

A Thursday that December. Charing Cross Road, the rumble of traffic, the tramping of crowds. The moon once more hung over the city, on the wane. Martine had just met Gerry Taylor. Good-looking and intelligent, *Small feet,* she'd noticed, but scorned the thing about shoe size, so they were moving on from a pub, letting the door go on the shouted conversations, cigarette smoke cooked with beer. She was laughing, her face flushing, knowing that it was.

The lanky Jonas suddenly materialised, across from them on a corner by the green man. When he saw them he tipped off the pavement, and a cab nearly hit him. He'd obviously been loitering on purpose.

Gerry stopped by a theatre, lighting a cigarette. Her eyes jumped over him: preppy; nipples hard as tackheads through that sweater. As they chatted, he nodded vaguely at her gloved hands like beaks, opening and shutting: as usual she saw her ridiculousness, but felt fine.

Gerry moved off at last. She steered them into a shopping street and spoke to him without turning, bowling along ahead of him, trusting he was there. Along the shopfronts, swags of coloured Christmas lights painted out the grime around each windowframe, a rolling purified filmstrip of her beloved London. Then she saw Jonas, still walking the pavement opposite.

'We could find a...' she started.

Gerry interrupted, 'Everywhere's busy near Christmas.'

Martine saw that Jonas had been diverted by a jogger with a false white beard, a Christmas pudding in his hand. She guided Gerry into an alley with a bar. Jonas stumbled past, oblivious. It didn't help: minutes later, Gerry made excuses and left.

Jonas had been a draftsman before he'd lost his job in Chicago. His mind worked in lines, making intersections, and Martine guessed that it had occurred to him that from her college and its nearest Underground station, Russell Square, the Piccadilly line ran her direct to Leicester Square. That there it was crossed by the Northern line, where she could change trains to hurry home. Covent Garden was too close to work for dating, but she could emerge at Leicester Square: the network of streets between the Square and Cambridge Circus was perfect dating middle ground.

Smart guesswork, she admitted. She imagined Jonas systematically scoping the bars and pubs. Her thoughts circled Gerry Taylor, the preppy journalist who'd got away. She suspected Jonas's stalking had transferred itself to pressure on her, indirectly putting Gerry off. She wrote a personal ad for her escapee in *Time Out*, and he rang up.

On a night in January 1983, Martine kept Gerry Taylor waiting. Her umbrella blocked the rain-etched moon. When she got to À Bordeaux, he bought them lagers at the bar.

'"Reported missing in action."' He smirked at her ad, which he'd marked with a circle, one hand cupping her elbow. "More coverage wanted."'

She shook her head, rueful. 'Crude come-on.'

While Gerry was at the cigarette machine, the Aussie bar boy said, 'Dunno if I should mention. A bloke left these.' He pushed two book jackets towards her. 'Said, ring him if I saw you.' They were the covers of her books, *Research Methods in Education: A Student Guide* and *Training: Structure v. Process*. He grinned. 'That's you.'

She felt the blood rushing to her face, reclaimed her author mugshots and stuffed them in her bag.

In her mind's eye she saw Jonas and Mum's life together. Flying lessons from Mum so they could talk about horizon lines (Jonas had wanted a pilot's licence when he'd lived in Chicago). Companionship, Jonas's gift to Mum. Martine was glad they had each other; but still cursed, *I'm being besieged again.*

She had to get Gerry home. As she held a cab door open, he paused to tread a cigarette into the pavement. She visualised Jonas somewhere across the rainy street, reflective jacket jazzing from the theatre billings round him. He might have harassed her into this, but surely he'd want the best for her and hope that things went well.

2 The object

While Martine skirts her decision for Jocelyn Teague, the object of it is currently using an iPad. Skyping could alert the warders, as they're nicknamed, so the silence of Facebooking is safest – once the warders have gone to bed themselves. The object's woodsmoke fingers tap, messaging in the shadows on the lower bunk bed. The object's neon wristband glows, keys and feathers hanging from it. The bed occupant overhead jerks and rolls about to iPod beats as heavily as a mammoth in a sack.

The first Facebook message to be sent is for Luna. Luna is Sailor Moon's talking cat, *Sailor Moon* being the best anime in the whole galaxy of Japanese anime, so Luna is natural code for best friend.

'Been too long. Whatcha doin out there. While I'm stuck here.

'There's no wifi in this building and they've confiscated our mobiles and they ban the internet. But yesterday they took us out and you know me I got a bit lost and suddenly a phone shop. Bought a dongle (the same word, weird in English innit). So the others envy me and hate me. Think I'll call them the Dead Moon Circus, like in *Sailor Moon*.

'I'm swallowing the nothing English food and trying to be nice by laughing at the DMC's lame jokes. I know, I know, nothing makes me see funny.

'Write soon.'

The message gets posted, sent.

The object's dark eyes find an email from the family. 'Are you still not getting these, precious? Make sure you make the most of this experience.' Reading, the feathered head ducks, as if fending off a blow. 'What's been sorted for the 15th? Have they found you someone? Reassure us.'

The object intones a silent mantra, useful for anxiety. *Marche, liement, en garde. Croisé, coupé, doublé. Sixte, quarte, octave, septime.*

The fingers handle the doorkeys on the wristband, chinking them like a rosary, one by one.

Put on a brave face.

Fingerpads slide and tap again. 'There's plenty of time. Stop stressing. It's OK.'

* * *

Martine
1983

Back in her maisonette, Martine was conscious of Gerry Taylor's hand round the coffee mug. Smoker's fingers, manicured. His arm trailed along the back of the Sottsass sofa.

'So.' He laid one casually bent leg over the other.

Martine's pulse skittered. She sipped her coffee.

A flukeish find, she considered. *Catalogue handsome: lathed features, ice blue eyes, a promising physique.*

'Tell me what you've been doing since I saw you.'

For some reason she told him about her latest paper, her big-thumbed hands chopping air, trying to stifle the internal giggle, *Ali would probably say I look as though I'm already raring to remake the bed.*

Abruptly there was quiet, Gerry looking amused and baffled.

Martine flirted, 'Any dream dates – apart from ours?'

'Tell me about academe,' the journalist in him said smoothly. 'Why teach teachers when you could teach kids?'

Martine said, 'Done that. But once you've got the knack, don't you find you want to move on? And I still do it, kind of. Teach children by proxy.'

'The refuge behind the lens,' Gerry murmured.

'Anyway, teachers are just big kids, like us.'

'But who teaches you?' wondered Gerry.

Martine launched into a jittery tale. 'The other day, a lovely man was telling me his lesson plan. Another teacher piped up

and accused him of stealing hers. And before I could call time
out, they were more or less playground fighting. I had to comfort
him.'

'But who looks out for us, if we're such saviours of
humanity?' asked Gerry, which disorientated Martine. 'Or what
if we're not?' he carried on. 'Who saves us from ourselves?' He
was leaning forward, watching her. 'You seem different this time.
More human. Nervous. Nicer.' She was startled. He plonked his
mug on the low table. 'Would you comfort me if I seemed in
distress?' She laughed, a thick sound she hadn't heard before.
'It's hard on these assignments,' he said, his smile fading. 'When
I was in the north last week, I cried.' She couldn't see where this
was going. 'I was moved by the bombings. Not at the victims'
plight, I'm ashamed to say, but... I was just... terrified, frankly.'
Now Gerry was grinning, blinking down at the carpet.

Martine scooched to her seat edge.

'I don't think I can go back there,' he said.

Martine felt something unexpected.

She said, 'Are you all right?'

'I don't think I can go back there,' he repeated.

Martine put her hand out. 'Come with me.' What she meant
was, 'Let me help you.'

Gerry rose woodenly. She started the usual route march down
the corridor. Trembling, her hands turned on the lights: half-
spheres of milky glass, imitations of the moon, and more as they
tramped downstairs.

In her bedroom Martine baulked, oddly wary of his reaction
to the crimson alcove with its gilded, built-in bookshelves
arching over the mound of the velvet-covered bed. It had often
raised a laugh, but he slipped in past her without sound and
began undressing. Her body fluttered. She fumbled with her
dress and tights and couldn't think where to leave things. When
she pulled out of her bra, he was already naked.

He was almost hairless, a lovely phantom female quality, she thought. The penis was uncircumcised and tall. He tipped her onto the bed. If she was to help him, he couldn't take charge. They lay touching at the knees. She stroked him. She tried to slide an arm under him, but found no gap. She licked his jaw, tasting his aftershave in a draught of cigarette breath, then slid down, lips pinching each bone of the ribcage, and moved onto his pelvis, sucking in the leather-musk of soap.

He shrugged away. A manicured hand passed the pimples of her breasts, her fleshy hips and pelvis, her chunky, waxed calves, then just as her mouth went to his face again, he suddenly knelt up. He pastry-rolled her onto her side, slipping between her legs.

She wanted to ask again, 'Are you OK?'

He wouldn't let her hold him.

His penis riffled her labia and broke into her cunt. He glided in. They rowed together. Sometimes his eyes went to her groin to check she was keeping up.

Without warning he said 'Now!', and she mouthed, 'Oh, please!', and he spasmed, then slithered out. Her vagina throbbed, too late.

He hopped out of bed, fishing a pack of Camels from his jeans, his arse unbothered by her stare. Lighting up, he lay against the pillows. She felt held open. Sex was her unscientific outlet, a nearness to manhood so intense that it couldn't be dangerous. It was her far side – not her dark side: some friends could see that, under certain conditions. This was her portion that stayed unseen.

Gerry blew smoke at the ceiling. 'Feel better after. Thanks for that.'

She snorted silently, *Sex isn't a kind of medical treatment.*

'Basically, I'd like to do nothing but this.'

She teased, 'Have a lot of sex, do you?'

'Not sure how much is a lot.' His face was humourless, eyes squinting against the smoke. 'There's a neighbour, a nurse, who helps me out.'

She blinked. 'But you're trying to find someone supportive, to be with for a while.'

'Oh I don't know,' he said. 'Don't want reforming, that's for sure.' He yawned. 'Had a girlfriend once who tried that.' His arm slipped under her shoulders. 'D'you mind if we go to sleep?'

And then they nestled, his lap cupping her body, his balls rolling gently under her, and it was a novelty, because men usually went home. His form melted into relaxation, expelling noisy gases, and she stifled chuckles. Maybe, despite the countersigns, all this with her was what he sought.

When she dressed in the morning, his confession of weakness lingered with her, still massaging her need to offer help. She agreed he could leave later, latching the door on his way out.

In the kitchen, she left a note. 'I'm sure you will go back. Good luck in Sri Lanka. Help yourself to breakfast… Is it me, or did we make a connection? … Won't bother you again – unless you want to be bothered. If so,' and gave her number.

That evening the note had vanished.

She found it late the next night, in the bin she was emptying out.

In a reflex she rang her mother, then realised it was gone midnight. 'You were up because the phone went.'

'Ho-hum. Spoilt my punchline as usual.'

Her mother didn't need to ask how she was. She talked about a new neighbour, her day's shopping trip and Jonas, all with a ringing cheeriness.

While her mother's voice murmured, Martine drew back the sleeve of her kimono and pulled at the links on her armlet. She'd hoped she could take it off, maybe give blind dating a break. She felt the stitch-like pain that meant her return to egg production. Through the window behind her the moon was in its fullness yet again, still a teaching aid, no more. Meanwhile her mother droned like honeybees in summer.

Abruptly she heard her say, 'What about Jonas? Tum-tum.

D'you think he'll ever get the work he wants? I'm not even sure he's looking.'

'I could try to pull a few strings,' said Martine. The balled-up note for Gerry was scratchy in her fist. 'I know people – if Jonas wants to work in London.'

'That'd be great, love. He might let you.'

'D'you talk to him about Dad?' Martine urged.

Her mother hurdled this with 'Of course not,' and reverted to Jonas. 'Speak to him. I'm sure he's still up somewhere.'

Martine declined. He'd only refuse and pass a message: that was all he ever did.

People invent patterns. Martine began to spot Wyn Davies wherever she was in college: the library, the cafeteria queue, on the stairs, always wearing something bright, like a handwave. The teacher she'd mentioned to Gerry. In the staff lounge, where he shouldn't even have been, she sought a seat, and the red-shirted Wyn was the first person out of a chair.

'Crossword?' he sighed.

He flung her *The Times*, and a page spilt out, and a boy's face came towards her, a dark face, captioned 'Sponsored child, Peru'.

The sell line read, 'Would you like to get to know him – and help him at the same time?'

The charity offered a geographical menu: Africa, Indonesia, El Salvador, Sri Lanka. She hooked onto the last place on the list.

It offered her a way to spin the night with Gerry Taylor: to flip what she'd hoped to give him into real help. It would also be payback for the way he'd slithered off: a link, through the country of his assignment, that he'd never even know of. At the weekend, she sent off the coupon, thinking, *I've made a pattern for myself.*

3 Martine

Monday 4 February 2013

In her cramped flat, Martine's been cooking. If her relationships are to be real, to have meaning for her, food must be there.

In the 1980s she went for earthy, complex flavours. Duck with olives, almonds and honey. Beef, pickled walnuts and prunes under puff pastry. Terrine of cauliflower, tomato and broccoli with a sorrel sauce. These days she produces simple fare as well, calling it spontaneity. Pears on a board with cheeses. A plate of smoky antipasti. Fresh seafood on moist seaweed. Each dish she thinks about with care, slogging to express something. This time, it's to work out a dilemma.

Today she's turned over and over what Jocelyn Teague is asking, all while avoiding the spare room. She's cleaned the kitchen and the bathroom, sorted out papers in the sitting room, tried to push back the tide of clutter. She's mummified a ball of shortcrust pastry in clingfilm, laid it in the fridge to rest. This embryo of some meal reminds her of parenting, of her mother yet again. She doesn't know what she'll make out of the pastry. This is unlike her. Sancho draws attention to himself, raising a claw, leaving it suspended as if to scratch his head. Martine thinks and thinks. She thinks, *I'll check for the decorator's number, just in case.*

The *Für Elise* phone ringtone startles her, although she half-expected it.

'Look, we can't really wait much longer,' says Jocelyn Teague. Her voice isn't as shrill as last time. 'There's a family involved as well, waiting to know.'

'And you say it has to be this one,' says Martine. 'It's only that, ideally...'

'We've been through this before,' says Jocelyn Teague.

'I can't tell you just yet.' Martine puts down the phone.

Sancho scratches, and another limp joke comes back to her. *A chameleon's motto? A change is as good as a rest.* As a scientist, she knows that chameleons don't actually colour with their environment. Their chromatophores change constantly, according to their mood. She thinks, *With me, it's environment and mood: my decision-making powers seem to fluctuate with both.*

Tonight, the slip of moon is at the window again. And again, she tries to blank the illusion that it looks angled at her. She rings back Jocelyn Teague.

'I'll tell you by tomorrow,' she says.

* * *

1983–1984

In response to her *Times* coupon, from Sri Lanka InterRelate gave Martine a boy. She'd asked for one without a second thought. With the letter of introduction came a policy document and a leaflet.

His name was Liyanage Mohan, or Mohan Liyanage. He suddenly seemed a bit of an imposition. At college she'd just committed to more research; she was covering for a colleague, who was sick; then there was a conference in Stirling to prepare for. Most evenings she had her round of socialising. These were the movements of her life, frictionless and regular, as if it were a machine with its own beauty.

She put off explaining the boy to her mother, one of those parent-child mysteries that she shrugged off. She even turned to her address book for advisors on the ethics of cold feet. Sheila, Tony, Dawn and their undergrad entomology project came back to her: after the four of them had urged each other on through five long nights surveying nocturnal insects pricked out in glow-worm light, they'd celebrated by jumping into a freezing summer river. None of the other three was now a scientist but even today, they shared a house. Sheila, survivor of a near-fatal car crash and ardent cat lover, worked for a charity, which could be vaguely relevant; Tony, his love of Dawn still undeclared, was a counsellor, which might help.

Next she considered Rosemary, met during teacher training when they both got stuck in a lift – a nightmare for Martine, given her imprisonment years earlier. Rosemary had expertise in the gentle art of rejection, in her case though of men, not foreign boys.

In the end Martine didn't consult them, or her current crowd. They'd only have advised her to do whatever felt right. So it was mostly from cowardice that she got out a pen and paper and, sitting at her home desk, wrote Mohan her first letter.

Weeks later, his reply came.

'**To InterRelate parent UK 89375**

From InterRelate sponsored child 88 6502

15th April 1983

My good lady Haslett in England

Thank you for caring of me my sister says sponsoring. My name is Mohan Liyanage. I am living near Maha Nuvara town* in Sri Lanka. I am 5 years old. Here there is a photograph of me with my sister. I am waiting for your letter.

*Maha Nuvara is Kandy town

Writing in Sinhala by the boy's sister, Anupama Liyanage, age 12

Father: Farm labourer. Mother: Housewife.

Translating by InterRelate International, Colombo

Note. We do not showing wrong spellings. We do showing the child's punctuation.'

Martine thought, head shaking, smiling at herself, *I don't know children these days. The ones I see are filtered by classroom observation – and they tend to be teenage. Anyway, in school they're fish in a tank, while this boy's free in the ocean, a real-life person, in the round.*

She grappled with the photo he'd enclosed. Small and fragile at the corner of a wall, one bare foot covering the other, his face half-turned as if unused to the camera. Spindly arms. A sister of his, Anupama, stood apart, her chin a little down, a slide pinning her hair. Martine had worn them at that age, maybe a few years younger.

Her eyes skated over the girl's script of blue biro curlicues filling wide-apart lines, neat but somehow emphatic, energetic. The paper was as meagre as the photo. She propped the photo on her desk. Periodically she scanned it. The pair was unbelievable. Maybe it was the mean photo size, that or the black and white.

Next time she wrote, she exchanged her pen for typing. Maybe the machine would keep a protective distance.

'My good lady Haslett

Your letter is nice. You are sounding important. Perhaps you are having a secretary. In Sinhala your talking is funny.

'Anupama has an idea. She can say your photograph is nice. You will smile soon. Your hair is nearly long red or brown and you are having brown dots on the face and on the arms. Did you stay in the sun in your white skin. Your blue sarong is short. Why.

'About my photograph of me. I do not think what you are thinking my face is a heart.

'"It is an upway-down raindrop" my mother is telling me and "Your eyes are large brown like a spotted deer but your arms are long like a grey langur."

'Anupama has an idea. We can say Hanuman was a langur. He rescued Sita. It is Hindu. The langur is a monkey climbing high trees and I am not. I do not like my mother telling me I am the animals.

'My sister is writing quotation marks. This point is significant. Please notice.

'Please send a photograph of the husband in your house.'

Martine checked with herself for a minute, assuring herself that she had no aim to find one man. Having photos of no such person, she then wrote back informing Mohan straight that England had different customs, different ways. In fact few of her girlfriends wanted a permanent partner then, or so it seemed to her at the time. They got together and compared work and parties, and buying houses and flats, and commuting and family, and hobbies and love affairs. These were the lovely cogs and pistons to her life that she took for granted. But any point to them – to find a reliable lover, for example – they simply didn't discuss.

'My Miss Martine Haslett

I call you the name way you are asking.

'Sorry about there is no photo of your husband in the house. Send a drawing instead. Anupama has an idea and I say she can tell you. I am having two sisters and one brother. Upeksha, Anupama are the sisters and Jayamal the brother. 14, 12 and 8. My father is working hard. Also senior father and junior father and the mothers and five cousins are living by our house not our house but on the side. Anupama tells you the Sri Lankan fathers and mothers are the English uncles and aunties.

'There is a drawing here. It is an old flag. The sun is for the prince. The moon is for the old princess.

'Your question is "What is your village like."

'Anupama says InterRelate International says I cannot tell you where I live near Kandy. Kandy is a big town. There are hills. They fall down. There is a big lake. By the lake there is a Buddhism temple. Our village is very smaller. It is 40 kilometres from. My father has a bicycle.

'I am waiting for your drawing of your husband.'

These words, dictated to Mohan's sister, then translated, then typed up in some Colombo office, probably didn't even safely carry his voice. The jumpy typing gave the big facts from a life, age, name, large town, and Martine grew jumpy about that, sensing that with each of her letters, too, it was her identity that she was gradually sending. *Giving bits of myself away,* she blinked, *as if such fundamentals aren't important at all.*

Mohan's drawings flowed through the post, stuck with numbered labels like used Band-aids; alien objects in wax crayon, oversized, untethered to the page.

'The moon is for the old princess.'

Martine skimmed over the lunar references, still taking the moon for granted at her dark window. She chucked the pictures in a drawer. The drawer was below another, stuffed with embarrassing soft toy pigs and china pigs and flying pigs and pigs on mobiles and badges and pigs in snowshakers given to her over the years by students and friends who'd discovered, with a relief that she had frailties, her porcine fascination. Stashing the letters and the drawings was another shifty act.

The boy's letters mounted up.

'Dear Miss Martine

You are old with no husband in your house. Perhaps you are 30. I am sorry.

'My question is "Why are you having no husband in the house why are you having no children why are you caring of me." Anupama says sponsoring.'

Mohan was resisting her brushoff about husbands. She wasn't sure she wished to answer the question about her sponsorship, either. Gerry Taylor was too personal for a child.

'Dear Miss Martine

I am sorry you are 34 years old.

'My question is "Are you having fathers Anupama says in English uncles." They may have sons. You can choose one.

'I do not find your answer about why caring of me. Sponsoring my sister says again.

'Yes, my house is big. We have 6 sleeping mats. Good chairs. They are nice white plastic chairs. The food is cooking on a stove and milk on another stove. Anupama asks and I say she can write I am keeping your photo on the wall. I am happy about you like the garden drawing. Yes, it is a king coconut. Yes, there are flowers and other trees with fruits. Father makes many fruits and vegetables. Rice also in our field.'

'Dear Miss Martine

The photograph of your family is nice. Your mother is living far away for you.

'My question is "We have three good brown dogs your mother is having a funny one why."

'It is small and prickly. It is wearing a red hat and it has a white ball why.

'Tell me about your Christmas Festival.

'Anupama has an idea. I am drawing the harvest festival. It goes to the Temple of the Buddha's Tooth. The farmers are giving 80 measures of new rice. People are taking it along the path by the lake to the gold shrine. Afterwards we have our village festival.

'You are waiting for a husband very longer than the farmers for the harvest.

'My question is "When you get a husband can some ladies take 80 measures of husbands to say thank you in the temple."

Anupama says I am making a good joke but a nonsense.

'Please send your answer about why sponsoring me.'

'Dear Miss Martine

There are no cousins in your family. I am sorry.

'It is my birthday. I am 6. I go to school now. Anupama says we can say only the school is near not the school name not the village name. My blue shorts are nice. My white shirt with a badge is nice.

'Anupama says to me "You wait until you are walking to the bus to big school you will grow even very stronger legs" and I am saying "They are strong now from Jayamal kicking me and me kicking Jayamal."

'The bus is bringing our letters. Today it went past us then two houses on the snake road then the Post Office. Then Mr Semasinghe the postman is bringing your letters to me. He has new flip-flops because from all the walking to the villages. The bus is bringing any bigger parcels also.'

Martine was flummoxed by Mohan's questions; by his pity, too. A hint for a birthday present she thought she detected in the last letter precipitated her to Hamley's for the best child's paints and brushes. InterRelate wrote back.

'Dear Miss Haslett

InterRelate policy with regard to presents for sponsored children

Please find herewith the set of child's paints, brushes and paper that you sent us for forwarding to child 88 6502. As explained in the policy document with your initial welcome pack, we are afraid that no such gifts can be sent to children or families within the scheme – any more than we can allow endearments or other familiarities.

'As you know, the main benefits accruing from your charitable giving are those associated with improvements in the welfare of the whole community where your "adopted" child resides: cleaner and more accessible water sources; enhanced hygiene; better health for the sick and frail; higher standards of education; and much more besides. In your case, monthly donations contribute to a local latrine-building scheme. Personalised giving is not compatible with such initiatives.

'I enclose another copy of our policy document, along with our latest brochures.

'We shall explain the situation to the family, just in case the child was indeed expecting a present for some reason.

'Yours sincerely

Ibrahim Akhtar

Office Manager, InterRelate International Office, Colombo'

In her next letter, Martine blocked the slapdown from her mind, giving the laziest of news – 'I have been to a couple of parties... Work is very busy.'

The boy's reply seemed obliquely accusing about his birthday.

'Here there is a photo of my birthday. You can see all this family.

'My father is saying you will never send presents and Anupama is saying Buddhists do not need presents only for giving to people needing them.

'My question is "If you send a present what is it."

'My question is not about I want a present it is about I am interested in everything. Anupama is saying this very strongly and we are telling you that.'

Still embarrassed at her failure, 'What would you have liked for a present, supposing I could have sent you one?' Martine asked in reply, enclosing a list of prompts.

'Dear Miss Martine

Not a school bag not a cricket bat not paints not a T-shirt not a book telling about London not Kermit a frog. There are frogs here Big Birds also, for example cranes on the paddy.

'My sister Upeksha is telling me "Answer a television a skate-board" but no.

'I can answer "Something for a good boy at school for

example pencils a book" but no. Or "A present is my mother to go very more times away of the house" but Upeksha is telling me it is not a present.

'Anupama is saying you may think medicine for amma but the clinic and hospital are free. And I do not think medicine is the need for amma.

'Here there is the answer for your question about what present. To my tatta and amma and sister Upeksha and sister Anupama and brother Jayamal and senior father and junior father and the mothers and cousins and me Mohan. A very bigger cake.'

Martine read, and gave herself a ticking-off. *I mustn't let a small boy floor me with his impoverished life.*

She stuck to her textbook letters. 'There are six rooms in my flat... My best friends are Ali and Conrad, Claire, Bernard, Phil and Matthias, as you know, and two men both called Mark...'

Filling them with small facts that she felt safe to release.

In early August 1984, Martine met Jonas in a Notting Hill tapas bar, neutral ground, as if he was now wary of meeting her anywhere else.

The year before, she'd helped get him a job planning kitchens. He'd grudgingly accepted, and moved to London from her mother's. He seemed happier, if unhappy at the gifting. Between half-brother and -sister it had been differently uneasy since around that time.

In the bar Jonas twitched at waiters, pretty girls laughing, the street door squeaking shut. Martine tried to stroke him with her voice.

'You're the spitting image of Dad. Have you seen Mum's films?' Her smile felt stuck: she'd been three when Dad had left. 'The profile and the slouch.' He scowled, and she teased, 'You've got his scowl as well.'

'Mom has home movies? I guess she hid them. But then, I do

know how Dad looks.'

'Whereas I don't, except from the movies. How're the flying lessons?'

'Great,' he said, 'just great,' sarcastic for all she knew.

When the waiter delivered the anchovies and *patatas* she pushed the dishes at him, sacrificing her growling innards.

'And the dating?' he grunted, overriding their silence on the subject.

Once, Martine had seen Gerry Taylor on TV: he was back in Tamil territory, reporting, she'd re-entered the country of blind dating.

'Can I help you someways?' Jonas mumbled.

Martine was stung by the banned subject.

'How's the job?' she parried, alert too late to the fact that in recent months, he'd used that word 'help' often.

'Everything's great,' said Jonas, his voice gone dark and muddy.

'How's Mum?' they asked together – and at last they grinned because they'd found a common thread of chat.

They were both in contact with Martine's mother, just in different ways. Brother and sister nearly, after all.

Back at home, Martine stared again at the photo: Mohan and Anupama against that foreign wall. There was a tree behind them, its leaves like carnival feathers. From it hung a pimpled, ovoid fruit. Something about it disturbed her.

Brothers and sisters, she mused. *Sharing a space doesn't ensure a shared thought, a shared feeling, even a shared experience. On separate tracks most of the time, the different engines of our lives bump us along.* She wondered how they managed, those two children, how much they truly shared.

She thought, It should be easy to send out care or interest, at a distance. It was with Jonas, before I met him. And Mohan's just a new and distant brother. Just not mine.

4 Anupama

Monday 4 February 2013

Mohan's sister is part of Martine's tale.

On Monday 4 February 2013, she's thinking, *He is not here. The posters most definitely state the Sarasavi Bookshop at 10:30 am today, however it is 10:30 am now, and there is no table with a starched table-cloth stacked to the bookshop rafters with* Human Rights: Where to, Sri Lanka? *No white-haired man with large spectacles and most illustrious smile to autograph my copy, accepting the utmost height of my admiration. K. Sivapalan, Siva for short, where are you?*

'Auntie-Uncle Moon, he was a drop of water in my somewhat dry life.'

The moon receives this lament invisibly; it is currently elsewhere than over Kandy.

This is the same date, a few hours earlier, that Martine receives the insistent phone call from Jocelyn Teague. Anupama, these days a lean-cheeked, somewhat bulbous forty-something woman, leaves the bookshop amid the buzzing crowds and tuk-tuks along D.S. Senananayake Veediya.

On the first floor of Pizza Hut overlooking the busy street she takes a seat, defying the girl and boy waiters speculating audibly about a local woman of her age eating there alone. It suits her state of mind to rip great chunks with her teeth and hands out of a pizza.

The disc of tomato craters and cheesy seas is a travesty of Auntie-Uncle Moon, she thinks, *but we are connected, the moon and me. We always have been.* Originally, it was Martine who caused the link. Yet to Martine she barely existed: barely, still, exists.

Martine, a continent distant, won't look into that letter carton, and Anupama, too, tries not to relive her past. But like the moon with its rugged side and its smoother side, life has a symmetry. It obeys the near-law of it. Just as the moon goes about its functions in geometric complement to the sun's, night and day,

day and night, so Martine's life story has its opposite, and Anupama's unwittingly provides it.

* * *

1983–1984

It was the girl Anupama, not Mohan, who chose the photograph of the pair of them and the breadfruit tree behind them.

Mohan simply said, 'All right.'

The girl in cotton shorts and T-shirt, her shoulder-length hair held with a slide, twisted their tyre swing round and round, scuffing the cinnamon earth with her big toe. It was dark, soon after school. The crickets' hissing raked on like nails through gravel.

She whispered, 'I wish Miss Martine would write to me. However, I am Mohan's sister merely, and Mohan is the chosen one.' She looked up and the moon was there, in its first quarter. She silently addressed it. 'I cannot make you a penfriend but I shall make you my talk friend. I can even think of a name for you, a name like the Handamama name you had when I was little.

'As you know, I already have the mother species of auntie, my mother's two sisters and my father's brothers' wives. I also have the father species of uncle, my father's brothers. But a nanda is a father's sister, and I do not have that kind of auntie; and a māmā is a nanda's masculine mate; so I shall put the words with Handa, the word for you, for Moon. Handanandāmāmā: Auntie-Uncle Moon.

'You will be the Auntie-Uncle to whom I can speak about almost anything. I shall build you an album of facts, because I collect them.' She paused. 'Some will be scenes from the life of me and Mohan.'

She would have said more, but from the veranda amma quavered, 'Anupama! There is the food to serve. Come in.'

It was Thursday 24 March 1983. Later that evening, she talked to the moon again. Over the hiss of the cicadas, the collared scops owl was hiccupping from some treetop. She had finished her chores and homework; now she was hallooing for one of their dogs down the ridges of the paddy, under the stars.

She stopped, upturned her face and said, 'Handanandāmāmā, today was the first scene for our album. Did you see Mr Semasinghe the postman? He came earlier, in his blue shirt with the red badge and his nearly worn-out flip-flops, not the black shoes that he should wear. He walked up to our doorway with letters in his plastic carrier bag. I did not see him because I was at school, so were Upeksha and Jayamal. But Mohan does not go to school yet, as you know. He was with amma and the mothers, my father's brothers' wives who live here also, in the houses joined to ours; so he saw the letter when it came.

'From wherever you were in your orbit, Handanandāmāmā, did you see us two tired, hardworking sisters, Upeksha and me, trudging into the garden? Amma was sitting on her outside chair. Jayamal was home from school before us, leaning hard against her, spinning the baby coconut machine he had made, tick-tick-tick, faster and faster. She smiled at Jayamal and me because our uniforms were still spotless, but she grumbled at Upeksha because her white dress was not; she smiled and grumbled both.

'"A letter from the lady, like they promised!" Mohan cried.

'He ran into the house with his arms out, counting "40, 41, 42, 43", round the sleeping mats in the boys' room, where he will not often sleep, round the chairs in the sitting room, and squeezing behind them, round Upeksha's and my rolled mats: around mine in particular, where the letter lay. He is most adorable running and counting, always from 40 like that.

'I wondered why the letter was on my mat.

'"Leave the letter alone until your father gets home," amma said.'

Anupama left her retelling. The dog had limped to her from the stream at the bottom of the paddy. Dragging him by the scruff, a bone in his growling mouth, she returned to the yard and shut him up. She resumed swinging on the tyre swing.

'Just before you appeared in the sky, Moon, tatta came in. We showed him the letter. Most abruptly he stopped chewing his betel and spat it out like poison. Did you see that, Handanandāmāmā? He told amma to get up from her white chair, even though there was the other just beside it, claiming it for himself and opening the *Lanka Deepa*, giving a shakeout to its pages. Peering at it in the darkening light. On the edge of the rug with the cloves spread out, Jayamal and Upeksha had a coconut lamp and were already doing their homework. Evidently it was my job to read the letter.

'An official had stamped the envelope "InterRelate International, Colombo Office" with a most smart address on Park Road. Mohan pulled out three papers and an empty envelope, fastened by a staple – too roughly, I had to show him how. The top paper was thick and clearly from Miss Martine's pen, being in English writing. Unfortunately her script was spiky and joined up, not printed like in our textbooks, so I could not read it. The second page, thin and greyish, was written in our letter curls and arches (you know that they are formed in that way, Handanandāmāmā, to withstand the splitting of the straight veins of the Corypha palm leaves on which our forbears wrote). At the bottom was a sheet from the Colombo office. Its typing gave us, the chosen family, careful directions for writing replies from Mohan.

'"Read, read," said Mohan, jumping along beside me.

'I lit the kerosene lamp and put him on my knee indoors. From the kitchen the fumes of coriander and chilli roasting were making my mouth water. The others gathered round me, even tatta.

'When I had nearly finished, Mohan shouted, "Now I'm

excited! 40, 41, 42...", and ran off to play with his plastic truck around the firewood store and the chickens and the yellow flame tree and the king coconut tree and the breadfruit tree and the jak tree.

'Handanandāmāmā, that is the first scene for our album.'

Anupama stifled a yawn. Earlier, she had heard Mohan shrieking in protest about his bedtime, pleading to sleep with her and Upeksha as normal. Now, only the crickets. No one had missed her from indoors. She went inside.

A few nights later, the moon was waning over Anupama as she sat on a boulder in the stream.

She said to the moon, 'I forgot this washing so I could see you.'

It lit up a pile of white on stone. She began dipping it into the stream, drawing it out, rubbing and dipping it again. Among the black humps of the trees, a deer was barking.

She confided, 'I have been thinking. Below most of this island – the mountains rising near us, the paddy that tatta works – lie the most great, angled layers of rock. I collect rocks as well as facts. The layers are metamorphic. P.G. Cooray's book in the school library says that there was a post-Miocene uplift long ago, and that the mountains have three pereplains. The rocks have changed over billions of years, perhaps are changing still, because of heat, and pressure, and folding and re-folding. Each process affects the others. So are they stable or not?

'These are the facts: Miss Martine's letter arrived; amma and Mohan kept it for me. But the reasons why tatta pretended to read the *Lanka Deepa* hid in layers. They might have been the same reasons why he came inside once I was reading. Or various reasons might have pushed up against each other.

'Then there is amma. She wanted me to read Miss Martine's letter. I knew because she got me to bend so that she could smooth my dress and pull one dented sleeve. The reasons might be the same as why she now leaves the evening meal, apart from the grinding and roasting of spices, to Upeksha and me, and why, to my sadness, she cannot decide whether to smile or grumble when we come home – or much else, to be perfectly honest. Her reasons might have pressed against tatta's, or tatta's against hers, until those reasons shifted and changed again.

'Upeksha is older, and has more homework and duties at home than I do. Jayamal is a boy: tatta and amma listened when Jayamal said no to reading and writing the letters to Miss Martine.' She went quiet. 'There might have been other reasons, I suppose, why I was thought the best one. Reasons about me.'

Eventually, she stumbled home with the laundry. About her role, reader and scribe, it appeared she must stay unsure.

From then on, Anupama often sought out the moon and spilt her thoughts.

In July 1983, in the early hours of the morning, she began, 'Handanandāmāmā, this has happened.'

Stealing a plastic chair out of hearing of her sleeping father on the veranda, Anupama told the moon what it must already have seen.

'Last night, tatta and senior father walked home from town together. The rains were loud, but I could still hear tatta shouting. They burst into the kitchen soaking, banging their umbrellas, pushing us aside to dry themselves at the oven. I smelt the gusts of moonshine in the room. Tatta says he never drinks, but this is not a fact.

'He was shouting, "Motherfuckers! Bastards! Fucking sodomites!"

'I have never heard him angry till last night.

'Senior father dropped most wearily into a chair. "Yeah, yeah, they started all this, we know that."

'Tatta struck his drenched *Lanka Deepa*, or rather the news it had printed. "What have I been telling you all evening? *Our* people. Making things a hundred-shitting-fold times worse. Burning cars in Kandy, in other places digging Tamils out of buses, ripping at them like animals..." Uncle passed a warning glance from him to Jayamal, Upeksha and me, against the wall where horror had pinned us. And tatta saw Mohan and swore again. The little one had crept to the oven, and was feeding his plastic cars into the flames.

'We four dumbstruck, horrified children were hurried suddenly away.

'I whispered to Mohan, "You can sleep on my mat tonight."

'He has been dreaming awful dreams, Handanandāmāmā. He crawls onto my mat, and I allow him. He will grow taller and stronger, more like a little man, but for now he smells mostly of earth and smoky spices, Auntie-Uncle. Last night I stroked him until he flopped entirely.

'I am trying to help him, Handanandāmāmā. Do you think I am doing right?'

The months rolled on to 1984. One night, after the special curries and milk rice she had helped her sister Upeksha make, Anupama finished her homework by a lantern in the garden. Algebra; acids and alkalis; more of the island's geography. In that household, it was hard to get time alone, so she delayed, shaking out the peppercorn rug, feeding the chickens, sweeping up the yard. She peered between the blots of the flame tree, the breadfruit tree and the jak fruit true, but the moon was unseen because that night it was new. She realised that sometimes she'd have to talk without its presence.

She murmured, 'Handanandāmāmā, here is another, happier scene for the album. Mohan's birthday is today, 8 March. Up until today, Mohan has been quite annoying, to be perfectly honest.

'He has kept on asking, "What present will I get, what present will I get?" 'He has asked amma and Upeksha and Jayamal and me – even tatta and the fathers and mothers. He probably asked you also.

'This morning he was bothering us again. "Where is it? Where is it?"

'Tatta led him outside. "Well now, little one," he said.

'Tatta's bicycle stood against the house. Lashed to the back was a little cart with a seat. Tatta had made it.

'He pointed out, "Now you can ride with me sometimes."

'He has been building it at junior father's, round the side of our house, keeping it a secret. Mohan is overjoyed.

'This evening, before the birthday meal, Mohan found me near the rug of peppercorns, at my $x + y = z$. Did you see him? He gazed at me through those lashes. They fringe his eyes enough to melt anyone: they truly are enchanting.

'He said, "Will you write to Miss Martine? It's my birthday after all."

'Then I suspected why he had been pestering.

'"Did you think Miss Martine would send you a present?" I put on a stern expression – although I longed to tease him, to be perfectly honest. I said, "She will not know it is your birthday until you inform her, at any rate." At last he understood, and we settled down to write. "But you cannot ask for a present. It is not proper," I insisted.'

Anupama smiled at the moon with a contented sigh. 'That is a happy account of our family, is it not?'

The children's holidays passed; May came. Now that Anupama saw she could talk to the moon when it wasn't there, they also communed in daylight. One Sunday she was desperate to speak, so she scrambled, in drenching rain, far up into the montane regions. She sank to her haunches in the cool air by a waterfall, planning to return with bundles of brushwood to justify her absence. A green bee-eater dropped to her level then flicked past.

'I hope you are listening, Handanandāmāmā,' she began. 'This is a most dreadful scene for the album.

'During the April holidays, Mohan started wandering off. You would have heard us joke that he was playing in his mind of toys. When the holidays ended, he stopped attending school, even though, as you know, he had only recently started. I leave for big school earlier, so I made Jayamal promise to take him, but still, often the little one disappeared. No one sent a message from school enquiring after him; and despite tatta's urging, amma would not ask Mohan's teacher for advice. Another thing that amma could not decide.

'Now the rains have arrived, of course. So on Friday, we three tired, hardworking schoolchildren, Upeksha and my friend Harshini and I, were walking home from big school, from the bus station. A truck of bricks splashed past on the narrow road, soaking us, under our umbrellas, in papaya-coloured water. There was a screech and a bump. Fearful bellows from the driver and the man on the back soon reached us.

'During the rains, Harshini giggles that any vehicle is a "blind fish trying to breed with the snakely road". "Snakely road": that is what little Mohan calls it. I thought the truck had hit a pothole – after all, there are so many; but stumbling up a way we saw a hump, like a pile of dirty laundry amid the torrents of red. It was Mohan's blood, like the pulp of watermelons. One thin, long arm was gashed, and so was his left side.'

Anupama stopped, head in her hands. A tiny squirrel brushed through the wet undergrowth.

She restarted, 'We carried him home with the driver and his mate. We clapped to tatta down below us, under the shelter in our paddy. He rushed to discover what had happened.

'Jayamal worried, "Why is amma talking to herself?"

'Tatta took Jayamal and Upeksha in, instructing them to tend to amma and Mohan. Amma lay making the most frightening noises; Mohan looked like a branch a leopard had crushed, on his mat in the main room. Then tatta carried the outdoor chairs, sloshing through the water, to the shelter of our pouring yellow flame tree.

'He gestured me to sit.

'"Do you understand what happened?" he asked, pushing his soft voice against the most fierce rush of rain. I shook my head. "Mohan has been disappearing daily to the bus that brings the mail. He expected it to bring a present from Miss Martine." My heart began to thump. "Whenever he heard an engine, he ran all the way up our track and onto the road. And when the bus came by, without a parcel carried into the Post Office, he crept back home again."

'"Where were amma and the mothers?" I croaked.

'Tatta looked at me. He has most handsome teeth under his moustache, do you not think? Not one is missing, and the betel is a most beautiful, even stain.

'He said, "Amma was lying down, and the mothers were talking to her. Sometimes she doesn't feel well. And now, you see, she may feel a little worse."

'He has never before spoken to me for so long, Handanandāmāmā. It must have been five minutes: a significant point for the album.

'He asked, "Was there something you put in his letter, Anupama?"

'I said, "I'm not quite sure."

'My heart began to somersault, because then I saw what had happened.

'My brain must have been in my x and y and z because the most cunning Mohan had had me scribe, in the letter about his birthday, "The bus is bringing the letters first to the Post Office.... The bus also brings any much bigger parcels."

'Beneath the bus words, there had been a birthday hint: a layer.'

Anupama was mumbling now. 'Handanandāmāmā, tatta

drew his chair up close.

'He said, "When Mohan is better, write to Miss Martine with him beside you. Make sure he says he was not expecting, will never expect, a present. Do this politely, and in a way that Mohan understands." My face began to glow. "I'm going to tell you why no one should send us anything." His fists gripped his sarong; his thigh muscles twitched. "As your father, I'm the one who provides for this family."

'The rain plopped through the tree roof, all around us.

'Today I have done it, Auntie-Uncle. I have written for Mohan, "Buddhists do not need presents unless they are meant for other people, people who really need them."

'I am thinking, Handanandāmāmā. InterRelate International is about to bring our village the most wonderful gift of latrines. So even tatta's statement was not a fact. And another layer was hiding: tatta might not have said what he said, or not in the same way, if Miss Martine had been a man.'

5 The object

Monday 4 February 2013

The iPad, with its dongle plugged in, glares again in the unlit cell of the bunk room. The overhead monster is once more prone, heaving and humming. The object of Martine's indecision hunches under the monster's bed. If only there were total quiet. Quiet is dope. Then you can imagine voices, ones that could make your actor's name one day, the cool ones, the roaring drunk, the lovable crim, the misunderstood outlaw, whatever voices you want.

Facebook has a message, and a new photo: the family and best friend Luna. They're on the observation deck of the local tower at home, seated in its bar café. Their necks stretch towards the viewer as if bunched with cord, parental tendons straining, dark cheeks and Luna's much paler face bleached by the flash of the camera light. They all have red-eye.

The message is from Sister Number Two. 'We miss you. We're all worried about you. Even Creepy says hello.' Creepy is Sister Number One. 'D'you know yet about the 15th? Have they found you someone?'

The object's woodsmoke fingers write back, in the family's language, 'Miss you and Luna too. Creepy's still a total suck-up no doubt. I know this is an escape of sorts but it's shit here. Bastards. Still not sure about the 15th but shouldn't be anything to stress about.' The object whispers inaudibly a variation of the same old fencing mantra, handling again those keys on the neon wristband. *En garde, flèche, epée. Balestra, marche, attaque. Sixte, quarte, octave, septime.* The fingers finish, tapping out, 'If any of you ring, don't gab that I've got the net.'

Eventually the object pats out another message, addressed to 'Black Sheep Shit.'

'I hate you. The family hates you. I think even Creepy hates you.'

Why wouldn't they all hate him, the eldest brother who left home without a word, the brother missing for two years without a trace? The bile of the message is purging.

'Actually I miss you,' the writer adds, contrite.

After another pause, the object scoops up the string of words and deletes them with the tap of one dark finger. Black Sheep Shit isn't active on Facebook, email or Twitter. The family's given up looking for him: son and brother seems determined to stay missing. He'd probably never see the message, even if it went.

* * *

Martine
1984

'At least let it touch the sides,' Martine's mother said.

It was a Sunday in late August: Martine's birthday. All over England, mothers were serving up the traditional roast lamb with her same scolding to their children. Not many would be thirty-five tomorrow. Once a child, always a child: the truth in this brought Martine back to Harrow Weald once in a while but more often somehow kept her away, talking at least thrice-weekly down the phone. It was Jonas who, despite his move to Willesden, was the regular to what he still called home.

The women sat at the polished repro table with its centrepiece of late pink rosebuds from the garden. The dog snuffled at Martine's mother's feet. There was a mound of birthday packages on the sideboard.

Martine put most of her energy into eating because, at Harrow Weald, it was her mother who did the talking, with her unconscious trademark hum, leaving dotted-line type gaps for answers.

'Dum-di-dum. Jonas seems to love his job, doesn't he?'

'Seems to.'

'Did you know they're branching into bathrooms?'

'I told *you* that.'

'Dum-di-dum. The Willesden flat seems a bit squalid – or is that just me?'

'Nope, it's everyone except Jonas.'

'D'you think this girlfriend's serious? She's kept him away today.'

'You know him better than me.'

Her mother looked askance.

'Is your workload as bad as ever? ... How's Ali? Is she better? ... Will I ever get to meet Alec? ... Tum-tum. When am I going to see the famous roof garden?'

Recently there'd been a delivery to Martine's maisonette at Stockwell: obelisks of clipped box, the trained ball of a holly tree, and a male nude statue, which she'd draped with a wry boa of dried herbs.

The two went on with their familiar duet while under the table the older woman's embroidered slipper kept the beat, tapping the dog. Martine felt her body language being scanned for clues as to her degree of happiness. Martine thought she felt fine: happy and fine.

After opening her presents they entered with gusto into taking down a pair of curtains for dry cleaning, belatedly baking a birthday coffee-and-walnut cake, moving the garden bench under a window, shampooing the dog-stained carpet in the hall.

At the same time, Martine sponged energetically at the images of an era long ago, when all of a sudden things were moved from room to room in that same house, and – for reasons other than a dog – doors were abruptly closed.

Going upstairs, gathering up a stray woodlouse, her mother stopped.

'Dum-di-dum. Do you remember how, after Dad left, you began collecting insects?'

The bugs had to be caught in some act of success, her mother reminded her: an ant with a crumb, a spider finishing its web, a beetle mating, a bee loaded with pollen.

'You kept them in all sorts. Matchboxes and envelopes and film canisters. I told you that they'd die.' Her mother laughed. 'You learnt, then kept going anyway.'

Martine let her finish, though she'd heard it all before. How she'd coopted friends at school. In the playground, her employees would slide a page under the insect subject then crush it on her instruction, very gently, with a shoe. Martine drew her tiny victims, or got neighbours to take photographs. She decided early on that each must have an identifier, train numbers. Friends' parents would bring her the digital strings if they ever went on a train ride. She transcribed them onto the backs of the photos, the scientific way. Before he left, her father had been a line engineer, managing the rolling stock at Neasden. Her mother's umpteenth retelling suddenly revealed to Martine this time from nowhere that the insects, with their train labels, were for Dad.

On the beds in all three bedrooms, Martine and her mother laid out a shortlist of the older woman's outfits for a charity lunch she was going to, which made for lively debate. They walked Hairy to the top of Mountside and picked blackberries. Mum told Martine any news she had, gave her a health bulletin and shared a tale or two about the neighbours. She frowned at their short clinch when Martine left in her usual bouncing hurry.

At the beginning of September, Mohan's next letter came.

'Anupama is helping me reading your letters again. All. You are telling me about London and your family and your friends and you are working "as a kind of teacher for teachers". I do not understand. Please tell *about you*.

'Also I did not find the answer to my special question.

'Anupama says it is annoying I am still saying "caring of" not sponsoring.

'Anyway there is always no answer for "Why are you

sponsoring me."'

Martine gave in to Mohan's question, after some bulking chit-chat.

She said, 'I met a man once. The man has gone to Sri Lanka. That's partly why.

'P.S. The man said he was lazy and a coward.'

The 'lazy coward' reference she by now applied to Gerry's rejection of her, not the Sri Lankan war. And once she'd written her explanation, it was a fly flicked out of a window: her mind was clean, and Gerry was gone from view.

As Pimlico was on her tube line, most Tuesdays Martine called at her friends Ali and Conrad's on her way home. On the 25th of that September, the moon was in its new phase, out of sight and out of her mind. She'd worked late. She arrived breathless, somehow sensing before she could hear it that she was missing out on fun. The house door was ajar.

The narrow hall seemed at first glance full of mannequins tilted as if in storage, then they morphed, undulating and talking, into a mob of the usual Soho Sisters – dressed for their queen parts, which was unlike them, away from the drag-club scene. The Soho Sisters. There was Nev, stage name Old Sal, with her coltish legs in fringes of black leather, and Graham, in role as the cowgirl Araminta, in latex hat and studded sleeves and a wreath of chains. Fleur was exclaiming wildly with another tart whose name Martine couldn't think of, the latest prozzy Ali had taken under her wing. And there was Grand Dame Tattlemouse, Bernard's alter ego, head to sandal in gold lamé, false curves cinched in by a black corset. They'd been stooping towards some structure not normally in the hall.

Martine exclaimed, elbowing her way in. 'What the flamin' fandango?'

'Hi, gorgeous!'

'Mar, see what's occurring!'

Saila Billet-Doux gave a thin pout. 'We're havin' a guilt party, can't you tell?'

That explained the gold lamé and fetish gear – except for Saila, whose usual style prevailed, her midriff a fuzzy hollow under a sailor crop top, thighs like twigs in crisp white shorts and bright blue stockings.

The structure was a booth, improvised from cake cooling racks and broom handles and plywood. Beside it, a curtain masked a chair. Two raw sausages were crossed and tied above the booth, which Martine could now see was meant as a spoof confessional. Below one grille, someone had hung a postbox.

Fleur gave a demonstration in her broad Welsh yap. 'Take a gold scrap, look,' she plucked a bunch of shiny papers from one of Ali's erotic bowls, 'and write something on it. A thing you might feel guilty about, look. 's all anonymous. No need for details of who – tharris if you'd rather not. Then bin it in the box.'

'Confessing makes me feel goo-ood,' grinned Old Sal, plumping the tower of her leather-strapped wig.

Saila Billet-Doux shrugged. 'Was just sayin', I got nothin' to feel guilty about.'

'Whereas I'm guilty of just about every darn thang.' Araminta galloped a hip.

Martine assembled a mental list, admitting where her guilt lurked: in blanking Jonas's coded offers of closeness; in taking college envelopes, male porn to bed too often, the odd *vino rosso* overdose, Mum's support for granted. Alec, the latest boyfriend, met while swimming, had called her clingy at the weekend; bossy, too – and then he'd dumped her. She wondered briefly, *Is he another source of guilt, or a regret?*

Claire, her chief confidante at work, would have said about him, 'Are you going to try to tie with a ribbon every hopeful episode that doesn't work? Sri Lankan charity for the dishy Sri Lankan reporter – what for Alec: because he's in paper, plant a tree?'

Grand Dame Tattlemouse slithered against Martine, big lashes skating against her cheek, breathing her in. 'Girl, do you smell fine.'

Fishnetted arms wound round her. She sensed the unseen bulk of Grand Dame's genitals, strapped away. She smiled and stared her favourite queen in the face, because of them or despite them. She wanted to be close to him or to have him: the male in the female, the female in the male. Difference, opposites. They completed her, brought her to symmetry, in a way she couldn't explain.

She broke away from the Grand Dame.

Araminta was still focused on the postbox. 'If you're such a pure gal 'n' all,' she winked, 'just think what you should do for the poor miners and probably haven't.'

'Or all that famine in Ethiopia, look,' Fleur nodded.

'Yeah yeah, I give my whack,' smiled Martine.

She hurried into the main event. The walls of the high Victorian room clashed to Prince's *Purple Rain*, and Phil hammering *No Regrets* out of the piano, and knots of people howling Edith Piaf over shouted talk. Everyone chucking down drinks. Glitz and pancake makeup. Boots with killer heels, executioners' masks. Dog leads and handcuffs. There was no dancing, she saw sadly, although she was hopelessly clumsy at it, like someone suddenly blindfolded and spun round. Instead she mingled, trying to wave wildly at people, masochistically restricted – aptly – in her work suit.

Ali arrived in something black and ragged, reproachfully holding out a glass. 'They've told everybody now!'

'Told what?'

'Don't let Phil or Matthias spin you their disease line. It was all to get this party.' And she sped off.

Martine's friend Phil was busy at the piano; she looked for his boyfriend Matthias and found him sprawled on a sofa doing his famous pelvic thrusts. As some descendant of the slave Black

Bob, he got bit work butlering for the wealthy pretentious in eighteenth-century dress, which he seemed to relish in an avenging, sarcastic kind of way. Now friends had pinned him down convulsing, drawing convict arrows onto his white shirt and chinos, and he didn't seem to mind that either.

Martine quizzed him. 'What's going on?'

'Ask Phil. He's prepared a statement.' Matthias laughed towards the piano.

Phil's vest sported convict arrows too. A girl in a judge's wig dragged a stepladder past Martine, mounted it and began to paint a cherub on the ceiling.

'Oi!' Conrad roared hoarsely, draped over the piano, looking and sounding less buttoned-up than usual.

Phil tossed Martine towards him with his curls. 'Aha!' he greeted her. 'Someone else to tell!'

He went on bashing the keys, conducting the so-called singing.

'Tell what?'

His musician's talent wasted, he earned pennies playing piano in muffled hotel lounges and depopulated bars, craning among the longely regulars for signs of appreciation.

'It's decided. We've got the new disease.' He sounded reckless. 'It's all the rage for guys like Matthias and me.'

'Disease,' Martine echoed.

She felt suddenly overheated. She and Phil had been friends since their earliest London days; she'd helped him make his peace with coming out. She stared at his fingers scurrying on the keys. All at once they looked like shadows, as if they couldn't last. She blew cool outbreaths, fanning her face.

Phil bellowed, 'It's the plague to have.'

When his fingers stopped, she saw he was really angry. She tried to recall what Ali had said.

Phil wilted at her expression. 'RIV, Regular Income Virus, not the other thing. Matthias is going to train as a priest and I'll be selling these bad boys', he rapped on the piano hood, 'in Bond Street.' He looked suddenly deflated. 'A salaried job for both of us. Who'd have thought? The piss-awful burden of finally growing up.'

Martine gasped. 'If that was a joke it's way beyond tasteless.'

Leaning over the piano, Conrad slurred, his eyeballs rolling at her, 'He's trying to make us feel bad.' He meant, she and he had both got regular jobs. He gave the room the finger. 'He even conned us into this party. This party's a fucking con.'

Martine's hand fled from Phil's shoulder. 'And you could do that to your friends.'

Heart pumping, she stomped away.

She remembered, *Today, on a station platform, I saw a sparrow disappear under a train. There was no grind of machine parts, no crunch of tiny bones. Maybe nothing changed in the train or in the bird. But maybe something did.* She was angry not so much at Phil's trick but at his news. Other people's sensible choices dulled her existence. Phil and Matthias were supposed to elaborate on her life, to give gleam to her life's machine. The same she feared was true of the Soho Sisters. They'd become her friends originally through an adventure, an unexpected dare, and now supplied her with panache and colour. She swallowed down shame.

At some point in the evening a painted devil joined the cupid on the ceiling, and there were multi-coloured paint sprinkles on the floorboards, and the artist had disappeared. Standing with Martine by a shuttered window, Phil was defiant, laughing about one last flamboyant gesture, a holiday he and Matthias would take. She suddenly heard 'Indian Ocean' and 'Sri Lanka'.

'Don't go there, matey,' Saila Billet-Doux interrupted. 'There's troubles. Black July last year, the massacres of Tamils, the reprisals 'n' all that.'

Others constellated round them, chipping in about the island's civil war, and for Martine, the room just stopped.

She slipped away, wrote on a few gold papers, folded them

and dropped them into the box. One for not considering, till then, the effects of priesthood on Matthias's life with Phil. One for her dissatisfaction with them both. One for her descent into blindness about Sri Lanka, for not following its news: for maybe, deep down, not wanting to know. Some too for some of her other, lesser guilts. There should have been a note for Mohan, since he hadn't, as her mother might have said, touched her sides. But Martine found she couldn't write one, even that night. She posted three blank scraps.

At once she took the Northern line home. She resolved, *Write to Mohan's family asking how they've come through the violence. Interrogate InterRelate as well. That'll be contrition, of a kind.*

Martine preferred the tube to buses, planes and cars, and not just because of her father's ex-job with trains. She liked the smut invasion of her pores and the gusts from all directions, their conspiracy of chaos with her hair. Clattering rails, a whoosh and the dying wail of her ride as it whipped old tunnel air into the station. The heat of steel and the warm fuggy smog of hot rubber suspension. You knew where the train was going, where it had to go. A track couldn't be veered from; of all the forms of transport, a tube train shot along with the strongest sense of purpose.

In her carriage a boy with a bloodless face wheedled his sobbing girlfriend, 'You've got to come with me. I'll make you come with me.'

Influence, persuasion: it was what people did, more strongly than the moon's half-hearted pull. More like the sun, people were enforcers, intent on imposing love, and all the things they wanted to say.

Martine emerged from the tube at Stockwell. On an impulse she delayed heading home and, dodging the babble of traffic and dark and light, made it to the wedge-shaped island at the busy gyratory. The war memorial and clocktower guarded the war shelter in their lee. Traffic beams strafed the shelter's curved face, blanching out any moon or starlight. A youngster in a shabby suit was swigging from a can, his leg tucked up behind him, foot to the concrete wall. They nodded to each other. When Martine neared, he moved.

Inside her head the exhaust fumes and the traffic roar died back. Her eyes travelled over columns of names marching down the stone of the memorial. Car lights swept across them, hundreds of World War I fallen. She searched for any foreign name. Nadaud, she found: a name that to her, sounded like No Man. The dead soldier and her boy seemed equally vague with distance, sketched in the sepia of history and geography. She pondered how to plumb their depths.

She heard movements. Footfalls, a sideways pull at her shoulder-bag. She hung onto the bag, teeth gritted, legs riveted to ground. Sacrificing her briefcase to the pavement. Her muscles tightened, and she didn't let go. His wrench was now a wrangle, a knot of their four arms. They tussled, their breathing laboured. The youngster was pinned to the bag and her hands locked down around it. Martine determined to win.

Ferocity pumped the blood, flogged the sinews. She threw into her combat Phil's uncalled-for trick, his aggravating news, Sri Lankan massacres, Ethiopian famines and all kinds of self-disappointment. She wrestled on, until all at once she saw herself as she tried not to see herself, refusing to be fazed by anything, striving hard at everything. Battling for perfection. Battling to get through.

She stopped trying hard enough to win. Next thing, the boy had punched her to the ground.

In the morning she talked to the police and a doctor examined her.

'Who can I ring?' said the nurse.

Martine shrank from having friends at her hospital bedside in the vomit-and-pine-smelling line between Denise, who'd walked into a car or more likely her husband late last night, and Ruari, worsted in a pissed-up brawl with a pavement. She didn't want her friends to see her as she felt, defeated. Anyway, none of them she had in her life for their usefulness. But in the end there was no option, and she gave the nurse a list – excluding the Soho Sisters, nightbirds to a man-woman, and so mostly asleep.

Ali wasn't at her desk and Conrad was with a client. Rita, Claire and Lesley were in their usual Wednesday meeting. Leanne was ill herself. Mark 1 was on holiday, and Mark 2 had had to ring off: some crisis with a power cut. Discounting Mum, who she didn't want to worry, Martine had only Jonas left.

'On way,' the nurse reported.

Jonas eventually appeared, wide-eyed and smiling in fits.

Martine shrugged. 'He was wearing Doc Martens. What can I say?'

Jonas stepped outside the curtain with the nurse. Martine was separated from their low, serious voices. She heard him ask about 'women's injuries'. The nurse gave reassuring answers: only the legs, abdomen and groin and an unhealthy dose of shock.

Jonas handed over a big blue tartan dressing-gown, awkwardly helping her drape it around her vandalised clothes. He took uncertain charge of her medication, trundling her barefoot in a wheelchair out to a private taxi. Fiddling and fussing, he laid her on the back seat.

They crawled through the traffic, crossing a bridge, the Old Brompton Road, and on.

'Going north?' said Martine, bewildered.

'To my place, stupid. You'll get to meet Astrid.'

'I don't want to be looked after. Stop the car,' Martine directed. She told the driver grimly, 'I'm older than he is.'

The man pulled in, opening the *Evening Standard* as if he'd had this many times before.

'You're going to Willesden,' Jonas quavered, adding, 'You never talk to me.'

'What's that got to do with this?'

'You admit it.'

'I don't admit to anything. Now take me home.' Martine felt rough now.

'Talk to me.'

'About what?'

'I've been trying to talk to you for months. Let me in some.'

Martine had an urge to vomit. 'Not here.'

'At my place then.'

Martine tried to imagine Astrid, the angel she'd still not met who could transform Jonas's lifestyle with his flatmate from half flat, half jockstrap. And they'd no spare bed.

'Home,' she said.

'To receive is also to give dammit. Let me be a brother to you for Chrissake.'

'Maybe at home,' Martine persisted.

'No key. He took your purse.'

'There are locksmiths.'

'OK. Let me stay over,' Jonas said. 'I could care for you there, I guess. We can talk.'

Martine just couldn't answer. *So there has to be more conflict,* she accepted, *to end up where I want.*

6 Anupama

Monday 4 February 2013

It's 20:54. Martine has just put down the phone on Jocelyn Teague.

In Kandy town, Anupama's husband comes in from mucking about with a football with the boys along their lane and Anupama is, as usual, so stirred to see her beloved that her book-signing disappointment crumbles in her mouth into a disjointed anecdote.

Tailing off weakly, she says, 'I am absolutely determined still to be a barrister.'

But from her research into all that, there's something she hasn't told him.

Panting from his games, Asiri takes down one of his cuckoo clocks for mending, damming up his own space within the walls of her textbooks on the kitchen table. 'As you know, that is OK with me. You finish your A levels. Then, to fund Colombo and the Law College, let us look once more at sponsorship.'

It's a long time since the word sponsorship has affected Anupama's family – since Miss Martine and InterRelate, in fact. And about her plans, he doesn't know what she knows.

He says, 'I have a scheme for you... Remember the lawyer who helped us out with Jayamal's trouble?' The trouble is Jayamal's turtle-poaching, harking back years. 'Well, the fellow will have contacts. Let us...'

His plump hands leap on and off the clock gears, carving out tactics on the formica tabletop.

A phrase springs up at her: *Control freak.* He has an answer for everything. She thinks, *Too many people try to take over each other's lives – at least, the parts of them that seem useful. Why did Asiri and I have to fall in love?* she rails internally, and not for the first time. But she won't see herself as victim: her life is as much her fault as her husband's.

As he plots on, her mind flits away to the moon. 'Handanandāmāmā, I think I want to turn this new leaf on my own.'

So far, her life has been mostly endings of different kinds. She'd like it more full of beginnings.

* * *

1984

In August 1984, the young Anupama sought out the moon at the nearest shrine for the Buddha. It was late at night, and raining, and she placed in front of the plaster figure, among the brass lamps and statuettes and jewellery and flowers, a dripping breadfruit root. Her dark eyes found the moon, waning, behind the monsoon clouds.

'Auntie-Uncle Moon,' she whispered, 'I believe that letters are not like seeds.'

The cotton scarf covering her hair was clinging to her head. A forest eagle owl uttered its sinister, low cry.

Anupama said, 'You know it is our holidays again. Time for more album facts.' The owl broke off, exposing the gushing sound of rain. 'Do you remember the rains recently stayed off for two following days?' She went on, 'The grassy patch up the snakely road, with the washing stream on one side and the community hall on the other, was noisy with children delighted to be outside. Jayamal, Mohan, their friends and I were playing a game about goats and a leopard. I was the goatherd. Mohan's friend Marvan was the leopard, but without warning Jayamal took over. He pushed past me and grabbed Mohan, but to everyone's surprise the little one shrieked most terribly instead of giggling and wrestling, as normal.

'He screamed, "He's murdering me!" I tore them apart. He struggled, but I tickled him until he was smiling weakly. He whispered, "Jayamal says that Miss Martine's letters are his. He wants them, or he says he's going to kill me."

'Jayamal is most unpleasant at the moment, to be perfectly honest – but chubby also, and he can barely slap a mosquito. When I said so, it made the little one grin at last.

'That afternoon he helped me plant out seedlings, which some say grow better after you have been in fullness. Later I saw him making a figure from branches, painting a fierce face on a rag. Yesterday the scarecrow stuck out between the eggplants and the chillis.

'I told Mohan on the veranda, "That was a very good idea."

'He murmured, "It's to keep *all* pests away," his little ankles crossing and uncrossing, not indicating Jayamal, who was lazing on the tyre swing. Auntie, this made me smile; and he grinned also.

'I squeezed him. "Let's hope it's going to work."

'This is what happened tonight. We were sleeping on our mats. Suddenly something made me start. I arose, careful not to wake Upeksha. Looking round in the darkness, I realised Mohan's mat was empty. I peeped into the room that he should really share with Jayamal. Jayamal was bolt upright.

'He hissed, "I saw him take... I think it was the letters."

'He jerked towards the door.

'I stole past tatta, sleeping as soundless on the veranda as the Buddha. This rain had started falling. In the vegetable garden knelt Mohan with a coconut lamp beside him. He seemed to be digging.

'I crept a little closer. There was a heap of muddy objects in his lap.

'He was scrabbling at the ground. "Please let them be all right!"

'It was most pathetic, in case you did not see it. He wailed and would not stop. I dropped down at his side. He hugged me. We sat there on the wet soil for a while. I turned to his pile of objects, and helped him carry them in under the flame tree. Then, by the light of the lamp, he showed me what they were.

'Did you see the fearful mess, Handanandāmāmā? Miss Martine's letters and photos tumbled about. Their envelopes were grimed and soggy. With pieces of coconut shell Mohan had tried to enclose them, making a sort of casket for each one. On the day we had planted together, he had pushed them, without me seeing, into the ground. His scarecrow had marked the central point of their burial, some caskets in the chilli patch and others among the eggplant patch, the turmeric patch and the ginger.'

Anupama suddenly said, 'Excuse me, Auntie-Uncle.'

With steepled hands she chanted a *pirith* to ward off fears and sorrows. The owl had started up once more, an inauspicious sound.

At last Anupama finished, and began again, 'Letters are not like seeds, are they, Handanandāmāmā? I told Mohan, "Nothing can grow out of them." The pieces of coconut shell had fallen apart, letting the rain in. I asked on a sudden thought, "Did you want to hide them from Jayamal?"

'Mohan hiccupped, "Ever since my accident, I keep expecting more bad things to happen."

'"And what has planting letters got to do with it?"

'"Planting from full moon day makes the vegetables grow," he declared.

'"So they say," I replied – cautiously, Handanandāmāmā, because, please forgive me, this is not yet proved.

'"And fruitfulness is a sort of luck, isn't it?" he said. "I'm the opal boy: I had an accident and brought bad luck. Miss Martine has no husband, so she needs good luck also. If she got luckier, she might spread it out and send us things, so I thought if I planted her letters..." He really is the most bright boy.

'"But then tonight it started raining..." I suggested.

'"... and now I've ruined the letters!" Mohan finished, sobbing once again.

'Moon, they were damaged, but not ruined.'

Anupama stared into the moonlight, not heeding the rain in her eyes. 'I wish that letters were like seeds. As you know, Handanandāmāmā, I collect seeds also. A plant grows from a seed. It flowers, fruits and makes seeds in a cycle. That cycle is a fact. If letters were like seeds, they would take a way that we could follow. We could foretell what things will come. But out of Mohan's letter, no present had arrived.

'Our breadfruit tree does not have seeds; at least, that species does not. It grows, tatta tells us, from an injured root.' She reached for the root she'd laid on the heap of offerings, its splinters grazing her fingers. 'We can only grow more roots if we make more cuts. This is a jagged, wounding way towards new life. Its way might be the way of letters. I think I know this. Mohan might suspect, and yet I hope does not.'

Anupama stumbled up, her wet skirt clamped to her legs. 'Among the sodden papers, there is a photo on its own of Mohan's birthday. We are crowding round his cake on the veranda. Then, I still have the smile and rounded cheeks of a baby leopard below the sad eyes of a slow loris – so amma then described them. Now she has told me my jaw is changing, getting lean and growing old to match my eyes. In the same photo, Mohan is looking most enchanting. He was not worried at that time. That was the time before his watch for presents.

'After his accident, we put the photo aside for sending. He must have kept it back.'

And with those words, Anupama trudged home.

On a night at the end of September 1984 the moon was full, and Anupama was cooking with Upeksha. Pans of bean curry, green pumpkin curry and rice were clanking; Upeksha was scolding Anupama; amma was muttering from the mat in her own room; Mohan was brum-brumming his trucks on the veranda; tatta was telling Jayamal about a story in the *Lanka Deepa*; and Anupama realised that, even here, even from indoors, she could turn her mind from what she was doing to communicate with the moon.

'Handanandāmāmā,' she breathed mutely, 'Miss Martine's reasons for sponsoring Mohan have arrived. However, are they truthful? Even at thirteen years, I want to work this out. Mohan is a most adorable boy, most intelligent also, I love him most dearly, but I see more in Miss Martine's letters. If Miss Martine had been my penfriend, I would have said different things, given and requested more facts.

'She says, "I met a man. The man has gone to Sri Lanka." These seem significant facts. She also writes, "The man says he is lazy and a coward."

'She says she believes the man, but deep in her heart she might not.

'These are the reasons she might have chosen my brother:

Mohan lives here in Sri Lanka, where the man has gone.

One day Mohan will be a man (unfortunately I will not).

She thinks Mohan is not a lazy coward.

She hopes that he will not be, when he is a man.

None of the above.

'If I had been writing for myself, I would have requested Miss Martine kindly to tick reason 1, reason 2 and/or so forth. However, her answers might be slippery also, much like Mohan's snakely road.

'Those English letters might have misled us – as might our letters back. However, did we mislead ourselves at first? How should I help the little one, Handanandāmāmā? If I scribe to Miss Martine what Mohan wants, words might come back from her that mislead him or make him worry – or he might be worried if certain words do not come back.

'I could write more than he tells me to – or less – and keep facts from him also, and I doubt that he would notice. But is that idea proper, do you think?'

7 Martine

Tuesday 5 February 2013

Flapping about in her bathrobe to Van Morrison's *Moondance*, having picked it pointedly, now Martine's upbraiding herself. *Coward. Tomorrow Jocelyn Teague will give up on you, move on to someone else.*

Yesterday she fed her foetus of raw pastry to the pigeons.

It's gone midnight, the same night that the object of her indecision has Facebooked a sister and deleted a message to a missing brother. The moon is still a nudge in Martine's local city sky. She gurns on another unwelcome one-liner: *Definition of insomnia: unable to sleep till it's time to wake up.*

In the sitting room, an Asian mask and batik hangings line the walls. She starts laying photos on the carpet, not conscious why. A framed montage of her nieces from her bedroom, all phases of grinning and spoilt, little, teenage and grown-up. Next, a snap of her mother in her last years, in a car park, trouser-legs flapping. Her nostrils are flared and red with age; her eyelids give her an exposed look, albino-seeming, without the usual glasses. A mat of thinning hair, the ever-youthful cherub mouth.

Martine brazens out her mother's lost scrutiny. Now Astrid and Jonas, Astrid smiling, Jonas not, his arm too tightly round her. The next two shots are some party and some drag show, the details long forgotten. Feather fans and bustiers, false eyelashes swoopy as eagle's wings. Saila's there both times, but in the groupings it's Grand Dame Tattlemouse, Bernard when not in drag, whom Martine studies. The bulk of the genitals strapped out of sight and, in theory, mind.

She sits back painfully on her heels. Her row of snaps steers right to left towards the masculine. Freddy on a forest walk, turning towards her lens with stolid forbearance, a rucksack strapped common-sensically round both shoulders. Her long-ago first love. Solemn Mohan with a cricket bat, surrounded by an air of isolation. And last a snapshot of her father. She turns it face-down like the one playing card that will bust her. His portrait in the lobby is enough, the large black and white one at his office desk, a tube train on the wall behind him.

Now she sees why she's dealing out photos: to grapple with her old problem, her attraction to the male. Scanning, her lineup blurs from masculine to feminine just as the moon blurs from dark to light, its terminator indistinct. It's not that she doesn't like women, doesn't have oodles of women friends. It's just that... *Everything's a compromise,* she lectures herself; *so why, when it comes to male or female, do I get so sodding definite?*

She staggers to her feet. Thin moonlight enters the kitchen with her, and her mobile presents new messages.

Bernard texts, 'I'm scared, you're scared, we're all scared, girl. No one's gonna expire.'

The moon's in its last quarter: night by night its light is fading. For some reason, this makes her more afraid. She thinks of her mother, that she's no longer there. Beside her, Sancho shifts, giving her his inscrutable eye. She remembers, *Sancho goes darker when he's frightened. That way he thinks he looks less cowering, more certain.*

Impending blackness moves her towards her laptop. She sits down at the table and, trying to feel more certain, emails Jocelyn Teague.

* * *

1984

Discharged from hospital with Jonas, Martine lay unwillingly on the coloured blocks of her sofa pinioned by Jonas's dressing-gown. She'd felt pinioned in the white bed in the hospital, pinioned when he'd carried her into the flat. The unwilling sister bride. Absurdly, she'd longed to do her clumsy dancing. She fixed on her feet, shapeless in red bedsocks.

Jonas shifted on the sofa arm, fingers raking his thighs. 'I'm going noplace till I know you better.'

Martine raised a mental eyebrow. *Grit: unlike him.*

She snapped, 'Send me a letter telling about you,' a Mohan reference he wouldn't get. She said, 'I don't like being tricked.' First Phil's tasteless joke, now Jonas was abusing her weakness. 'And it makes me squirm when people try to help me. Is that confessional enough?'

'That's something.'

'You're bluffing about staying. You've got a job to get back to.'

'People's kitchen fantasies. They can wait.'

Martine and Jonas reared their heads at their stalemate.

'You insult me,' Martine said.

'What d'you mean?'

'You're implying I'm damaged or something. Everyone's flawed, you included.'

'That's not what I said.' Jonas jumped up and went to the French windows, blinking down at the back of Martine's building, its aerial view of garden walls and trees and gardens. The moon was out there, ignored. 'Tell me some things, anything, that made you who you are.'

'Not everyone goes around thinking why they've turned out the way they have, you know. Some people get on with living. They're too busy for all that.'

'Goddamn right. Busy busy busy.'

'Are you saying I don't have time for you or something?'

'No. I'm...' Jonas made a muffled noise. 'You're... driven.' He faltered. 'Or that's how you come over. I guess I want to know why.'

'Better driven than the opposite.'

'I'm not saying it's a bad thing. Wish I could be that way. All that nerve. I'm asking for pointers here.'

'Flattery. It'll get you nowhere nohow.'

Jonas left the room without explanation. Martine heard him

murmuring into the phone, having shut the door. She focused on the room enlargements in her mirrors. She always had to have a door ajar, couldn't bear the sensation of imprisonment. She pushed down the memories of ten years ago when someone had locked her in a lab storeroom. The school caretaker, who she used to kid around with, had denied it, said he'd have heard her calling if he'd done it, let her out. Five half-term days of thirst, hunger and excreting into beakers, of silence and the dark, in the time before mobile phones.

When Jonas came back to her she said, 'So you've explained that I'm your hostage. And what does Astrid think?'

'It's not all about you. Astrid just suggested moving in with me.' He continued, 'Stuart says he's moving on, so…'

Stuart his flatmate.

He re-positioned himself on the sofa end; Martine hunkered down in her dressing-gown.

'I still mourn Mom, my birth Mom,' Jonas began again. 'Never having had her. I guess that's why I sometimes seem… dependent.'

Martine imagined Astrid advising him in her Nordic lilt, 'You could try not asking, only telling. Trading feelings?'

'More blackmail,' she snapped. 'You know my weakness on Mum and Dad, so now you're heading for that.'

He didn't deny it. 'You let your Mom kind of adopt me. That's amazing.'

She rolled her eyes. 'Skip your Mum, died giving birth to you, blah blah blah, and Dad's Merrimac woman with her own kids, not that bothered about you, blah blah, and how my Mum saved you, more blah.' Jonas twitched. 'Get to the Dad part.'

Jonas gave in. 'I let you keep the wrong picture of Dad.'

'What picture? I was only three when he left.'

'I wonder' – ('Go gentle, Jonas,' Martine decided that Astrid must have advised) – 'I just wonder if you…'

'You think I'm a daddy's girl? That I've glamourised him,

across the pond and all that? That I think he's perfect just because Mum's said so?' Jonas didn't respond. Martine snipped, 'By the way, you know that for Mum you're his stand-in, don't you?' He still didn't respond. She said, 'How dare you presume to know how I feel about him?'

'Now you're assuming what I was trying to say.' Jonas cleared his throat. 'I'm gonna tell you about him.' Martine fell silent, waiting, heart mysteriously pumping. 'He has to be early for everything. Drives me crazy. Claims he needs time to get used to situations. Basically he's a buttoned-up British guy still learning not to be shy – according to Merrimac Mom, anyways.' Jonas rambled on, and the facts kept on falling. Martine listened. 'He loves kids, too. Turns to mush when he's around them, forgets his hang-ups. But he lost interest in me, I guess as I got older. Then Merrimac Mom and her own brood came along.'

This was all new to Martine. 'He left me when I was little,' she said flatly.

'It must've hurt him like hell.'

'Dad's letters stopped when I was eleven.' Jonas shrugged, clearly not knowing why. 'Mum tells me', Martine seethed, 'when we were still a family, whenever they started an argument, one of them would take me out of the room and shut me in another. After a bit, one of them would come to me and toddle me back in. They did it to shame themselves to stop. But then they would re-start. And the same all over again.'

Jonas shook his head. 'Dad told me. He says they moved you around to save you grief. Then he'd stress about you on your lonesome. He said he couldn't stand either.'

'I wish she'd never told me. Shuttled backwards and forwards.' Martine mused, a faint light dawning. 'Small wonder I don't like wandering off straight lines.'

The door buzzer sounded.

Martine brightened. 'It's probably someone checking how I am.'

Jonas made no move to rise.

Martine levered herself up. 'OK then, I'll– ...'

He stood in front of her, blocked her. She struggled, swearing, but eventually sank back. Jonas retreated to the French windows.

It was night-time. They were oblivious to the moon, a silver rind draped in black clouds above the parapet outline of the roof terrace, wire-brushing the housing estate rows angled towards a slab of low-rise flats. Jonas pulled the blinds, muffling a tide of city noise.

He fell into the Eames chair, his legs flung out before him.

'Someone'll ring,' threatened Martine.

He got up and flicked out the living room phone cord. 'I wish we could be… friends. That's why I'm trying to talk.'

'You think we don't get on, that I don't want to?'

Jonas said, 'I'm working my butt off here.' Martine didn't speak. 'When you ask me I tell you about my love life. I trust you. I trusted you to get me work.'

'You're saying I don't trust you.'

'D'you trust anyone?'

'Look, I don't even trust myself.'

'Or don't like yourself.'

'I'll tell you what I don't like,' Martine started. 'My love life, so-called. Hunting for a man. Pretending that I'm not.' Words were erupting out of her. 'Getting used to disappointment. Ignoring people's hints, the clock they're tapping behind their eyes, as if there's some imperative about it. The fact there probably is. Laying eggs and banging a gong I never asked for every bloody month. The pain. Dressing myself for it, medicating myself for it, like a wounded gangster. Sorry, but fuck,' Martine said. 'Pretending I want a relationship more than sex – unless the bloke wants sex more than a relationship, and then pretending that. Pretending he's fantastic. Trying not to think how fantastic I'm not. Keeping busy to block that thought. Being on my own or idle, because then I can't block it. Depending on people like Mum to block it for me…'

Jonas murmured, 'She stresses about you.'

'I know that! And how fucking guilty do you think that makes me feel?' A braying noise came out of Martine. 'I could tell her what sex does for me. That it pours me away into the man I'm with. That not being myself, not being by myself, is pretty much all I work at. D'you think that'd reassure her?'

Her hand was spooling tissues from a box now. She listed her reams of failed male encounters, then heard herself describe in gruesome detail how she wanted to be touched and smelt and tasted, and in what way, and more.

Jonas tried to hold her. She beat him off. He sat, drooping chin on steepled hands.

All at once, Martine ground to a halt and she thought, vividly as a storm in sunlight, *Noah sent a bird over flooded wastes to search for something solid. I've just flown the savagest bird. I'm on a vast, empty prow with the memory of its claws, of what I've said, anchored in my palm. The useless memory, since I've let it go.*

Jonas suddenly walked to the kitchen and stewed them apples with cinnamon, more or less the way she'd taught. Martine was relieved. She'd swamped him with the sump oil of her life, he'd surprised her in the rough grass of his stubbornness. They'd crossed into regions of each other that they'd never guessed were there.

With things so raw, Martine wanted him gone from her flat. But the fact was, someone had to help her move around. Every night he supported her to the bathroom. There was intimate laundry, things in her bathroom cabinet that made him blanch. Sleeping in her impersonal spare room clearly rattled him after her mother's, the guilelessness of Mum's fussy, unsure style.

Over the days Martine tried to shove back the entrails of what she'd lately exposed. 'It's not about sex. I'm not a… I just need…' 'Of course I want someone permanent…' 'It's not that I don't like being helped, it's just that I'm not used to it.'

Jonas twitched, looking unconvinced.

One day, eating their signature chicken with grilled peppers, he said, 'Why did you never offer me a home when I got here?'

Martine clattered down cutlery. 'I never thought you'd think… You and Mum seemed to feel the loss of Dad even more than I did. And you needing something of her was exactly what she needed.'

'You don't need me?'

'I don't know how to answer that at all.'

'I'll take that as a no.'

'That wouldn't be quite right.' That was as far as Martine could go.

She knew she was being stingy with her feelings. To compensate, she found herself admitting, 'There's something you don't know.' She tried to twinkle at him. 'I've met a boy.'

She sent him to the study for Mohan's letters, drawings and photos.

Swilling them on the coffee table, something came over Jonas. Martine saw it. The drawings roused him especially. His arm crept to his chest and lay there gently clutching. Later he'd tell her that they presented him with a vision of the life he wanted: Astrid and three children. Girls, he'd tell her later, just like in the stories.

'The boy's not a substitute son,' said Martine. 'I still don't know how I feel about having children.'

'What did you write the little guy about me?'

She told him. Then he wondered why a boy.

She shrugged, 'Why heads, why tails?'

There was a lot more to an answer that she didn't know herself, and the question stayed inside her.

8 Martine

It's the small hours. In bed, Martine can't sleep. She lies on her side, switches onto her back, rolls onto her side again. She's trying to conjure back the Sri Lankan dream that she has sometimes: not just to have it, but to finish it. She fixes on the stimulus of the tropical curtains. She's shivering. To have the dream she should be steamy-hot, but the heating's off, and despite two extra blankets, she can't warm up.

Sometimes dribs and drabs of the dream trickle into her sleep and trickle away again, unresolved; sometimes the narrative begins and gathers pace before shearing off like fabric; sometimes the dream plays out at length until some logic in her brainwaves refuses to believe in it, and the dream turns on its heel and ambles away from her, whistling nonchalantly to itself. So she has never known the ending.

She pours more water from a carafe into the glass on her bedside table, drinks it down. She remembers and notes wearily, puzzled, *The dream never leaves me thirsty*. The dream in its entirety is a problem she hasn't solved yet; the ending seems a key to something important. One of these nights she has to perfect it, complete it, get it right.

* * *

1984–1985

Martine was supposed to convalesce gently, so Jonas stayed on and helped her, if inefficiently, to a soundtrack of tuneless whistling and bad jokes. She shook her head despairingly sometimes at the void where his self-belief should have been, but she began to see new things in him, tact maybe, or at least the discretion to withdraw, and appreciated him for them. Nonetheless they moved apart again. She slipped into a tunnel, went back to self-contained. The roar of their recent clashes died away. In its wake, there was the odd spark on their lines and a distant rumble.

One day, Jonas slipped Martine a sheet of paper. 'Might amuse the little guy.'

A cut-away map of the Underground, quirky, non-mathematical. There was a tube train with an animal face, burrowing through the network, and London landmarks like molehills on the surface.

'It's wonderful,' smiled Martine.

She added a stick figure of herself, on her route to work. She wrote a letter to Mohan asking about the civil war, inserted Jonas's map and sent them on.

'16th November 1984

'Dear Miss Martine

I did not hear from you a long time. Then your letter came. Anupama took me upways the snakeish road to the temple. We put flowers at the shrine.

'I have a cough.

'Your journey in the tubes is nice and walking on the dots. The head is a melon and the arms are sticks and the legs are sticks.

'My question is "Why are you going in the tubes with ointment? Do you like it?"

'My question is "Do you have a car? What is it?"

'My question is "Describe to me your buses."

'Anupama has an idea. She can write I ride my tatta's bicycle, on the behind. I am a king on the cart. I ride with my father only in the village. Tatta is saying very strongly we are not going towards Kandy except Anupama and Upeksha safely on the school bus.

'It was indeed most fearful last year, July. Tatta and senior uncle heard about some people gave bad names to some people. Some cars were fired also. There are some torn people in the tea plantations not far up. Tatta does not talk about it. I request you most ardently do not ask because I am most youthful and I am quite worrying.

'My sister can make punctuation marks and this point is significant: please notice.'

Martine murmured in distress at her own insensitivity when she received this. She could understand the knockback, but InterRelate soon hammered Mohan's point home.

'Dear Miss Haslett

Organisational changes

I have pleasure in introducing myself as the new Programme Manager.

'Thank you for writing to our London branch.

'We fully understand your concern for the political situation in Sri Lanka and your desire to support your "adoptive family" in troubled times. However, I should be grateful if you would re-familiarise yourself with InterRelate's rules. These require sponsors to refrain from communicating with "their" children on political matters. Charities such as ours can act, indeed can exist, only thanks to a bond of trust with, and the full endorsement and support of, the government of the day. This necessitates an undertaking on our part to remain politically neutral in all dealings at every level.

'On a positive note, we have been restructuring. This extends to the translation of letters. Our own, expanded team of highly qualified personnel will henceforward interpret the letters between you and "your" family, checking them carefully to ensure that their meanings are as clear as they need to be.

'Rest assured that the welfare of the families is always our primary concern.

'Thank you for this opportunity to make myself known to you.

'Yours sincerely

Anura de Silva

Programme Manager, Colombo Office, InterRelate International'

And yet Martine had only been trying, or so she felt.

Her return to college was phased in, so even in the new year she had more time to write, and a lingering need for penance made her strain.

Warned off by InterRelate and Mohan, while sparing the boy hard news such as her mugging, she still tried to elaborate in her letters. 'Happy New Year! We don't celebrate much here, but I suspect you do... Here's a photo of my new Mini. The driver sits very low to the ground. I dodge in and out of the traffic. The car's so small that it's easy to park. Mostly it's quicker to use the tube, though – but it doesn't hold ointment. We call it a tube because...'

Writing to him came slowly, mentally and physically. Mohan's replies surged back. It was an ebb and flow, every four to six weeks: the ebb in Martine's case, depleting her, because, to her frustration, no sense of connection grew.

'Your letters take a long time. Anupama says not to worry, then I play with my cars.

'Your Mini is fantastic. The tube is nice with no ointment.

'How can you celebrate New Year if there are no new things?

'My question is "How does a tube work? Is it dark inside?"

'What do you like? I like cars, lorries, shrews, cricket, football and Upeksha's curries – nearly all.

'About our new latrine. It is called a pour flush. The walls have holes at the top. There is a metal roof. They dug a septic pit. They put in an S-trap. They put in wire mesh. A bucket made a hole in the middle. They poured concrete in around. It dried. They put in a squatting pan. They connected it to the S-trap. We pour water down. I watched the men building. It was nice.

'Mr Semasinghe does not bring your letters now. Mr Mendes from Colombo. He drives a LandRover more than 120 kilometres. Amma says he is the man who came to talk so that you could adopt me. Mr Semasinghe still brings our other letters. It is a change. I ask Anupama why. She says do not worry.

'Tatta and the fathers want a tractor not two bullocks.

'I have thought of another thing I like: machines.'

Jonas pored over these letters as they got more detailed.

'Now I am seven. I was absolutely not waiting for a present.

'It is nothing important, but my sister has grown big.

'When is your birthday and other special days? How do you celebrate them?

'You told me "I like fast cars, swimming, pigs, the full moon, the colour green, most children and most of my own cooking."

'That is nice, but I like the part about tubes.

'We celebrate most numerous festivals about the moon. I kindly request you describe your moon festivals.

'I am excited for New Year. A prince will come from the sky riding in a white carriage. He will wear a white crown. He will break through the sea of milk.

'Anupama says "You are making a story. In Buddhism it is about the sun."

'The ladies will put out the fires except one log. They will wash and clean the house and get all the food and water into the house. The family will wait. We will have sweetmeats and games. Then we can throw firecrackers. Amma will light the stove and boil the milk over. We will throw a present in the well and take up water. We will give presents on betel leaves. We will eat milk rice with plums and sesame seeds. There is a play day with pillow fights and I can hit Jayamal with a bag.

'Firecrackers are loud. I liked them last year. This year, I do not think I will.

'What things do you not like? Here are mine. Coughing. Cobras because they cannot be good spirits in the house. Anupama says yes but I say no. I do not like Buddhism lessons. Anupama is writing that I do not like her curries but I want to.

'If possible, I kindly request you to put outstanding stamps on your letters – showing seeds, insects, reptiles or minerals.'

Certain phrases stood out. 'I kindly request you to describe your moon festivals... put outstanding stamps on your letters.'

Martine registered, Mohan's getting more demanding.

Then there were his questions, 'What do you like?' and 'What things do you not like?'

She thought, Like a date showing off his emotional literacy, male to female. As if trying to make a good lover's impression.

Through the spring, leaving work, Claire, who lived two stops from Martine, offered, 'Stay on the tube and walk home with you?'

Martine said she was fine, happy and fine; but fear from the mugging was still in her somewhere, like an undeveloped negative.

Mohan's fears seemed to lie elsewhere than the civil war: coughing, firecrackers, people talking fiercely, sharp swords and in his dreams. Reading, Martine thought, *Comfort him. Why can't I comfort him?*

Whereas Jonas's fears started to touch her. Of not belonging anywhere. Of finding no one liked what he could offer. Of disintegrating into no one in the sight of everyone, especially himself. Unlike her he seemed to need love, had to have it, maybe couldn't even otherwise survive.

The differences in Mohan's writing seemed to become more marked.

'Mrs Thatcher opened the Victoria Dam on the Wimalasiris' TV. It is an arch dam. Here is my diagram.

'Amma did not do the things at New Year. Anupama says do not worry about amma.

'It is raining. Anupama says it is not English cats and dogs but Sri Lankan boar and bullocks.

'Your letter said "I get a bit foolish sometimes when it is full moon."

'That is funny.

'What I do not like. Answer. Being made to do things and not to do things also like you. I do not like people playing tricks on me also. But I like people trying to help me and being kind to me. That is a strange thing not to like.

'Anupama wants to write about the Buddha's birthday, the first day of full moon this month. But I do not want to tell you about the thorana by the snakeish road and paper lanterns with candles and the seven lotus-flower steps from the feet of Prince Siddhartha and being kinder to ill people like amma. Anyway Anupama promises strongly that amma is not ill. I am not interested, only in my birthday.

'Anupama says "How absolutely typical of a young and foolish boy. You are for certain not the young Prince Siddartha."

'She is laughing. I tell you that she took a long time to write about full moon.

'Here are two more things. I do not like it when people tease me and when they talk fiercely in quiet voices.'

Martine couldn't quite put her finger on the letters' evolution. And she was chastened that Mohan had picked up on the thing about her craziness at full moon. It had just been a cheap remark to fill up the page. She began to search out special stamps, as he asked.

'28th July 1985

Dear Miss Martine

I am happy Jonas lives closer to your house and you like him more and more. Anupama says she understands.

'My question is "Was he naughty before?"

'My question is "Why is he in a house away from your house?"

'My question is "What does he work?"

'I have made a model of the tube. It is bamboo. You are a nutmeg and cinnamon sticks. You cannot go in. I cannot send you a photo. We are waiting to borrow the camera from the Jarasinghes.

'Here is my drawing of our lands. I am a pilot looking down. You can see the mountains. They stand near our village. The snakeish road goes up and round. Some people call the mountains the Knuckles Range. It is better to call them Dumbara Kanduvetiya, or the most admirable geologist P.J. Cooray says the Mist-Laden Mountains, because there are no knuckles on our side of the ridge.

'On our side under the scrubby summits are the cloudforests, the high montane region. The tea plantations grow in the mists of moisture also. In the high hills are ferns and mosses among the waterfalls. There are evergreen and semi-evergreen and coniferous trees. There are the red flowers of big flame trees. Below are the lower montane and tropical regions and our village and other villages and paddy and many tropical plants. The paddy of the fathers is on a terrace. Look, you can see the rice stalks sticking out. The snakeish road goes down to Kandy.

'Your stamp of a dragonfly is outstanding. It might be the scalloped spreadwing. The water lilies look like ours. Sometimes I climb to the streams very far. There are bright birds and many dazzling insects. Among the dragonflies there are dark forestwraiths, mountain reedlings and numerous others – 117 species, in fact.

'The nymph lives in water for up to four years then crawls out, shedding its skin on the stem of a water plant. The adult lives only one year. I remain puzzled. Which part of the dragonfly changes, and which part stays the same?'

Another letter came with it, impatiently, in the same envelope. This was a new development, too.

'30th July 1985

Mr Mendes is still here and Anupama wants me to write to you again. She wants me to tell you about the Esala Perahera festival. It is about the rains. There are processions near the Temple of the Tooth. The elephants wear bright coats and jewels. I do not like the flames jumping about in the fire dances. The men with sharp swords who go to the river and [*girl's writing incomplete*]. We are stopping now to talk about my dreams.

'We have finished talking. The swordsmen cut the river, nothing else.

'I utterly enjoy the fact called surface tension. It is a skin on liquid. If it is cut, it grows together most rapidly. However, once again I am puzzled. Is that skin, healed over, the same as the skin before?

'I tell Anupama that my letters are growing longer.

'Anupama says "You are growing longer too, so this should not surprise you."

'Please be gentle with your brother, because you are older. Anupama says she is gentle. She is not crying.

'I wish I had told you more about growing big. I wish I had asked about growing big in England.

'What I like most is writing to you, to be perfectly honest.'

One August day, soon after getting these letters, Martine gave up her seat on the tube to a pregnant woman. Minutes later, the train braked in a tunnel. There was a forced roar from the engine, then a death-throe ticking.

She smiled at the man jammed up against her. 'My watch has stopped.'

He sighed behind unnecessary dark glasses, showing her his watch. She had a meeting at Waterloo, tendering for the teacher development of a whole outer London borough. *This can't happen,* she thought.

The crammed carriage was sweltering. Some passengers closed their eyes or stared ahead, buried themselves in books or papers or the jangle of their Walkmans, but the rest stared wildly or smiled like sudden friends, trying, against tube protocol, to connect.

There was a clank then sounds of tinkering. Martine's fears of a lock-in didn't take hold on the tube unless, like now, an engine ceased its chuntering. Blood pumped into her ears, the life plea of the hostage. The expectant woman pushed at her cuticles. A boy fanned his girlfriend; laughing, she fanned him back. A mother gripped her toddler's teddy bear too tight, fumbling the beads around her neck.

Feeling rammed up against the black brickwork through the windows, Martine cast about for a calming strategy too.

From memory, she clutched at the questions in Mohan's recent letters that had stood out: 'What part of the dragonfly changes, and what part stays the same?'; and, about the surface tension of water, 'Is that skin, healed over, the same as the skin before?'

Teaching was her standard act of giving, so she prepared her answers ready for writing down. That occupied her until the train was fixed.

Revisiting the letters that day started something. She didn't know it at the time. It was as if their details began to irrigate her, at the same time rusting the cogs of her current life. She was being primed. Inside her soon would rear up Mohan's scrubby summits; his cloudforests and tea plantations; his ferns, mosses, waterfalls with dragonflies: a whole new landscape, bathed in an angel light.

9 Martine

Jocelyn Teague responds to Martine's email.

Martine screens her scratchy voice, enthusing to itself. '...I just know you'll both get on... I'll send you directions on buses, tube and so on... Have you got a digital photo that I can take in? Could you ping it through?'

Martine feels for her heart: to her surprise, it's beating just the same. Sancho is roaming his cage more than usual though, back and forth, up and down with stop-start deliberation, as if he knows something is up.

She's texted Jonas that she's said yes. He's pleased for her – *And probably*, she thinks, *a bit relieved for himself.* To celebrate, he texts back, he's coming over later, and will try to bring the girls. Martine sidles past Sancho, foraging from the cupboards and the fridge. For the family she makes more pastry, and frangipane this time, and bakes them into little, fat plum tarts.

Jonas hasn't visited for a while: too busy getting ready for America. A month ago he broke the news. Him and Pearl: in Pearl's case, for a holiday, at least at first. Jonas hesitated after he'd told Martine, then tried to pat her hand. She remembers pushing her chair back, pretending it was to offer him a beer, and yet she liked that brief male touch.

Now that she's emailed Jocelyn, she has to broach the guest room. It used to be her home office before last year's crisis and she retired and her mother went. Four boxy walls and one small window, a single bed and a narrow bedside table, a desk and chest of drawers. The paintwork looks dejected. She's rung the decorator, who says that, for a price, his nephew can fit her in.

She blinks at the clutter she'll have to move. There's a scrumpled scarf in a bag, which Martine was going to frame. Her mother's golf clubs and the now unneeded clothes, Mum's dog bed and secret trophies, in paper in their box; and of course the letter carton. Another cracker joke torments her: *What's spring cleaning? A sign the laptop is broken.*

She picks up the carton and heads towards her bedroom. She elbows open her wardrobe door. There isn't room on the top shelf. She rests the carton on her white duvet. From the high storage space, she tips out a plastic bag, full of scarves and hats and gloves she never wears. She'll take them to a charity shop or somewhere. Swiftly, she hefts the carton round and up. For a moment it feels supernaturally heavy, the weight on a pulley inside a pendulum clock. She pushes it into darkness. The letters are once more hidden, but they're attached to her life; and despite her resistance her life, wound up like a dead weight, is starting slowly to drop.

* * *

1985

It was a mid-September Sunday in Harrow Weald. Empty bamboo steamers, blue and white sauce bowls, sesame crumbs, fortune cookie wrappers and starched red napkins littered Mr Wu's best tablecloth. Jonas and Astrid smiled with Martine at her sixty-year-old mother in her new violet dress.

'You deserve the best for all you've done for us.' The three said variations on this theme.

Martine's mother seemed serene, happy to have them round her.

That day, Astrid unofficially entered the family – to Martine, another cause for celebration. She saw her as quirky, calm and sure. Her own life could continue on its oiled tramlines now since, with Astrid, Jonas should be like she was: happy and fine.

He took Martine aside. 'This one's on me.'

She opened her bag. 'I'll do it.'

His shoulders bunched, and she got a pang she recognised by then. She'd nearly refused his lift to Harrow Weald, too.

'OK, let me pay half.'

The words of Mohan's recent letter reminded her, 'Please be gentle with your brother, because you are older.'

A sister could affect her brother too much. In recent months she and Jonas had strung a line of effort between them; there was a little more give and take.

She took out a credit card, Jonas started a cheque. He turned to her.

'15 September,' she supplied.

He grinned. '1985: who'da thought? Only a year back, we...'

Martine sat with Astrid in the back of Jonas's beaten-up Capri on the return to London. At last her mother knew about the letters: Martine had assured her that they didn't mean maternal cravings.

Now she showed a couple to Astrid, who was a plumber. 'Here's one about latrines.'

Her Debbie Harry hair shutting off her little face, Astrid read.

Then in her seesaw voice she either stated or asked, 'You do this to help the boy's people.' She addressed Jonas at the wheel. 'You could draw for her a latrine. Like the Underground drawing you told to me.'

He said, 'Don't read back there. It'll make you sick.'

Astrid sat back giggling, 'Only his driving, it does that.'

She studied the latest letter. 'Conflict is there with the sister.' She quoted from it, '"Please be gentle with your brother."' She winked out of sight of Jonas and made a neck-wringing gesture. 'What is "growing big"?'

Martine shrugged. 'Growing up? Which seems to worry him.'

Astrid gave a little exclamation. '"What I like most is writing to you," it is the most sad sentence.' She cocked her head.

Martine's gaze rested on Astrid; later, she took out the letter and looked at it again.

Another question had been picking at her mind: Jonas had asked it himself, a while ago. *Why Mohan? Why a boy?* She'd asked InterRelate for one – unthinkingly, she felt. Also, she found herself puzzling, *In that did they oblige me, or was a he their decision?* In the end she'd asked InterRelate.

She got the answer just after her mother's birthday.

'Dear Miss Haslett

Excuse this hasty scrawl. We have little time for individual correspondence. Attached is a photocopy of a proposed official response to an FAQ – suggested by a Colombo colleague – which might answer your query. I have highlighted the relevant section. Please forgive that it is addressed to colleagues. I should have Tippexed out the comments meant only for us, which may be a little blunt, forgive me, but I am, in haste,

'Sincerely

Derek Ffrench

Public Relations Manager, InterRelate International, London'

'Dear Derek and London team

Some thoughts re: the FAQ "How was 'my' adoptive family/the location of 'my' adoptive family, and/or 'my' adoptive child/the gender of 'my' adoptive child chosen within the family?"

'Sponsors can assume that all our local efforts are undertaken primarily on their behalf. They may find it hard to see themselves as anything other than clients; they may regard us more as a service than a charity. This is natural. Theirs will tend to be the market-orientated perspective of the affluent, commodified, "developed" world.

'That said, they may on occasion ask for some account of how we identify the beneficiaries of their generosity, and perhaps they are entitled to know more than we currently tell them.

'Would there be mileage in updating our FAQs to include

something like the text below? Our field officers consult with a) other NGOs and b) communities, community organisations and groups in the locality. Through this process, plus their own systematic, on-the-ground research, they establish key areas of need, e.g. education, sanitation, health education etc.

'InterRelate Colombo analyses the officers' quantitative and qualitative findings. The local needs identified are ranked in terms of urgency and severity. From this process, one or more spending priorities, e.g. sanitation, are ascertained. Achievable objectives, including the budget/funds needed, are articulated, e.g. "Build x latrines @ x cost in x locations."

'Existing funds are allocated, and/or essential fundraising begins, e.g. advertising for more sponsors in countries we choose to target.

'With the locations for new projects now identified, field officers return to those communities. Through house-to-house visits, they identify a) families who are likely to prove committed recipients of communications from overseas sponsors, and b) children, one per family, whom parents and officers agree would be suitable 'readers' of, and respondees to, such letters.

The choice of child is a delicate matter, and needs sensitive discussion with parents and other respected elders linked to the home. Within any community, particularly in a country like Sri Lanka with its current ethnic and religious tensions, an equitable spread of children should be sought – in terms of ethnic origin, religious affiliation and gender.

Concerning gender, traditionally Sri Lankan families accord boys more choices and privileges than girls. The eldest boy, especially, has a particular status among his siblings – but for InterRelate, in some cases he may be less appropriate as a writing partner than, say, a younger brother (it is to be hoped, after all, that the relationship with a sponsor will last and develop). Attempts to persuade families to nominate a girl over a boy should be made circumspectly, with due regard for prevailing local views on gender roles.

'Educating sponsors more fully in these realities can only help us by engaging them still more. If we explain things diplomatically, perhaps we can also start to shift their perceptions of their part in the process of charitable "adoption".

'Good wishes to all in London

Anura de Silva

Programme Manager, Colombo Office, InterRelate International'

This answered some, but not all, of Martine's puzzles.

Then there were more undercurrents in Mohan's latest letter.

'25th September 1985

Your typing is different. Anupama did not notice.

'My question is "Our mountains do *not* sound beautiful. The jackals and the bats screeching and Jayamal copying me talking are annoying."

'Anupama says that is not polite and not a question. I can see her writing that. I say she must put what I ask.

'My question is "Do you have a computer typing? What kind is it?"

'Happy birthday on 27th August. Anupama asked me to say, but I have agreed. I could not send you a present. Anupama wishes we had.

'I have a cough again. Anupama is cuddling me. I am watching her write.

'If we could send you a present, mine would be invisible ink. I dilute Coca-Cola with water. I dip a stick in it. Then I would write over it, and you of course would type across. To see the writing, we would heat it in the oven. We could find translators. They would be our special agents.

'Here are the reasons why I would choose this present.

We could communicate most secretly.

Things that are there and not there, both, intrigue me.

'Are the things we hide still real? Are they still facts? I entreat you ardently, please tell me your opinion.

'I am annoyed. I want Anupama to write that. I have checked. She has written it. But she will not tell you why I am annoyed. She will only write that she will not tell you. She has gone to start the baby jak fruit curry. Now I am *very very* annoyed. I am writing this part trying hard.

'My question is what does your brother do if you do not do what he asks.

'She is coming back. I will hide the letter. I will say I have lost it. I will give it to Mr Mendes when she is not here.'

'29th September 1985

P.S. I know that Mr Mendes has the letter. I told him that this is another part. I request you to believe strongly that this is indeed another part, absolutely essential. This is a fact. I have most numerous things still to say to you and ask you. I wish we had shared more facts. I ardently wish you were here so we could talk.'

'What does your brother do if you do not do what he asks?'

Martine answered Mohan when the letter came, but inwardly. *Well, sometimes Jonas digs in his heels. And sometimes, I register his long, stricken face and know that I'm not giving him what he's asking for.*

The letter came in early October, with the cold nights drawing in. Martine was at her swimming pool surging up and down in the butterfly, trying not to think of Charlie. The moon was shrinking down beyond its last quarter, blinking at her churning progress through a skylight, at her thrashings of mind and body away from Charlie.

For mental distraction she thought about contraception. She

was three months on the diaphragm, having left the pill. She felt in some sense whole again, her ovaries dragging at her abdomen. And then there was a moment, an instant of fantasy, uncharacteristic, that to this day she no longer even remembers. To her eyes breaking the surface, the broken pieces of the moon flashing in the water in their uneven rows became the blisters in a pack of Loestrin.

She aimed for the pool end, another swimmer fighting her to it. Her palms pressed the cool tile of the wall, and she crouched and kicked off and twisted, but the pill images stayed with her, dot-dashing along the lane beside her. She pulled herself onto the ladder. The word *monath* came to mind, *month*, connecting her cycles to the word *moon*. After that brief hallucination she'd be attuned to the moon as poetry, not just as fact, for always.

Monath. Mona. The words evolved in her brain into *Mohan.* As her feet slapped to the changing rooms, frustration returned about him. There was something wrong between him and Anupama – *And*, she cursed, *whatever it is you can't do a sodding thing about it.*

Swimsuits flopped over cubicle doors. The tiles bounced women's halloos, laughter, shouts, gossip, reminding her of something about the letters. There were things about them she couldn't fathom. Mohan seemed to speak in several voices, some of them almost lover-like, or adult. Apart from the familiar interrogator with his 'My question is', of late she'd picked up the oddest tones: philosopher, scientist, bad dreamer, Buddhist – who disliked religion, even so – and to her the weirdest, with its talk of invisible ink: secret agent. As if he'd refracted into various personalities, become a puzzle. He was no longer what he'd been, revolving in a corner of the gadget of her life, a routine widget, an unremarkable little part she needn't be too concerned with.

She assumed with an inner shrug that the alien voices came from her, a kind of splintering effect of the mugging or her recent combat with Jonas.

She reclaimed her clothes and armlet from her locker. As she did, the hook on her cubicle door caught her and scratched a finger. A red drop oozed. She reminded herself, *Concentrate on Mohan, not on Charlie.*

'What I like most is writing to you... I have things still to say to you... I ardently wish you were here.'

'It is the most sad sentence,' Astrid had pointed out.

An enigma of a boy, delicate and thin, under an alien tree, its leaves like paws. Out of nowhere he broke through Martine like a bead of blood through a membrane. From then on, she really did want to share herself with him.

10 Anupama

Wednesday 6 February 2013

It's afternoon, and Anupama's husband Asiri is at his job on reception at the Suisse Hotel. Before he left, they kissed long and deep. Her groin still tight, Anupama paces their corner of garden to the tooting of the birds, fanning herself with her iPhone clone. Her washing is drying over the hibiscus: she still prefers the old, country method.

She's been rehearsing, for the hundredth time, what she knows. She's discovered the narrowness of the ways that a forty-one-year-old Sri Lankan, a woman who is only now taking her A levels, can train to become a barrister. She thinks of Asiri. *Husband.* She hasn't yet told him the narrowness of those ways.

'Handanandāmāmā,' she remembers, 'there was a time when I was most fascinated by the crust movements of this island. Our metamorphic rocks, lurking in layers. Gradually I discovered that even before their time it was sand and clay and silt that went on to make the rocks that went on to make the metamorphic layers. And these facts feel to me as deeply hidden yet as significant as that original silt.'

She resolves, *I cannot put it off any longer. I must tell him.*

* * *

1984–1985

October 1984, and Anupama was on the laneside after school. There was a bees' nest in a high tree, the bulbous sac pendulous from an inaccessible branch. Her brothers wanted to help their neighbours build the dislodging fire. Jayamal pushed and Mohan darted among grown men positioning brushwood and a ladder, but Anupama fished a half-written letter out of her skirt pocket. Although it was light, to her mind the moon still watched her.

'Handanandāmāmā, here are some pleasant facts for our album,' she started inside her head. 'When amma was young, she used to clamber up behind her family's house, following mountain streams for water. The streams were pure, especially at that altitude. Times are different now, and we live in a different place. Amma is not happy.' She tried to smile. 'Still, you see me climb to her old spots, to think of her and watch the dragonflies. They are magnificent.'

She shook her head. 'Unfortunately there are other facts also. Have you noticed,' she asked, 'that Mohan's sleep, since Black July, has grown still worse? Also he has a cough like words he dare not speak. Of course, there has been further hideous news since Black July.'

'And now Miss Martine has written, this long time after, about it. She is asking, "What has happened to you since July last year, I mean 1983? Is your family all right?"

'I know some facts about our troubles. Unfortunately, Mohan knows a few also. Because facts are rare and precious, that does not mean that when we learn them they cannot hurt.

'So I have not read Miss Martine's questions to Mohan. I am writing, in Mohan's name, merely enough to warn her not to write that way again.' Anupama frowned at the paper in her hand. 'I hope it is the proper thing. Auntie-Uncle Moon, I am still only thirteen.'

October 1985. A year had passed, and Anupama hadn't talked to the moon in all that time. She had her reasons.

The stars and its waning oval lit the rain stabbing the dark as, heedless of her soaking, she hauled two pails of water from the nearest village stream.

Without greeting her Auntie-Uncle Moon she threw down the buckets and burst out, 'At last I have the courage. I have been too ashamed to speak to you until now. When tatta has sometimes said, "Come and sit under the black umbrella," meaning the night, I have not, for fear of seeing you. When Mohan and I wrote to Miss Martine about the Buddha's birthday, and I had to write about full moon, I felt unworthy to write your name. The other day I saw you in the stream in pieces. Of course it is most unscientific, but for a moment, I thought it was because of me.

'I know you watch me and see everything. Nothing is concealed from you. But I believe that the Roman Catholics have a practice they call confession; and now I must confess to you anyway, to try to make myself better, although you know it all, of course.

'Last year I began something not right. In scenes I was involved with there were untruths that made changes. I know I made the dishonest details; what I do not know is when those details, like the edges of P.J. Cooray's metamorphic rock, moved, and pushed, and started to heat and carve the events around them, step by step, until things became the unbearable way they are.

'I took step number 1 for the protection of Mohan, or so I thought. It was when I asked Miss Martine not to mention our political troubles to him, hiding my strong plea in his words. Remember, I talked to you about it. She must have listened: she has never written again on these difficult matters. But Mohan's fearfulness continued, as you will have noticed. He ordered me to tell her his cough was serious. Then that a cobra came to his bed that could say his name. Then he wanted me to ask her whether his foolishness in wanting a special present had taken InterRelate's letters from the postman. Then, whether the swordsmen at Esala Perahera were bad men. I did not write these things. I disobeyed to protect him – perhaps Miss Martine also, if I am perfectly honest.'

Far off, a barn owl lowed.

'You shine on the mighty Lion Rock at Sigiriya also. I went there with my school once. What I had done was one shallow step through the water gardens beneath its cliff and giant paws.

And yet it was a step.'

Anupama's hair hung in wet hanks. She straightened and took up the buckets and began to carry them home.

She went on, 'And then I took step number 2. I helped Mohan write more interesting letters. I have to explain.

'InterRelate's latrines arrived in the village a while ago, remember. No more bushes for the women, no more polite pretence of calling them the bathroom. Mohan joined the boys and men to watch the builders. He threw them numerous questions; sometimes they let him load a bucket with cement. He learnt everything, as you know, about latrines.'

'You will remember one day. Upeksha and amma and I took our pails to the well, in the grass where we children often play. This takes up the water from the ground, whereas our tanks, which receive the rains, were rather dry. Amma sank down to listen to the ladies. There was auntie Sashi and auntie Nilu and auntie Prema and their daughters, washing their hair and clothes in the stream, and the venerable mother of auntie Nilu, like a cluster of bright fruit. They studied me in an utterly pointed fashion.

'"Soon someone will be back here for a different reason," chuckled auntie Sashi.

'Auntie Prema nodded. "A few months? I give her a year at most."

'They were staring past the InterRelate badge below the collar of my frock to my own Mist-Laden Mountains taking shape. Up till then I had myself been fascinated about them. Upeksha stuck out her front and pouted. Even amma cackled.

'I knew to what time they were referring. Suddenly I was not quite sure about it.

'"Well, I'm ready for my next stage of life, working in Kandy and earning a wage,' taunted Upeksha.

'Amma made a noise. I put my arms around her: so my sister

was thinking of leaving, school and home both.

'Auntie Nilu teased amma, "You once said you couldn't decide whether Upeksha should speak less and think more, or Anupama speak more and think less!"

'Everyone stared at me again.

'Tatta and amma hope that Jayamal will go to Jeshta Vidyala College; Mohan too. As you know, Upeksha and I go to a Kandy school also, for girls only. Several of our ladies, including Prime Minister Sirimavo Bandaranaike, have become most powerful people. I am not foolish: I may not achieve as much. However, I want to try.'

Anupama tripped on a tarmac patch, recovering at a run, raising her pails to prevent spillage.

'You are waiting for my confession, Handanandāmāmā. How the latrines led to step 2.

'By last January, Mr Mendes had started bringing our foreign letters. Mohan was utterly brimming with questions for Miss Martine: about the slowness of the English mail, and numerous other topics. But he did not think to tell her about the latrines – even though they had been his lifeblood, as I say.

'When I reminded him, he said, "Oh yes!"

'I asked, "What shall I put in the letters about them, little one?"

'He merely suggested,"'They built latrines.'" Then he shrugged, and because the rains had eased, ran to dig in the garden, not so far from our latrine.

'I was most frustrated, Handanandāmāmā. Those words were not the truth of who he was. So I bribed him with halapes to describe septic pits and S-traps and wire mesh and so forth; then I wrote her this retelling. I must confess, I bribed him for other letters – although, once the kikkul treacle was melting in his mouth, he got more and more unwilling.

'So step 2 went by, lifting us, like the Sigiriya boulder gardens, somewhat above the truth, because I was not absolutely honest.

I showed a joyous boy, bursting with curiosity, but not the fact that his interests could as suddenly vanish.'

Anupama stopped, resting her burden in the road. A moonbeam lit a creature that slid ahead in the darkness.

'A water monitor!' she exclaimed. 'I studied a chameleon this morning. Until today, Mohan used to bring me their shucked skins.'

'"Look! He was just about to eat it!" he would sometimes crow.'

She stared at the white egg of the moon reflected in one of her brimming vessels. 'Handanandāmāmā, your light can penetrate chameleon skin: it is ragged and transparent, like a veil.'

'I use our latrine to store such finds. Mohan helps... used to help me.' Anupama made a small, ragged sound. 'As we entered the stink, Mohan would pull me down and pinch my nose against it, making me splutter. Then in the dark round the back he would spring onto my hands. We have nailed rough planks across the back wall, making narrow shelves. I have lined up my rocks along them. I have old tobacco tins and jars for Miss Martine's stamps – as you know it is I, not he, who love them – along with the skins I collect of lizards, snakes and dragonflies. Mohan lifts... used to lift down a jar for me, placing the new skin inside.'

She hefted the buckets and set off again. 'But I must stick to my album of facts.

'We have all been nervous lately, because amma is worse. We hear her screaming or slamming her shutters for no reason, or find her on the kitchen floor. The mothers and fathers wanted to perform a thovil to drive away her bad spirits, but tatta will not. He enters her room and talks to her, then scowls and goes to his chair with the *Lanka Deepa*.

'Upeksha and Jayamal have cared for themselves for a while; up until now Mohan has had a person to care for him, and that person is me. But the mothers think I am strange. Auntie-Uncle

Moon, where is my mature and caring lady? It was this that caused the third step, I suppose.

'Already Mohan was content to say much to Miss Martine the way I suggested it, because he is so young.

'But I began adding more to the letters. Without Mohan's permission I told her about your significance to our people, and enquired about her birth, moon and other festivals, and requested stamps, and described our dragonflies and what happens to the nymphs, and outlined, in case she did not know, the fact and mystery of surface tension. I even got Mohan to write more letters than he wanted. By now I must have been climbing the narrower, steep stone steps of Sigiriya, but I am afraid I barely noticed.'

The rain was falling heavily now. Howls began from a wooded slope.

'Jackals,' Anupama commented. 'Then', she carried on seamlessly, 'I crept up to step 4 – because I longed to share how I felt and thought.

'It began from the latrine.

'One day I discovered Mohan most furtively using my store-shelves in the same way I did. Along the lower planks he showed me a toy car and a lorry, his favourites; the raw kernel of an areca nut, marked to look like a cricket ball; a picture of a football match from the *Lanka Deepa*; and Upeksha's eggplant curry, still steaming and sweetly fragrant, in a banana leaf. And something in his fist.

'"A shrew!" he whispered, peeping under his thumb.

'These were not objects merely: he had chosen them as symbols of the delights of his young life.

'He whispered, "I don't want them to break or disappear."

'I deduced, '"Because of Jayamal."'

'"Or an accident, or anything." His fearful condition had arisen again. "Will you borrow the Jarasinghes' camera? If we could take a photo, then I'll always have them."

'He is excellent at technical things. I found a broken toddy crate, which he upended. We put each item in a compartment, and Mohan designed a door on a string to prevent his shrew escaping. When we raised the door for the photo, however, it still escaped.

'I suggested another way to preserve his treasures. "We can write a list, even send Miss Martine a copy."

'That idea bored him utterly, to be perfectly honest; but me it had most suddenly inspired. While he was dictating this list for Miss Martine – his dislikes, also – I could insert into the writing "What do you like?", "What things do you not like?", the questions to get her answers. They seemed quite natural, really, Handanandāmāmā, like a buffalo's horns before their reflection in water, and Mohan, still learning to read and write, was not aware; nor of some further questions I decided to add. Little queries, about changes in larvae, and in liquid.

'Moon, as you know, Miss Martine answered! She even wrote about you.

'When she said, "I get a bit foolish sometimes when it is full moon," it was surely meant for me.

She told me she liked her brother better now. I was proud she thought I understood. She explained that liquid particles could not be cut with swords; about the agitation of liquid particles also: how, if disturbed, they moved; how some might even escape into a gas, despite their molecular constancy.

'Now I was at the steps wrapping round Sigiriya. But I did not see my mistakes around me, or my now dizzying height. Instead I hugged the famous mirror wall along to the walls beyond painted with stories: my stories of growing big.'

11 Anupama

6 February 2013

A small voice stops Anupama pacing her garden. The other side of her luxuriant green boundary, the elderly woman, her neighbour, is quavering out an old village song.

'Boatman, I can see a figure on the far bank. I think it's your wife, waving you home.'

Stiffening at the melody, her mobile to her lip, Anupama shudders at the image.

She turns away with a look of determination, recalling instead two powerful Lankan women: Shanthi Eva Wanasundara, first female Attorney-General, and Dr Shirani Bandaranayake, the first woman Chief Justice. There's always injustice and inequality to fight. She thinks stubbornly, *Sri Lanka has a history of such women, and I could add to it.*

'Handanandāmāmā, their success should give me hope.'

The hot air is thickening; the sky begins bruising like mangoes, and soon it will shed its contents. Anupama pockets her phone in her apron, gathers up her washing, takes it in. But the boatman and his wife and their separation by water follow her.

'I might like to be with someone, but – if he is often apart from me, or sad – I will not like the state of being married.'

She owns up to herself, *I said that long ago. It was part of my confession to Auntie-Uncle Moon. And now,* she thinks, *for my honest remark, I must absolutely pay.*

* * *

1985

The young Anupama stepped up her pace, now slopping her load of water, unburdening herself to her Auntie-Uncle as rapidly as she could. 'For a while I had been crying when I was happy, laughing when I should cry. On 15th February this year I visited the latrine. I felt sick. I saw pink spots in my knickers. I confided in Upeksha.

'"Oh for goodness sake," she tutted. "Another thing to think about."

'She went to amma – to my distress getting no response; so she fetched Mohan.

'She told him in a hissing way, "It's nothing important, but you'd better tell the mothers that Anupama has grown big. And auntie Nilu. And auntie Prema the elder.'

Mohan was staring at me.

'"Don't worry," I smiled bravely.

'Upeksha warned, "Stay away from small lady for the moment. So must tatta and the fathers and Jayamal. From today you're a little man, so keep them off."

'Mohan dawdled off on his errand, gazing back, his arms of a langur dangling, a young boy to me still.

'In our house, no room does not lead to others apart from the cupboard, with its door from the outside merely; but you know this. This was where they placed Upeksha at her time. It has no windows, no way to see you, Handanandāmāmā.

'Mohan sobbed at the door. "Let me in. I can protect you. Surely I don't matter, since I'm not really grown yet."

'I pressed my eye to a knothole. "Imagine this is just an exciting story."

'Upeksha was supposed to be with me. She should have led me to the latrine under a cloth while the mothers and aunties made me the most mild curries and planned what would happen to me next; but soon she grew bored and, unknown to them, she often left me.'

Anupama's sandals were full of water. She slowed down, shaking out her feet.

'One day, using one of Miss Martine's London envelopes, Mohan slid a key on a string under the door.

'"Put it on," he hissed. "To protect you from the yakshas."'

Anupama stopped, put down the buckets of water and clutched her belly, remembering. Rain full of moon glints was gushing down the road ahead of her, and the jackal foxes were still yapping.

She puzzled, 'The breadfruit tree has male and female flowers. But people often put themselves in separate places: the little men apart from the small ladies who fetch firewood and harvest vegetables; women, who bring water, apart from men, who build the wells. While the latrines were being built they were places only for men, but mysteriously, once they were done, they were transformed to places mostly for women.

'I still remember long ago, our family discussing which child should receive the letters, and Mr Mendes reminding amma, "It could be a girl, you know," and amma saying, "But Anupama can be so naughty. She lost her tie on school prize-giving" – which was unjust, she had misremembered; whereas Jayamal had just broken Mohan's cart and was now refusing outright to receive the English letters, and yet – apart from tatta – the family disapproved not at all. And in these times, the fathers frown at my fascinating questions but not at my crying, and at Mohan's crying but not at his many questions: Handanandāmāmā, does that seem fair to you?

'I sat and thought such things in the cupboard. Every day, Upeksha opened the door and fired at me, "Are you clean yet?"

'Fortunately, from utter disdain she had not requested my dirty cloths for washing; I say fortunately, for since the first day there had been no signs in my knickers.

'The only escape from her question was yet another lie: on the fourth day I told her, "I am clean."'

Anupama moved on, but at the Post Office she stopped. She wandered under its roof and, back against the wall, slid down till she was squatting on the ground. She picked up a leech with her fingers, and squashed it with her thumb.

'Here is what happened next. The astrologer had set an auspicious day. Senior mother and the ladies led me under my cloth, an extra white cloth on my head, up our lane and up the road, to the well. Unveiling me, she doused me in cold water from new pots. She broke them, and the ladies led me home. She gave me a knife. I hacked a coconut in two. Both halves fell inside the doorway. A late marriage.

'"Did you want to be on the shelf?" teased Upeksha.

'I know the answer. I might like to be with someone, but – if he is often apart from me, or sad – I will not like the state of being married. As for babies, Lankans adore them, even silly unfeeling boys, but I find them mostly of scientific interest. So I do not think I want a husband at all.'

Anupama drooped, and the leeches teemed around her.

She remembered, 'All the males of the family were gathered: tatta, the fathers, Jayamal and Mohan. They watched me enter through the veranda. The ladies dressed me in a new red dress. They sat me on a mat, requesting me to stare into a mirror. Junior mother passed me a comb. I drew it through my wet hair. Upeksha took away my hair slide.

'"Grow your hair now, small lady," she smiled knowingly.

'I blew out the lamps. Then people gave me earrings and a necklace and we had a party, all. I felt the same as ever. But since these events were not truthful, since they came from my mistake, they are improper for the album. They were nothing, a painted story on a wall.

'You know what happened next, Handanandāmāmā. A month passed, not much more. Now I found my knickers full of blood. To me I seemed the same, but everyone else seemed changed, even Mohan. If I had spoken about this to Miss Martine in writing, I would have been discovered.

'The paws of Sigiriya's stone lion were waiting to bat us higher still.'

Anupama mumbled her story into her lap. 'In May I spotted Mohan questioning tatta, then tatta and the mothers talking. On Friday 24th, the little one accused me of tricking him in my writing. I am so sorry: I denied it. We started to quarrel horribly about what words to write in the next letter.

'My feet had touched the clifftop's metal stairs.

'Soon, the little one was definite that our letters had got longer. The stairs trembled under me. I longed to tell Miss Martine that I would turn fourteen in three days' time, but I no longer dared say anything for myself.

'Then, Mohan was most certain about me. I refused to tell Miss Martine. He passed Mr Mendes our latest letter – containing some secret message I never read.

'I smuggled a P.S. to Mr Mendes pretending it was from Mohan. '"I ardently wish you were here so we could talk."

'My one last call for help.'

Anupama was almost home now, her excuse to leave the family over. She roused herself and lugged her buckets on.

'The mothers and auntie Nilu have just been to see me, as you have witnessed. It was Mohan they sent running, a grin on his face, to summon me. He led me through these most grim, clapping rains. I stood on the veranda before the ladies, with amma nodding dimly, all sagging like wet fruit.

'"About your letters to Miss Martine," auntie Nilu began. "You know what you've done wrong." I also knew what you call the lowest part of your body, the hidden part, the part where blood appears. For some reason, my heart drummed hard in there.

'Senior mother clasped Mohan. I stared at him, and Mohan stared at me.

'"Lajjawa, Anupama, humility. This one's a little man now. He'll read and write his letters from today."

'He hid a smile. The thumping grew inside me.

'"Another thing," junior auntie muttered. "It's no longer proper to be with him at night. Take care this doesn't happen from now on."

'Mohan looked horrified. My hammering speeded up, exciting and terrifying both, making me hot and strange. Seeing the fullness of what I had destroyed, I ran to seek you somehow, to confess.

'I used to collect seeds, remember; but humidity sprouted them and changed them. Rocks and skins are better: they stay the same. In liquid and reptiles, both, their changes are under the surface and not fearful at all, whereas in people, it happens the other way round. I am the same as always – except that no one says so; and if that is the case, then perhaps I am not.'

The sky flooded out the moon as Anupama's hand pressed against the gate of home.

'Where are you, Moon, where are you? I shall be punished by the aunties. I have climbed away from what is right. I am teetering on Lion Rock, with darkness and a pouring sky around me.'

On Sunday 21 October, Anupama and Mohan were pulling his cart among the forested streams. Every now and then they stopped, loading up wood. Anupama toiled with the cart downhill while Mohan gambolled about, whipping the treetrunks with a switch.

'Handanandāmāmā,' she whispered, 'do you see how Mohan is now that he controls the letters? His head is dancing like the mosquitos.'

On the Tuesday after school, Anupama was gathering nutmegs on the plantation of uncle Kumara, a generous neighbour.

The vegetation rustled, and Mohan plunged in through it.

His gaze on her was gleeful, half-afraid. 'My letter from Miss Martine must be coming soon.'

He batted his lashes, cocking his head. 'My, me,' Anupama repeated to herself. The nutmegs lay under the trees as if they were hard egg yolks splitting open. She parted a swollen casing, threw it away. The mace enclosing the nut was like the vessels of a heart.

She said quietly, 'I wonder if you have fed the hens.' Mohan scampered off. 'Handanandāmāmā, turn your eye away from these scenes. Oh Handanandāmāmā,' she keened inside herself.

On the Wednesday and the Thursday and the Friday, Mohan asked Anupama, 'How long since we sent the last letter?'

The first time she said evenly, 'Well, Mr Mendes was here on the day that it was done. 29th September. Can you work that out with your maths?'

The next day she just snapped, 'Twenty-six days'; and the third day she told him, before he'd got through asking, 'Mohan, it has been twenty-seven days. I have assured you before this, little one, that you just have to wait.'

'I'm a man and not a little one,' he said.

That Sunday Raththota held its market. The Liyanages were all there, but for Anupama's mother. Among the stalls they met their friends and neighbours, most buying as little as they. The eyes of Anupama's mothers followed her. Between the lines of flip-flops and salt fish and piles of soap, she spotted Mohan by a heap of pumpkins, head upturned, in animated conversation with their father. Tatta answered Mohan in monosyllables, unbending, meanwhile waving at some friend.

Anupama pointed out mutely, 'Auntie-Uncle, Mohan is trying not to cry.' She deduced, watching his lips move, 'He is asking tatta if he absolutely must write the letters on his own.' Her stomach fluttered. 'Perhaps they will let us go on as before.'

The following day, there was a lunar eclipse. In Anupama's village a young woman was getting married; in another, not far off, there was a funeral at the same time. Tatta would attend the funeral as a drummer, while Jayamal and Mohan and Upeksha chose the wedding. Amma refused to leave the house.

Anupama confided in her Auntie-Uncle, 'I want to stay with amma, to lie beside her and wait for Miss Martine's letter,' but senior mother said, 'Young lady, you must choose.'

She fled to the latrine and held the door shut.

'Handanandāmāmā,' she breathed, shallowly, 'I do not know which is less painful, to celebrate a death, or the married state I do not want; that I may have sent my last letter to Miss Martine, or that I may never read her letters again. I may be running out of time to have my own thoughts to share with her. At school, I have learned about air pockets. I think I am breathing in one of those.'

She went to the funeral in the end. The leaders of the procession drummed their drums and laid a white path of cloths along the lane in front of the dark blue coffin held high. She thought, *At least the little man isn't here.* Mohan had a fancy that the mourners scattered fried paddy that he could eat like American popcorn. *Even so,* she thought, *these days all death deters him; and for once, I am most glad.*

In the cemetery, she put her burning spill to the pyre. Well-wishers offered messages for the dead man, slipping them into plastic and pinning them among the white bunting hanging limply on the perimeter.

She scribbled her wish. 'To all the people who are dead to me. Perhaps we may come back in another life.' She spelt out silently to the moon, 'This may not be in invisible ink as I once wished; but still it is a code for Miss Martine.'

When the family got home she went to her mother's room, looking for the mound of her, but amma wasn't there.

'The others must have taken her to the wedding,' said tatta. He acted disappointed in her these days. 'And, small lady, you are coming too.'

Changed into coloured clothes, the fathers and Anupama walked through their village, emerging out of the lane onto a house yard at the roadside. The rituals had finished under the corrugated-iron *poruwa* cascading coloured paper. The couple were taking their throne, and people were clapping and cooing, and Mr Jarasinghe was acting the showman with his camera. Anupama hung back.

'I do not want my finger bound to someone else's with a thread however golden,' she told the unseen moon. Soon the crowds snaked along to the community hall where the feast and gifts were waiting. Darkness drew in, thick as paint, on the laughter of adults and milling children. The full moon rose, silver-rimmed, making a black woodcut of the forests high above them. There were the scents of curry cooking and frangipani drifting.

Anupama stayed at her mother's side. Her mother gorged herself with her usual glazed expression, nodding at anyone near them. Harshini, Anupama's friend, tried to tempt Anupama away, but she wouldn't move on to the singing and the dancing.

After several hours the quacking pipes and bonging drums faded away, and eyes upturned to the grey screen crossing the moon. Some guests began low murmurs of incantation. Anupama looked steadfastly at the ground.

'Why aren't you watching?' a deep male voice asked.

'Because I am not interested,' she said. Then she corrected, 'That is not a fact.'

'And what is fact?' the young man asked.

She turned to him. He was towering for a Lankan, cumbersome, at least twenty to her fourteen, alert looking. He had an aura of applied musk, of careful male preparation.

She said, 'We have to be honest. What else is there?'

The ground took on its auspicious russet tinge, and the chanting grew.

The young man said, 'You think that there is something that we can call absolute truth? I'm not so sure.' The glow picked out his cleft chin. 'Take the bride, for instance. She's my friend's cousin, by the way. I have heard people saying that she is not pretty. Perhaps objectively she is not. But to the bridegroom, I expect she is. Facts change, depending on who believes them, if we need to believe them. And we may find that we change with them.'

'I do not agree,' Anupama began, just as a Land Rover rolled onto the verge.

Mr Mendes prised his bulk out of the seat, the sails of his eyebrows flexing, mesmerised by the moonlight. He made Anupama a distracted mock-flourish, absently patting his pocket, which had an envelope sticking out.

She gabbled to the young man, 'I am not watching because, in a way, I have stabbed the moon,' and hitching up her sari, she broke into a run.

She skirted the back of the hall, following the village stream uphill. Clouds rolled above, darkening the tint of orange, and whenever the moon came out again the falls were flaming fringes. Soon they began to silver, and she risked staring up.

'Handanandāmāmā,' she said, 'I did not want these last days in our album. They have been full of scenes I did not want. But I know I must continue with my truths, for truth is everything. If I do, please give me one last chance: let me keep my special contact with Miss Martine.'

Harshini arrived, her plait loosening dangerously, full of a friend's concern and news of Mr Mendes. They talked but argued, and Harshini stormed off.

Anupama sank down by the water and looked up. 'So there will be no bargain with you, Moon. Which is just as well. Because I do not wish to dwell on what Harshini told me. That Mr Mendes sauntered up to amma and pretended to flirt with her, as he normally does. That he presented her with the next envelope from England. Or that of course she muttered back nonsense. I do not want to tell you that he looked uncomfortable and went with the letter to tatta, with Mohan tagging along beneath him, craning up most avidly. I want to forget tatta speaking to him and Mr Mendes swivelling his head around – Harshini said, as if searching for me. Of tatta frowning, and Mohan tugging Mr Mendes' shirt to get his attention, and Mr Mendes starting, as if he had suddenly understood, and...'

A fish jumped with a plop.

Anupama spoke with a clenched jaw. 'Mr Mendes bowed a foolish bow, I hear. And Mohan bowed a foolish bow also and snatched the letter from him and teetered off on tiptoe so that everyone would notice, with the letter balanced childishly on his head.' She added, 'You must know that Jayamal teased Harshini with, "Now Mohan can be free at last."

'And that when she repeated this, I said to her, "Well, that is nonsense. I do not know what he meant."

'Or that she said in a quiet voice, "Oh, Anupama."

'Or that I said rather formally, "Please explain."

'Or that she replied to me most sadly, "Are you sure that you liked talking to Miss Martine merely? Is it possible that in writing those letters you liked to hold Mohan under your thumb?"

'Auntie-Uncle,' said Anupama, 'we quarrelled then. You saw us. It is true that I shall miss Mohan if we cannot meet over the letters, but that is because I am his sister. However, need that prove Harshini right?' She eyed the current dully. 'Very well. Just as these waters carry sediment and plant matter and detergent, I am not pure; nothing is pure. That young man may be right. I enjoyed my power over Mohan.' She turned from the stream. 'I do not need to ask you whether I shall see any more of those letters or write to Miss Martine ever again.'

Anupama never re-met the young man, but she found someone quite like him: philosophical but more practical, a little less cumbersome-looking. His name was Asiri. They met at another wedding, seven years thence.

12 Martine

Friday 8 February 2013

His name is Matt, and he's here to paint the guest room. Martine thinks, somehow taken off guard, *A boy, not a man.* Milky jowls that don't seem shaven, shrinking eyes. Nearly twenty, apparently.

She rushes, 'I won't say matt not gloss,' and winces.

He's unamused. He picks up the roaring crowd behind her, chucking his head.

She grins, 'The cricket.'

It's the last One Day International between Australia and the West Indies, and Sky Sports has been on since early. She's still not sure she's doing the right thing, taking the foreign visitor; and she's anxious to get the spare room as it should be, so the jokes clunk in in force. *The room was so small, when he put the key in the lock he broke the window. Hospitality: making your guest feel at home even if you wish he was. Eat everything up: visitors are coming.*

Her mother's stuff now crowds her own bedroom: golf clubs, suitcases, dog bed and the woman's secret trophies, wrapped up in their box. In a separate bag lies the scrumpled Amelia Earhart scarf, which Martine was going to get framed. It's quite hard to reach her IKEA four-poster.

The boy's all right with the pocket size of the task. He fumbles with the steaming mug and homemade biscuits and wodge of lemon cake but gracefully spreads out dustsheets, sets down paintpots, tray and brushes. He barely looks at her. It's a habit of the young that, as she gets older, she's still never forearmed for.

She also gets easily hurt by the young's absence: in the end, Jonas came alone the other night.

He'd said, making no bones, 'I guess the girls have something better lined up.'

To congratulate her on her Jocelyn Teague decision, he'd brought a bunch of narcissi – and a jar of Marmite, bizarrely.

She'd made too many plum tartlets. Those tartlets, if not eaten, soon go stale.

She goes back to the TV. The West Indies' Tino Best bowls full to Finch, and it hits Finch on the pads and rolls away to the fine-leg boundary. Tino appeals for leg before, but it's not upheld. Martine mutters agreement. Suddenly she senses Matt beyond the threshold, trying not to be seen.

She turns in her chair. 'Interested?'

He chucks his head as if winking, so she beams back, then realises that it's a tic that he can't help. But he doesn't move away.

'It's a kind of battle. Each over is a tactic, a separate skirmish. But you probably know that.'

He stays at the door.

'Over?' he frowns.

She smiles, still feeling he's someone younger, imagining grubby knees beneath the paint-splashed jeans, a liking for conkers.

Tino bowls like lightning, and Finch tries to whip it to the leg side, but it comes at him too fast, hitting him on the thigh pad.

'150 kph,' the commentator says admiringly.

There's a hollow clanking through the heating pipes.

'Yeah, yeah, Mr Olfonse,' Martine smiles.

The Jamaican patriot upstairs likes to make sure that she can hear him during a match.

At the corner of her eye she studies Matt. He catches her at it, chucks his head again. They grin. The next ball is quick, too, while the next hits Finch's pads, and Tino appeals, and Martine sucks her teeth, but the ball was going down the leg side, so Tino doesn't win. Matt folds his arms and leans against the doorframe. Best to Finch, another back-of-length delivery, and Finch is struggling, the ball again skimming the inside edge of his pads.

'152 kph!' the commentator whistles.

Mr Olfonse's heating pipes are tolling in ecstasy.

The next ball is slower, and Finch drives it hard away, towards

Tino, hitting him in the chest. Tino, startled, fumbles it and drops it. The Sydney crowd jeers, and Mr O's heating pipes fall silent.

'Leg side?' Matt surprises her. 'Back of length?'

'Sounds like gibberish, doesn't it.'

Now Matt has crossed his legs, and Martine and he grin, and as Johnson bowls to D.M. Bravo, and Darren hops and jumps, Martine finds herself sharing cricket speak.

As she translates and explains, three letter bundles, as if no longer in the wardrobe, appear behind her eyes. The jargon becomes their wavelength, hers and Matt's. It begins to matter. *But so*, she owns with a qualm, *does the fact that he's a boy.* Then she relaxes, for the first time in a long while.

* * *

No balls

(No ball: A failure to bowl within the rules of cricket)
1985–1986

It had all changed for Martine after her mother's birthday, then the night at the swimming pool.

'What I like most is writing to you… I have things still to say to you… I ardently wish you were here.'

The words of that letter had hit some soft spot. They brought back to her moments, important moments, when she'd felt needed, with someone begging for help.

'Would you comfort me if I seemed in distress? … When I was in the north last week, I cried.' That night with Gerry Taylor, for instance.

It was as if she'd been jetting along buffered by cloud when all at once, thanks to Astrid and a blood drop, white wisps had drifted aside to reveal dark, solid parts of Mohan far beneath. His veins were Sri Lankan mountain streams, or tendrils of some island creeper. She was seduced by a need she thought he had for her help – actually, by her desire for his dependency. Like his landscape, it began to grow inside her.

With so much riding on it, Martine's next letter wouldn't come. 'Mohan. Dear Mohan. Dearest Mohan. Hello, young boy.' In the end, with a 'Sod it,' it was time to go to work.

On the journey she decided she might write better with less: a pen, not the computer. The tube carriage had an Audi ad, *Vorsprung durch Technik*. A woman and a schoolboy vibrated slightly beneath it. She didn't speak German, but she looked knowing, pretended she knew what it meant. She thought, *We're surrounded by artefacts and artifice; civilisation makes so many artefacts, no wonder we pretend and make things up.*

There was another overhead graphic, crayon-like, of a man and a woman on separate, parallel escalators, a heart above their heads. 'Dateline: Don't let love pass you by.' *But if we just correspond in letters,* she objected silently, *we so easily might.*

The biro jogged in her hand. 'Dear Mohan. I'm paying attention now.'

At work Charles Colgan, Lecturer in English Education, finished their discussion in his reasoning Irish brogue. 'Sure and it's a shame we're not involved is all I'm saying.'

He turned on his heel and closed their conversation and the door of her office with deliberate neutrality. He'd just complained that without his knowing, she'd pressed the button on LIPSS, the Language In Primary and Secondary Schools project. (He'd resequenced this to 'LISSP', surely on purpose.) Martine's team should have involved him.

'A shame we're not involved': the phrase with its double meaning stayed with her when he'd gone.

She tore up the latest try-out letter for Mohan on her desk. She'd been finding Charles difficult – 'Charlie' in her head only – not because he kept complaining to her and about her, or because they differed about multi-cultural education or the methodology for longitudinal studies. He was her junior in age and status, so that shouldn't matter. But there was something about him that was undermining her warmth with all her other colleagues, too. A friction. It was obsessing her. Along with the wave in his hair.

When she'd activated LIPSS without telling the English lecturers, it wasn't to nark him specifically: she'd simply hoped to avoid him. Hadn't she?

That day she tried to forget him. She moved from their stiff discussion to advising Joanna Bacchus on revising her research proposal, then collected the overhead transparencies and handouts for her next workshop. In the staff lounge, wielding an egg and bacon sandwich, she claimed a seat beside Claire.

Claire announced, beaming, 'I'm moving into a house. And Rollo's moving in with me.'

'That's wonderful!' Martine said, but the news felt like another gear change in her life.

Everyone's moving, she supposed, *just not in the same direction.* She was moving, though not necessarily forward. She was blind dating, still, and throwing herself into work as ever. She'd begun a research paper on market forces in education, a college lecturer's oblique act of defiance, and a book compilation of games for the classroom, her retort to the coagulating seriousness of many people round her. She was adjusting in her small if growing family; refreshing her friendships; provoking Charlie unthinkingly; avoiding Charlie thinkingly; trying to link to her far-away boy.

It was as if she was on the diagonal of an escalator, and vertical in a lift, and sliding along a belt on the horizontal, and spiralling round a staircase, and shifting in other planes too, on her own private Underground, all at once. Mohan's life must be as complex. She thought, *What chance then that my letters can ever land in his footfall – I mean, really reach him? It's a miracle that his have ever touched* me.

She confided to Claire, 'Charles Colgan's just had a go at me about my communication skills.'

She knew they needed work; surely everyone's needed work. Yet she'd tried and tried with this new era of writing to Mohan with real intention, drafting and re-drafting.

In the end she wrote, 'You say you're annoyed. I don't know how to make you feel better. Anupama sounds unhappy too....

'You ask whether your hidden thoughts are real. They are. Consciousness is part of reality. Your consciousness is part of reality. I know it's a very grown-up idea.'

He replied; but now, inexplicably, all his intriguing voices vanished. He sounded peevish, starkly different.

'Now I am writing the letters *by myself*. I can read and write fairly. Soon I will be better than Anupama.

'I am *not* annoyed. Now I sleep in the boys' room with Jayamal.

'My question is why are you writing with a pen not the Amstrad PCW 8512.

'My shrew is dead. I still have a cough.

'Your letter is not interesting. I do not understand consciousness and reality. Jayamal read me the words. I do not know about special ink either. Do you have a husband yet.

'I do not understand the stamp. The man with a shield is on a horse. The lady is behind his back. She will make the horse tired. Is he brave.

'Tomorrow I will make a shield.

'I am going to play with Nalin.

Mohan

Letter written unaided'

'*I do not understand*'?, she queried to herself. She didn't understand, either. Mohan seemed to be rebuffing her just when she was interested. She thought, *He's writing now without his sister's help: maybe that has somehow changed things.*

Charlie sent her a memo, typed.

'Presumably you're familiar with R.Y. Hirokawa: "Discussion procedures and decision-making performance". His finding that more effective group decisions are made when all views are fully aired beforehand? Can lend you his paper if you like...'

Barbed and nasty, she thought it. Of Mohan and of Charlie she found she wanted the same thing: that they'd stop it and be nice.

In the staffroom she passed Charlie marking student assignments. His green pen chased through the pages with underlinings, exclamations and vehement, dark scribbles. She'd expected his critical style to be deliberately light.

Writing she judged was fickle; with Mohan, it had uncontrollable effects. She asked him about growing up: 'growing big', as he seemed to call it. Perhaps her visuals, her special stamps, would encourage him to open up.

He didn't, much.

'My question is what shield. No I did not make one.

'My question is why is writing better than a computer. I used to use a pencil now a pen. A computer is best.

'About the stamp. Why did Lancelot take Guinevere. Rama rescued Sita. They were Hindu. I could not rescue Anupama. My question is was Lancelot brave.

'I *know* you like writing to me.

'Your brother *is* grown-up. How can he grow up more.

'I *will* tell you about growing up. The story of the ten giant warriors. Their enemies tried to kill the king with arrows in the mouth. So they fought with arrows and swords. I am big for my cart. A grown-up king. I do not want an enemy to kill me in the mouth. These nights I hear the rain. I think it is arrows.'

His rudeness was rather wearing.

'You sound a bit cross,' Martine wrote. She tried to reassure him, to help him. 'Whatever happened to Anupama, I expect you wanted to rescue her. If you failed, well, sometimes, you know, you have to count the thought, not the deed.'

But how could she really help him with whatever he needed help with, if he was going to be like that?

Jonas and Astrid paid her a visit.

'Now we will have a child.' Astrid's Nordic inflexion sounded uncertain where there was no doubt, and Jonas looked transformed.

The pair had first got together like clockwork; as if she'd helped or planned it, Martine had been content.

She was going to say, 'That's wonderful!' but recently, with so much news about, she'd been saying it so often that she was worried it wouldn't sound true.

She started with 'That's won...' and ended with 'one down, just two to go.'

Astrid looked startled, revealing that she didn't know Jonas's three-point plan for children. Martine hurried in with an awful, crude plumbing quip about smooth junctures of male and female terminals.

Astrid's pregnancy felt like a landmark. Martine deliberately took a while to find fizzy drinks for them to celebrate. She told herself, *I'll be an aunt soon, so all must be right and good.* But somehow she felt dented. First Phil and Matthias getting sensible, then Claire moving in with Rollo; and now this. How many knocks could her lifestyle withstand before it seemed defunct? But then she thought, *I don't want to trade it in.*

1986, the start of the spring term. Cool sun on Hampstead Heath, and Martine was walking with a date, a talkative man with earlobes like fruit called Justin. They found an artist working on a tree. Andy Goldsworthy, famous now. He was lining the channels in the trunk: with hogweed stalks, he told them. Silver-green infills, they seemed to spread their own light, to ripple in the bifurcating grooves. Justin philosophised about what was true and what was false. Also, what was natural: always the opposite of false? The tree was natural and unnatural at once. Martine thought of the wave in Charlie's hair. Its effect on her was powerful but wrong.

Mohan's next letter came.

'My birthday. I got a man in army clothes. Marvan's brother had it before. Jayamal said great present soldiers are killing machines. I wanted a model jet kit. Also Upeksha's eggplant curry and bitter gourd curry and milk rice. But Anupama cooked. I said the *pol sambol* has a strong taste of coconut. I did not mean the white part.

'I am *not* cross. I am 8. Soon I will learn English.

'The thought not the deed. I do not understand.

'Upeksha has gone. I said to tatta is she in nirvana. He said in her opinion. She is working in Kandy. The mothers and tatta are cross.'

Late April came, and in Professional Education, Leanne was ill again; so was Pippa, assistant to the team. The LIPSS project was overloading them. Management proposed seconding Charlie in from Teacher Training.

'Surely a coffee and a chat about it can't hurt, now,' he said outside her office. 'You know you're safe with me.'

He grinned, his broad fist twisting towards her in a dummy punch. It was another kind of visual: a gold band on one finger, flashed in her direction like a talisman. She didn't flinch; her mind was racing, all the same.

Images are no more reliable than script, Martine thought. *I know the ring could mean much or little.* When he grinned, his teeth were gappy. The ripple in his hair had a sandy glint, tucked behind his ear now, growing longer. She hadn't known until the ring flash he was married. A month or two, apparently. Something in her thudded down a shaft. He had no children to suffer, or so she hoped.

Together they bypassed Martine's habitual Luigi's for some large, 1960s bland hotel. Its lounge was where besuited, commission-only salespeople went to look salaried, talking the sales spiel talk. She couldn't help her usual evangelising for LIPSS.

'It's the perfect way of improving classroom conversation.' Her big-thumbed hands chopped air. 'It's real action research for real practising teachers.'

Charlie argued quietly but forcefully for the social mediation of English texts in multi-cultural classrooms. His wave wouldn't stay behind his ear and he kept winding it back. She felt odd, feverish. She thought, *What are the two of us saying, what are we hearing from each other? Not just what we're saying.*

She got up. He got up and clamped her hand to the table. He grabbed their cups of coffee and swaggered off, stealing them, bold as brass, out into the mild spring day. She was flustered by his grip but even more when it went. She found herself pursuing him down the pavement.

On a bench in the nearby square she reclaimed her cup, which he'd put down. It slopped as she took a gulp of filthy coffee.

Now he was speaking about some project called Erasmus. 'It's a university pilot. We're still planning and talking, but.'

A hand's breadth on the bench away from her, he was behaving as if nothing was happening. The hand of the breadth was Charlie's, broad, coarse-pored, flecked with hairs like a dune with grasses. Erasmus was an initiative to link English students with those from other countries: Martine took that much in.

Charlie wasn't niggling her that day. Maybe he'd never intended to, and maybe nothing would happen. *Keep looking about the square,* she told herself. She looked about distractedly and decided, *Nature doesn't belong in London*: *London's a place for buildings and people and machines*. There was budburst into flower on the trees. Her inner voice word-played out a warning, *Nip it in the bud*.

She spouted on, 'For the moment the teachers are just baseline calculating the teacher: pupil talk ratios,' advertising LIPSS again.

Talk, talk, talk. It was their subject and their medium, yet she couldn't even focus on Charlie's fervour for it across whole cultures and continents.

Her mind escaped to Mohan, the way he'd talked of talk from far away. 'I said to tatta is Upeksha in nirvana. He said in her opinion.'

His words were always processed through hearsay, translation, editing, even censorship for all she knew. Media more distancing than a slab of hand on a strut.

Two people startled a bird from the path, a black man and a white, runners in bright Lycra.

Phil and Matthias surfaced in her head, shaded with sadness. 'There's a friend I miss. He's changed.'

'Sorry to hear that. But that's about your friend, now,' Charlie said, adding, without missing a beat, 'not so much about you.'

Martine's heart sped. 'Whereas shop talk is?'

'Well you're one for this work now, aren't you? You mostly care about that. We both mostly care about that.'

He didn't say they were passionate about it, but the p word sat between them, with his hand.

She grabbed their cups and walked away. She found herself at a tree-stump. She put the cups on the blank face of the stump, giggling in a way she never did. Beneath their circles placed like eyes, she veed the spoons for a mouth. He was close behind her, scrabbling in leaf litter. She smelt the odour of flesh as an arm wound round her, offering a cigarette stub for a nose. She stopped giggling, suddenly. They left their artwork and circuited the square, and the traffic circuited them. They walked round twice, in silence. Then they returned to work.

She wrote to Mohan, 'Are you all right? What can I do for you? Your letters seem much shorter.'

Straining to help him. 'Shorter' seemed more tactful than 'rude' or 'unengaged'.

Now if she and Charlie met, they talked or argued about work, nothing else. And Charlie was seconded to her team.

13 The object

The object of Martine's decision slips into fencing breeches, Hi-Tech shoes and padded jacket and picks up mask and gloves, shuffling down to the gym hall, where they're allowed to practise. In the lodestar of all animes Sailor Moon has sword fights too, with Prince Endymion and many others. A fencing bout always brings out bravado, if not bravery: it's good to have somewhere to stay soon, but it's still an unknown woman, an unknown place.

The object's relieved family has emailed, full of obvious tips for behaviour. 'Take her a present. Take an interest in her. Come to table when she says it's time to. And of course never go out unless she's with you.'

The last is because of Black Sheep Shit. In fact, these days every bit of advice is because of Black Sheep Shit. BSS was his own boy, with his own style and ways, and for two years now he's been and gone. Parental fears are stressful. Stupid bastards, to believe that keeping his siblings boring will stop them vanishing too.

An email has gone back to them: 'Whatever. Lots of love.'

Fencing is a help. The cut and thrust get the frustration out, and the fencing terms are soothing when you get anxious. But also, when you feel that you don't belong they make you feel that you do. They're a cipher, known to a privileged few.

The opponent today is Dietrich, slight, fair, rather pasty-looking.

He hisses in English, before they draw their masks on, 'You are shy and horrible.'

Foil salutes are exchanged, and their feet squeak on the piste. The tinny engagement and disengagement of weapons, termed in the sport a conversation; the occasional grunt, shouts from the referee. The jargon repeats itself in the object's head. *Attaque, parry, balestra, counter-attack with a glissade, parry, riposte.* This is just a knockabout, as the English call it, but for thirty minutes or so, the combatants share something.

Afterwards, drawing off their masks, Dietrich recants, explaining surprisingly, 'I mean, shy and horrible like me.'

The object retreats to a private space, feeling a bit less beleaguered. The gloves come off, and the neon bracelet, threaded with its keys and feathers, goes swiftly back on the smoky wrist. Most of the keys are mortice keys, clunky and dramatic, a style statement, but one, a little padlock key, belonged to BS Shit. It's a recent discovery that no one else even knows that the object has. It fits BS's gym locker, back home.

* * *

Martine
No balls continued
1986

In June 1986, Martine was called to a LIPSS school in Hackney that Charlie had just visited.

'He may be charming, but that man thinks he knows everything,' the headteacher complained.

As Martine left through the playground, Charlie walked out of a bike shed by the gate.

'You're rubbing people up the wrong way.' Martine had just ambushed herself into silly thoughts of touch and texture.

She explained things to him as gently as she could, making some professional suggestions with dry humour. He looked at her as if her advice was odd.

'We can all learn, now,' he said. 'You can even learn to like me, if we practise.'

Without warning he was moving, manoeuvring her into the cliché of the bike shed, tugging at her shirt collar, fumbling her towards him, and she saw his mouth looming, puckering absurdly, presumably moving to kiss her, and beat him off. She stalked away, her heart pile-driving her chest.

'Dear Miss Martine

No I do *not* like the stamp. It looks like two things on fire the comet and the spacecraft. Jayamal is reading layers of gases surrounding the compacted nucleus of Halley's comet consisting of rubble pile but I do not understand. You say I am interested in minerals. I am *not*.

'My question is come. I will try and find you a husband.

'Jayamal said she must not take an Air Lanka Tristar L-1011 jet. Or she must look in the hold and if she sees any crates of vegetables they might be hiding something so she should get off and run away then row a boat then take a bus then take a tuk-tuk instead. Tatta said Jayamal stop that. I do not understand. A jet is best.

'An elephant got into a village near. It did not kill any farmers.

'My letters are *not* short. I am writing as much as I can.

Mohan'

The letter confirmed Martine's doubts about visuals, since Mohan had spurned her stamp of Halley's comet – not to mention her talk of minerals, a topic she thought he'd raised. And his demand that she come to Sri Lanka sounded bossy, not needy at all.

Just for a while, what with Charlie, it suited her to believe that. She'd booked the Nile and the pyramids, a trip with Ali and Conrad. She'd done longer journeys before – South America with boyfriend Lucho, New York with boyfriend Patrick, Australia for a conference, beside her holidays in Europe – but she told herself now, *I can't go further than Egypt: I need to be closer to cope with Charlie.* She ignored a smaller voice: *If only to distract yourself maybe you should go further, make yourself remote from Charlie, see the boy.*

So she told Mohan, 'You know I'd love to visit you. But it's a long, long way, and very, very expensive.'

There was a guest lecture by Gunther Kress, the rising star on social semiotics, just flown in from Sydney. Afterwards, a group of colleagues hosted him at a restaurant. Charlie was in the group.

Since the bike-shed episode Martine had kept busy not thinking about it, not replaying it differently. He sat across from her. His square head, the hair by now pulled back into a ponytail, exaggerated the fleshiness of his face. She couldn't miss its male-female quality. His big mouth working fast, Charlie demolished a noisette of lamb on aubergine purée. He started to lyricise to Kress about language as ideology. His foot knocked against Martine's, she assumed accidentally, but for a long second, unabashedly, he stared at her. She went hot. She sidled her fork under the table. She ploughed his thigh with the tines. He snorted with laughter, throwing back his head, startling the restaurant. Then he went on chatting, ignoring her again.

At first glance, Charlie was not what she wanted. Any new lover should be more exotic: someone remote from what she was, someone with stories from other worlds or a taker of risks she'd never take. Someone to oppose her, not necessarily comple-mentary: someone who could be the other half she couldn't be. On the far side from her female. *I can't help it*, she thought helplessly: *I'm an extremist, a romantic.*

She'd never been with a married man before. She thought, *Maybe as a lover he'll know things I don't: he seems to with so much else.* Whenever this occurred to her she got a frisson of something. Not exactly fear. Married life was another culture, far away – which maybe made him exotic after all.

Meanwhile in the letters, Mohan was full of fear – for Jonas, for Astrid, for their unborn baby, at his own dreams – yet still didn't spell it out for her. Apparently, his yearning tone had gone.

'My question is will you leave your brother because he will have a baby. Do not leave your brother. The lady Astrid will hurt. It is suffering. Anupama says that Buddha says all life is suffering.

'Tell the lady Astrid not to clean the cobwebs. It is bad.

'You are doing very boring things in the college. Anupama does also. She roasts the spices cooks cleans picks the vegetables fetches water does the washing feeds the chickens fetches firewood. I do not understand a man helping you, My question is does he not have his own work.

'I am a little man helping Anupama carrying the firewood for my muscles. Jayamal chops the wood and we put it in the oven and Jayamal lights it. Jayamal laughs. The axe is very sharp.

I have an idea about the wood. I am not going to tell you.

Mohan'

Martine missed the variegated tones and voices in the letters, even missed her puzzlement about them. Then she began to doubt herself. *Did I imagine it, that night at the swimming pool? Did he ever turn to me at all?*

The week after the Kress dinner, Martine followed Charlie into the student bar.

'So shall we…?' Her mouth was dry. 'Is there somewhere here we could…? Before work? At the end of the day?'

His wave was still tied up.

'Not at work, sure enough.' He chuckled, turning back to his pint.

In July, he loitered after a meeting. 'How about a hotel, now?'

Her stomach flipped.

'How trite,' she said.

Another day came.

'Do you have a big car?' she asked.

She was thinking an ample back seat.

'You've got to be kidding, now.'

More days passed.

'What's wrong with your place?' was the next thing he suggested.

All those other encounters there, she supposed.

Most people want what they can't have. Martine wanted what she could never be, and one thing she could never be was Charlie. Where she believed herself light, he seemed to her dark and threatening; when she felt dark and unlovable, he seemed to her bright white. If ever they came together it would be at the terminator, the line between dark and illumination. That meant she had to go for him, she knew.

One August day in 1986, after her Egyptian holiday, Charlie's Irish lilt through the phone slapped her from her chair. She could hear his untransmitted voice as well somewhere near in the college buildings, through an open window. Charlie in stereo.

'How much longer will this take, now?'

'What are you on about?' she floundered.

He laughed. Despite his hints, and her misgivings, that he had higher powers of communication, apparently he thrived on uncertainty and double meanings.

She stammered, 'All this ramping up and backing down. Are we ever going to...?'

He shrugged invisibly on the phone. 'If it happens, so. I'll not be the male Neanderthal brandishing the club of my will to drag a woman home.'

Testosterone seemed to course along the line.

If she said 'I'll set something up myself, shall I?' she sensed he'd only snip back with 'Don't come the old colonial with me' or something, at once belittling and charming her.

One of his main attractions was his abused-by-the-English, war-torn, sea-separated country, which she felt outshone her origins by miles.

She stood over a paper on her desk: a statistical breakdown of so-called 'illegal aliens' in the school population of London. Charlie was as alien as a man could be, tempting her from his unknown element.

She played him at his vagueness sport. 'There's a parents' evening coming up, to explain LIPSS.'

She named the Hackney school of the bungled kiss. In fact, neither of them had to be there; she took deceit a step further, giving him the wrong date and time.

Deserted netball courts and red, blue and yellow game markings on melting tarmac under the hot stale air of a London evening with the sweat glueing Martine's armpits. *Will Charlie come?* she wondered. *Does he already know my game?* Her heart skipped at the sight of his kicking walk. When he got to her he leaned back, shielding his eyes, and skimmed the high blank windows of the school.

He stared at her, laughing. 'But it's all shut, so.'

She'd thought that sex somewhere like this would shake the routine she'd recently got stuck in, except that, as he was pointing out, the gates were padlocked and the walls were topped with wire.

He turned away from the main entrance, set off along the pavement at a lick. Martine never normally followed, but this time she followed. They entered the wide field of Victoria Park, swathes of parching grass on unbuilt land. He headed for the skate park in the middle. The concrete ramps were empty, graffitied. He kicked his way towards a ramp. He looked at her, laughing again. He began to unbuckle his belt; it jangled. Her throat went dry.

She lay down on the baked ramp, swearing when she banged the back of her head, folded up her skirt and found a condom from her bag. Charlie snorted with amusement or annoyance. Someone kicked a football and a child hallooed in the open pastures of the park. She felt on view, and yet that seemed a good idea.

'Wankers Unite!' yelled a large graffiti slogan, the i phallic, its dot a spray of sperm. She reached up, hooking Charlie by his belt-loops towards her face. There was a windless heat. She unzipped him and reached in and pulled his genitalia out. She weighed their ripe smell in her hands and studied the cock, curving, beginning to stir over the huge swell of his balls.

He pulled away with a grunt and launched his trunk at her, winding her and banging her head again. He smelt of a butcher's shop. He tried to kiss her, but their teeth clashed in a meaty gust and his tongue slopped away. She moved to untie his hair, but he growled and wouldn't have it. He wrenched up her blouse and bra, strangling her chest, ogling her breasts, paying her back for her earlier stare, then let out a bellow of laughter into his armpit. She wriggled out of her knickers. His fingers manhandled the condom, refusing to let her dress him, blundering about.

He wouldn't let her guide him, mishitting many times, and when he found her, his entry was painful. He slammed her legs . down on the ramp, wouldn't let her wrap them round him. They went on, Martine trying to rise, he shoving, jerking, out of time. He pinned her hair down with a fist but she croaked and tossed her head, needles stabbing at her scalp as strands of her hair tore out. He twisted and cursed and ejaculated, eventually.

Later that evening, back in her Stockwell home, she sprawled in her Eames chair fingering her near concussion and reliving the encounter. She'd found it disgusting and delicious, offs and ons and ons and ons and offs, an uncouth binary code. She pondered what the act had been: either mutual bullying, or mutual self-expression. She thought, *Why can't I tell?*

After dark she opened the windows onto her roof terrace and stepped out, and the moon had emerged as if to meet her, full. For the first time with total consciousness she recognised its romance. She smiled to think that it might be pointing at her. It wasn't that time in her cycle, but for the first time she wanted to sense the lunar tug at her abdomen, an ovum budding inside her.

First touch?

Mohan's next letter touched her with hope.

'Dear Miss Martine

I have seen the two-wheel tractor. It is a Jiangxi Kaier PP-151L. Tatta and the fathers use it in the paddy. They share it with four friends. It is very fantastic. I am not allowed. It has a 4-stroke diesel engine. It is 15 horsepower. It [*boy's writing incomplete*]

'I went to watch again. Here is a drawing.

Mohan'

It was a flicker of the eyeball from him, a possible sign of life up close.

14 Martine

First touch? continued
1986—1987

Martine and Charlie broke their location rules in stages. She hired a BMW and parked it away from work. He hired a campervan, parking it closer. He got a key to the post room and, arriving early in the morning, they laid bubble-wrap on the lino. When they got up printed with dimples, he guffawed so loud she had to gag him with her balled-up knickers. In the service lift, in the working day, she squatted over his mouth and, with a fitting hand, hit the door-shut button for a full twenty minutes. Every time, the perverse attraction of his abbatoir stench.

'I mustn't be late home, now,' he'd say, but they ended up many evenings at her flat.

He was so arrhythmic that they tried moving to music. *I Heard it through the Grapevine*, *Every Beat of my Heart*. And afterwards, she thought, *We make a kind of poetry, how corny, I love his lap cupping me like the birth sac cupping the embryo, me grazing his testicles like netting over fruit.*

One night, just as she was drawing him into her, Charlie noticed the bite-marks on her bicep where the armlet should have been.

'You took it off.'

'It's about a time I don't need to look back on.'

She didn't say, *Now you're here.* The oval inset into the armlet had displayed an *Orthocarpus imbricatus*, mountain owl's clover, from her father, sent to her, pressed, in a letter long ago. The beaklike lips, pink and peeping from the bracts, the yellow pouch underneath each, like a surprise. As a child she'd liked the name, hoping that her father had meant some message for her, something about wisdom and its rarity maybe. A visual she'd relied on for a long time.

Freddy, who worked mostly with Kew's tropical plants, had

told her that the flower wasn't that rare, certainly not on the west coast of America, and she'd quashed her disappointment. He'd had it set behind glass and made into a pendant, but she never wore pendants. She'd got it remade as an armlet, and after they broke up, in memory more of Freddy than Dad, still rarely took it off.

That night after Charlie had gone, she left it in its padded box.

Out of guilt about Charlie, Martine cooked for Jonas and Astrid. She was into Middle Eastern then: leg of lamb in yogurt with garlic, cardamom, cinnamon, cumin and saffron; rosewater-scented rice pudding. They sat on the roof terrace on a few balmy evenings with the grey estate below them under the haze of a London summer, and she grinned at Astrid as she seemed to her to bloom. Despite the impending birth, she'd been neglecting them for Charlie. She felt she couldn't tell Jonas about him, but these days wished she could.

In bed, she taught Charlie. He was surprisingly docile. Before and after they talked shop, argued about it; he challenged her thinking. She wondered, *Does this compulsion we have stem from him teaching me, me teaching him? The titillating cliché of canes and blackboards? Strange. In the bedroom, but not elsewhere, I don't mind teaching as power, learning as submission.* With no other teacher had she ever made love.

Although she didn't tell him, it felt to her like love. As she saw it, direct current began to pass between them. Sometimes at night, when he was flexing her over the kitchen counter or she was being coy with him out on her overlooked terrace, she glanced up and gave a tacit nod to whatever moon there was.

They both seemed to go for an unsafe closeness: his hand around her neck, thumb resting, never pushing, on the lethal vagal nerve; her jaws around a testicle, tacitly threatening the fig of flesh. She thought these and other lyrical things about him, laughing at herself. *Lyricism isn't necessarily safe, though,* she cautioned herself. *It's a symptom of romanticism, which can be an extreme condition.*

'This is going to sound like crap,' she announced one night. For a long time now he'd let her free his ponytail, and his hair, male and thick, long and female, spread around her, in her mind like sand. She went on, 'It sometimes feels as if writing, imagery, talk, food, music, all our messages, even the things we think but never say, everyone's versions of reality, just flow in different frequencies in some invisible ether.'

Charlie curled a lip. 'Parallel worlds theory. Not an unusual notion.'

He fisted her hair – *Like a bunch of flowers*, she thought.

'I'm not sure I mean that,' Martine said. 'I'm talking about every message aimed at us, every version of every message aimed at us, whether at some level we take them all in.'

Charlie lay back and yawned ironically, flapping a hand at his mouth. 'Don't forget sex. Sex pheromones,' he said. 'There's another kind of transmission, now. Winnifred Cutler. Between males and females. We pass them in the smell of sweat, so she says. You know your female ones mean readiness for breeding.'

He rolled in her scarlet bed, and with his meaty tongue circled her armpit.

In the next few days, Martine read the research. Pheromones affected the menstrual cycle, even synchronised it in women living together. *Embarrassing*, she thought, *that I haven't kept up with my own biology.*

Charlie taught her many things, casually, in bed. Through a story of his uncle's cat, or someone's eureka moment in a lab, or an eccentric ex-colleague's mistake, or his one-time accident opening a bottle. She learnt that castles were ancient hubs of power, sucking people and resources out of their surroundings. About the various types of bet, something she'd never grasped. That photonic crystals would be the big thing after fibre optics. About the prevalence of diglossia, of separate forms of language in one place. That G. Gregory Gallico III was working on synthetic human skin. About the UN Charter, whose declaration for the self-determination of peoples he seemed to know by heart. About Shulman's new concept, pedagogical content knowledge: that teaching, more than imparting content, was about knowing how to impart it. Inwardly she smiled about this: *Charlie seems adept at both.*

Travelling on the Underground, its warning to mind the gap rang false to Martine because gaps meant limits, whereas she felt close to everything. She was on a constant high, as in her time with Freddy.

Hormones overran her, too many for just Charlie. She treated Mohan as if she were wooing him and believed she could easily win him.

'Do women work in Sri Lanka?' she wrote. 'I mean, alongside men?'

She was scratching a flirting itch, and it was all about Charlie. Mohan replied.

'Yes of course ladies work here. Upeksha makes clothes. Jayamal says it is Victoria's secret. I say tatta have you met the lady Victoria. Tatta says Victoria is no lady so there is no lady to meet.

'Ladies have some work and men have other work. The best is a pilot or an air steward.

'We were playing cricket. I shouted *corre corre* run run. I shouted *que captura espantoso* what a catch that was amazing. I think I learnt from Cruz at school. I did not notice the foreign words. Mr Mendes was there with your letter. He said where did you learn Portuguese you must have the ears of a parrot. A parrot does not have ears.

'Last month I had to go to Esala Perahera. Amma stayed. One elephant did not want its chain. It stamped. It stabbed a sack on its tusks. The sack was a lady. It was a dream. I do not like to sleep [*boy's writing incomplete*]

'I lost my soldier. It does not matter.'

A message that coughed from indignant to newsy, maybe another splutter of real contact. At the bad dream part, Martine's pulse quickened: was it the cry for help she'd craved?

She told Mohan the man and butterfly paradox, explaining, 'Your fears and dreams are real life too. If you can think what they mean, that might help you.'

What she got back was,

'You say the man was dreaming he was a butterfly or a butterfly dreaming he was a man. Jayamal says you are trying to help me. My question [*boy's writing incomplete*]

'Your amma cannot fly an aeroplane. It must be a story. Why did your brother stop flying. Is it because of the baby coming.

'My question is is your brother suffering is the lady Astrid suffering.

'A baby from senior mother died. Jayamal told me.

'I got a branch. I fastened it to my cart. It is our yoke. Jayamal laughs. I pull with Anupama. It carries more firewood. We are the bullocks.

'A mother I do not know brought Tharindu from another village. He is a cousin. He tickled me. They talked to Anupama. She went behind the latrine. She broke some jars. I do not like him. I tried to cuddle her.

'Come here. You can leave teachers not like leaving rice plants. When you have a husband you can go back.'

Martine was encouraged by Mohan's encouragement.

She asked him, 'How's your mother? I've been wondering about her... How many cousins live near you, and how many friends? ... Tell me about your hunts for butterflies and dragonflies. The ones you talked about sound very exotic.'

But her Charlie hormones made her tantalise Mohan, deliberately not answering his plea for her to visit.

Pippi's birth, early in 1987, wasn't as she expected. She'd dreaded the hospital run, having to smile as if from a stable doorway at the holy family of her half-brother, Astrid and the child in a halo of happiness. She hadn't anticipated the baby handed to her, to herself painted into the picture. The density of the wool-wrapped construction, breathy, smelling of fresh skin and sour vomit, warm and downy, in her arms. The assumption that there'd be no problem with her accepting it or photo-posing with it.

Most of her relaxed then, and enjoyed. Just one tiny fragment wondered how Charlie would behave if he was handed this same gift. Whether he would be delighted or clumsy, at ease or unwilling. This wasn't a fantasy of them together as parents. Presenting him with a baby would have been a test of character: mellow and accepting, good; nonplussed or grudging, bad.

Every time Martine paid a visit to their now pristine, organised flat, Jonas and Astrid gave Pippi to her, expecting her to hold her, to part-own her. When the baby wasn't asleep, the pimpled face screwed up and she squirmed in Martine's arms and two slits of eyes glinted at her. Martine absorbed the small, bulky life and had to remind herself that her niece was, well, her niece. She'd never thought she'd handle a baby with grace. She had an inkling that Pippi was a question, one that as yet she couldn't answer.

Through the gate?

(Through the gate: Successful ball from the bowler that travels between the batsman's pad and bat, putting down the wicket)

On Martine's news of Pippi, Mohan seemed to sit up, very suddenly, in the letters, any clot somehow massaged out of his communications.

'Dear Miss Martine

The photo of the baby is very very nice. She is tiny and crinkled up and fine for holding gently. The lady Astrid is smiling sweating. Her hair is messy nearly white.

'That name Pippi. It is funny. Anupama says you could write most people find babies adorable in Sri Lanka even cruel boys. I am hiding my writing. My question is about Pippi. Is she all right.

'The stamp is very fantastic. The plane has a target. It is a Hawker Typhoon 1B. Lord Tedder looks nice and smiling. My favourite is a P-40 Warhawk with teeth painted a Flying Tiger.

'Amma. Sometimes she gets up. Anupama or tatta or the mothers take her to her mat. I do not get sad.

'Harvest. Tatta let me lead a buffalo for threshing. I went round. Jayamal hit me with his stick. He said you are a buffalo leading buffaloes. Because I pull the firewood with Anupama.

'7 cousins and 17 friends. We could make 2 cricket teams a score-keeper and two umpires except some cousins are girls. Their names are [boy's writing incomplete]

'The raining is not hard. I am going to play cricket.

'P.S. I was bowled out.

'P.P.S. About pulling wood. I do not look for dragonflies and butterflies. My question is what is exotic.'

'1st March 1987

I am happy your brother is happy. I have looked in your letter but I cannot find when you can come.

'A message came from Harshini's amma from Anupama's school. The others sent me away. I went not far. Harshini's amma said the message was why is Anupama not at school every day if her amma cannot do the work Anupama must ask her mothers and neighbours. My question is will Anupama go to prison.

'I am going to find new jars. I will get her some more things. I will put the jars back on the shelves.'

So it was that, like a chameleon's front foot making its journey, his letters tapped the air, paused, withdrew like a film rewind, paused then pushed on, fully extended, again.

'18th April 1987

I did not get your letter for a long time. Jayamal said at your age go to the shrine by yourself.

'Now I am 9. I am nearly taller than Jayamal.

'We are learning English *where is the pencil it is on the desk there is a textbook it is under the chair*. It is not interesting. But I can say also *I want to be a batsman when I grow up who is your favourite player shall we have a match*. I know the words because Cruz's uncle works in a tourist shop so Cruz says the words and I have parrot's ears.

'You are going to say do you want to be a batsman or a pilot and my answer is a batsman. Jayamal told me something bad about a Tristar jet. I have changed my [*boy's writing incomplete*]

'There was a noise in the kitchen. I saw tatta and amma. The pot fell off the stove bricks. The coriander fell on the floor. Tatta said I was taking the pot to help her. Upeksha will do it amma is tired she must lie down.

'Because Upeksha is here. She says only visiting. Anupama and Jayamal are happy. Tatta is cross and happy. Senior mother and junior mother can stay more in their houses. Upeksha is making eggplant curry and pol sambol and all my favourite dishes. She says her face is Fair'N'Beautiful. She has a ring with a golden stone.'

Mohan's reference to English was another trigger to Martine, and whenever she couldn't see Charlie she began staying late in libraries, searching out glossaries that might hook the boy some more.

'7th June 1987

I have made a bow and arrows. Here is a drawing.

'I shoot when it is not raining. I use a photo from a magazine. I put it on the coconut tree. It is of jet trails. They cross like a star. Yesterday I hit Anupama in the face. I said sorry sorry. Today an arrow fell on Jayamal's head. He said what star tatta will make you see stars. It was not on purpose. I was trying to [*boy's writing incomplete*]

'Jayamal has taken the bow and arrows.

'The cricket words you sent are funny out for a duck, silly mid-on, daisy cutter, dibbly dobbly, chin music. My question is how can you know about cricket.

'I am using commas in lists. This point is significant. Please notice.

'The juice is from a jak fruit.

'Upeksha has gone. Anupama is too busy. Jayamal is doing his homework. Tatta is working. The rains are raining.

Mohan'

Love made everything, in Martine's eyes, seem right. She saw the signals crisscrossing between her and Mohan as if at last, between them, they'd hit the target on that tree. And her holiday in Egypt went ahead without, it seemed, deflating Mohan much.

'Dear Miss Martine

No I did not see stars. Tatta smacked me but not as hard as he smacked Jayamal when he was 9.

'I am sorry you are having a holiday in Egypt. You are saying Sri Lanka is double the way. You are saying Egypt is different and strange and beautiful. My question is is it by the sea is that what you mean exotic.

'You have not said about Pippi. My question is is she big enough for cuddling yet is she all right.

'Anupama says it is Miss Martine's birthday on 27th August please wish her a happy birthday from me. I am wishing you a happy birthday from myself. I have cut 27th August on the breadfruit tree. Next year I will remember without her telling me.

'The English words. I am learning them but they are not about cricket. You say you do not know about cricket, you found the cricket words in a book, cricket is not interesting. You say when I say cricket is not interesting I am copying what you sometimes say in your letters. My question is but everyone likes cricket is that a joke.

Mohan'

One October night, Martine lay in bed without Charlie and heard the wind roaring and glass smashing and the creak and crash of a tree below and sirens wailing and the clipped box bordering her terrace toppling and rolling and fences hurling themselves to the ground, so many boundaries gone. The storm somehow confirmed that things had permanently changed. When she resumed life after that weekend, she felt again the lack of boundaries between people: at work; in her time with Charlie; in Jonas's new family; and now, between Mohan and her.

The next weekend, with his wife away, she persuaded Charlie to a garden-centre trip, looking for replacement plants. The expedition made her uncomfortable: it was too couplish and domestic. She headed for the *Buxus*.

'Sure and isn't that what you had before?' said Charlie, casting around as if he wanted to do mischief, big hands straining at his pockets.

'If it ain't broke,' Martine shrugged, but of course the roof terrace was.

She'd imagined her box obelisks replicated and her roof terrace restored, but actually, abruptly, she didn't want that. She wanted to tell the world, *I'm moving on, making my kind of progress*.

'God's sweet bejasus, isn't that...?' laughed Charlie, ducking down.

He'd spotted one of their colleagues with a student, also looking illicit. The others loitered by the box plants, deep in an argument.

'Something else it is then.' Martine grabbed some purple heucheras and lugged them onto her trolley, hurrying on to lavender and rosemary.

Charlie lurked behind her, gurgling with laughter. On their way out, he splashed her from the Butterfly Fountain, an ornamental feature in carbon fibre.

Martine was disappointed with Mohan's blunt dismissal of his interest, the dragonflies and butterflies, and still longing to talk with him about his native species.

The next weekend she returned the box, the lavender and the heucheras. Mohan's landscape letter of a while back was by now unfurling inside her, drawing her towards a different kind of garden, a new start.

'Dear Miss Martine

The October storm. Your roof is a rubbish heap. You are smiling and shrugging your shoulders. You are saying you will get ferns. My question is why like ours.

'It has been the Cricket World Cup in India and Pakistan. One day it will be in Sri Lanka.

'Jayamal says each match is a war with many battles it can take one bowler or batsman to twist the knife and the wound is bloody, sudden and fatal and tatta says parrot ears remember now stop that.

'You are teaching me English so I will teach you why cricket is interesting.

'Tatta says the cricket field is the hills and mountains and the pitch is the paddy and cricket is a struggle for the paddy. One side is the elephants, rabbits and rats and other hungry animals, the pests and the diseases. The other side is the govigayas* like us. Our captain is a govigaya*. All must eat.

'First the enemy. Sometimes they do not trouble us. Sometimes they come and eat a little sometimes they trample and destroy or blight a lot. That is their side of the match.

'I am saying wait I am trying to write this down.

'Second the govigayas. Sometimes they guard the crop in trees or guard huts. Sometimes they put up electric fences. Sometimes they put down pesticides or poison. This may work or this may take a long time or this may fail.

'I am saying go slower. I need more time like poison.

'The govigayas also try to frighten the other side. They burn fires. If the fires spread wrongly or go out they have not worked. But sometimes the fires do frighten. Or they may use a gun or guns to frighten or destroy.

'In the end if they can harvest enough paddy then they have won.

'Whoever wins the match does not really finish. Australia won but the struggle must go on. It is no one's fault. All need the paddy. All must eat.

'These are tatta's words. My question is now do you think cricket is interesting.

Mohan'

*Note from translator: *govigaya* – **farmer'**

15 Martine

Matt has just left, so Martine's cricket teach-ins are at an end. Since retirement, her mind as buzzing as ever, she can't get used to the longer hours alone. She doesn't know who she is when she's by herself. For her the silent times are the rag-and-bone times, the bits and bobs that she feels she can't admit to, can't make into anything.

She switches on the kitchen radio. An interviewer is talking.

She scrolls through My Pictures for a photo for Jocelyn Teague. It isn't easy. These days she avoids being captured on film. And she's become distracted by doubts: maybe Lemon Tropics brings sun into the guest room in a way that's try-too-hard. And then the letter bundles in the grey carton, labelled with cricket terms, are now in her head again – or, more telling, the knowledge of what's revived them. The getting close to Mohan, that boy.

She moves to the decorated room with the furniture stacked at its centre and takes a snap on her mobile, sending it to Ali. She rings her.

Ali breaks into song. 'Bring me sunshine,/In your smile…'

She groans. 'That's what I was afraid of.'

'Yellow's not very you.'

Martine thinks, *As time speeds up, so many more things seem uncertain: history, places, relationships; what works for me, what I want.*

Matt's only just gone, but she's already missing him.

'Went off the railway tracks, didn't I,' he's confided.

When he was young and a dick, he told her. He chucked his head, and they grinned.

He'd picked up on her background in education and told her about the teachers he'd hated, confining his evolution to the school experience: she found that sad for him, but for herself too, what with her background, supposedly trying to improve it. *What went wrong could also be about his parenting*, she'd thought, but couldn't ask him about that.

This Friday, her foreign visitor comes and she'll be the surrogate parent. When she worked with children she was used to them. Teaching was, up to a certain point, entertainment, yet somehow she's gone blank about how to entertain a youngster. Surely, at her time of life, she should have learnt the difference between parenting and teaching. She challenges herself, *But is there one? Surely only in the degree of love.*

For Jocelyn Teague, she settles on a photo from her retirement do last year. She's posing as if to twirl in her favourite mint-green skirt, which, admittedly, only just fits her. Artificial light washes out her eyebags nicely, and the lifted wine glass magnifies her smile. Her eyes she knows were wondering whether retirement was the right thing.

On the radio, the interviewer is following an eighty-year-old woman whose litter-picking rambles have become a way of life. They talk as they stroll briskly up some glen.

'How did you start?' the presenter asks.

The woman begins, 'Tra-la-la. I think it was 1999, dear, and...', and Martine hears her mother, the way she used to hum, too, in her speech. It feels somehow like sacrilege.

She wishes the moon was out. Like her mother it's somewhere else, shrunk into the void, as if to remind her, *What you do with your young guest is up to you.*

Parenting. Martine ransacks her brain, *How did Mum do it?* Before the visit of the object of her decision, she must get her mother's scarf framed.

* * *

Cricket terms
1987

Endings and beginnings. Early November 1987. St Mary's, Battersea. Not HIV, certainly not RIV, but carelessness in a club had done for Phil in the end. Martine hadn't been there for the accident in Heaven. From a midway row Charlie and she sang pulling faces at each other, groping for the tune to *My Song is Love Unknown*. She pictured Phil dancing barefoot over that broken vodka bottle to infected cuts and, she hoped, a more permanent, fun-filled, irresponsible heaven.

She hadn't gone to the crematorium. Jokes had come to her as usual, inappropriate and clanging. *Definition of a cremation: more heat than light at the end of the tunnel. The trouble with a cremation is that for all you may put into it, you don't get that much out.* Not going had only brought guilt that there wasn't much guilt, because all around her, change was happening. There was a gulf where Phil had been, but an even deeper chasm between that time back then and her present. She was really happy now: happy and fine. That guilt party, with Phil at the piano? It had been three years before.

She knelt pretending to pray, but she wasn't sure what there was to pray for. To be thankful for, maybe: a sense of the real Mohan trilled in the back of her head, other-worldly, like her lover's reedy singing, heard today for the very first time. The moon would be full later that day, she knew, the image of how she felt.

Many of the Soho Sisters, a familiar tumble of names and faces – Fleur, and Bernard/Tattlemouse and Graham/Araminta and Nev/Old Sal, and Saila Billet-Doux, and the tart, who'd turned out to be named Evie, and several more besides – had decided on a joint tribute: alternating outfits, white and black. They swivelled like dominos to file out of the pews. She thought, unable to stop herself, *There's got to be a better way of getting people together than dying*. The sleeves of Bernard's black jacket were actually printed with piano keys and she grimaced at being schmaltzed out of the building to Michael Jackson's *Black or White*. The black note of Matthias was missing: ordained now, he had a spanking new disapproval of the family's choice of church.

Bernard approached Charlie, fingering his leather jacket. 'So this is he!'

Martine wanted to hurry home, but Ali took her arm. She steered her away from the bow-windowed overhang of the porch. The two of them faced the wide, wrinkled road of the Thames twisting away in the direction of the past evaporating from the roof of Ali's Pimlico flat.

Ali burst out, 'This is probably the wrong place. I'm going to let Conrad make an honest woman of me.'

Something in Martine stilled. 'And you'll be thinking babies.'

'*Naturellement.*'

Ali's eyes rested on a nearby group of moored-up houseboats, railings and gangways with padlocked bicycles aboard, the stolid hulls with their flower-sprigged curtains pressed to dusty windows. She must be awaiting congratulations.

Martine met her gaze with her usual sideways look. 'The kitchen-sampler approach to life,' she remarked. 'They say it can be very...'

'Meaning what?'

Beyond the hulks grinding together, a mini speedboat chipped the waves, snagging Martine's attention.

'Sew in the traditional emblems in the order husband, home, family, pets, grandchildren, then you can rest your eyes for what's left of your time on earth, let everything go, potter about with the background stitching, the filler.' She knew she was being naughty. 'Rewarding: they say it can be very rewarding.' A realisation came to her: *And Ali's younger than you are, like most of the rest of your friends.* 'I don't even know how you sew a sampler,' she conceded pathetically.

Ali grabbed her by the shoulders. 'Dear patronising bitch.'

They hugged, Ali bountiful with her forgiveness. Martine heard Conrad behind them, talking to Charlie. But her smile was with the driver of the boat in the grey churn of the water, blinking down to a white pixel in the distance.

With Charlie around, all new ideas stimulated Martine, so when Mohan's long-distance cricket lesson arrived quickly, in mid-November, cricket took hold of her. This and Anupama's jars inspired her to batch the letters of 1986 and 1987, the ones that Mohan had begun to write alone.

She wasn't clear from the letters what Anupama's jars were for, but she liked to think of her not as a Lankan skivvy, drearily bottling chillis or whatever, but using them for some Zen-like ordering exercise, something that pleased her: painting them, maybe, or keeping science experiments in them, as she, Martine, might once have done herself. Anupama must have gained a chink of time with her liberation from what Martine saw as the drudgery of letter scribing for her benefit. Maybe the jars were her celebration of that chink.

The earlier letters Martine put together with blue ribbon threaded through a gift tag. On the tag she crossed out a birthday wish of Ali's, inserting the cricket term, 'No balls'. The later ones she trussed up with string and luggage labels. On the first packet, she wrote in her jagged script, 'First touch?'; on the other, 'Through the gate?' Cricket terms charting three phases in their connection that she hoped and believed she saw. Mohan's cricket letter seemed a crowning triumph, seemed to share something important. With that he'd surely lowered his guard, let her through the gate?

These are the three packages now in the carton on her high shelf.

One weekday evening, the buzzer sounded.

'Plant delivery for Ms Haslett!' Ali Cockney-hammed through

the intercom.

'Right so. I'll go if you like,' Charlie offered. He was several hours early: his being there hadn't been planned.

Driving to Suffolk to see her sister, Ali had agreed to collect Martine's plant order for the roof terrace from a specialist local nursery. She appeared at the top of the stairs with a tray of ferns, unfazed by Charlie wading towards her, hoisting himself into his jeans. They smiled.

'I can bring up the rest. Throw us your car keys,' said Charlie, and went down.

Martine bobbed about making hot chocolate and finding the homemade gingerbread. She returned to the sitting room as Ali was reaching for the windows to put the fern trays onto the balcony.

She twisted back, indicating the forest in her arms. 'Why these?'

Martine bent over, breathing in chlorophyll, running greenery through her hands. The stipes of some ferns were fleshy, the leaves of others glabrous and hairy. Some felt to her like braid, or waxen ruffles.

A letter seemed to speak to her. '*In the high hills are ferns and mosses among the waterfalls.*'

She said vaguely, 'They're something different, aren't they.'

In her head, in her customary way, she reeled off her shopping. *Cyrtomium caryotideum*, clean holly fern. *Pityrogramma*, also from Sri Lanka: cocoa-coloured stipes and waxy yellow farina on the undersides of the fronds. Three *Thelypteridaceae*, three *Hemionitis tomentosa*. Cliff brake fern. Maidenhair fern. Bird's nest fern and lion's mare fern and *Blechnum* silver lady: even their English names sounded exotic – and there was that word in her mind again.

A damp, cold mist was suffused by the city lights and the last of the waning moon, which Martine could sense, even though she couldn't see it. She imagined how the larger shadowed portion would seem to jut from under the slip of silver, like a coin trick about to be explained. There were new modes of life all round her; her rusty old life was no longer right. With the ferns' delivery, she felt the onset of something.

Ali re-entered. 'You haven't been to see us the last few Tuesdays. And you haven't come clubbing either.'

They carried mugs and plates to the sofa.

'I've been with you in spirit.'

Ali choked on a crumb of gingerbread. 'Poppycock. I demand an explanation.'

Martine said, 'Cock certainly came into it.'

The real reason was that she'd feared talk of Ali's engagement. Ali might blather on about it or be quietly smug, or worse, protest that marriage wouldn't change her, trying hard to seem the same.

Charlie swung the ferns past them, dissolving into the fog.

Ali started, 'It'll be the same, you know. You and me.'

Protestations then, thought Martine. She jumped up.

'You're always in a rush,' Ali called after her. 'Sit down and talk.'

But Martine pushed out through the windows. On his haunches with a torch, Charlie was hitting the ferns thoughtfully with a small pool of fluorescence, reading the plant labels. When she came out he stood.

'I must get on with the planting,' she said.

'*Stenochlaeba palustris*', he informed her, 'likes to grow in trees. And it can get tall.' He held his arms up from his sides.

'Will you help me?'

'And Brake T.G. Walker prefers the clefts of rocks. *Marsilea* has to be in water, look.'

'Ali's being...'

Charlie said, 'For the ones you *have* got right, you'll need to protect them so. In a herbarium. Which will need building. Drip irrigation, probably: pipes, all that malarkey. Why didn't you do that first?'

Martine said, 'You're not even a gardener.'

'Nor, I see, are you m'darling. They're beautiful, so. But some are entirely wrong for here, and you've bought way too many.'

She asked herself, *Why do I feel thwarted? I just want to have my own miniature landscape.*

She said, 'Ali's getting married.' She hadn't told him before.

Charlie's arm came round her. 'Ha. We can escape everything except our own biology. That'll be you but, in a few years' time. How old *are* you, exactly?'

He'd never even registered that Martine was older. Till then their relative ages hadn't seemed important. Instantly she saw that, whatever her difference from her friends, he saw her on their conventional treadmill, just the same.

She wrote to Mohan, 'Dear friends of mine are getting married.'

Hoping to keep him and her focused on the same page, she described wedding customs in England: the bouquet throwing, the foam on the getaway windscreen, the boots and saucepans running on strings behind.

19 November Martine would never forget. On the 18th, Jonas had rung with his news of the second expected baby. On the 18th, Claire had also told her – too smugly, Martine felt – that she was getting married. But the 19th – for her – that was the unforget-table day.

In many ways it seemed like others, hanging from a rubber grip with the *Standard* in a crowded Underground carriage. But the paper showed the ruins of King's Cross. Thirty-one dead from a cigarette or match. It had happened the previous night, around seven-thirty: she'd passed through the station herself not long before, travelling from a school, taking the Victoria line home.

A horrific accident, probably. On the train, shocked, she tried to think about change. How it was like fire. How people could want it, or it could happen despite them, or it could start, like the *govigayas'* fires in the paddy, because they felt it must. *I wanted it,* she reminded herself: *I chose love with Charlie over the dross of dating. And with a bottle smashed in Heaven, Phil's dead, whether anyone likes it or not.*

The day before, she knew she'd started change of the third kind. She'd heaped up the way that Ali took the basis of their friendship for granted, and Charlie's assumptions about her, and Claire's self-satisfaction with her engagement, and Phils's death, that ex-fellow spirit, and the sense that even her half-brother was progressing far beyond her. Useful tinder, all. And she'd gone home and waited for Charlie. And while King's Cross was burning, she'd fucked him like she'd never fucked before.

The 19th was the day that she could see what she'd done. She'd copulated without her cap on purpose. She'd made a spark because she felt she must.

16 Martine

Matt reappears at the door with the flicker of a grin. 'Decorator's back.'

Martine's mind flips to the conspirators' codes of the fertile female. *Got the decorators in again. Shark attack, jam doughnut, crimson tide.* Decades free of pain and blood loss, she feels, are no compensation for her sense of post-menopausal shrinkage.

The boy Matt – Martine still sees him as a boy – takes a comic little sideways jump over the threshold, his hand to an imaginary forelock, lifting his things in after him, and her anxious gut stops churning. As he starts the re-painting and they chat through the guest room doorway, gradually her self-doubt melts away. She shows him her mother's scarf, which at long last she's had framed.

This fills up her day nicely. Supper and TV as usual, then it's time for bed. She doesn't know if it's Matt's doing, but Martine is wishing hard for that dream again. And wonderfully, as she drifts off in her four-poster, it does start. First there's the work part, all that stuff about water and the mountains; she gets as far as the hotel; then an elephant trumpets, except it's a baby crying, and someone screams out 'Matt!', and there's blood, and loss, and pain, and it's scrambling into some acid trip through a looking glass, and out of desperation to uncurdle it, she wakes up.

And so the dream is not resolved, again.

* * *

Inswings

(Inswing: A bowler's pitch that moves in towards a batter in the air, like a curve ball in baseball)

1987–1988

At the end of December 1987, Mohan wrote Martine a letter.

'About your friends getting married. Anupama says tell Miss Martine getting married is different here. I am writing this for Anupama to be nice because [*boy's writing incomplete*]

'The lady on your stamp remember. A man on a horse rescued her. She escaped from a fire. Hanuman and Rama rescued Sita. She came through a fire also.

'Tatta was working. Jayamal was playing rugby. I was doing homework at Nalin's. Anupama had to go washing. Amma started cooking. The fire. Amma burnt in the kitchen.

'No one rescued amma. Tatta says amma has gone to nirvana.

'When can you come.'

At about the same time, the Saturday before Christmas 1987, the A23 from Brighton funnelled Martine's car into Streatham High Road then down Streatham Hill. Ragged red-brick frontages crowned a mass of tacky stores that lined the roadside with evening shoppers. The moon was in its new phase, blotted out. Even if it hadn't been, given her current state Martine's mind would have tidied it away.

In the shunting traffic, her new Astra jerked and grunted. Drizzle veiled the dark, and the bright squares of shop windows, and filmed the metal pod of the car. Exhaust smog and the bitter taste of tyre rubber clogged the vents. She hadn't worked out the car's finer points so it was hot in there. The showroom-new interior added its reek to Bernard's Chanel No. 5, and Fleur's L'Air du Temps, and Saila Billet-Doux's double dose of AllSpice and musk perfume, and the after-stench of egg mayonnaise from the picnic sandwiches Fleur had insisted on bringing, munched earlier on wet shingle. Hard behind them in Graham's Golf GTI crawled Graham, Ali and Conrad and a pile of carrier bags.

Martine's suggestion, Brighton promenading and Christmas shopping in the Brighton Lanes and beach huddling, had filled up some of her thinking time. But Bernard had split up with his girlfriend, and Fleur was missing her boyfriend, who was away, and Ali was still trying to get pregnant, so the gang's mood has been up and down and the expedition had been bearable, no more.

'More music,' chirped Martine.

In the front Saila, today bare-scalped sporting dungarees over his sailor top, put another tape in.

'Not Vivaldi, you insensitive git,' muttered Bernard from the back. 'Something we won't slit our wrists to.'

'Oops, sorry.'

Bernard and his vanished Jenny had often made out to *The Four Seasons*.

Fleur noisily lipsmacked the horn of his nose and patted his leopardskin jean-leg. 'Git-ess.' She was needling Saila. 'Insensitive git-ess.'

In Brighton the gang had suddenly all guessed why there were Thailand brochures in Saila's Soho bedsit.

'I would've told y'all,' snapped Saila. He slotted in another tape. 'Just not yet.'

Martine hadn't told them her secret either. Only Charlie. As time went on, it was accreting physical mass, a tissue-thin coating of lies.

The Pet Shop Boys launched into *Heart*, and for that one upbeat song they all joined in, upbeat; but the next track was *King's Cross*. Martine's hand darted out, ejecting it.

Bernard's nylon leopardskin seemed to glare at her in the mirror. She imagined its fibrousness, and the window she'd just tried her cheek on was cold and clammy, and when she unpeeled her hands from the wheel they ripped away with a brief feeling of damage; and she was enduring the scurf flakes on Saila's shoulders almost as much as the dense seed in her belly, low low down. The last few days, ugly sensations had displaced all else.

Fleur fumed at Saila, 'Since when do you not trust your friends, you s-s-s...'

She prodded the back of his neck with a sandcastle flag.

'What're the timings? I suppose you'd have hormone therapy first.' Martine tried to brighten the mood.

Saila mumbled an answer.

The car was hemmed in by a double-decker. Her prisoner's claustrophobia mounted. The bus discharged its passengers. No ill-timed jokes this time came to relieve her. She couldn't ignore her own timings. She couldn't stop her brain rehearsing, *This Wednesday, around 11.15, some doctor at 108 Whitfield Street, London W1 will hand me over to some other woman who'll also write '23 December 1987' and my name, birthdate and age of 37. I'll claim not to know the date of conception, but she might pause there, detect in me the thin veneer of a lie. She'll record 15 November, the start date of my last period. 'You've come to us very quickly'* – *I hope she won't say, 'too soon.'*

Yanking the wheel, Martine overtook.

'Dunno I'm even havin' the surgery, goin' ahead yet,' Saila snapped.

Martine asked herself, *And which of my two options should be called 'going ahead'?* From the bus exit, a woman with a buggy landed in front of her. The Astra stalled again.

'Once it's done there's no going back, look. Who knows how you'll feel on the other side, like?' Fleur harangued Saila.

Bernard began an effeminate rendition of *I'm a pink toothbrush, you're a blue toothbrush,* waving the others to join in. No one did.

Beach grit in the foot well, grinding on Martine's boot soles. The smell of brine was with them still. She turned the key with a pressing wrist. As the engine expectorated back to life she pictured the second woman at Marie Stopes. *She'll be dressed in blue and green,* she foretold with an odd certainty; *she'll be young and small, not unlike a child herself.*

There was a tearing sound, the others ripping something. There were 'Aha!'s and limbs bumping together and the crumpling of paper and a slurping. Then Fleur's purple fist was under Martine's jaw, thrusting an oozing doughnut at her.

'There you go, darlin'. Nice'n jammy.'

Martine's throat kicked up resistance. 'Still full from the picnic.'

Actually, she'd eaten as little as she could. She pushed the sugared bun away.

She couldn't push away more premonitions of Wednesday. That the woman would crouch towards her under a poster of the ova, or the next phase maybe, sectioned through and hanging there in a fleshy, cutaway funnel. That she'd murmur about 'doing the tests anyway', and calculate the due date. That Martine's rebellious brain would replace the desk and chairs of the consulting room with the colours and talcum-powder smells of a cot, mobile and changing mat. That she'd defend herself against the woman's euphemisms, 'the father?', 'your situation?', 'close family, or a friend?' That she'd answer none of that. Evasive wrappings, building up.

To the left of the Astra, a man stretched up to the rear doors of his lorry. Its back end sloped the way the car was aimed.

In parallel Martine saw the woman writing 'Full-time job', and 'Father married – no prospect of paternal input', and...

Fleur was still carping. 'What happens to "Bill'n'Coo with Billet-Doux"? Don't you wanna do drag no more? An' will Bernie and the rest feel the same about you after? Have you thoughta that?'

About her problem, Martine had certainly thought. How friends and family and Charlie's wife might feel.

Beside her, Saila hugged his bones. 'Don't wanna be just what people think of me. Can't stand it any longer.'

The carload considered what to say.

In a Goon voice Bernard took on *I'm walking backwards to Christmas*. Outside on the road, the overalled lorry man hooked one lorry door open. In the mirror, nearside wing, Martine glimpsed something in the interior of the lorry. It glinted, seeming to shift under the streetlights fuzzed with rain. A tall, metal cage appeared, pivoting slowly then sidling a bit and trundling down the lorry bed, gaining momentum, loaded high with groceries. Beyond the soundproofed capsule of the car someone, some silhouette against the Safeway window, mouthed at the driver. He stopped his move to activate the tailgate, cowering and bracing his raised arms. Martine twisted, compelled to watch; and the trolley halted at the rim, just for a second.

And she knew that on Wednesday she'd tell the woman briskly, 'Of course I can cope; I mean, worse things happen,' which the woman would note as 'Client masking distress' or something; and that then she'd gabble, 'Better me than all the others who'll suffer if I go through with it.' And that would be the decision made, her choice framed as a controlled detonation, bearable, a practical plan for going on as before.

But then the goods cage crashed down, trapping the man's torso on the tarmac and voiding shrapnel into the road, milk and apples and cabbages and cartons of eggs, smashed eggs – Martine found herself gagging again; and there was ruptured cellophane, paper, cardboard, packaging; and a van, trying to park in front of the lorry, reversing without looking, smacked back into the wreckage. And the Astra sat there shuddering.

Saila's door clanged against the cage as he scrabbled from the car. Bernard and Fleur were screaming and pummelling the seats. Martine's hands wouldn't leave the wheel. Whatever she'd tried to protect had gone now, whatever it had been. Outside, people ran to help. Inside, she was already with the woman on Wednesday scribbling something like 'Refused further discussion.' There on Streatham High Road, she already held dead weight.

'Sorry? What's so friggin' funny?' Saila hissed, his face ducked into the car.

He thought that she was laughing, she supposed.

In January 1988 Charlie drove Martine to the clinic. A residential road in Wimbledon. A narrow front garden with a shrub or two. He was considerate in a measured way, but he wouldn't come in. There were beds in the ground-floor room, one for her, one empty, the other two occupied by teenagers. She offered a packet of wine gums, forgetting they couldn't eat. The girls glumly ignored her. Beyond the bay window cars sauntered by, a woman walking her dog. The room reminded her of the dorm of a small girls' boarding-school or some other wrong place, of having taken a backward turn.

She was whisked to the procedure pleasantly, as if to have a tooth out. The nurse loosely held her hand. Martine thought about touching women. Her girlfriends hugged and stroked her and she hugged and stroked them back. She'd never sought an intimate woman's touch.

'Treat yourself to something nice when you get home,' the nurse said matter-of-factly.

Martine thought, *I just have to unblock this minor congestion on life's route.*

'A bath with candles; your favourite music; a lovely meal.'

'He can cook,' said Martine, joining in the fantasy.

'*Bouillabaisse.*' The woman pronounced it oddly.

'*Soupe au pistou* with *aïoli.*' Martine played up the accent.

Nurse chuckled softly. '*Boeuf Bourgignonne.*'

After '*Crepes Suzettes*', Martine remembered nothing.

When she came round, she knew she wouldn't recall the staff there. This would become a sleepover to forget. Each visitor would have left a small gift and those who'd supervised would fade into the background. She got a taxi home.

It was only Charlie who ever knew. Insofar as Martine called it anything to herself, she called it the excision. A medical diagnosis would have been moderate depression, but she didn't go to the doctor. She felt numb. The option of children had clouded, might no longer even be there; her sense of direction was fogged up.

And just then came the news of Mohan's mother's death, stirring something under her emotional freeze-up, so she revealed, in allegory, what had happened to her.

'The news about your mother made me so sad for you. I'm so, so sorry – and sorry that sorry is my best word. I wish I could come and see you.

'I'll probably write little you want to read. I'm going to try to talk to you like a mother, a mother you might have had in another place or time. If you were an English boy, for instance.

'When a woman's expecting a baby it's a different, new feeling: she's going to have a better present than she's ever thought of. She's alive with it, she feels ill with it; she sees everything as changed. That's how your mother would have felt about you.

'Then, almost at once, there are threats ahead. Others will have to see him and hold him and know a lot about him; when he comes most people will be happy, but some may be upset or jealous. For these and other reasons he'll grow and change despite his mother – change in himself, and in her mind. In an eye-blink, he'll no longer feel like hers; this sudden under-standing will break some inner part.

'Even without your mother's illness, which made her distant from you, she was losing you from way before you were born. Her illness only dug the loss more deep.

'Maybe you wake with your stomach lurching as you realise she's gone. Try to blot that feeling out. Instead think of your mother with what love and pity you can, because she had that losing feeling long, long before you.

'Upeksha or Anupama or your aunties, probably your father too, will aim to mother you. But you're changing – growing up. Gradually you're leaving them, though maybe you haven't noticed.

'Have you been to the shrine and thanked the Buddha for your mother, and for being her best possible present? She's still around you somewhere, and she's missing you so much.

Martine

'P.S. I'd sign off differently, but it's not allowed.

'P.P.S. Here are some old cricket centenary stamps.'

The waiting for his answer was another little lack. Then a letter came, one that was hard to read.

'How could you know about an amma? You are not one.

'You say I am changing. I do not understand.

'Anupama is saying "of course you are changing, we are all changing, every cell in our bodies changes every seven years."

'She is pushing her nails into her hand. She says she is looking at the cells.

'My birthday was not interesting. I got a camera. It is for all of us and it is not new.

'You must not come. If you come you will go. Stay in London then I know you are in London.

'I forgot to turn your photo on the wall. A dead spirit might have climbed in. My question is are you all right? I dreamt about the paddy. The mothers fried it and we threw it on the road from the coffin to the cemetery. But it was your coffin. It is too far from your coffin to our cemetery.

'Cruz told me about Easter eggs. I would like them. I did not look at the egg they put in amma's coffin to keep the spirits away.

'I cannot sleep.

'P.S. The stamps are all right.'

Certain phrases were like a carpenter's nails, banging into Martine's hand.

She wrote,

'Dear Mohan

It's so important to sleep. I know you're 10 now, but is that too grown-up to take my suggestion, the only one I can think of at this distance? Ask someone to sing you this – or any lullaby.

'Lavender's blue, dilly dilly, rosemary's green,
When you are king, dilly dilly, I shall be queen.
Who told you so, dilly dilly, who told you so?
T'was my own heart, dilly dilly, that told me so.'

'This is one my mother sang. Maybe your mother sang to you too.

'Try filling bottles – or Anupama's jars – to different depths. When you tap them, each will make a different note (you'll need seven, as the music shows).

'Lavender and rosemary are English plants; they have the tang of our summers. "Dilly dilly" is just English nonsense. You're the king of course.

'I don't want to talk about eggs, I'm afraid. Can I use our old joke and say I don't find them interesting?

'I can be upset, like you; then certain music makes me feel a bit better. I'm not grown-up, even at 38.

'You'll probably say that a lullaby isn't interesting either, but try it, just for me.

Martine

'P.S. Who's the better cricketer, Ranjan Madugale or Arjuna Ranatunga?

'P.P.S. How are Upeksha, Anupama and Jayamal? Please send them all my thoughts.'

She wondered, *In this state of mind, where does my patience with him come from?*

In their letters, the two of them pushed through as if chewing their tongues with concentration over Upeksha's sewing machine. If there'd been a treddle, Mohan's foot would have been stamping it to destruction, but Martine's letters back stayed gentle. A needle might have been looping their messages together, catching one up with the other, the other with the one, banging them out in a holed yet whole straight line.

Easter 1988. Martine's cycle of work, and swimming, and friends, and phoning her mother, and spending time with Jonas's nuclear family, even her and Charlie, had resumed much the same. Her periods were much heavier and more painful. She blamed the moon somehow. It was punishing her, dragging her bleeds more fiercely because of the excision.

In her crimson bedroom, Charlie rocked her.

Whenever his wife was away she heard herself whining, 'Stay the night,' like a toddler begging for the light on.

They both called the wife *she*, like a long line of adulterers. *She* travelled a lot, training horses in Ireland. *She* didn't want a family, contradicting Charlie's line on female biology, but he seemed content with that.

Martine never told him that she'd set aside her diaphragm that time. They avoided talk of the excision. A short stare at each other, a wordless clearing of the throat, a particular embrace: in these ways Charlie and she consoled each other for any loss they'd shared – or so she chose to think. She saw that he assumed with nonchalance that, should she ever need one, another chance for children would come.

Mohan wrote,

'I am *not* upset.

'I am fully grown up. I am not a king for a cart. There is no prince in the sky in a white carriage. Anupama was right that is a New Year story. I broke the cart. The axe is still sharp.

'I collected toddy bottles with Anupama. She filled them from the bucket. We all sat on the veranda because tatta has still not finished the kitchen even though the fathers started it.

'Tatta cannot [boy's writing incomplete]

'We listened to Anupama. They said the music was silly.

'Once she had time to sing it. I went to sleep. When she went, I woke. Suddenly it rained. The rains do not sound like arrows, they are flames.

'About Anupama and Upeksha and Jayamal. The mothers are here often. Upeksha is cross. Anupama is tired and working more than Upeksha. The mothers are cross with Upeksha. Jayamal is always busy at school or talking to his friends.

'I am better at punctuation. This point is significant. Please notice.

'About amma. Anupama says she did sing sometimes. I say amma was a big dark lump in the corner.

Mohan

'P.S. Madugalle is not good when we go international. I wish I was half as good as Ranatunga, or his bat, or the tree that made his bat, or the seed that grew that tree. Etceteraaa, etceteraaa. My English teacher says that.

'P.P.S. Sometimes Ranatunga gets angry like tatta.

'P.P.P.S. Do you really have no dead spirit inside you?

Enclosure
'Sli- sli- sli- Sleep, baby
Ba- ba- ba- Babby, baby
Where has your amma gone?
She's gone to fetch your milk
But the pot of milk is lost, runs downstream,
With only a flock of cranes overhead to see.
A M.'

Martine had long ago forgotten about the variegated Sri Lankan letter voices: how she's wondered where they came from, what they might have meant. Astrid was expecting another child. Martine didn't have one. Mohan was reaching out to her now: he needed her, she could see that. Maybe now she needed him. Against the odds, overriding his truculence, she simmered with tenderness, felt... tenderness.

She started watching cricket on TV, bought the odd cricket magazine, even took out Surrey County membership.

17 Anupama

'My father's going on pilgrimage,' says Asiri. 'We should visit amma.'

He flexes his short arms with a crack and, with Anupama, leans over the wall at the top of the giant white Buddha on Bahirawa Mountain. Normally she'd be elsewhere, the only adult in long desk lines of schoolchildren at her A-level tuition class, scribbling and paying close attention, but it's Asiri's half-day from the Suisse Hotel.

Below lie the town, the lake, the ants of traffic, the outlines of Kandy prison. The towering tree beside them blocks out the bright lime light, its branches thick with screeching bats, dangling like long, black marrows. It isn't done for couples to touch in public but Anupama thinks, *I desire Asiri's hot arm round my shoulder, the fingers dallying most invitingly near my breastbone.*

Asiri's an only child, a mother's boy – Anupama suspects ever since his illness as a child. She adores his twinkling amma, her little acts of kindness, her tactful self-censorship when Anupama asks for critical comment, but Anupama still baulks at their duty visits because the woman reminds her that she doesn't have an amma of her own.

Asiri says, 'What is it?'

She thinks, *Those most pensive eyes.* They squint a bit, but she didn't fall for his looks: she fell for his sensitivity and thoughtfulness.

They've prayed under the massive seat of the Buddha, in the temple, on the way up.

When they were chanting their *namo tassa* she also whispered to the unseen moon, 'About becoming a barrister I must tell Asiri the truth.'

Her attention snags on a colony of stick insects stumbling among the branches of a sapling that has forced through the concrete balcony.

'You know what my life was like before we met. After amma left us, with Upeksha gone and tatta drinking and seldom working, I had to do many jobs at home.' Asiri does know, but listens. 'I left school after O levels. I worked on our neighbour's plantation, also.'

He murmurs, 'The past. Let's try to be in the present.'

Anupama tugs a leaf from the weed, using it to fan herself. 'Mohan seemed no longer my friend. I did not speak to Miss Martine again. I do not know if she ever discovered my false part in the letters. I had only the Buddha, and the moon, to talk to.'

Asiri says, 'Miss Martine would never be told. InterRelate, and Mr Mendes, would have lost face.'

A couple of American tourists, wheezing from the stair climb, nod in unsmiling greeting then, nestling together, stare into the case of tributes to the Buddha. Asiri's arm shoots up, pressing a tuft of hair to the crown of his head: he's conscious of his looks in front of strangers. At his reflex, Anupama observes how one stick creature freezes.

'*Thanatosis*, it is called,' she explains. 'You see? It is feigning death most convincingly. After the letters, before we met, I believe that I was doing the same. Doing merely what I had to do, trying to stay quiet.'

He laughs. 'Which for you cannot have been easy.'

She notes a drunken glaze cross her husband's face: he wants to do that thing he does, cupping the knot of hair at the back of her head, pinching her chin between thumb and forefinger before stooping to brush her sunken cheek with his lips. He thinks she doesn't know that when he does this, he also tidies away the hair strands at the nape of her neck.

'But this is now, us.' Asiri winks his point, nodding down at a male stick insect, thin and spiny, hooked on the back of the female, which is stouter. 'That's us.'

Anupama sighs to the moon, 'But we two are the problem.'

She declares aloud, 'I am most glad that we married. You are most adorable and I love you. You have helped my family: Jayamal out of his turtle poaching, and much more; Upeksha with her trouble at Victoria's Secret, before her boss decided to be honourable and became her husband.

'You have never held me back. You found me work in a legal office for which I typed somewhat badly. However, they were not always fair to their clients. The estate agents were no better: I witnessed money being passed that should not have been. Dishonesty and injustice. So I left, as you know. That was six years ago.'

Asiri's listening. 'But soon you will take your science A levels. Then you can apply to Sri Lanka Law College.'

Anupama's gaze alights on another stick insect. *How to say what I must say?* Gingerly, she lifts the twiglike object.

'Handanandāmāmā,' she whispers soundlessly, 'this can be like a test.'

She drops the creature into her husband's palm.

He picks up something from her manner, looking closely and saying almost at once, 'There's something wrong with it.'

It's coated in a sheath like perished plastic with thin, shrivelled extremities, twitching faintly. *Once,* she thinks, *I would have examined this creature, placed it in a jar.*

She watches her husband.

She messages silently to the moon, 'I hope he sees that the nymph is being strangled.'

He hesitates, then exclaims and, with nail-bitten fingers, tries to tug the old skin off. Anupama breathes.

'Handanandāmāmā, I thank you and the Buddha,' she confides mutely. Then she tells Asiri, 'My love. For the last few years I have been held fast, as if near death. Unlike those other years, I must stop pretending. You may have to save me. You may have to let me go.'

* * *

Pie-chucking and slogging
(Pie-chucking: Poor bowling, slow to medium pace, easy to deflect;
Slogging: Poor batting, often disregarding technique)
1988

'21 May 1988

Dear Mohan

I'm sorry the lullaby wasn't very successful. What was that that you slipped in for me, a lullaby of your own? It was beautiful.

'You write as if you hated your mother. I know that isn't true.

'Loving a person who's not with you can feel especially hard. If people cry or shout or argue, it can feel as if the fielders are closing in on you while you're at the wicket, batting on and on. Ranatunga was very young when he began to try so hard. All we can do is try.

'One birthday when I was little my mother gave me a black-board and chalks. She sat on my special chair, looking too big.

'She said, "Teach me about fairies."

'(Fairies are tiny winged spirits that English children like to believe in.) I drew on the blackboard and showed her pictures and gave her my best lecture on the subject.

'She said, "So fairies have eight legs."

'I made a face. "Haven't you been listening?"

'She said, "And their wings are made of cheese."

'I saw then she was teasing. She pounced on me and squeaked me in the middle. I remember her hair tickling my nose. That was the best part of our conversation. Remembering a person, trying to see the whole truth of a person, helps to keep them near you, however far away.

'Have you got any stories about your mother and you?

'P.S. Here's an interview from *The Cricketer International*.

'P.P.S. But how is Anupama, really?'

'13th June 1988

   Dear Miss Martine

   I did not slip anything in.

   'The interview is brilliant. First there is the writer's question, then Ranatunga and his answer. I read it in English. I am Parrot Ears and also Bullock Stomach different stomachs for different languages: Sinhala, Tamil, Portuguese and English. Also Hindi from the Wimalasiris' TV. My English teacher says "*Vell done old chap*, ne?" Please send more cricket writing for my English.

   'I do not cry. Sometimes tatta is smiling and sometimes [*boy's writing incomplete*] Crying is for [*expletive deleted*] sots and girls.

   'I do not understand about the whole truth of a person. Amma was not funny except when we went to wash with auntie Prema, and amma fell in the stream and pretended she had not.

   'About Anupama. She is not at school. She works here and on uncle Kumara's plantation. About the <u>boys</u> in this family. Jayamal is golden because of winning prizes and being in performances at school, but he is cunning, he does it to be gone. I may be the opal boy, but he is not brave. I come home straight from school and I will try and try.

   'Here is a picture.

   Mohan'

It was a warm June day in 1988 and Martine had run out of alcohol, so she, Astrid and Jonas were sipping drinks outside the Canton Arms on the corner of Aldebert Terrace, her street.

   'You will take Gretel and I pee.' Astrid thrust the baby at Martine but, as its body heat hit her, she thought, *This being isn't mine*; also Gretel was a baby, which somehow, abruptly, she knew wasn't what she'd want.

   ''tine!' Pippi flapped disapprovingly at Martine's finger antennae behind her baby sister's head.

   Pippi wasn't Martine's either; moreover she was a girl. Suddenly Martine knew that a girl wouldn't do, wasn't what she wanted either. She wiggled her ears and made Pippi shriek as the revelations spiked her. Meanwhile she saw Jonas and Astrid taking in the carelessly cropped hair, the few more pounds, the lack of makeup, the shapeless logger shirt.

On the phone Mum quavered, 'Jonas says hum-hum, you're, you seem different. Are you all right?'

The abortion, the excision, was closed and gone; she couldn't tell Mum about it, so she couldn't explain the longing it had set off. Pippi and Gretel weren't enough, and writing to Mohan helped, but now... She asked herself, *What do I want?* She assumed that what she had to want was Charlie.

There was a game in playgrounds then: Contaminator. The It sprinted to tag another child. Once she or he was infected, the two had to hold hands. They raced to touch more children, to expand the chain. It lengthened, swirled around them. Dwindling numbers were free to bounce like molecules. The unclean whirlpool spread from a single source.

Charlie still wouldn't stay the night. Martine tried to keep him, suggesting new things: his hair swept back, his fleshy odour confused by a dose of Poison, her scent, clad in her fuchsia dress for instance. She felt she was trying to get a purchase on his masculinity, blatant and foreign, inside the slick bright satin. The moon winked in on them, taunting her with the far side she couldn't reach, spangling his get-up as he joshed around and blighted the attempt. That led onto role-play clichés, judge and convict, damsel in distress, which again felt like pollution. Which made her oil her fingers, riding him in a male way, repelling him then her. Then they started fretting over which room, which furniture, which sequence of positions. They galloped hard and rough and Martine couldn't help thinking of racehorses in Ireland, of *her* putting Charlie through his paces, and he growled, thrashing about, and before Martine could say 'Let's stop,' he threw her.

She began to think they were competing. Maybe they had

been all along, and weren't trying to communicate at all.

As the wheel of education turns, the government reinvents it. At the time it was touting multiculturalism and a new National Curriculum. In college, there would be new funds for both. Scenting money and promotion, staff jostled and manoeuvred, tendering for the finance and their futures. Grimly, Martine took proposals to her boss; eagerly, Charlie did the same with his. The two directors and their committees weighed the options. Charlie wouldn't share his thinking with Martine; they argued about anything and everything.

One night in early July. Martine's boss John Brough, Head of Research and Professional Education, invited her to the main lecture theatre. She met Charlie coming out, pressing his lapels out of her way. In the arena the rostrum glared, spotlit. John Brough, who was at the back, gestured her to the stage.

His muffled words came down, 'Tell me again why your way and no other. Imagine I'm your jury, if you will.'

At first Martine thought that he must know about the excision, that he was referring to that. She stilled in the bright white circle. Then she recovered and began her arguments, urging a roll-out of the LIPSS programme into each subject in the planned new curriculum. Talk should be made more important in chemistry, geography, art, history. Brough questioned that there was enough multiculturalism in it. Arguments blundered from her. Her idea was to fund more bilingual assistant training, to celebrate the languages of all pupils.

Above her she sensed Brough scowling. 'So we'd be prioritising language over students' cultural values, their religions, their backgrounds?'

A stock debate. Which was more crucial: did communication trump culture, or culture communication? She stammered that in language, there was the culture of the message as well as the medium, the word; that you could explore cultural diversity in and through them both. She met with no response.

As she hurried out, Brough laughed. He stepped out of the dark, and was instead her father, Verdon Haslett.

Her office had shifted too: the desks were outside the theatre, where Rita, Claire, Lesley, Leanne and Pippa flocked around the seated Charlie.

She overheard him kidding, 'Will we move with the times, or stay in the same old rut?'

He wooed them with a wink. It seemed a jibe at her age, which he now knew. She guessed his proposals had found favour with management; she also guessed he'd take her whole team with him.

The mound of his hand arrested over a piece of paper. He turned but oddly he was Jonas now, not Charlie. On the page a drawing came up to meet her of the lecture theatre with a man on the spotlit platform, his hair thrown back, exuding macho confidence. There was a figure high in the background. Not John Brough: it looked like Geraldine Bowker, Charlie's boss, the Head of Teaching and Learning. The fall of seats was thick with flame trees, in red flower. The woman morphed into Bobbie, Martine's mother.

A fantasy about work conflict, maleness, parenthood, or was it Mohan's landscape taking over? Anyway, it seemed like the far side of the moon. Of course it had been a dream.

'9 July 1988

Dear Mohan

Your photo made me smile. I barely recognised you. You're very tall, and thinner than Ranatunga. Are you eating enough? Is that your own bat?

'By the way, I'm sure you *are* brave.

'I've been saving something to tell you. Jonas and Astrid have had another baby, Gretel. Here's a photo of Pippi, me and her. I gave Pippi the toy pig in the car. Gretel has Jonas's high forehead.

She's cute, but so is the way Pippi staggers towards me (not often in a straight line) and points at me and everything else. She says some words now. Soon I hope she'll learn to say my name.

'I was wrong about Jonas: he hasn't grown up that much. Perhaps it's because his mother, an American woman, died when she had him (Dad left us when I was three, ending up in the United States). Jonas calls his girls his storybooks-come-true and talks to them like a baby – mind you, so do I.

'Do you say you're the opal boy because people say they're unlucky? You're not unlucky to me.

Martine

'P.S. I'm researching more cricket writing.'

'30th July 1988

Dear Miss Martine

Thank you for the baby surprise. The fathers and mothers saw the photo.

'Jayamal said "why has she rolled her jeans up? She doesn't wade in the paddy."

He calls you "she", as if you are below the lowest mountain. I did not answer. That makes him more annoyed.

'I like Gretel like Pippi. Gretel could make laughing. That car is wheels with stuffing. Is Gretel really all right? Are Jonas and Astrid all right? I do not understand about storybooks-come-true. Do you still like Jonas?

'I did not know his amma is dead. He has your tatta in America, but that is probably why [boy's writing incomplete]

'The bat is cousin Thurindu's. He comes again and again. He lent it for a reason about Anupama.

'My English teacher has the hair of a macaque. He says cricket is "vizard". I also like football, but he says "it is not wery proper for English gentlemen, ne?" What sports do you have in England?

'Cruz and I saw a Sinhalese boy in the town. Pieter. Cruz says he was in a convent. His parents are his parents and not his parents Dutch. Cruz says you do not have to be rich or the same colour for rich people to adopt you. Pieter looked happy.

Mohan

'P.S. I am not writing about a girl having a toy car because I am thinking about it.

'P.P.S. Happy birthday for 27th August.'

'2nd August 1988

Dear Miss Martine

Uncle Kumara can see Mr Mendes in Colombo. So here is another letter.

'The fathers have finished the kitchen. I wish tatta was [*boy's writing incomplete*] Tatta says the Kaier has broken. He says his arm hurts also.

'I said "it is strong enough for crates of moonshine."

'Jayamal said "what do you know, you little [*expletive deleted*]?"

'Upeksha has gone.

'I went to the fast deep part. I caught three Martenstyn's barbs.

'Anupama said, "Their coats look like pineapple scales."

She cooked them.

'Jayamal said, "Tasty for something so *small*. Thank you Anupama."

'I did one thing better. I caught a hare. My trap was bicycle cable.

'Anupama smiled and said, "Well done."

'I did a thing even much better. I went to [*boy has deleted his writing*] with Nalin and some friends in the mountain. We [*boy has deleted his writing*] a big sapphire. We hit it in pieces. We shared it.

'Anupama said, "What have you done?"

'I said, "We found it lying."

'She cried. "I do not believe you."

'She bought a cow. She called it Raththi, Russet. I said no,

Nila, Bluey. It is more interesting.

'I wanted the money.

'Jayamal says, "How sweet. Boys and girls playing mothers and fathers."

'I do not answer. That way he gets annoyed. I should be the leader of this family.

Mohan'

By the end of August, the gist of Martine's confused dream had happened. Management had approved Charlie's ideas: beside being teacher trainer for English he'd head a working group embedding multicultural content in each new school subject, trialling it across the teacher training programme. Through one of his contacts, the results would be fed to government.

So much, Martine railed at him, for his tirades against what he liked to call 'the unassailable monoculturalism of our education system, now'. Miraculously a bit of teaching about another culture here, another culture there were suddenly not, as he also said of her letters to Kandy, 'sops to assuage your nation's guilt about your cultural imperialism, look'. All along, he must have seen her LIPSS project as her opening hostilities with him, and his sell-out now was his revenge for that. To add insult to injury, his new group would take LIPSS over: another swerve.

'"Multiculturalism, multiculturalism": from now on you'll have to parrot that frigging mantra,' Martine raved in bed.

Charlie shrugged, 'I won't say "It's just politics."'

He locked his shoulders and turned his face away, offering her up the thick veins in his neck she loved, and told the wall a story she admittedly found funny about John Brough.

And still she didn't know what the machinery of her life was whirring towards, where it had still left to go.

It occurred to her that she needed... not necessarily a man, but someone male, something male; at least, some alien counterpart. Mohan, maybe: she certainly wrote to him that way.

'Dear Mohan

Two whole letters!

'Thanks for your birthday wishes. You remembered, as you promised.

'I'm sorry for the slight delay, but I've got a few problems at work. Some people seem to think it's a competition: between men and women, or younger and older people. Some behave as if being young, seeming young, is better, and that the things I do, the things I try, need changing. I assumed they wanted what I did but that's not true.

'Please don't compete with Anupama. It could destroy your friendship.

'Sometimes these battles follow me home. I often wonder if I'll ever feel at one with other people, or if I should just admit I'm on my own in the end.

'The family are fine, although I don't see them enough. Jonas is great – except he could work a bit harder. I'm so glad I've got to know him. He might never have existed if our father hadn't left me. It's a strange thought.

'As for your father, it sounds to me as if he's struggling with his sadness about your mother. Try to admit that that's how you've felt too.

'Your teacher's English is unusual, by the way. Could he be teasing you?

'English sports: yes, football! Also rugby, tennis, swimming (as you know, my favourite), athletics, cycling, golf, hockey, horseracing... I could go on but I've had a visitor here, and it's late, and I'm a bit tired, sorry.

Miss Martine

'P.S. Tell your father I'm sending him good thoughts.'

'Dear Miss Martine

I dreamt I was at Pieter's house. It was very very nice.

'I tried for the scholarship to big school.

'I did not know the macaque's English was wrong. The interview is wrong also. Ranatunga's first half-century was 1982, not 1981. I am looking at it under the breadfruit tree.

'I am explaining to Anupama, "In an interview one person tells, one person asks. No one should only ask or only tell. I do not like it."

'Anupama is milking the cow and saying, "Sometimes breadfruit trees bear leaves but no fruit, sometimes leaves and fruit. And when the wind throws away some leaves, they more clearly show their branches. All the things people say and the messages they send are absolutely significant."

'She says she was talking about our letters, the stamps you send me, the drawings I send you and the cricket writing, even the interview.

'You are talking about a competition. I do not understand.

'Jayamal tells me, "She only likes you because you're far away."

'"She" is like the unknown mother of our cow.

'He was in the Esala Perahera because he is older. The parade is in the family but tatta would not [*boy's writing incomplete*].

'Senior mother said, "J looked so manly, drumming and dancing in his thuppottiya skirt."

'Manly is not brave.

Mohan

'P.S. I still want cricket writing.

'P.P.S. There is horseracing at Nuwara Eliya. Pieter goes with his nearly parents. You can take me.'

Martine, offloading about work, didn't notice her pie-chucker's aim, how ragged and misplaced it was to a receiver of only ten; nor did she examine Mohan's strokes, slogging some misguided message back.

18 The object

'Let's go on with the birdboxes. Meanwhile, our friends from abroad can label these birdbox diagrams with the English words.'

The male warder, the technology teacher, hands out papers to the seven foreigners he is asking to stay at their desks. The English majority moves towards the clamps and saws and chisels, looking back with sardonic pity.

Among the abandoned group Martine's visitor-to-be mutters, '*Friends* from abroad my arse.'

Fencing opponent Dietrich signals agreement with a pale eyebrow. Even the rest – the hostile Dead Moon Circus of fellow inmates, i.e. foreign students – sniggers in appreciation. They study technology as a subject in their own countries, are perfectly capable; they even mostly speak good English. There's no reason for the teacher to give them a separate, easier task.

'Roof', 'platform', 'entrance hole', 'nesting space', 'dovetail joint': their pointless labelling begins.

This morning the object of Martine's decision doesn't recite the calming mantra of fencing terms or use the rosary of feathers and keys, instead resting a hand on the comforter of the bumbag that is slung under the desk. It holds a piece of paper that no one, not even the family, knows exists. It came to light using the gym-locker key on the wristband, the one for the locker that belongs to the object's brother, Black Sheep Shit.

There's also a print-out of a photo in there, brought to prison – school – by Mrs Teague from the agency. The woman's name is Martine Haslett. She looks older than expected, but seems to enjoy a party. The viewer's hoping for minimal fuss during this upcoming stay, and preferably quite a lot of silence. On second thoughts, the hand unzips the bag. Fingers take out BS's paper, unfold and spread it on the desk for reassurance, masked by the birdbox diagram. The dark eyes focus intently.

It's an impressionistic map. BS Shit's coloured penstrokes start at the family home: the pool of blood surrounded by a police cordon, not a real one, but obviously meant to symbolise family tensions and conflict, makes home easy to spot. Through Japantown, the part of town the viewer loves, an ambulance races, BS's distinctive booted foot with its green bootlace sticking out of the back, pouring a trail of gore, again symbolic of family damage. At the entrance to the hospital, a cartoon BS lies prone, the ambulance gone. His face is grim, his body a bloody mess.

The clear message is, 'You bastards. Yes you, the family, did this.'

Next a blood trail points to the doctor's surgery, along another road. BS the cartoon figure is leaving, swinging the door with a jaunty air, his bandages soaked red, suggesting he's on his way to some kind of teenage freedom. From there, crimson droplets fan out along various streets and roads, but there's no more sign of BS. The edges of the paper are vague, just empty swirls of colour. They lack satisfying detail, the smashing crystals and tall white pillars and butterfly skies of *Sailor Moon*, say, but BS's sibling likes to think that this is the boy's alternative heaven, his escape.

The police haven't seen the map of course. Anyway, it doesn't really tell you where he is.

A paper pellet plops onto the desk. Dietrich's head bobs over his diagram, at his desk over to one side. He looks up and winks.

The photo: Martine Haslett. What will her landscape be? The city or the country? Garden or none? House or flat? Somewhere to be comfortable in, to be quiet in, to be shy in, or somewhere to escape from? What will the bedroom be like? Not painted, the object hopes, in the foulest of colours, yellow. As long as the walls aren't that toxic colour, it'll be a refuge from Dead Moon Circus, this shit lot.

* * *

Game of two halves
1988–1989

One October night in 1988 the door buzzer sounded during Martine's bedroom persuasions.

Charlie sighed and swung his legs over the bed edge, pouring himself more wine. 'That'll be your alter ego, now.'

Saila Billet-Doux had been visiting Martine often late at night. Sure enough she pushed past her into the flat. She had less stubble already, already looking more female.

'Ken's plannin' to come to Thailand, be with me every step of the way, says he wants to hold my hand.'

'Not a bad sort of problem to have.'

Saila dragged off her beret and wig. She hunkered on the sofa, crushing a posy of mixed flowers. Last time she'd brought a kitten. Martine had rejected it gently: the ferns and mosses were all the pets she could cope with, a kitten somehow seeming too much and not enough.

'He thinks we'll live together when we get back. He's already found a flat. In Kensington.'

Martine buttoned her man's shirt, in other words Charlie's. 'Again, sounds—'

'It's not how I pictured it.' Saila gripped her flaking skull.

'Ah.'

Saila groaned. 'I've seen the flat. Like Saila the woman, all paid for.'

'Oh.'

'It feels real now. Borin'.' Shivering, Saila hugged her raddled bones. 'You have a definite idea of what you want, the boyfriend you want, don't you, and then…'

Below Saila's layered skirt Martine registered bare feet. They took her back to that first Sri Lankan photo, the little boy with one set of dusty toes roofing the other. These were contorted and grimy, with flaking purple paint. *Saila's more screwed up than I knew*, she thought. She realised that no one ever hugged Saila but

Saila. She thought of the boyfriend, Ken, acknowledging *My craving is Ken's, but homeless.* Unlike Saila, she had no idea what she wanted. She'd given up on Charlie, but this nameless yearning made the ice inside her creak.

Earlier, she'd stirred parsley and cream into garlic mussels and baked two sticks of bread, all barely touched by Charlie. She warmed them now, again, and Saila and she talked, and, for mutual relief, she speared each yellow morsel and fed her like a bird. But Saila wasn't hers, and it wasn't Saila she wanted.

Charlie straddled the doorway, naked and unbothered.

'I'll away now,' he said.

Martine shrugged, as Charlie had before her. 'I won't say "Don't bother coming back."'

If she could bring herself to look back, she'd admit that she didn't trouble as she should have, writing to Mohan.

'How full and long your letters are. I'm ashamed: this one to you will only be long in arriving.

'I'm afraid I'm tired because things in my life are difficult – nothing for you to worry about.

'Sorry about the races, but I don't want to go to them, never will.

'Here's a leaflet about the Oval. English women play cricket too, you know. Men and women could use more middle ground.

'Next time I'll try to write a longer letter.

Martine'

Her letter was scattered and distracted, subconsciously assuming that the writer of the reply would return to their old philosophical bent. Mohan didn't.

'Thank you for the very brilliant Oval leaflet. Asgiriya is a big stadium. It is still quite far. Tatta says he saw a Test series against

India. It was a draw. I was five too small.

'All cricket fields are circles or ovals. I found a dictionary. "Oval" comes from a Latin egg.

'My teacher said "That is poppydash, ne?"

'But I will not talk about the not interesting eggs. Have you been to the Oval?

'About the Asia Cup. I watched at the Wimalasiris'. Sri Lanka did not win, but at least we flew to the final.

'I am not writing about women in cricket because I am still thinking about it.

'You say "Men and women could use more middle ground."

'There is mid-wicket, mid-off and mid-on. Macaque will say, "Get your facts right."

'P.S. Cruz saw Pieter in the British Council in Kandy. He says his nearly parents are very nice.'

Martine still failed to spot the subtext. She was preoccupied, new ideas and possibilities maybe activated by something in the letters. She even forgot to write.

'Dear Miss Martine

Your letter did not come. Mr Mendes is here. So here is another letter.

'I dreamt you slept on the veranda. A jackal and a leopard ran away.

'I argued with Anupama.

'Yesterday I said, "Miss Martine's tatta left her to have a baby with another lady. The baby Jonas grew up and went to find Miss Martine. He made her a bit happy. So the tatta of Miss Martine died to make him happy."

'Anupama said, "Nonsense. There's nothing that magnetises our lives as the moon does the waves, pulling them in a planned, neat straight line. One event causes another, and that may cause another. Everything's absolutely unpredictable."

'I read your writing to her. "I am so glad I've got to know Jonas. He might never have existed if our father had not left me."

'Anupama said, 'Miss Martine does not mean what you mean."

'I did not tell her something else. Jonas's amma died so he had to find another lady. He found one and began a family so now he is happy. So his amma must have died to make him happy.

'I went away and mended Nila's milking post. Anupama does not know what we know.

'Do not get tired. Play your certain music.

Mohan'

Seeing Charlie at college was like grit in a soft scab. Martine decided that she'd given up on men, that the compulsion to breed had left her. *But*, she thought, *I still need an outlet for whatever's brewing inside me.*

The Arctic in her heaved, green buds beginning to nose the ice. She started to do research and to make some phone calls, a new idea rising in her. She felt a bit delirious, found herself wanting to walk alone in Vauxhall Park. Its leafless trees promised to burst soon, one day soon. She tended to her ferns, and looked out for the moon.

'8 January 1989

Dear Mohan

I've taken especially long to write. I'm sorry you had to write me two letters. I've been busy. Much in my life has been changing – still is. No time to visit the Oval for the moment.

'It warms me that you think about my family; even more that a dream about me can help you feel protected.

'I'm still tired, but only on the surface. By the time of my next letter I'm pretty sure I'll have exciting news.

'I read in a book last night that we can be like migrant geese, somehow knowing the season to travel. We have a voice inside us if we'll only listen that tells us when to go out into the unknown. The book took me beyond Anupama's words about fate to somewhere much more hopeful.

'I'm not sure what you think we both know, though. Please explain.

Martine

'P.S. I've let you down – again – with this letter. But the next one really will be special, I promise.'

'1st February 1989

Dear Miss Martine

About the scholarship. Now I go to [name deleted] big school in Kandy. Everyone was happy. They gave me a game in a bag, yellow hoops and sticks. I am going on the bus with Jayamal. I must wear black shoes. It is my exciting news.

'You have been writing about fate and birds and a voice and a competition and men and women and middle ground.

'I do not understand. Send properly *your* exciting news and asking about me. Then I will tell you what I know we both know.

Mohan'

As the months went by, spring started in London, Vauxhall Park and the gardens of Aldebert Terrace pushing into leaf. Martine excused herself for her Sri Lankan radio silence on the grounds that she was too busy with her secret plans to write, and also, her plans felt too indefinite.

At last though, she saw they were clearcut.

'2 April 1989

Mohan, happy birthday for 8 March. So you're eleven. Secondary school! What did you do on your birthday?

'I feel embarrassed. This is not only late (again), but you're right: I haven't been attending. My letters have been aimed at someone that you're not. I've been talking to you as I should talk to myself. How could you understand that? I think I felt I could trust you – more, sometimes, than I trust myself. And there I go again.

'You ask for a proper letter. Here it is. And I'm keeping my promise: I've got something to tell you. It's important to say first that it'll make no difference between us.

'As you said, I'm a bit happy: i.e., not nearly as happy as I have the power to be. So I've decided to work a bit less, and – without a husband! – to adopt a boy. He'll probably be between 5 and 11 and come from what we call a foster family, somewhere in this country. I hope for almost some English Mohan with me. Once he is, perhaps you can write to each other. He can be for both of us together.

'First I went to meetings to make sure I wanted this. Now a woman, Rebecca, visits me once a week. She asks me what sort of child I'd like; who'd support me bringing him up; what I think about schools, and money, and religion, and hygiene, and discipline. I haven't told her about you yet. In a few months, she'll tell me whether I can adopt.

'Each time I write there'll be more news of this. I hope you're as excited and happy as I am. The main thing is, you and our letters will always be important, more than important, to me: nothing of that will alter.

'If InterRelate would let me, I'd finish this letter "*Fond wishes as ever*."

Martine'

She could never pin down where her adoption plans had started. Maybe from Mohan's talk of Pieter; or from her self-discoveries over summer drinks with the family; or from someone at work mentioning an adoption and fostering agency, or dropping the unsuspecting word 'adopt', as in 'adopt a policy' or something. Or maybe from all those.

These days, to Martine, the moon seemed fully blown as spring.

19 Martine

The room's finished. Matt has finally downed tools, and is crouched with a mug of tea and warm caramel slices over South Africa v. Pakistan on Sky while Martine appraises the finished bedroom, hands on hips. Through commentators' banter and waves of clapping she can hear his shy tries at remarks, sometimes on point and sometimes not.

She's content with the green she's gone for, Enchanted Eden, but the paint stings in her nostrils. She tuts, *No one could sleep in here.* She negotiates the piled-up furniture and shoves open the small high window, and cold air rushes in, but with her guest arriving tomorrow, a thought that makes her throat clench, she concedes, *On that timescale, it'll need more than a blast of air to mask this turps taste of my neuroses.*

Taste. Her words chime with a sudden bong from Mr Olfonse's heating pipes and inspire her. She hurries to the kitchen.

'*Hola*, Sancho.'

She begins chopping and stirring, throwing bones and vegetables into pans, mixing dough. Stock bubbles and bread proves under a cloth, and she starts knocking on doors up and down her landing, then the landings above and below.

There's a choice of broad bean 'n' borage soup or chicken 'n' cider. Her relentless brain quips, *What's invisible and smells of chicken? A fox fart.* She flings wide the door to the spare room, brandishing the pans, flapping the cooking aromas in on purpose. She loathes artificial fresheners, and she's always shunned indoor plants as captives, but maybe tomorrow, she'll break her embargo and bring in a scented plant.

She calms herself in front of the mirror, tries to tidy her oblivious hair. With her fingertips she pulls up her face to eliminate, for a minute, the puckers like yesterday's tapioca above the nose, around the eyes, along the lips.

By 7:40, neighbours are crowding in: Jess and Tracy, Mrs Landor, two of the Gibbins boys with their mother, dragged along under sufferance, Renée with her sleeping baby, and Nigel from number 80, who has also prised out Mr Olfonse. A few of them visit at Christmas, or on one of the children's birthdays. They've never been *en masse*.

The neighbours overrun the sitting room, tongue-tying Matt, slurping soup from mugs and bowls, mopping it up with fresh-baked bread. Martine bounces about topping them up, talking and smiling too much.

'What's this in aid of?' Mrs Landor asks, casting around for clues.

Martine feels she's begun to tick, a stopwatch till tomorrow night. 'Nothing really.'

The gathering somehow adds weight to the imminent arrival. Awed into near-silence by her mysterious occasion, the locals could be tribal elders round a camp fire, attending a rite of passage.

Which maybe it will be. Martine won't know until her guest is there.

* * *

Wrong foot, best foot
1989–1990

A letter from Mohan crossed with Martine's, the momentous one announcing her plans to adopt.

'4th April 1989

Dear Miss Martine

I saw mr mendes at nalins house I said still no letter from miss martine he said no I said *miss martine esta cansada* she says shes tired on the surface thats the skin *ela deve estar doente* she must be ill with skin disease please let me send another letter again I made myself look sad he said well write it quickly so I am writing quickly

'you might be too tired to hold your pen or you might be upset

'I told A still no letter I told her my last letter she said it sounded rude

'J followed me opal boy she will probably not write to you again

'I did not mean it please write and I will never ever say write a proper letter or I do not understand

'Also about what we know I will tell you

'A and I argued she shouted it was not planned in the stars that our amma had to die theres no magic reason that you got to know miss martine she was not meant to be english so youd want to learn more english from cruz and become his friend just because miss martine is english nothing decrees she will want a foreign boy even if he is good at english just because she has no husband and no baby nothing decrees she will take notice of parents like pieters who arent parents but can be miss martine will not ride down from the sky in a white carriage to take you amma did not die to make you and miss martine happy

'but I know you know

'I knew that one day you would come for me you will come'

The hiccup in this timing turned Martine's head abruptly in the direction of understanding. In case it hadn't, InterRelate's letter followed.

'17 April 1989

Dear Miss Haslett and Master Liyanage

Administrative error

Your last letters (2 and 4 April respectively) have crossed. Our sincere regrets.

'To avoid confusion, we suggest Miss Haslett resumes the correspondence.

'Once more, our apologies.

'Yours sincerely

Anura de Silva

Programme   Manager,   Colombo   Office,   InterRelate International

'P.S. I have just read copies of your letters and am concerned at the turn they have taken. I entreat Miss Haslett to refrain from implying in any way that Master Liyanage could be considered a member of her family, something he now seems in danger of assuming. Our Field Officer will visit to ensure that he understands the limits of the relationship. It would be very regrettable if your correspondence had to be curtailed.'

Martine hadn't been attending. Attending, which is more than reading and writing, as she knew. She certainly knows that now, in 2013. She'd misread Mohan, in fact hardly read him at all. He must have convinced himself she could adopt him: it was the only explanation for his outburst. With the rest of his family around him no one would have let her, even if she'd considered it. And of course she had her own plans.

Mohan had to be harmed by her blindness, and she tried in her new-style letters to mend things.

'Dear Mohan

As you'll know now, your letter arrived here probably almost at the same moment that mine arrived with you. I've sent you news that I now see you may find difficult. I so much hope you don't.

'I think we need to start again. I'm here in England, and you're there. It's sad, but that's how things are. You have a loving family. It has problems, I know; but in various ways I wish mine were more like yours. So many of you live close. You see each other often. I have no uncles and only one auntie, who's far away; I have no cousins. You have a father with you, and I don't; unlike me you have two sisters – all, with your brother, older than you, able to guide you in what you do. I feel like a mother with no children.

'I hope you'll see that I need to find, to make for myself, a family of my own.

'I'm ashamed I didn't spot sooner what you were trying to tell me. I now think I can guess. I'm so so sorry, but we mustn't talk about the hopes you might have had: not just because they're impossible but because InterRelate wouldn't like it. The main thing is to make sure they let us keep writing.

'What I should have said more often is thank you. Your letters over the last few months have been even more special: I think it's partly your talk about Pieter that made me think of adoption – plus you've taught me truths about myself.

'I'm wishing hard for a letter from you. Can you forgive me? Please try to understand.

'P.S. Here's a drawing from Jonas. Casey Jones is from *Teenage Mutant Hero Turtles*, a cartoon on TV. The turtle Raphael persuades him to punish criminals without killing them. Jonas has drawn your face on his mask because one of Casey's weapons is a cricket bat. Casey's another person who tries and tries.'

Mohan's letter back read as if he'd pressed a button sardonically and slunk off.

'Dear Miss Martine

Mr Mendes is waiting.

'Here is a copy of my English essay.

The true story of Saradiel

The Portuguese and Dutch and British rulers robbed our lands. The British growed coffee and tea over the lands. Saradiel hated the British rulers so he became a robber also. He robbed from the rich people and gave money to the poor people. The policemen catched him. They killed him in Kandy. It was in 1864.

'*In 1864 also, two Lankan cricket teams played cricket together at first. What a coincidence. They were St Thomas's Collegiate School Mutwal and Small Pass Cricket Club Colombo. It was the Battle of the Blues. The first big match was the Central Province against Colombo. It was in Kandy in 1867. The match ended by a tie.*

'*The British robbers brought cricket but the British robbers and the Dutch robbers and the Portuguese robbers were still bad.*

'The story was to practise the past tense. I got 65%. I was supposed to write about Saradiel.

'Pieter has Kermit the Frog in Sesame Street with Ali Baba and the turtles video game. So he knows about teenage ninja turtles and mutant. He has seen real turtles at the beach.

Mohan

'P.S. I did not say "I do not understand." This point is significant. Please notice.'

'The British rulers... The British robbers': Martine noted the robotic pointedness, felt the hatred. *My fault*, she knew.

'Dear Mohan

I was really glad you wrote to me. How are you getting on at school? How's the cricket?

'You sound so far away. I think you're angry with me; if so, believe me, I'm still angry with myself. Yes, the British stole Sri Lanka, to my shame; then again, if they hadn't you might not have cricket and maybe you wouldn't be learning English. Then we might not share the things we do.

'You may be fearful how to write – although you may not want to talk about that. (I used to teach teenagers. I know.) Please send me your news, or questions, or pictures. What can I do to make things better? Just tell me, and I'll try.

'I've taken some pictures of the Oval for you (sorry, no match was on). The walls curve high round the ground. Behind a pub with big, ugly blue signs, overlooked by huge, cylindrical gas holders, you can see the pavilion peeping up. I visited the shop for you, and enclose some pages from the catalogue. We both know I can't buy you anything, but what would be your top choice?

'My news so far is good. Rebecca has finished seeing me. There'll be an important meeting soon to decide if I can adopt (I'm not allowed to go). She says I stand a good chance.

'The boy will be younger than you. Imagine having someone younger to send news to, to advise and possibly share your love of cricket, who may have had a much, much sadder life.

'P.S. Give all good wishes to your family.'

Martine agonised, *Can I ever be contrite enough*? It felt hard not to misstep in her letters, even now.

Meanwhile, Mohan's anger seemed to be getting him into trouble.

'Dear Miss Martine

I did not want to do it. Year 10 saw the school bus with no driver. Nalin and I were lookouts. Plastic bags were masks. Viraj jumped in at the steering wheel. The others made us get on. We thought we were going to the sea. The bus crashed at the girls' school. The girls laughed and screamed. We did not want to tear the books or break the windows or carry the toddy. Nalin ran and found some people. Mr Mendes promised he would not tell you, but someone else might tell.

'I had twenty strokes in assembly. I have not been expelled. I saw Pieter. Now he does not like me. I will be better. If you go on writing, I will try harder in English and write more in my letters.

Mohan

'P.S. Do not be angry with Jonas for the mask idea.

'P.P.S. Happy birthday for 27th August. You will be 40. I added all the years.

'P.P.S. Nothing from the catalogue. A piece of turf from the Oval. British land.'

Martine sensed a thinness in Mohan's armour plating: at least he'd told her what he'd done. Was it a small sign of progress? She felt her old urge to give again, welling up.

'Dear Mohan

I sense you're still fearful how to write. About your bus escapade, it troubles me you're so anxious about my reaction. I'll always try to put myself in your place. You must have been terrified, and I can tell how sorry you were. I suspect you're also angry – still angry – with me. It'll take time for those feelings to improve. But I'll still write: nothing you do or say could ever stop me.

'I'd love to hear how, in other ways, you're getting on at school (if that's not too boring a subject).

'For me there's fantastic news: Rebecca tells me her office has approved me and I can start to search for a boy, first in the local area. Actually she does this for me. No sign of anyone yet.

'All other news seems less important. Jonas, Astrid and my mother are well. Jonas would like another baby.

'Here are Pippi, Gretel and me by a paddling pool at the seaside. Maybe my coming boy would fix their sailing boat better than I did. The English sea is often far too cold to swim in. Have you ever seen your own?

'Now I look more than a bit happy, don't I?'

Recently, Martine had begun to think that people aged more between the memorable events, in the static times of their lives. She dreaded losing momentum, being inactive.

On 26 August 1989, twenty-four hours before her fortieth

birthday, she found a crease. Freddy – the Smooth Shit, she dubbed him now – had described the entire surface of her body as a scarcely set cream dessert, freckled as if with nutmeg. But now, after the times of Freddy and Charlie, the first significant groove had appeared. It travelled down from the left corner of her mouth, as if she grimaced on a regular basis. And yet she'd been smiling more, not just from hope but as though that would somehow hurry her real boy, as she thought of him, her English boy, into coming.

There again, she had spent the last few months sitting about being dissected by Rebecca, her social worker, waiting weeks for approval from Rebecca's office then waiting again for the office to find a match. By August, Martine wasn't convinced they would. It felt like stagnation, loss of momentum. If she wanted to postpone more creases, then her fortieth, she decided, would have to be a memorable event.

Before midday, the buzzer sounded.

'Your second birthday I've remembered.' It was Charlie's voice, with an edge to it.

Her thumb sprang back from the door button. 'I'm getting ready for a party.'

'Let me come up, now. I've to give you—'

He was interrupted by shuffling sounds on the pavement, Astrid's voice, Pippi whining and an unclear conversation. Martine thought how at once to bar Charlie and let the family in.

Inevitably, amid the staircase percussion she heard his kicking tread: Charlie was climbing with them. They were far too early, Astrid and Pippi with presents, Jonas with his arms full of Gretel, her mother with her arms full of Tupperware. In her doorway they stood around this man they'd never seen before holding a bottle and a pot plant. She fumed, *Charlie should remember that I pity indoor plants.*

His stare moved from the little-girl frock to the kiss-curl styled for the party. She thought, *You dare touch it.*

'Looks like grey paint.'

'I missed a bit in the bedroom.'

An eyebrow shot up. 'Bordello gone, is it?'

The adults guessed more about him than Martine wanted. Pippi grabbed his jean-leg. Martine loosened her and hustled them inside.

As her door levered Charlie out he growled, 'You didn't tell me you were adopting.'

'Why would I?'

These days she told him only work things, when she must.

He clumped away handling the painted tongues roughly, shaking his head and blurting over his shoulder something pointed about 'the imperialism of need'.

This from him, anti-establishment vagabond turned establishment darling. Still, it was damning. She thought, *As if I haven't questioned my motives: whether I'm trying to adopt to express love or its lack; out of a need to give or a need to own, to oppress with my own need.* She'd taken to incanting, *If I had a boy, I mean really had him, I wouldn't grip him as I gripped onto Charlie.* At least, that was her firm intent.

20 Anupama

Asiri nodded and smiled on Tuesday as Anupama explained; as, over the vast head of the Buddha, the moonless night dropped like a mosquito net while, in the town below, a thousand lights pricked on and traffic headlights crept, outlining the black trapezoid of the lake. Although she knew he was listening, she was thinking, *He always reacts behind the news: like one of his clocks, there is a pause, a grinding whirr, before his 'Cuckoo!' noise comes out.* Sure enough it's now Thursday, but here she is explaining patiently again.

At the Buddha, the statistics poured out of her to Asiri; tonight, in the kitchen, she shows him the proof on a print-out. 'You see. In 2002, the Law College admitted 344 students through the Entrance Examination that I am planning to take, whereas now, the numbers are down to the low two hundreds merely.'

Asiri abandons the wallpaper paste of her basmati and her bland lentil slop of *parippu*. 'What fruit do we have?'

Anupama continues. 'Before you speak. You may say that there is also Colombo Faculty of Law, that I might do a law degree there and transfer to Law College to study for the bar in my last year. However, as you see, the Faculty also admits barely two hundred.' She says, 'Facts are everything. We cannot deny the facts.'

Asiri sighs. 'We have had this conversation.'

Anupama knows from many previous marital debates that Asiri thinks like his precursor, the young man at that wedding long ago: 'You think that there is absolute truth? I am not so sure.'

Asiri says, 'There is a man in an English novel, by Charles Dickens I think. His motto is "Facts, nothing but facts," or something similar. But the man is not the author. The author argues that there are two separate things, a wisdom of the head and of the heart.'

Anupama snaps, 'And how does that help me?', plonking down an uncut papaya. At once she mutters contritely to the new, invisible moon, 'I must be kind. I have to do this right.'

'Very well.' Asiri looks unruffled. 'Let us try another English saying, "Knowledge is power." Sir Francis Bacon, 1597. If the numbers into law study are so tiny for this whole beautiful island, as you say, this land where the need for justice is so strong, that is utterly unacceptable. We should mount a campaign. *You* should mount a campaign.'

Anupama unburdens to the moon, 'All I have ever wanted is a voice. Not my little brother's, not Asiri's: mine, my very own voice.' She explains to Asiri, 'Understand me, please. I want to fight the battles I can win, and on this one, the laws of probability are against me.' Asiri doesn't start slicing the fruit. His teeth bear down on a hangnail, a sign that he is starting to take things in. She continues, 'I shall of course still take the Entrance Exam. But if I fail, which is most likely…'

Asiri brightens, raises his head and beams. 'Of course. You have another plan.'

'The best alternative, as I say, would be to go to England.'

Anupama thinks, *Soon, in Asiri, the rupee piece will drop.*

* * *

Bringing on a substitute
1989–1990

Martine downed quite a few before her fortieth party started.

Grey clouds filed above the roof terrace like traffic. It was a breezy Sunday but warmish, fine enough to use the birthday barbecue Jonas had built (actually he'd begun it, Astrid had put it together). On the terrace, Jonas lit it with Pippi's hindering help. The chargrilling carcases in tyres that were hopefully out of Mohan's range were five thousand miles from smoking sausages and chicken. Martine felt herself revive, with a sudden sense of blessings.

Friends clattered into the maisonette with presents.

Her heart lifted at parties, especially her own. She pushed for universal happiness, wading through noise and activity and people, spreading outwards like a firework spreading light. For once she'd brought everyone together: the family, the college team, the core of the Soho Sisterhood, other London friends – although Rebecca, her social worker, couldn't come.

Mark 1 arrived at the door and took in her Yellow Brick Road gingham. 'Very Judy Garland.'

In fact, most had flouted her dress code, As Young as You Want to Feel, for summer shorts or denim. Among the kitchen and living room masses, still-torn Saila did sport a mullet wig. Mark 2 in a nappy was one idea that Martine should have banned. Leanne had pinned her hair with a token bow. Martine's mother wore jeans and a T-shirt, a youthful look for her. It was a surreal mix but they made polite if quizzical chit-chat, somehow got along.

Wherever Martine went she overheard her mother vetting someone with a bemused, 'How do you know Martine then?'

Martine heard Bernard answering as she slipped past, 'Our shared interest in all genders – that and having fun.'

He didn't goose her with his hand as she'd expected, his genitals today an unremarkable bump in his stone-washed jeans. As the years went by, he was defaulting more and more from Grand Dame Tattlemouse, gender adventurer, to just another greying, slack-faced man.

Martine drank, wandering about, the party fragmenting in her head. She backtracked. *When I first explained my adoption plans, which surprised this lot more, my news or my sudden concession that I have needs?* She'd written many of her friends onto the support network diagram that Rebecca had had her draw, and a well-chosen few had justified her faith in them by vouching for her convincingly at Rebecca's interviews.

For Rebecca's records, Martine had outlined the long phase of blind dating and the short thing with Alec. She'd also given highlights from her love history – leaving out the unsuitably married Charlie and a certain excised child.

'OK,' Rebecca had accepted, 'but what if you met someone now?'

'The child would always come first.' The answer had arrived in Martine's mouth without any hesitation or forethought.

She fizzed with impatience for her new adopter's life, as if it might arrive even that day.

She registered several of her guests wishing her, 'I hope it happens for you,' and toasted each endorsement with a swig.

Tipsiness took hold of her, distorting the party, breaking it up. In the living room, her fluorescent red sneakers looked inflated with Pippi's feet inside them, paddling about. Gretel was bawling, she heard. Catching Jonas's clouded eyes fixed on Astrid and the children, briefly she saw a tremor under the crust of someone's happiness.

She began obsessing about the donor of a birthday card that said, 'There's a boy out there. Just believe.'

'D'you send this?' she slurred at people at random, 'or d'you know who sent it?'

Someone turned down *The Raw and the Cooked*; she turned it back up. Ali paid her scant heed, forever shuttling to and fro to the bathroom, changing the longed-for baby, which had finally arrived. Children everywhere.

'Have you got Ribena?' Mark 2's partner wondered.

'Mum wants some kitchen towel,' sulked Leanne's little boy.

Stupidly, Martine hadn't planned for children that day.

She meandered back, in an alcoholic fog, to the mystery of the card. In her study with a bottle of Tempranillo she started ransacking drawers, peering at documents that might resolve it.

Eventually she re-emerged no wiser, strolling poker-erect

through the living room to find the tired-from-standing on the terrace parapet kneeling to the vivid ferns and mosses in their built-in glass frames. Pippi, agog with responsibility, gave her a dragonfly, self-crafted in translucent fabric, and Martine helped her plant it in the ferns.

'Send in the clowns!' she yodelled.

She was still impelled by that card. She toppled away again to the study.

Her mother stopped on the threshold. 'What a mess. Whatever the heck are you doing?'

Martine bundled her papers together guiltily.

Her mother perched on her desk. 'Who was that man?'

Martine burbled something about having scribbled on the Charlie page for too long; that adopting was replacing him with a clean, fresh sheet.

Her mother started something she'd clearly rehearsed. 'You'll feel I'm treating you like a child, but...'

'You're my mother. Don't worry about it.'

'This adoption. I can't bear you to... hurt or disappointed.' Martine's brain felt out of tune for her mother's lecture. 'Your work and social life are, well, your life. A child... change everything. Sometimes, you make decisions so... Are you really sure ...?' Then the tone changed. '...probably being selfish... maybe want to keep my single daughter single... Jonas has become the next-generation parent, the provider in this family... How will he feel, or me come to that, when...?'

They pressed together, mumbling unconceding, reassuring things.

Martine hadn't wanted to listen anyway. She slumped in the study and woozily reminisced. *After Dad left, whenever I left my bedroom, day or night, it seemed, I'd find Mum right outside the door, looking guilty. Her listening seemed more powerful than just being there: she was being constant, sending out a pulse of constancy, I suppose.*

But people want to be doing: she knew that they found transmission more glamorous than reception. Listening: the LIPSS project, her project, had been intended to foster listening as much as talking, but the teachers that she worked with had rarely taken that on. She feared now that she was much the same.

Restless kids and flagging adults gradually left between five and six, leaving greasy paper plates and wine-glass rings and children's fingerprints. Half an hour later, someone was at the door again.

It was Astrid. 'The others are playing in Vauxhall Park. Jonas is saying this is hokum, but... Now the people they are gone...' Downstairs she flitted ahead of Martine, revolving in each room. 'This will be the boy's, yes?' In Martine's bedroom she mused, 'You have painted grey: green is better. Place a dish of pomegranates. For children, for fruitfulness.' Then she tuned in to Martine's state. 'Make coffee. I will clean this.'

Martine burbled, 'What d'you clean, mean?', then went upstairs and faffed with the coffee pot.

From the stairwell, incense suddenly stung her nostrils, then came the sound of incantations. A sense of hilarity mounted.

Astrid called, 'Come down in the study.' Martine obeyed, swallowing giggles. 'There is not good energy for the boy. Especially here it must be cleaned.' She accused Martine's papers, the chaos she'd stirred up during the party. 'Which writings from people did not go well? They will hold you backwards.'

Astrid seemed to mean, which papers held malevolent forces? Martine removed the letters from Mohan to a safe place but meekly condemned other messages, the penstrokes blurring before her. Various scribbles from Lucho, including the one ditching Martine and university with broken English excuses about the Shining Path and his Peruvian family. Swimming tips and stilted postcards from Angus, her drug-squad lover and first real swimming coach. Impersonal florists' cards from Patrick, her flashy diamond broker. Precious words from Freddy, in her

imagination during their three years, less of a Kew horticultur-
alist than a dashing plant hunter-explorer. The only scrap from
Charlie, his birthday scrawl of the year before from someone
called Chaura-Panchasika, hard to say when you're drunk: 'Little
lonely one,/You cling to me as a garment clings, my girl' –
double-edged, as he so often was. Freddy and Charlie, her two
broken passions.

The lovers' words strewn in the study made her reel more.
Evidence of so much sex, and some romance. All those
encounters had somehow built into decades like train cars then
passed along beyond her, a bygone era. *Charlie will be the last
man*, she felt. *But is adopting a romance of a different kind?* It was a
thought she'd scotched before.

Most toxic were her father's letters from Milwaukee –
especially the last one, from 1957. His woman Phyllie wanted
him to move with her and her children to Merrimac by then.
Astrid's presence inhibited Martine's usual Dad daydream over
each airmail, the way she liked to picture him pausing his and
Phyllie's debate about more life changes, withdrawing to some
male domain in their Milwaukee house, greasy forelock inter-
fering with his glasses as he bent to the blue page.

She knew the letter's words by heart.

'Happy eleventh birthday... little book... *One-Liners for No-
Hopers*... a token that you may find amusing... Jonas still assures
you that he'll visit you some day... You may find it problematic
to correspond... It's testing to express oneself, perhaps especially
on the page... my only girl in perpetuity. I'll persevere with
writing. Indeed in my head I do so, at least once daily.'

That letter was the end with him, she thought, and then, *I've still
got that trashy book somewhere*, suspecting that it was where her
bad jokes came from. For the first time, there with Astrid, she
understood that her father's stilted language may have hinted
that he was in trouble, not just from the lack of her replies but
from a lack of words he longed to use. She thought with

wobbling perspective, *Have all those writings shapen me – or misshapen me – too much? Have I let them?*

From her yellow bag, Astrid took a pouch; she poured out five crystals.

'They will make a grid for cleaning.' She pointed Martine at the door. 'Take the bad papers outside.'

Martine did that, swaying with them on the terrace, the platinum sunlight cooling on her skin. Next thing she knew, Astrid was with her having used the stones somehow, cursing with distinct aspirituality, trying to revive the barbecue with a spilling box of matches; then she had Martine offer it the offending letters and cards. The wind got up. At some point, the moon was overlooking her, a fragile waning dish.

Martine woke to the sparkles bouncing off a glass of water by the bed in her grey room, still chemical with fresh paint. The moon at the high window, thin and leaning. She no longer felt drunk: more revived. Almost imperceptibly, she had drifted even further into lyricism. *Forget the poxy pomegranates,* she smiled inwardly; *things will all work out.*

She got up. From the window, her dreamy gaze caught a scattering of pale squares on the shrubs and paths of the estate, like discarded postage stamps. She smiled at the moon and made a little joky baying sound. Then she went back to bed.

Setting off for work in the morning, a page flapped on her front step. It was some prize draw offer. *The litter I saw down there last evening wasn't mine,* she wavered – *was it?* She resolved, *Adopting is what matters: not whether yesterday will be a clearly remembered day.*

Like a miracle, Mohan started to empathise about an adopted child.

'Dear Miss Martine

The boy must learn how to make and mend things. When he is older he can do this for you. Also, he must be healthy and laughing, not angry and sad. He must be 8 or 9. He must like lullabies and cricket. Also, he must adore babies, especially the little girls. Also, he must be able to write.

'I wish [*boy's writing incomplete*]

'About school. I am in the middle of the form except English. In life skills I made a bell and a coconut spoon. I am best at cricket but that is not a subject.

'Here is a match report.

Eleven-year-old Mohan Liyanage scored a magnificent 439 in our school's three-day match against St [school name deleted]. It was in the Battle of the Brave. What an incredible match. He faced 421 balls. He hit 12 sixes and 56 fours. That was a nearly triple century in fours and sixes only. He smashed the last record of an under-12 batsman from our school. That record was 401.

'I got 90%. The teacher said "What a corker, ne?"

'That was not true, just my dream.

'P.S. I have not been to the sea. I had a cough when everyone went. On the beach the turtles come to lay [*boy's writing incomplete*]

'P.P.S. I am asking you for Nalin. Do you have games with a computer and a helmet and gloves called virtual reality.'

Mohan's proprietorial air made Martine grin.

Her progress with adoption threaded through the next letters; so, too, did Mohan's growing up.

'Dear Mohan

The bridge on the stamp is an aqueduct with a canal boat moving along it.

'Tell Nalin that yes, as far as I know virtual reality games are coming, but no, I haven't seen one.

'Your match report reads well. I'm sure your batting will be great too, some day.

'We can't find anyone locally for me to adopt. The next stage is to look around England: there are plenty of boys, so it shouldn't be hard. Like the catalogue pages I once sent you, a magazine arrives in my post, full of photos and details of children who need a family.

'You have strong views about my coming boy; so do I. I find myself thinking "No" to one child and "Maybe" to another. Then it feels like shopping. I can't promise he'll be exactly as you or I would like. I fear we shouldn't expect to have all the things in our dreams just because in our dreams we find we can. I'm writing in an adult way again. Maybe Anupama can explain.

'How's your family? I never forget about them, or about you.

Martine'

'Dear Miss Martine

You must get the right boy. It is not shopping. If he is not healthy and laughing and cannot mend things, he will not make you happier. If he cannot write, he will not write to me and make me happier, then you will be upset. If he is a Buddhist that might help.

'It was the Nehru Cup. England beat us.

'We have much older aqueducts. We made them before the British, Dutch and Portuguese. Also we have tanks. They hold the rains. They are older engineering than the ancient Egyptians' engineering. They are made of stone and earth. Some not here have sluice gates letting the water onto the fields. If you do not believe me, here is a drawing.

'I am going to build [boy's writing incomplete]

'About the family.

'Jayamal is in the cricket under-15s. He is top in nearly all subjects (not English). He and his friends start swearing and look for me and my friends and [boy's writing incomplete]

'Tatta is often [boy's writing incomplete] Sometimes Nalin helps me find him and then we carry him from [*boy's writing incomplete*]

'Anupama used to borrow books from Shashika. Now he does not come.

'Upeksha visits Kamani and Geetha our cousins. She has many sarees and jeans. She never cooks here.

'I am trying for the under-12s.

'P.S. The writing about the family is because you asked. They might not like some of it at In... [*boy's writing incomplete*]

'P.P.S. I told Nalin there was virtual reality. Also you can make the computer look like handwriting.'

'Dear Mohan

I'm sitting in bright sun beside a swimming pool in Florida (America). My mother and I are on holiday. The plane on the stamp might carry our letters one day. They call it hypersonic.

'I picked it because of this holiday. We hire a plane nearly every day – a Piper Archer PA28-181, 180 horsepower, Mum says to tell you – and fly over a wide green waterway called Indian River. I was nervous at first, but now I just enjoy her skill. Down below are lagoons and swamp and stretches of sand and out beyond, the dark blue ocean. They remind me of your aqueducts and tanks. We've seen a dolphin and lots of alligators. I think you have those too.

'There's something on your mind about computers and my writing. Do you doubt I'm real? It isn't easy to reassure you. Scientists wonder whether, from reading written answers, someone could tell which was a woman out of a real woman and a computer imitating one. A computer mightn't be as clever as a woman but it could pretend successfully to be one. Sorry, it's complicated and you may not understand this.

'Would I be this honest if I were a computer? And computers don't peel from not wearing enough sun cream.

'I found a boy called Kieran. He was eight and healthy – and could write, I expect; but I don't know about the other things you're keen on (although I must warn you, there aren't many Buddhists in England). The people who had to agree whether I could adopt him decided I couldn't. I never met him. This was hard, which is why Mum insisted on this holiday.

'How's school? I hope things are much better.

'I've asked about another boy. Bobby is six with curly fair hair and a crooked smile. He has a sister. Wish me luck.

Martine'

21 The object

Dietrich's method of making friends seems to be boasting.

Yesterday he told the object, 'My stepfather invented 3D printers,' which is patently untrue.

He's also crowed over the weeks about his unicycling prowess, his sixth toe, his latest Playstation, the designer brand of his luggage, the new go-kart that he's been promised and latterly, about the place where he's staying from tomorrow, over half-term: a big house in the country with a large family, three cats and several llamas.

As opposed to a half-term with Martine Haslett, who seems to live alone. Hearing lists of Dietrich's successes and acquisitions doesn't help with the apprehension that from tomorrow, for a week, they'll both feel like commodities: parcels, bundled off for convenience somewhere else.

Since his pellet flicking in the classroom, Dietrich has popped up four times to surprise the object when no one else was about: by the lockers, in the empty dorms, on the deserted sports field, at the end of the school drive, which had seemed a safe enough place to suck on a smuggled cigarette and contemplate release. This time he's materialised in the school vegetable garden where, behind the greenhouse, there's a bench. It's a cold evening, but the crafty fag helps you to forget that; the open iPad with its Dongle warms the knees.

Dietrich sits down uninvited, fingers poking out the corners of his pockets, his brow ceaselessly crinkling. 'Gonna be an astronaut. Although I could be a fencing champion, probably make it to the Olympics if I wanted. But no, it's an astronaut. Because there's gonna be a new push on exploration...'

He burbles on, and it has to be tolerated, because although he's probably ADHD or autistic or whatever, they're connected, because they both find friendships hard.

In his defence, he can also shut up.

'What are *you* into?' he attempts, and then the shutting up happens, Dietrich with his mouth clamped, like a cap over a drain.

'Um. Acting.'

Dietrich's blonde eyebrow rises, but he stops short of speaking. Through their staccato conversations he's already heard about Sister Number One, aka Creepy, who does every-thing that's asked of her, and Sister Number Two, who's cooler, a co-conspirator; even in broad outline, without the melodrama of his disappearance, BS Shit. Dietrich's own family naturally is great in every way.

Martine's visitor-to-be mumbles on about acting. 'Back home I try out for the cool parts. Demons, thieves. The kid that no one likes.' The last without irony. Another pause, and, 'Want to go to drama school, but doubt my folks will let me. Bastards.'

It may be taboo to tell strangers about BS's disappearance, but somehow it's OK suddenly, here with Dietrich, to reveal something of the paranoia at home, the early curfews, the ban on sleepovers at friends' houses, the rules and regulations since the BS went.

The chatting lurches onwards for a while. They even exchange email and Skype addresses.

Dietrich insists, 'We can talk over half-term,' pointing out that then he too can rejoin the living on the internet.

He leaves, and it feels good to be alone.

On the iPad, there are more instructions from home.

'1. Make sure you've got the cash to pay Miss Haslett for any extras. 2. Don't ask her to help you with too much laundry. 3. Take your best clothes. 4. Don't forget to take a present. 5. Offer to help with things like the washing up. 6. Do whatever she tells or asks you to. 7. And, again, please don't go out without her.'

Sailor Moon will block out these parental tyannies. At the press of a few buttons an early episode races across the screen, the

Sailors trying to overcome the evil Falion. Falion blocks Sailor Venus's crescent beam, blasting Sailors Venus, Mars and Mercury. Sailor Moon dodges Falion's onslaught, and mysteriously, from somewhere, a white rose hits the ground. In a tree above, the Moonlight Knight appears, destroying Falion's energy wheel. He vows extravagantly that he'll meet Sailor Moon again.

* * *

Martine's boats
1990

By January 1990, adopting Kieran hadn't worked out, so Martine was set on Bobby, the boy who had a sister. As ever, Mohan had his point of view.

'Dear Miss Martine

Kieran would be better. A bent smile would not be nice. You must not adopt a boy with a girl. About Bobby's hair. Is he white-skinned? Why no for Kieran? I do not [*boy's writing incomplete*]

'Tell the people that you are working less now and have a big enough flat and know about boys who are 8 because I have been 8. Do not forget, he must play cricket.

'About school. I am still mostly interested in cricket. Here is a report in English.

[*School name deleted*]: *a magnificent one-day match*

On the 18th of December the under-12s of [deletion] played the under-12 reserves. The reserves won the toss and went to bat. Nalin Jamasinghe opened. He scored a delicious 95 from 110 balls. Then he hit the ball for a six. It was magnificent. Asela Kudararalage was third man and he was near the boundary. He ran, fell and stood up. He jumped and flyed and caught the ball. It was magnificent. Nalin was out. Next Mohan Liyanage batted. He batted carefully and sometimes he batted fiercely, and he got 25 runs from 40 balls. He scored two sixes.

By the end we had 150 runs from 150 balls!

'The reserves took a magnificent three wickets in 45 balls at first. (The under-12s scored only 28!) But then the under-12s scored 83 more. We dropped two catches and made many no balls. The under-12 batsmen tried and tried. Our fielders did not try enough. Mohan Liyanage was not fine leg but bad leg. He missed an easy catch. At the last Nalin caught the batsman out, but it was a no ball. So the match was a draw.

'This was a *real* match. About this draw and our draw in the First Test against Australia in December. Which would you choose?

'I will look hard at your answer. Computers are clever.

Mohan'

'Dear Mohan

Yes, Bobby was white. It's been decided that no one can adopt him. His sister will still go to a family. That makes me feel much more for him than for myself.

'Anyway, here are Tate's details and picture. He's nearly eight and loves football. Is that a teenage mutant hero turtle on the grass?!

'I've told the people who arrange these things about the size of my flat and my lessened workload and you – even what you'd like in a boy. But I'm afraid it isn't simple. Over here, not so many boys like cricket. You and I may have to convert him.

'Your cricket report was *magnificent* and *delicious*. Your question about the two draws is obviously a test. Before you look at my answer, ask someone else who cares for you the same question.

'(Here's a pause. Imagine me waiting.)

'Now here goes. I'd choose the match you played in – like anyone who cares for you, I expect (wouldn't a computer choose the more skilful, exciting game?). I hope you're happy with my answer. If not, please don't stop writing – or decide I'm a cunning computer.

'Warm wishes to your family as ever.

Martine

'P.S. Another good reason: getting to your match would be half the distance of Brisbane. (Only joking. But here's a point: can computers joke?)

'P.P.S. People say they must separate Bobby from his sister because of the hard life they'd had together. And by the way, white English "parents" mostly adopt white children: the people in charge here feel that white people wouldn't appreciate a dark child's background, and that a family's colours should match. Some of us think we notice colour too much. How about you?'

Martine might have had fractured memories of her fortieth birthday, but Saturday 31 March she knew she would recall.

The moon was new, keeping its distance. It was 9:30, and near Stockwell, in Kennington Park, crowds were gathering to march against the poll tax. Friends were going; she'd thought about joining them. But she was a single householder, ambivalent about the issues. Anyway it was a fine spring day with other possibilities, other reasons to be out there.

The day before, Norwich had rung her. Fiona, the woman she'd been dealing with, had said that with Tate, they could 'proceed to the next stage', which was showing him a photo album and a video about her. This wasn't the same as it had been with Kieran, or with Bobby. Martine had sat about for them, head on her home desk or the kitchen counter or between her legs on a deckchair by that Florida pool letting out obstructed grunts, hearing how ridiculous they sounded and admitting defeat: that she couldn't force a boy to come, couldn't even force tears. Mohan's letters of opinionated support were pegged to a wire along her study wall, now seeming almost like prayer scripts she could turn to. With Mohan behind her and the Norwich news of Tate, something really felt promised.

With the college videocam, she bowled from home with a slew of ideas for her film. For the muddy-kneed boy who, according to the snaps they'd sent, could land a ball in a net she shot the sun-drenched opening to Stockwell tube. For his hopes to do it again in front of someone caring, she panned round the double platform, the posters and waiting travellers. For him she took off her hat, fiddled with her hair, then couldn't find somewhere to rest the camera to film herself. She recorded her hello to him unseen.

'We're going to travel under the River Thames. I hear you're keen on trains.'

She merrily ignored other people's glances. She explained that the station was hers, then corrected that it could be Tate's and hers. She found herself describing her father's old job, managing the Metropolitan and Bakerloo stock at Neasden. Tate's dad hadn't managed anything, including drink or drugs. *Both men are lost to us*, she thought.

There was a shake and a violent rattle and, like an emblem of her future, a train shuddered, unretractable, out of the black hole of the tunnel. She filmed its squeal to a stop and swung into a seat.

She popped a couple of Feminax for the grinding menstrual pain. Thousands were mustering overground, crossing the water over bridges, and still the train was almost full. The later Saturday workers, shoppers and stray protesters with placards and banners, jolting from time to time under the white light of the carriage.

A black woman reading the Bible threw back her head and beamed at Martine as if she radiated something.

Nodding at the camera in her lap, a youth addressed her, breaking tube etiquette. 'You coming?'

'Nah.' She smiled.

Reflections of faces turned to her, stretching in the window opposite, their elongated eyes seeming to take particular meaning from the pork pie hat and petticoat dress with its carnival citrus fruit and flowers: surely she'd got to be going somewhere. She romanticised, *And I am: to my own demonstration, a demonstration of the new page I blathered squiffily to Mum about; I'm going to fold it, shape it, make something magical of it.*

From her bag she flipped through the morning's post: a resubscription notice, a card from Matthias in Rome and a letter with a London postmark. InterRelate. Mohan's spurts of script showed through the envelope. *Why diverted through London?* she wondered. *An official scolding again?*

She tackled Mohan's letter first.

'Dear Miss Martine

Brothers and sisters should stay together. How could that life be too hard? I do not [*boy's writing incomplete*]

'About white people having dark children. Nalin and I found tatta as usual. Tatta said to senior father, "Pieter's white nearly parents have stolen him from Sinhalese people who could have had him." Pieter doesn't talk to us any more.

'Tatta said, "The Dutch and the British will always patronise us. They still think they need to rescue us from ourselves."

'I do not [*boy's writing deleted*] know some of the words.

'Senior father sometimes says "unhygienic ugly swarthy people". He does not mean the Dutch or British.

'Tatta says, "They're [*expletive deleted*] no such thing. They shouldn't harm us, we shouldn't [*expletive deleted*] harm them, deprive them or even insult them. One nation should stick together."

'Also he says the Indian soldiers are taking something from us. I do not [*boy's writing incomplete*] It is confusing.

'You can adopt a white boy. What a pity Tate is not 8. In the picture he is scoring a goal. He might make a good batsman.

'I am going out to [*boy's writing incomplete*]

'About your answer, the two matches. Nalin says think about

it, a computer would say Miss Martine prefers not to travel to the sea and America and other places or get an English boy. It would say you prefer to come and sleep on our veranda. So you are probably not a computer.

'Tell those people your boy must write to me soon. He must come soon.

'I am going to practise my [*boy's writing incomplete*] Mohan'

Martine's grin hardly shifted reading the formal letter attached. She thought, *With Tate on the horizon everything's OK: nothing can puncture me – not official words, not anything.*

She roused herself. Most passengers were leaving, and confusingly she was on the Northern line, not the Victoria line she needed for Tate's video. She'd been autopiloting towards work when she wasn't going to work, and now they'd stopped at Oval, and she registered the human swarm bearing placards away towards the surface, making for the park, the rallying point for the protest. Out on the platform, in the scrum of marchers, she laughed at herself and re-thought: if she went up too, she could walk the rest of the way.

At street level, through the drumming of tin cans and the din of practice chants, someone shouted, 'Martine! Over here!'

She spotted Claire. Her workmate was in the sun-filled entrance craning over the mob, waving a balloon printed with the words, 'Blow up the poll tax.' Some of Martine's co-passengers called out to Claire, elbowing past. There was a knot with Claire already, hyped-up for marching. Claire called out to Martine, assuming she would join them.

Martine shuffled to her as the mob channelled round them. Over the road, against the budding trees of Kennington Park, humanity seethed. Home-made flags, jugglers on stilts, costumes, one wild trumpet. Martine shouted in Claire's ear the reason she couldn't march that day, that her plan was to go shooting the Tate for Tate.

Claire looked at her beadily, so Martine thought she'd understood, but then she grabbed her arm. 'Come on!'

Claire hustled her with husband Rollo and their sheepdog and her gang across the road. Rollo and she were extolling the protest to the dog: *Their doggy child substitute,* Martine smiled. She felt weird, as if she was in two parties at the same venue: the crowd's excitement wasn't hers.

She shook off Claire's grip. 'I have to make this film.'

Claire looked slapped and turned her back on her. 'Fine. See you on Monday.'

Martine called out, 'What is it?'

Claire faced her again. 'You have to have a plan, don't you? You can never just go with the flow.'

Martine apologised, regaining balance. 'You go on the march. I can't. Today, Tate's my true flow.'

At college the next Monday Claire would apologise, shift to another grievance. 'I could have helped you. Come with you. Outside work, you never want help.'

But for now the sunshine warmed Martine, striding off for Vauxhall Bridge. She passed the gas holders, the synthetic ocean blue of the Surrey Tavern and the brick wall round the Oval. For once she was feeling of the crowds without needing to be with them.

Below the bridge the Thames glittered, and Martine experienced a clear lyrical vision of her pristine page origamied into a boat, cruising towards this adoption. She thought, *Hope hasn't just sailed: I've probably always been moving towards a special connection with someone. It's just that recently, like activating a sluice gate, a tide has been released, bearing me along.*

The wind caught the InterRelate letter flapping in the mouth of her bag. She pushed it down.

At Millbank, she mounted the steps to the Tate Gallery. She'd imagined filming Tate's name as a light-touch hint that London called him, but there was no carved building name near the portico. Uterine contractions grabbed her and twisted hard. She ran inside, letting blood pour into the lavatory, changing tampons just in time.

When she re-emerged, the embankments towards Westminster and Lambeth Bridge were fluid with a mass of dots of protest. She thought, *Filming the crowds might alarm him.* At last she found Tate the name on a banner at the entrance, zooming in. Balancing the camera on a step, she ran down to the pavement so that she could film herself. A snap-happy tourist moved her glowering little boy around herself like a chess piece. Martine talked to Tate and smiled.

A few streets away was Ali and Conrad's flat. Ali opened the door, beaming to hear of her progress with the adoption. Children were babbling inside.

'Conrad's on the demo, which leaves me holding the little'un. Got a few friends round doing likewise,' Ali said. As Martine stepped over the threshold she added, 'Jonas is here.'

Martine hadn't known that Jonas saw her friends without her. He was with a circle of mothers at the low living room table, feeding cake icing to Gretel on his knee. He and the others were chatting and laughing easily, with their mouths full. Children shunted toys on the carpet. Invisible tracer seemed to course between the parent-child pairings.

Martine crept up on Jonas. 'Don't look now.'

He murmured, 'Woah! Surprise!' his face clouding.

Astrid and Pippi were on the protest; Martine explained why she was there.

'That's great,' he said into Gretel's hair.

Talk was of Thatcher and the tax, children's development and food fads.

'Soon I could be in this club,' Martine said, feeling an inner leap.

Jonas laid an arm across Gretel. 'You'd want that?'

Gretel was squirming for release. The ceiling devil had long since gone, but Martine filmed the painted cupid still reaching a chubby arm for the cornice. The adults nattered with mouths full of crisps and chocolate, and she recorded a commentary for Tate while processing other thoughts. *Jonas is put out: I've invaded what he sees as his domain.*

Ali was sitting across from her with a woman and teenage girl, their hands locked together with what seemed to Martine an unnatural air of dependency. She got up to go, maybe to walk downriver, and the girl gave a squawk, and Ali raced towards her with a flannel and a blush.

The mother said, 'Love, don't worry but I think you might be having a...', and the daughter wrinkled her nose, and Ali asked, 'Are you OK? Maybe we need to get you to the...', and someone mumbled, 'Should I call an ambulance?', and Jonas dropped his head. Then Martine recognised the warm, drenched sensation and saw the red stain on the cushion she'd been sitting on.

Emotions can stream along in parallel. In Trafalgar Square the mood of the march was festive-angry, Martine would find out later. A rabble of marchers was kicking three bells out of Bernard, dressed as a comedy Thatcher. Police horses reared, protesters fell; scaffolding poles hurtled through windows and flames through portakabins and the high-ceilinged rooms of the South African Embassy; exultation rippled through two hundred thousand people. And Martine's mood took two channels, each running straight on. There was an undertow of panic about something – the maternal life nearly on her, the letter in her bag – yet at the same time, with the blood loss, a kind of breaking of waters, a vast sense of release, of the onset of everything she'd wanted.

Ali trailed her to the toilet scrubbing at the defaced lemons and oranges with Martine declaiming stupidly, 'Out, out, damned spot!', and once she was seated and alone, the blood came gushing out.

She re-read the official letter.

'28 March 1990

Dear Miss Haslett

Sri Lanka

The political situation in Sri Lanka has been volatile for many years and NGO work there has been under review for some time. The decision has been taken that our Sri Lankan operations and therefore, of course, communication with your sponsored child must cease. You will understand that, for reasons of confidentiality and security, we are unable to supply the family's contact details.

'We thank you for your support to date and hope this will continue. I attach a list of countries where we are currently active, and look forward to your decision on a new link with a child.

'Many thanks again for your help thus far

Gavin Godfell

Public Relations Manager, InterRelate International, London'

Martine's hopes and plans still flowed, but Mohan had dropped from her, a shard off the edge of a cliff. She couldn't swallow. There was a dam of giant pebbles in her throat.

22 Anupama

Thursday 14 February 2013

'We have said that if you live in Colombo to study, we can find a way to manage,' pleads Asiri, referring not just to money but to separation. 'But England...'

'You have heard me talk of Thurindu?' Anupama asks. 'The cousin I did not know we had.' She asides to the moon, 'You were there sometimes when that vain brat came to the house, glancing with disdain at my figure. You shone on me as if you were trying to calm me when he gave the little man sweets and lent him a cricket bat and talked to me of relationships with his ingratiating smile. His mother was most forceful. He was a bullet I dodged. He, and since, the bullet of having children. I have often thanked the Buddha.'

'My rival,' Asiri jokes in a leaden tone.

'He is married now. Because his wife has family there, they live somewhat near London.'

Asiri ransacks the England idea for obstacles. 'The money it would take! And it must be hard to get a visa.'

'Not a student visa, as long as I absolutely fulfil the criteria. And...' Anupama hesitates. 'I have already written to them. His wife is homesick for Sri Lanka. They are willing to let me stay. If I have to, I could say on the visa form, with a little truthfulness, that my cousin's wife is sick.'

Asiri's face is a helpless blank. Anupama thinks, *A dream becomes a need when it is capable of fulfilment. Till now, I have had no dreams like that.*

'Handanandāmāmā,' she questions silently, 'is it so wrong to follow my needs? To replace Asiri's with my own?'

'Have I lost you?' whispers Asiri.

She imagines the lively, thinking world of Miss Martine. She already knows how to answer him and the moon. Her will must supersede Asiri's: he's had his wishes for long enough.

She puts her lips to the rigid neck of her husband. 'My dearest,' she whispers, 'if I stay here, I hope no. But to be perfectly honest, if I go to London, possibly yes.'

* * *

Knockabout
1990–1993

At a few keystrokes Mohan was gone.

Some hurts come and go but some, like bootprints on the moon, impress people for all time. The blue manila wallet long unopened in the carton in Martine's wardrobe is like that, the dust of loss even now drifting across it. From 1990, over the next few years, it came to contain official letters: from Social Services offices, from children's homes, the press. Messages from friends too, and her mother.

'Dear Miss Haslett

Sponsored child 88 6502

I am sorry, but as previously stated our policies prevent us from giving you any contact information for the Sri Lankan family, or conveying a message.

'We note you have not yet opted for another country for child sponsorship, and look forward to your choice.

'Regards

Gavin Godfell

Public Relations Manager, InterRelate International, London'

'18th May 1990

Dear Martine

Possible adoption of Tate

Our ref: WW 33

Yes, I had received your letter. As she will have explained to you, you should not communicate with Fiona or me but through Rebecca Ng'ang'a, your Adoption Officer. I can assure you though that there are always sound reasons for delays.

'Yours sincerely

Nikki Leach

Placement Manager

Shoehorn House, Norwich'

'27 August 1990

Dear Martine

Tate (Norwich), our reference: PA/NHA/14/45

Although we've discussed the situation in person, my manager has asked me to write to you. Bureaucrats, eh!

'Please make sure your phone calls and letters always come to me. Of course it's disappointing about Tate, but agencies up and down the land would be overwhelmed with correspondence if every prospective adopter rang and wrote to them when things didn't pan out.

'I look forward to working with you towards a more successful outcome.

'Yours sincerely as ever

Rebecca Ng'ang'a

Adoption Officer'

Enclosure *[handwritten]*

'Martine,

I shouldn't be doing this, so keep this to yourself.

'I feel frustrated too – but my job is to help you overcome such feelings. We approved you as a single adopter – so why, you're asking, does Shoehorn Homes seem to operate to different standards, as though they value a couple over someone single? A couple who haven't even been found yet. From all the information I have it wasn't a simple 'couple vs. single' decision. It was also about your style of parenting compared with another, given Tate's needs. In other words, you must trust me to trust the agency for you – if you have his best interests at heart.

'If you're now thinking, "Well she would say that – they're all in this together," please think again. Having helped you through the approval stages, I'm now your advocate (although I must also weigh the needs of any child). You can rely on me being honest – or as honest as I can be.

'Your distress for Tate – the agency showing Tate your video as if it was more or less a done deal – I've written to them asking why, if they weren't sure about you even then, they did that. If I get a reply, I'll let you know.

'As for the delays, I'd say I'm sorry – except that I can't do anything to shorten them. I definitely shouldn't be mentioning this, but you've been so lucky to keep me as your social worker without disruption. This job takes a heavy toll in staff changes, unfilled jobs and sickness. And that's why crucial meetings are often postponed etc. too – not helped by the inevitable knots and snares of red tape!

'I know you can get over this.

'Fond wishes

Rebecca'

'2 October 1990

Dear Martine

Gary (Liverpool), our reference: LSS/71/15

Rebecca is having some time off work so I'm just writing to let you know that the meeting about you and Gary has unfortunatly [sic] been postponed until Thursday 22 November. Well [sic] be in touch as soon as we con [sic] after that.

'We do appollogise [sic] for the wait.

'Sincerely

Camilla Nixon

Manager, Adoption and Fostering'

'19 December 1990

Dear Martine

Gary (Liverpool), our reference: LSS/71/19

Writing formally with the outcome of our meeting on Gary as explained on the phone last week. His foster carers have discoverd [sic] a medical problem that may or, may not, be serious. Untill [sic] it is dignosed [sic] Liverpool feel they can't proseed [sic] with any possible adoption and have withdrawn him from there [sic] pool for the forseable [sic] future. This is a shame but Im [sic] sure is for the best to avoid rising [sic] false hopes. Please continue looking through *Take Me In* and we will help you all we can.

'Good news though we have apointed [sic] a new Adoption and Fostering Officer. His name is Francis Motti, he will be in touch very soon.

'Sincerely

Camilla Nixon

Manager, Adoption and Fostering'

'29th January 1991

Dear Martine

I may be a stressed-out red-tape merchant but *of course* I remember you.

'Just to say I was really really sorry not to say goodbye – and I still think of you. Use the phone number above (home, but that's fine) if you need to talk.

'I believe it will all come right for you. What they disliked us telling you is how different every child agencies' standards and procedures are, how long it all takes – and how many disappointments there'll be along the way (please eat this when you've read it!).

'I think I'm on the road to recovery at last – or will be if I change to a more stress-free direction. Desert island surveying? Maybe a project with teenagers somewhere? All ideas welcome.

'Keep on keeping on.

Love Rebecca'

'20 February 1991

Dear Miss Haslett

Stuart (Exeter), our reference: PPHE/73/3

I could not find you on the telephone the last few days.

'It is the greatest of pleasure that the meetings about you and Stuart have a very positive feeling to them. Now it would be helping the local Social Services if they can see an album of your photos of you and your family and friends.

'I can advise you on how to put this up if you like. I will telephone you to talk about it.

'All my very good wishes

Francis (Motti of course!)

Adoption and Fostering Officer'

'5 March 1991

Dear Martine

Stuart (Exeter), our reference: PPHE/73/4

I am very sorry I was not here when you were telephoning me. I have a busy job, you know!

'I am very sorry I did not know we were keeping an album of yours for all of these times. Please be sure that we have not lost this precious thing. I will put it into the post to Exeter as they are asking us for this straight away.

'All my very good wishes

Francis (Motti)

Adoption and Fostering Officer'

'11 April 1991

Dear Martine

Stuart (Exeter), our reference: PPHE/73/7

It is a very sad outcome I am very sorry to say. Although

Stuart was often having accidents you were content about, it will be a very different thing since the fire in the Home. I am sure you can see this.

'I think a conversation with you would be a very good idea and I would see you very soon. I have new ideas to give to you about the kind of child and so on.

'I will find you on the telephone as soon as possible.

'Once more very sorry, with all very good wishes

Francis (Motti)

Adoption and Fostering Officer'

'13th May 1991

Hi hon.

'How are you after the Thames booze cruise?!!! – I was wrecked. Do hope it did you some good – it seemed to. Didn't we tear off the world a strip!! – and also I think a man on some bridge and a hen party from Essex – ABOUT A LOST BOY CALLED STUART AND THE CRAP IN THE SYSTEM AND A CERTAIN PERSON'S EX-BOSSES??? (Although – to be fair – Camilla does her best, poor love.)

'This Francis bloke sounds bright-eyed and bushy-tailed, but make sure he listens to you and doesn't impose things on you – that's the key. As I said, if you don't want a girl – or you're a bit unsure – don't even go there. Really – trust your instincts.

'Thinking of you loads.

Love Rebecca X

'P.S. Also, stop thinking adoption for one minute of the day and go to your doc again. You can't carry on like that. Apart from the pain and blood, the loss of energy – I'd have slit my wrists by now. (Actually I wouldn't – because a) that would be even more pain and blood, and b) it's not what any self-respecting ex-Adoption Officer would ever ever advise.) Go to the doc!

Love Bex (again) X'

'18th June 1991

Martine

About our last phone call. Row, I suppose we have to admit.

'I've been trying to sleep, but something's come back to me. Before Uncle Simon died and Auntie Louise moved to Scotland and became such a hermit, when they lived in Birmingham, they looked after the little boy of a neighbour sometimes who had what we'd probably call now post-natal depression.

'Whenever you saw him at Auntie Louise's you'd handle him in a careless way, almost. (You were never interested in dolls or things like that, that I remember.) But one time, you must have been about six, the neighbour suddenly appeared at Auntie Louise's. She wanted him back unexpectedly. And you screamed and held him and wouldn't let him go and made such a fuss that I was embarrassed. I wonder now if some protective instinct had alerted you that her maternal drive wasn't quite reliable or something.

'You'll think I'm being old-fashioned. ~~I can't say this very well~~. I'm sorry, but I've always thought you'd be better off with a girl. I may not have said before, but I won't unsay it now. ~~What I meant was~~ I suppose I was trying to say how different from mother and boy the mother-girl bond is. I don't know how much science lies behind it but most girls seem partly mothers-in-waiting, primed to feed and nurture, as if they share some collective memory of mothering. And I don't think it's just their physical makeup. Surely almost any girl you adopted would share that with you already – just as you have some of me, and I have some of you.

'You're right though, I shouldn't tell you what to do. I know you're bombarded by "advice". Your mangy old Mum can't help it. Sometimes she longs to take over the flying for you through all this turbulence.

'Please don't stop our chats. I don't care what you say to me – even that stuff about night-time with your magazines. Anything, you can say anything.

'Good luck, darling, whatever you decide.

'Love always

Mum X'

'18th August 1991

Quick p.c. Not-so-sunny Spain, but Nathan – fondling bits of yrs truly at this very mo – is my sunshine, so no probs. Got answerphone message before leaving. Menorrhagia? Tranexamic acid? What the bejasus is those? Oh well, if dropping acid stops the monthly heeby-jeebies – and them wanting to rip your women's bits out, like you say... A girl, eh? Helen sounds promising – ish... Hon, about her tho. Stay hopeful but on an even keel of hope, if that makes sense. (V. poetic, no?!) Talking kids – got a bit of news too. Be happy for us. Be happy-careful for yourself. Bex X'

'29 October 1991

Dear Martine

Helen (Belfast), our reference: BGS/27/3

Our phone call was too quick, but as I said you must give the same answers again onto the new form from the St Anthony Children's Trust I am very afraid. I know you have given them to us mostly before, but they are wanting to see all of these again, in your handwriting not computerised. So you should write these again and send them to me.

'Also the new answer about why you are now thinking of girls not only boys is important. This is because you are now hoping for Helen of course! Please tell me if you want help with that.

'On the positive side, all seems to be going very well from their side.

'With my very good wishes for that

Francis (Motti) (as usual!)

Adoption and Fostering Officer'

'14 January 1992

Dear Martine and Francis

Helen, your ref: BGS/27/5, our ref: HR-LR-D-28

This is to let you know, formally, that we cannot proceed with placing Helen for adoption. This is owing to an allegation she has made concerning her current foster brother. It turns out that at the very least she is more the product of past experiences within her biological family than we had appreciated, and at worst... It is all very sad. Whatever the findings of our investigation, the outcome for Helen is a great deal more work with her before she can be ready, if ever, for a permanent family.

'At least we have informed you at a relatively early stage. Hopefully you can move forward swiftly with other candidates without too much sense of disappointment.

'Wishing you all the best, Martine, for an eventual adoption.

'Yours sincerely

Jago Penberthy

Child Placement Department, St Anthony Children's Trust, Belfast'

'24 February 1992

Dear Martine

I have tried to find you on the telephone.

'About what you are saying in your letter. You must be very upset at the moment. Please reconsider again. I am very sure there will be a child somewhere if only you can be patient for a little while longer.

'Perhaps I can help you even more than I have been helping you in these times so far. I will try to find you again on the telephone to give you some hope and more good ideas.

'With my very warm wishes

Francis (Motti)

Adoption and Fostering Officer'

'4 March 1992

Dear Martine

Closure of file

Francis (Motti) and I are writing to express our regret that you will not proseed [*sic*] with seeking a child to adopt for the forseable [*sic*] future. Francis says you have found the dissapointments [*sic*] rather dificult [*sic*].

'As he has told you, we will keep your details on our books. You will remain an approved adopter and if you change your mind you can always contact us again.

'Good wishes

Camilla Nixon

Manager, Adoption and Fostering'

'8th March 1992

Dear Martine

I am sorry about the children.

'Love Pippi X and Mum and Dad and Gretel XXX

'P.S. Pippi chose the elephant and pig theme for the card. Can you read her tracing? The letters are a bit wobbling! Astrid X'

'28th March

Not at home, or just not answering? No one's seen you – although we know from Pippa you're still working some days a week. You don't answer there either. Conrad and I are miserable for you and without you.

'Will ring buzzer as many nights as I can pop round till you answer.

Loads of love, Ali XX'

'7/4 5.30 Martine, going home now:-

Mark 1, Saila, Matthias, Graham, Conrad, Bex, Ali... Not writing their frantic messages down again. Get a new slave or deal. We have other work here at College, you know. Pippa X'

'22 May – 7.40 pm

Hon – Calling by quickly – Nathan and baby in grumbling competition in car. STOP SCREENING MY PHONE CALLS! There's more to life than work and swimming.

Bex X'

'18th July 1992

Martine, Hope you like the postcard. ~~With B~~ With a friend finding old furniture in salvage yards and auctions. Great market! The flowers!

'Come for the weekend again when I get back. Always good to talk, love. Mum X'

'18th December 1992

To open on Christmas Day

Martine

Don't apologise. I understand you wanting to get away in the holidays. Teachers' stories of their cute and funny charges must become hard to take. And if you'd come, Jonas's magic tricks and Pippi and Gretel's antics, all that "child-centred activity", as you call it, plus Astrid's aura-reading, would have grated I expect.

'You said you didn't want more "things" for Christmas. But when you weren't looking I got the details from your spa brochure. You'll just be up and down the pool day after day unless... And vouchers aren't really things, are they? They're just ideas for you to choose to give yourself. Flotation might be worth a go. Or I see they sell some gorgeous-looking bath and beauty products.

'When is a "thing" a "thing" anyway? Is love a thing? Is care a thing? We certainly need them enough.

'Here's one more unwanted gift: advice. (You know I can't resist.) Don't try to think about everything, and don't try not to. Don't try so hard. Don't try. Just wait and see.

'With all my love and then some, Mum X'

'4 March 1993

Dear Miss Haslett

Your submission to *Take Me In*

Of the several stories of non-adoption offered to us recently, yours struck me. It's a harsh attack on "all those agencies whose work seems to consist of grubbying the dreams of children and adults before rebuffing them", as you put it. We believe in showing all sides, in being honest with our readership. If you'll agree to some minor editing, we'd like to publish it.

'The aspects that need attention, in my view, are:

Your insistence on damping down the hopes of children awaiting families as well as those of potential parents. It's obvious that it's a cautionary tale. No need for so many warnings.

Your references to the murder on a Merseyside railway line of the toddler Jamie Bulger. The case clearly has great resonance for you – has proved some kind of turning-point in your decision not to adopt – but that paragraph is muddled, dare I say a little hysterical in tone. Perhaps we can work on this.

'I include the marked-up text, and look forward to discussing it with you. Please do ring us.

'Yours sincerely

Rose Barron

Editor, *Take Me In*'

'16 March 1993

Dear Martine

Your article for *Take Me In*

Our phone discussion was useful.

'So your point is that the public face a choice of feeling either for the toddler as victim or for his two young murderers, also victims – in their case, of a social system that has let them down? And that this strikes you as a parallel for the choices would-be adopters have to make between one child distantly known to them and others, distant and unknown?

'I still wonder if that's it. You seem to have some Jamie Bulger figure in mind.

'I'm afraid the whole comparison is still a bit abstruse. Given that the murder still features large in the media, it might even provoke the kind of publicity *Take Me In* wouldn't welcome.

'All in all I'm still going to cut the paragraph – but the rest is good to go!

'Yours sincerely

Rose Barron

Editor, *Take Me In*'

'13 April 1993

Dear Martine Haslett

Letter on adoption

I was struck by your indictment of our adoption system, and should be pleased to publish your experiences on the *World* Letters Page.

'Your "enforced abandonment" of a boy in Sri Lanka seems to cast a long shadow. You explain that you feel for him more deeply than you felt for your potential adoptees, but I won't include that part of your letter: it detracts from the account of the failed adoptions.

'On a personal note, it does make me wonder what you will do next about the Lankan child. I wish you the best with your decision.

'Yours sincerely

Adam Rotherhithe

Deputy Editor'

23 Chasing the wickets

Some nights, 1993–Thursday 14 February 2013

Matt has left, the neighbours have filtered away and Martine has retired to bed. Her mother's silk scarf in its frame is propped in the lobby ready for hanging. She can't stop thinking about tomorrow's arrival, which skis her around in her four-poster for what seem hours, until eventually she slides down into sleep.

There's a niche on the far side of her bed where pipes have been boxed in, a useful bookshelf. It holds a complete Shakespeare placemarked at *Romeo and Juliet*, a recent school production that she's seen. The tab is a strip of bark: according to a Kandyan stallholder, a twig smashed by a leopard. Beside it, an album of recipe scraps, handwritten in Sinhala; a book of folktales titled *Mahadenamutta, The Great Know-all of Sri Lanka*; and a roughly folded map of Kandy.

While she sleeps, as a scientist she knows that charged elemental particles run through her skin and blood and bone at 130 miles an hour. The poet in her also knows that her dead mother courses through her at the same time, by a kind of incontrovertible magic. No longer guiding her, but still.

From New Year's Day 1993, she began to dream the Sri Lankan dream, her needs travelling to their fantasy conclusion, to the far side of the moon. Tonight, before her visitor, she feels herself plunging into the dream again like a spacecraft gravitating to the moon's basaltic basins. As she's drawn under, again she hopes that she will finish it.

Mohan will be seventeen now, in 1995, Martine dreams, incorrectly. She dreams, *I have to dream my way to him, get to him before he makes those key life choices – or before someone makes them for him. I've got to help him.* She corrects herself to, *I've got to be there.*

To dream herself in Sri Lanka, near Mohan, she resists playing the part of cultural tourist, a voyeur to the island politics of the time. She must approach him for an authentic reason, obliquely, but with sincere intent; so somehow in her dream, her London life has been scrubbed out. She's acquired a new qualification, and is now equipped for a serious long-term role: an aid job, close to Kandy.

'The Effects of Third Sector Intervention on Children and Intrahousehold Inequality' could have been her thesis title during her development studies, preparing herself for aid work: so she dreams. And just supposing it were, then for her the ex-student, Mohan's unequal position in the Liyanage intrahousehold will have been the product of several things. Of the destructive behaviour, as she has perceived it from the letters, of Mohan's father; of Jayamal's apparent dominance in the family, the unfair licence he's been allowed; and of Anupama's struggle, according to Martine's impressions, anyway, within the limits of her home. Is Mohan even still at school? In her waking hours, Martine has read statistics for the island: after the age of twenty-five, his literacy is likely to decline – at least, by her standards. ('We should do more to foreground the alternative literacies of developing countries. Discuss.')

Martine first dreams the aid office, a cement floor, tables and filing cabinets. Through the window, from some sultry, leafy outside, a leonine man regards her, a driver who, in her dreamed aid role, takes her out to the paddy farms. He's often there, she infills in this dream, and she always calls him Santha. In versions of this dream she's had before, other people mill and melt, come and go. This time there's Lakshman, a researcher whose limp is his penalty for army duty and who's helping her find Mohan; a man and a woman; and other people known to her only as Extension Officer, Plant Protection Officer, Agriculture Animator.

They circulate round a man whom Martine dream-senses is her boss, solidly built, teak-skinned, with a close-cut beard and wirebrush hair: Gerald, from a metal label in front of him, 'National Expert, IPM'. She dreams, inaccurately, that he's the source of the recipes and the folktales by her bed. Integrated Pest

Management, IPM. The names of the insects that demand this IPM intervention buzz in Martine's brain: the yellow rice stem borer, the brown plant hopper, the rice thrip, the gall midge.

The dream focuses, suddenly pin-sharp, on the detail of a fruit on Martine's desk, rotund and green and barnacled, similar to the fruit hanging over Mohan in that first photograph. It will soon go soft and mushy. She dreams anxiety at that.

There's a map spread out on a surface, anchored at the corners with bottled water. The female colleague overlooking it has a wide smile, like a child's naïve drawing. The Mahaweli River, on the map printed blue and splashed with reservoirs, parallels a grey road at a distance.

Gerald mentions something about evaluation sites, and Farmer Field Schools. 'The trainers will begin to guide the farmers away from the unwise use of pesticides.'

'Guide away', 'unwise': *Loaded words,* dreams Martine.

If she did train for this for real, maybe she wrote an essay once: 'Participatory Rural Appraisal can coopt rural communities into neo-liberal development agendas. Discuss.'

These people never get on to proper work, though: instead, talk blurs into helping her find Mohan. On the map, Martine's gaze swerves to the Mist-Laden Mountains, the Dumbara Kanduvetiya, their contour lines like rag-edged fingerprints. They conjure up cloud mist, waterfalls and butterflies, children scrambling for wood.

The dream rolls into some hazy explanation of Gerald's that wherever Mohan is, there's obviously, from the letters, no need of irrigation, of reservoirs, sluice gates and canals. He's pointing Martine to the wet zone of the mountains, suggesting that it might have a need instead for latrines. Which Mohan's landscape did. She suddenly sees, *So the trail is all about water.*

The people around her swig from water bottles. She drinks deeply from one herself.

Gerald says, his rasping voice quite clear, 'Mohan's family

will be *anda govigaya*, tenant farmers.'

So tatta and the fathers don't own their land. Martine dreams that this is something she should have realised. In sleep an image comes to her: a gaunt girl, arms pulling at prickly vines and branches. But she mustn't waste her dream time on the sister.

She jolts, limbs starting in sleep. In the office, a man with erica-nut cheeks and a fine line of moustache is shouting like a shot boar, banging the drawers of a filing cabinet, and Lakshman, limping, reasons with the man. She's aware that the man is Tamil. There's a sudden change in the atmosphere of the room, and on the Tamil's face a smile. He clasps Lakshman's shoulder, and the two young men shake hands. *A British gesture*, Martine dreams.

There's another lurch in time and place, and tonight for once she does dream on. Now she's entering the Queen's Hotel in Kandy, about to watch the Esala Perahera. At first she's disappointed not to be searching for Mohan in the mountains, then is overwhelmed by unexpected excitement: Lakshman thinks that Mohan could be here, not there.

In the dream, she's wearing her clover armband under a cream linen suit. Jonas is with her, supporting her search for Mohan. She dreams, *All dreams should feel this close to reconciliation.* They're entering an upstairs room together.

Jonas shouts, 'Hey!'

'Hey!' friends imitate, raising hands in greeting.

There's Vijitha, an astronomer, and his wife; Thilangani, an astrologer; Lakshman the researcher, who's organised the room; and Gerald, her new boss from her work. She knows these people, but dream-puzzles that she does: she's dreaming them, after all.

'Here we are again!' Vijitha's wife says in Sinhala, letting out a trilling laugh she sounds as if she's been practising for years.

The group is at a lamplit table by the French windows. Some images are sharp and filigree. Waiters are ghosting in and out leaving dishes of peeled rambutans with mint, slices of mango and savoury snacks. At Martine's sandalled feet, the threadbare carpet is patterned with medallions, gold and red and blue. A chair has been placed for her close to the windows, flung wide to let the night in through the balcony.

The others talk and laugh. She and Jonas slip into the opening and look. She dreams, *I'm on the inside looking out.* She seeks the moon and finds it, waxing gibbous, almost *poya*, its swelling edge embedded in black sky. She can't focus on the party, turning down the snacks. She can see the throng along the street and hear the masses under her below the hotel colonnades, around the hotel corner, opposite the avenues to the temple. Thousands of voices babbling, the odd excited shout. Fringes of coloured lights swathe the facade of the street.

She says over her shoulder, 'Not watching?'

Cigarette smoke roils in the room. Only Jonas is transfixed by what's below.

'We've seen it all before, darling!' Thilangani shrugs.

Martine wants to be down there, maybe only metres away from Mohan and his family, but it's less likely that she'll spot him on the street than she will up here. Anyway, she's got only a few old photographs to go on. She dreams her fear: *I won't find him. Or before I do this dream is going to end.*

A glass of mineral water and lime appears beside her, held aloft on a waiter's tray.

'We know the festival. We always know what's going to come,' Vijitha's wife sips her smuggled-in whisky. 'At least, I always do.'

She's engrossed in a game of *vingt-et-un* with Vijitha. The astronomer stubs out his Marlboro. *She's like a slow, fat moth,* Martine decides, *sticking to the light source of husband Vijitha and to speaking in Sinhala, which Jonas doesn't understand.*

'Mmm. "Know",' Vijitha muses in English. His imposing head turns in its European suit, addressing Martine. 'It might be better for science, at least, if more people interpreted the word as something less definite than knowledge. I wonder if you agree.' His wife demands more whisky. He replenishes her tumbler affably from their half-bottle of Jack Daniels. 'How often we deviate from truth.'

Gerald, the boss and IPM expert, nods gravely. Martine smiles at Vijitha's obsession with deviation and deflection.

If his wife is a moth in her burnt-orange saree, Martine dreams Thilangani the astrologer as a butterfly in her spotted yellow T-shirt emblazoned 'Sunday is a Funday.'

The woman breaks in, also in English. 'Darlings, one year I was in a stand round the corner, opposite the lake, and I swear, the thing that most entertained me was a pickpocket. He had a stealing rhythm, honest to God. First money, then an item of clothing, then a toy or souvenir, then money, then a piece of clothing, then a souvenir... It was quite something.'

Vijitha says, 'Every year is special. Remember the time some of the elephants turned back towards the Temple?'

Vijitha says, 'Once, it was in all the papers, the beggars wouldn't move from...'

His wife objects in Sinhala, 'Stop being silly now. When I say we always know, you all know what I mean,' whereupon Thilangani and Vijitha tease her over the word 'know' again.

Gerald tries to smooth things over. 'It's true that even if we were blindfolded, we'd probably guess what was happening.'

Thilangani laughs, 'Let's do it! Our newcomers could tell us if we're right.'

Vijitha suggests, 'We could each predict how soon something out of the way might happen.'

There are murmurs of approval.

'Or,' Thilangani enthuses, 'we could guess what that might be.'

Gerald twinkles, 'From what I understand, that's your province,' referring to her astrology.

'Camels,' Jonas posits.

All laugh, except Vijitha's wife.

'Fireworks,' proposes Lakshman.

'Darling! Fireworks would be so beautiful, over the lake,' says Thilangani.

Vijitha says, 'For those without your expertise, precise predictions are difficult.' His lips purse in a smile. 'Can we not go with our plan A?'

His wife glowers, but the others agree, and they begin to bet. 'Ten-thirty-two and three seconds.' ... 'In twenty-five minutes.' ... 'In mole past hair! I haven't got my watch!'

The wife says, 'This is ridiculous,' unpins a large emerald brooch and places it on the table. 'I wager this that before something new will be a long, long time.'

People counter-stake, heaping up assorted matches and lighters.

Then Jonas breathes 'Get this!' which returns Martine to the glittering dark.

The crowd noise drops to a murmur, and a rhythmic cracking hits the street. Lines of men in Lankyan dress are inching forward, whirling whips and lashing the tarmac, somehow avoiding slashing each other and themselves.

Lakshman sends a waiter for blindfolds. The whipcrackers herald the procession, promising thunder, lightning and the rains.

Martine rhymes, 'Thunder and lightning/Truly bloody frightening.'

In her dream, for some reason Lakshman is watching her.

A waiter brings napkins, but they prove too short to use for blindfolds. Another brings dishtowels, and the friends find that they work, and Vijitha's wife fusses, but at last the group is masked, ready to play. Martine dreams a moment of revelation: that their carelessness of the parade is nothing but tact, a way of letting her search for Mohan in her own private space.

Music whines, and approaching lights stipple the threshold.

Jonas snaps with his camera as files of boys advance revolving, spinning flames, some tossing fire wheels into the darkness and catching them with a bounce, others yoyoing fireballs on wires around their waists. Martine tries to glimpse each shadowy figure, comparing it with the photographs she's taken from her bag.

Vijitha's wife picks up at the light-level change.

'Seven minutes,' her husband states, monitoring his Rolex.

'This will be the flag bearers!' she predicts.

This dreamed Martine understands Sinhala, and translates for Jonas. Acrid smoke drifts into the room.

'Wrong!' Jonas chimes gleefully, but then corrects, 'Wait up.'

Behind the boys, men step out in lines at either side of the road bearing the decorated standards of the ancient Kandyan provinces.

'Next there will be an elephant,' says Lakshman under his blindfold.

His voice is quiet, as if he's also on the alert to any sounds from her.

Vijitha intones, 'Thirteen minutes.'

A clatter of drums and the wheedling of instruments gets louder. Mohan's family could be drumming; maybe he is himself. Martine's pulse speeds up in sleep. She dreams, *Let me keep the dream; let the dream go on to the end.* As Lakshman has predicted, an elephant begins to sway along the street escorted by a mahout and attendants, its headdress studded with lights, in a robe of gilt and red. A bare-chested youth straddles its back, staring up at the flag he's holding.

'Now the Permunerala,' Thilangani singsongs.

'Twenty-one minutes.'

The hubbub from the hotel arcades boils upwards. Thilangani's right: another sparkling elephant is swinging down the road, the official rider bracing a scroll between both hands.

'This is boring!' Vijitha's wife complains, even though, for everyone else, the suspense is building to the impending ultimate, the tusker with its palanquin cradling the symbol of the Buddha's tooth, on which, according to Lankans, the rains and harvest depend. 'Make it a race to speak. Martine can be our referee.'

'She's kinda busy,' Jonas says.

Vijitha's wife gets up protesting, fumbles to remove her blindfold and accidentally pokes Thilangani's face with her elbow, and Thilangani shrieks, and Gerald concedes that the game isn't much fun, trying yet again to keep the peace.

Rows of drummers and musicians are noisily advancing. Martine is breathing fast and shallow in her sleep. In the dream she kicks her unused chair out of the way. Boys are beating dawulas; more boys and men rap tinny thumps and baritone bangs out of the two-cupped tammattammas; yet more blow the globular horanawas, sending out their whingeing, baffled notes. The players bend and turn, keeping their lines. Martine is dreaming the music as something else at the same time: the dawulas are stones knocking in a current, the reedy horanawas, the yodelling of teenage boys as they tombstone into water off a ledge.

In the room, the friends have removed their blindfolds; tonight in her sleep, Martine struggles with hers. And yet in the dream and out, she isn't wearing one. She feels Lakshman easing past her into the window as she tries to pull the blindfold off. She senses that he's scanning the performers. She must get free. She tears and struggles, but now the dream is getting tangled. With one last wrench, she opens her eyes in the darkness of her bedroom. She's back in her flat, and once more the dream has knotted, then frayed and torn and gone.

24 Play stopped

Martine has dreamed this dream, in fragments, since 1993. Actually, in 1993 her real life continued, without poetry.

By 1993 she'd given up on adoption, bared her feelings to the press and heard nothing from Sri Lanka for three years. Despite the tug of Mohan and Sri Lanka, her far side, she couldn't leave family, friends, work, social life, depart from her orbit. Something in her said, *That would be mad, a slingshot mission. I'll let my far side stay my far side: let it lie.* She neglected the moon, which was not the same as forgetting it.

In 1993 Jonas and Astrid split up and he took it badly, so Martine spent more time with him; with the girls too, when they came to see him. There were fewer parties to go to, and fewer friends without ties to cook for at her flat, but she filled her diary with meals at their homes, among their growing families, the odd drag show or wedding or christening, and long nights of morale boosting for Saila in his resurrection as Pearl. She saw Charlie with a woman once, walking away from college. That sandy paw on her waist. The woman, his wife, was pregnant. Martine worked harder, swam more often and began to brush up her Spanish in an evening class.

At Harrow Weald, sometimes she would stay the night, and her mother might take her out flying. On the panel she'd stare at the altitude indicator, her adrenalin cutting in. As they bobbed and wove in the air currents, any slide off the horizontal seemed to set it jabbing. Her problems had come from her swerves, from making radical decisions, she believed. *A happy future depends on staying level,* she assured herself. She'd keep busy, too busy to think what she'd lost, but she mustn't move house, change friends, change job: she must do nothing extreme.

It was a hot day, her mother's seventieth birthday. Gretel had turned six a while ago, too. Martine had planned a special day for both and Jonas. First there was a trip to the RAF Museum, then Pinner Fair. At last they ended up in Windows Street, a converted garage showroom on the edge of Larkford village.

'It's as hot inside,' Mum complained.

Artificial light blazed out, irradiating them. Strip lights, halogen spots, fairy lights festooning beams. Doll's houses stood in streets, backlit, many also sparkling from inside. A toddler and her parents, hushed by the display, padded up and down.

'Cool,' breathed a seven-year-old Pippi inaccurately with her dancing hands, long pale ringlets and vivid stare.

After an angina scare the year before, Martine was keeping an eye on her mother.

Crouched level with the girls, Martine enjoyed their baked white faces hypnotised at the house windows, eyes flashing in Pippi's, Gretel solemn and comical and spiky-haired, still pudding-cheeked at six. Her own glee looked as childlike, she was aware. Far above, it seemed, Jonas, hands in pockets, swayed along the rooftops peering down at them, letting out chortles like a jolly giant who might jolly well soon stamp on them. Avoidance and denial. The errant city-dealer Nick Leeson came into Martine's mind, still on the run, somewhere in the world, from everything he couldn't account for. The latest breed of presumptuous British imperialist, Charlie might have said.

Martine fell for a moss-tiled house with a library, Gothic and dark, or even more, a cottage with diamond panes and wonky half-timbers.

Gretel's eyes were hotplates. 'Marti-ine.'

'Ye-es.'

'Can I have them all?'

'I don't think anyone in the world could possibly afford that.'

'Ou-ww.'

'Anyway, Dad's going to make you one, remember. Pick one you think he could copy.'

With Mum and Jonas trailing after, Gretel began circling,

homing in on a cream palace with a rooftop helipad.

Pippi's arm hung off Martine's back as Martine opened her crooked cottage, absorbing the crooked flames in the crooked stove.

A version of Mohan's words appeared. *'A bent cottage would not be nice.'*

Pippi swung her slim frame round her, a compass-point toe divining for something. 'I want to know...'

'Hmm?'

'Time is going by...'

'Mmm.'

'When will you be starting to be old?'

Despite still swimming, her body was changing. To crouch was getting harder, the manic dancing was losing its comedy value and there were more facial creases. Martine registered the harsh side of the compliment, as uncalculated as Pippi's cheek grinding into hers.

Jonas scuffed from Gretel to the woman on the till. Martine could hear him trying for a deal on a miniature rocking-horse, a TV and a tiny doll's house, accessories for Gretel's eventual mini-palace, but the woman's only concession was mock-gold.

'The chocolate's rather soft I'm afraid.' She held out the foil-wrapped coins, smiling towards the girls. 'Tell them to eat fast.'

Martine found herself at Jonas's lean forearm, smelling his sweat. 'Don't want to pry. About Astrid.'

She saw his hand squeeze round the coins.

'I'm going away,' he blurted.

A squirt of dread surprised her. 'We need you. Mum's not very well.'

Jonas countered, 'She doesn't need looking out for, not by me.'

'This should be easier,' stumbled Martine. 'Maybe if we... We might...'

'Might what?'

'We still make a pig's ear of talking.'

He laughed, 'Right. Pork. So?'

Martine was flushing. 'You sound like you mean something.'

He stacked the coins on the counter, lining up the rims. 'Folks want perfect. You want perfect. But mostly things're just not.' He growls, 'And leave it about Astrid.'

Mrs Haslett appeared. 'No seats.'

Her breathing was fast and shallow. Martine felt paralysed, but Jonas swung into action, bringing out a stool from behind the counter. The older woman perched on it, gazing up at them.

'Hum-hum. Don't know what's the matter with you two,' she said. She sipped from a glass the saleswoman brought her. 'It's me who should need holding together, instead you're the ones looking tragic.'

Martine stared at the iron-grey strands stuck to her crown like weeds where a stone had been removed.

'We're just concerned for you,' she simplified.

'Lum-ti-tum.' All at once her mother was brisk. 'I may have had to stop the flying but I have got other interests.' Her eyes nailed Martine then Jonas. 'Bill Kidmay, for instance.'

'Bill Kidmay and you,' Jonas repeated, eyeing Martine.

Mum just let them take things in.

Long ago, the geriatric shorthand of wrinkles Martine has seen once recently in her mother's kitchen stretching out a gammy leg had done no less than shape her life: the father of her schoolfriend Alice, he'd get them to work out his inventions, a retracting pen-top, a handbag with a shopping section that folded out, not pontificating, asking them questions – real questions, as opposed to ones to which he held the answers – wanting Martine's and Alice's advice, treating them like adult thinking beings.

Mohan's voice suddenly drifted through her again: *'No one should only ask. You should also tell.'*

Martine admonished him dumbly, *Filling the empty vessel, the behaviourist view of education, is outdated – and, from a post-colonial product, ill-advisedly submissive.* Her viewpoint still had traces of Charlie after all this time.

Mr Kidmay was never a teacher, although he was better than all her teachers put together. He was why she'd become a teacher in the end, and yet when she'd seen him not long since he'd looked at her through his own disappointments, she'd thought.

'I do up a bit of furniture now,' he'd said.

From her resting place in Windows Street her mother mused unexpectedly, 'Your father. It turns out I was looking in the wrong place.'

'Will you...?' Martine asked.

'Oh!' she laughed. 'I like my freedom. No no, tum-tum.' She pondered. 'Back to you. I might find it easier not to worry about you separately if you got on better together. Have you thought of that?'

'Unselfish as ever,' Martine said, touching her arm.

The girls bounded up. Their hands delved, and reappeared from their grandmother's safari-jacket pockets with a miniature four-poster, a tiny spinning wheel and a bird in a diminutive gilt cage.

Gretel made an assumption. 'Thank you, Gram!'

'Where are these from?' Pippi handled the bird cage thoughtfully.

Martine's mother deflected baldly, 'By the way, they say my angina's well under control.' Without warning she sprang from her stool.

Jonas stepped back. 'Weren't you just sick?'

'Ho-hum. I was just getting your attention.' The old woman shrugged as Jonas stalked away. 'Sorry he's shocked. A little subterfuge.'

Jonas didn't go away anywhere after all. Meanwhile in her life, Martine knew something had stalled.

One day she visited a secondary school in Tower Hamlets. She rarely went to schools these days. She saw other people's children often enough, she felt: Pippi and Gretel, and Mark 2's boisterous offspring, and Leanne's boy and girl, and Mark 1's teenage stepkids, and Ali's only daughter – only child. Working with schoolteachers, as long as it was in college, usually buffered Martine from a sense of all the other children she couldn't have. But this time she was running a course on teaching scientific investigation, and one of her teachers was doing action research, and had to be observed.

The teacher met Martine at the spacious new reception, the shined-up face of the school. Hurrying down the hallways, Martine was hit by noise. The children funnelled round her, their shrieks and curses bouncing off the walls. There was that institutional smell of nothing special. The fenestrated corridors seemed to jog past with the spangled light of night-time trains. The gleam of the school approach gave way to grime and grey. Her senses operated in a muffled way, as if ice crystals blurred her. These days she was inured to most sensation, but something about the surroundings intensified her numbness almost to a sensation of its own.

Two floors up was the cavernous classroom, the desks pulled back against the walls. At one end stood a lectern with a microphone, and rows of chairs laid out in front. Martine noted, through her furred internal lens, the woman's enthusiasm, her tense little movements as she explained her lesson idea.

'I'm playing an infertility doctor.' She took a white coat off a chair and shrugged it over a low-slung bosom, her voice deadened by the expanse of carpet. 'She's grown cells from defective human embryos *in vitro* to the 32-cell stage. Now this is the press conference. I want them to air the moral and scientific questions about cloning, to think what makes a good question.'

She handed Martine a mocked-up press release and her lesson plan.

Martine heard herself say, 'Looks good.'

She read that in pairs, the students would plan questions, interrogate their teacher in role as members of the press, probe her answers and, at the end, evaluate their efforts. Such creativity in lessons wasn't uncommon, but Martine still found herself willing this to work. The teacher was muttering about some box of equipment that hadn't been delivered, and Martine dragged a chair to the side of the room to watch.

A bell pealed out on the corridor, and there was the slow tidal rush of feet. The teacher took to the lectern to enter into her part. Boys and girls of fifteen or sixteen burst or straggled into the room and stood staring at the layout and Martine.

The teacher said, 'Please take your seats, ladies and gentlemen. The press conference is about to begin.'

Mumbling and giggling, the pupils scooped up the press releases from their chairs. The woman introduced Martine and the lesson started.

There was nothing different about this student cohort from others Martine had met. There was a mixture of ethnicities; many pupils looked dirty and malnourished. Some larked about and giggled; others pretended a disinterest in the lesson.

Once the teacher had explained the lesson and playacted her conference announcement, she got the students, in pairs, to read their press releases and write down questions they could ask. Martine noted one boy, Damion, who'd had to join a pair and make a three. His partners didn't like it, and she heard him swearing as she threaded between the rows.

'How are you getting on?'

In the first pair she approached, a girl retorted, 'Nosy!'

The second she talked to sniggered and said nothing.

'Why are we doing this?' another girl challenged Martine.

Martine said, 'To help you learn what makes a good question.'

'Shouldn't we have tape recorders or something?' her partner asked.

'That's up to Mrs Willshaw,' Martine said, but now the group started heckling the teacher.

'Yeah. Microphones to hold...' 'We should be rushing up to you, you know...' The children became galvanised, overturning chairs and lobbying Carolyn Willshaw at her lectern. 'This is Fatima Szarowicz... very important breaking news...' 'Give us a TV camera. On one of them stick things...'

The teacher kept control. 'You're right everybody, and IT was supposed to bring a box of stuff, but it hasn't come.' She paused. 'Would Miss Haslett by any chance be prepared to...?'

Martine found herself agreeing to mind the class while the teacher sought the props.

Carolyn Willshaw had stranded her between the front and second rows with thirty-one adolescents. Her surroundings crept into her cerebellum. Temporary hardboard smacked at holes in the windows, and a chill draught stammered in. The nylon carpet, spotted with fossils of chewing-gum, squelched abnormally under her feet.

She persuaded the students to a game of Chinese whispers. Damion sneered. She took a seat on the end of the front row next to him, conscious of a fair fringe and a masculine jaw emerging out of puppy fat. She started the whispers with him, facts about cell division and clones. He passed on her messages in a reluctant growl. The lines of children sabotaged them into nonsense and obscenities, cackling. Martine calmed them down, but had to begin the game again and then again. She noticed that Damion's neighbour was anchoring his foot down with a heavy, scuffed shoe. Damion didn't object.

Carolyn Willshaw returned, and the children mobbed her, and she herded them into their places and handed out her props. There were complaints about the equipment, but the teacher restored order, and Martine retired to her corner, and at last the lesson resumed. Apart from a few shouted exchanges, the students became absorbed, grilling the teacher in their roles.

Note-taking and observing, Martine folded in on herself.

The school bell shrilled. Although the lesson was a double period, Mrs Willshaw and the children broke off. In a matter of seconds they were all on their feet under the corridor wall as, beyond it, howls and cries came nearer and feet thundered. On the other side of the high windows heads appeared, pogoing up and down and jeering at the class.

The teacher explained, 'The sixth-formers. They know the lesson's something different and you're here.' She rallied the pupils. 'Cupboards to doors!' She grinned at Martine. 'A precaution.'

While a brigade of adolescents hauled two tall metal cabinets in front of both classroom exits as if they'd done it before, and with fists and feet already pounding on them from the other side, Martine said, 'Tell me about Damion.'

The teacher sighed. 'Middle-class Anglo-Saxon parents in the media, sent him here on principle. Not very literate but bright. A bully in his time, now probably being bullied. What else do you want to know?'

Martine looked at Damion swaggering among the children drifting back to their seats as the lesson stuttered into life a second time.

Eventually, it was all over. Carolyn Willshaw still needed to work on probing and open questions, and must include quantitative as well as qualitative data in her findings, Martine had decided, now ready for feedback in the staffroom. The cupboards were pulled aside, and Martine left beside her. The students ebbed along the corridor, but Damion wasn't with them. She had an impulse to go back, and mumbled to Mrs Willshaw that she'd left something behind.

The boy was on the far side of the room. He was crouching by a radiator, his backpack flung away from him, arms flopped on his knees. Martine crossed and stood nearby, resting against the sill of a blocked-up window. She was wary of being too close to him.

'Are you all right?' She wasn't surprised when he said nothing. 'If you'd like to talk…'

Her elbow was painful on the window ledge, picking up a smattering of grit. She realised that the radiator was dribbling water onto the floor, which explained the sodden carpet. There were skidmarks on the green walls; in one corner, an empty Sprite bottle and a Coke tin; along the skirting, a jetsam of sweet wrappers and paper clips. The place flared in her consciousness.

The boy hoisted himself to his feet, shooting her a knowing smile. 'You're weird.'

Martine beamed. 'So people sometimes say.'

For a moment, she was still sure of it later, his eyes melted into that look that a male lover can have, a gaze without concealment.

Then his lids dropped, and the jaw set. 'I don't like being here.'

'It must be hard for you.'

'I don't mean here. I mean *here*.' Turning his head away, he stabbed a finger at the carpet.

Something in Martine lurched. She registered, *He thinks I'm being inappropriate.*

Damion twisted his head convulsively and flicked his eyes round for an escape route.

'I just thought it might help to talk to you,' she said. 'Teachers can be your friends, too, if you need one.'

She waited, but he said nothing.

'Can I go?' he said abruptly.

She let him, her inner voice berating her because he'd had to ask.

When she left the teacher later, Martine wished she could give back the building, the classroom and the boy, but she still felt in the thick of it, and suddenly knew that this ugly-beautiful landscape was a useful sort of poison, would do as well as anything else to propel her forward, alone as she must go.

She began to look for a job teaching biology and general science. She'd taught before, and she could do it again. In the end she found a Lambeth school, similar to the one in Tower Hamlets, that couldn't deny her credentials. She hoped to make a difference, but maybe almost more, that her new setting would make a difference to her. Just to be safe though, the place taught only girls.

The phases of the moon, its eclipse cycle, earth's tides, the colour coding of land and sea and swirling cloud around the globe, everywhere there are patterns, but for years, Martine avoided philosophising about hers, blanking out any overview of what had happened to her. She couldn't afford to be a satellite, looking down on all her failures.

In 1994, the newly appointed President Kumaratunga pledged to end his island's war. In London, Ron Dearing published his aims to revise the National Curriculum. Martine got on with the routines of daughterly care and singledom and working life and adulthood.

By 1995, she was busy re-learning her job. She skated over red dwarfs and black holes in the curriculum, a thin chapter at the end of the GCSE textbook. At home she read *Men are from Mars, Women are from Venus* with its claim that now and then, men like to back away from intimacy. She wondered, was male distance, not difference, what had attracted her all those years?

In Sri Lanka, rebels sank two gunboats, sparking the Third Eelam War. A bomb wounded President Kumaratunga, and a suicide attack at Colombo airport maimed a large portion of the Sri Lankan Airlines fleet.

The voice of Mohan's letters, which she'd not touched for years, hallooed from far away, '*Sometimes I am quite worrying.*'

Her Sri Lankan fantasies spread in sleep, now always including the permanent move to Sri Lanka, and sometimes some sign of detente between the Sinhalese and the Tamils, like

Lakshman's with the Tamil in his office.

The suck and drag of globalisation and capitalism, of oppression and resistance, violence and change, continued in the world.

25 Road

(Road: A hard, flat pitch for a run-up)

1997–July 2010

On Thursday 1 May 1997, Pearl suggested drinks to Martine at her Bohemian flat in Seven Sisters with 'whoever you fancy bringin'', cautioning that 'You know I don't do eats.' Eyes only half on the TV, an ill-assorted gaggle would drink to the results of the general election as they came in. His depression permitting, Jonas might even join them.

Abigail Gilmore, who lived downstairs from Martine at Aldebert Terrace, was a feisty sixty-seven-year-old with a spinal problem she didn't want to admit to; Geraldine was the Head of IT at school, a flamboyant fashionplate with an air of need Martine couldn't quite pin down. She decided to take them along. Back turned on the last shaving of moon in the city sky, she prepared seafood stew with coriander pesto, but it turned out that Mrs Gilmore didn't like fish, so she rustled up fried potatoes and beans instead.

On the tube, Mrs Gilmore was describing her attempts to dig her own grave in the garden when Geraldine said, 'Fun fun fun!'

The train was wailing to a standstill at Finsbury Park. As the doors hissed back, Martine's gaze followed Geraldine's. Across the island platform, on the eastbound Piccadilly, a shimmering troupe was arriving for a train. A stentorian voice sang *The Galloping Major*. The gang wore costumes in Tory blue or Labour red. There were bangs and raucous laughter as someone killed a drift of balloons with a stilettoed shoe. They had a banner, 'Bugger Blair', and bottles, clinking hazardously in rustling plastic bags. Before her train doors rumbled shut, Martine caught the echoes of a Welsh accent, and realised it was Fleur's, and that Evie, Nev, Graham and Bernard were also in the group.

Her train drew out, and her default of flat contentment drained away. She didn't crane for the vanishing point on the platform where the coiffeured Bernard in a red catsuit was mounting his carriage gracefully. She thought, *The Soho Sisters are my friends; why didn't I say so?* In her mind, the group branched away on another track.

Many years before, in a cabbies' caff, Tiny Tot, who was, with Litolita, one of Madame Dada's double acts, had overheard the bourgeois prattlings of an intoxicated Ali and Martine, guffawed and flourished her little sequined arms, and dared them to enter the Soho world of Madame Dada's club, Grand Dame Tattlemouse, Old Sal and all the rest. That foggy two o'clock morning led to friendships, firm and true. Now though, many were speeding into the distance.

By just gone ten o'clock at Pearl's, BBC News was predicting a landslide Labour victory, and Pearl was wound around Jonas – odd, although it seemed to mean nothing to them. The evening was strangely hollow for Martine.

By 1998, Martine's designer maisonette no longer seemed to suit her Puritan work regime and lifestyle, so she bought a flat on the seventh floor of one of the Brandon Towers in Kennington, skyscrapers on an ex-council estate. Two small bedrooms and a private balcony, netted to keep out pigeon onslaughts. She left all her ferns, although, if she'd looked inward, they grew on in her imagination. At night she stared out through the wires, across the estate with its squares of grass and high-rise flats, over a jetsam of lower buildings towards the Thames and, beyond its unseen water, the City to the left and Docklands to the right, not acknowledging that she shared this view with the moon. Slowly she replaced her furniture with junk-shop pieces, French country and shabby chic. She made her changes without fuss, as if slipping a ball between a succession of cups.

Meanwhile, the Blair government introduced the National Literacy Strategy in schools. In Martine's job there was plenty new to do.

She suffered plague and pestilence in 1999, as if, as Mohan

was to her, she was a landscape. Her precious MGB Roadster was blighted by vandals, and she decided it had to go. There was a flood in her flat from burst plumbing on the floor above that filled her dreams of finding Mohan with the topic of water. Bill Kidmay restored a chest of drawers, her bedside table and a bookcase. While everything was sorted, she camped with Claire and Rollo and their dogs and bought more functional, water-proof furniture, some tubular, some glass. By then Jonas, listless and morose, was back living with Martine's mother and McLairy, the latest dog.

Dead flies poured out of her lobby's ceiling trapdoor, swarming into her dreams as the tropics' pestilential yellow rice stem borer, the brown plant hopper, the rice thrip and the gall midge, authentic details for her Sri Lankan job in aid. Her menorrhagia was modulating into the milder, erratic bleeding of the perimenopause, but that meant heat waves at night and seesawing moods by day. She had bouts of laryngitis from colds caught at school, made worse by raising her voice in hectic class-rooms. She still revolved through school, friends and family; she found it hard to focus on much else.

At the Millennium, a quarter moon oversaw a fraction of Martine join Pippi and Gretel, her mother, Jonas, Bill Kidmay and McLairy round an undersized bonfire on Harrow Weald Common sipping acid punch with sparklers in their hands.

There was drought in Sri Lanka in 2001-2, to the island a blow more crushing than the attack of 9/11. Jamie Bulger's killers were released from custody on life licence, their identities kept secret. With the National Literacy and Numeracy Strategies rolled out in secondary schools, Martine began to feel new pressures: before long, the NLS would apply to science. Change, change, change.

In 2002 Martine was promoted to Head of Science, despite initial resistance. The Sri Lankan government signed a ceasefire agreement with the Tamil Tigers, who'd dropped demands for a separate state. The road from the Jaffna peninsula reopened. In 2002-3, rains in Sri Lanka brought a record rice harvest. Martine heard that her school might soon take boys.

In all the years after Mohan, Martine was trying to be pragmatic, down to earth, but her poetic side remained, albeit in the dark. She surfed the net at night, moving unblushingly from online male titillation to researching Farmer Field Schools, the Temple of the Relic, the Mahaweli Project, the Esala Perahera, and bread-fruit, and dragonflies. Her researches fed her dreams, and without knowing it, she began to shift through the spheres of her resistance, from a kind of troposphere to a kind of exosphere, up and out of her own earthbound grip.

2003-4 you might call her troposphere. Her internet wanderings told of floods in Sri Lanka. Then, newsfeeds brought her tales of Sri Lankan drought, the Indian Ocean tsunami and the end of the ceasefire. At home, the Children Act and the Tomlinson report promised yet more change in school.

She travelled through 2005, as it were her stratosphere, the assassination of the Sri Lankan foreign minister and the tsunami clean-up, and the island's feuding over a rebel deal on aid.

In London, bombs went off on buses and trains; the Tomlinson reforms were stopped before they'd started; Martine's school became a Beacon School for Technology and Science, which meant extra work again; and it began admitting boys. She had to confront what she knew: that she, if not her lessons, favoured male students over girls. Garey, who used every piece of her advice; Kumar, almost her stalker for a term or two; and the Ravi she found ravishing, whom she was careful not to see alone. Amal, the leader of a group of girls, accused her outright of being sexist.

One weekend, Jonas visited. 'Um, Samantha.'

A large presence with piled-up, slipping hair and a surprised expression thrust Martine a bottle of goji berry juice and forged her way into the small living room, bearing Jonas in her wake. At fifty-six, Samantha was older than Jonas by some twelve years.

'Living here must be some middle-class guilt fest, yeah?'

Martine stammered, 'Not exactly,' forcing a grin for Jonas's sake.

Samantha refused coffee in favour of her juice, and made more laughing, terse pronouncements, taking in the flat with a piercing eye. She had a successful shoe shop chain, and Jonas was moving in with her in Weybridge. He was being saved, apparently from something that might include Martine.

Martine pushed through 2006. She'd always resisted Googling for any trace of Mohan, but absorbed that a suicide bomber had attacked Colombo's main military compound; that the government was still striking enemy targets; that the rebels had attacked a naval convoy close to Jaffna; and that fighting had worsened in the north-east.

'*It is indeed most fearful*,' Mohan whispered in her head.

Samantha had a daughter, Bryony, older than Pippi and Gretel, now eighteen and seventeen. Things turned sour between the girls, and forty-five-year-old Jonas removed from Weybridge back to Harrow Weald.

Into Martine's mesosphere, so to speak. Her father was suddenly dead. To her, the news was a brick falling down a well that still hasn't reached the bottom even now, in 2013. While police were forcing Tamils out of Colombo, her school signed up to the Building for the Future programme. In 2008, the Sri Lankan government launched a large-scale offensive, and an international panel on human rights in the civil war left. There was a new National Strategy. Her staff revamped their teaching plans again. She still avoided Googling about Mohan.

'*Stay in London then I know you are in London*,' his ever-present ghost assured her.

2009, Martine's thermosphere. The Sri Lankan government captured Tamil Tiger headquarters and overran rebel-held land. London stopped imposing strategies on English schools; instead, it announced, schools must begin to support each other. At her successful school, Martine had a demanding role.

In July 2010, Martine escorted a school trip to an activity centre on the Costa Brava. The students had just taken their GCSEs. Many had never been abroad; the aim was to help them bond and grow, to enthuse them about staying on at school.

A girl called Sophie trailed her with sulky questions. 'No boyfriend?' 'You wasn't on any of the banana boats.' 'The problem-solving was boring.'

Martine smiled and deflected, but Sophie's grilling began to sap her, turning her hypercritical of herself.

One beachside morning Sophie's bikinied shadow, indignant hands on sunken hips, fell across her. 'Why are you in them cabins? The rest of us is camping. Except Mrs and Mr Alwyn. And Mr Keene and that woman what looks like a prozzy. But that's probably because...'

In her overseer's deckchair, Martine raised her sunglasses. She let a saggy arm drop over the perished elastic thighs she was all too aware of.

'Because I'm old and need looking after.'

'So why are you still teaching us?'

Martine hauled at her turquoise and orange one-piece. She'd be sixty-one in three weeks and could retire now if she wanted, but what could she do afterwards that would keep her so immersed in all the rigours of the mundane?

That night the moon was in its third quarter, and she met someone. Overseen by a dozen adults, sixty-two teenagers, boisterous with familiarity and texting and sharing music on their earphones and doing anything to stall organised games, were massed around three campfires on the beach. Cross-legged beside Martine was a man younger by over two decades, tall as a spindle, his features bleached in the firelight. His languorous chat had everyone laughing. Dark, glinting eyes. He introduced himself as the adventure company's PR Co-ordinator, new to the job, half-Spanish by birth, and there on his first visit.

Martine gurned. 'The devil's work. Or is that advertising?'

'There are fewer negatives than in my previous job.' He frowned. 'This is mostly positives.' He stared at her. 'More fun, for definite. I like fun.' Martine grinned. 'Would you like to have fun later? I could show you the late-night action in town.'

Sophie's goading had primed Martine to respond, 'That sounds great.'

Later he approached her in the dark, where she waited in the lea of the campsite office.

'Gavin; Gavin Godfell.' He shook her hand limply, unsmiling. 'I looked you up. You're Marianne.'

She was about to correct him when she recognised his name, registered what he'd done to her over Mohan. A sensation came to her at once muffled and piercing, like a tooth being pulled under anaesthetic. She calculated quickly, *If I correct him, he might recall my name, what from. Screw resurrecting Mohan with the ex-jobsworth who curtailed him.* She said nothing; then she got curious with curiosity about what kind of person Mohan's virtual executioner had been.

On their way to his car he patted his pockets. 'Sorry. I've left my car key in my cabin. Bear with?' She followed him to a cabin on its own, set between trees. 'Come in! I'm harmless.'

Inside was a neat, utilitarian sitting-room. A kitchenette lay off to the left, bathroom and bedroom to the right. Gavin disappeared to the left, a *Mission Impossible* ringtone sounded and he reappeared, talking in fluent Spanish into a mobile at his ear, balancing a wooden board loaded with sausage and Manchega and a hunk of bread, followed by glasses and a bottle. He laid them out on the low table beside her. Some woman was asking where he was; he made excuses to her about an unavoidable meeting, which he must have thought that Martine couldn't translate.

Martine gulped her Rioja, and thought, *Fitting, his capacity for lies.*

When the call ended he apologised. 'But can we talk shop for a moment? Ask you what you think of us before we venture out.'

As he joined her on the small sofa, Martine raised an eyebrow, recognising a workaholic when she saw one. She remembered his talk of the negatives of his last job. *To be charitable,* she supposed, *one minus could have been stopping my correspondence.*

She blurted, 'I'm not sure I can help you. I'm not sure I'm myself.' Abruptly this seemed true. 'I could give you some blah about your pre-publicity and welcome pack, but I'd only be going through the motions. I don't regard this as my real life.'

Unexpectedly, she was sharing: *Perhaps because he's who he is; perhaps because he's so much younger and I'm away from London,* she decided.

Gavin proffered a large knife. 'The only one, sorry.'

Martine hacked at the chorizo, hungry despite their recent fireside supper.

She struggled to explain. 'Being abroad must make me feel guilty or something.'

'A destructive emotion.' Gavin knocked back his wine, staring with his round eyes.

'I should be doing something else. Or more. A job like yours seems play dressed up as work.'

'So much for my client survey.' Gavin sighed and picked up the knife. 'But you do like fun?' he checked.

Martine shrugged her agreement.

Gavin said, 'In that case, I must just...' He laid the blade down, eyes flicking from it to her face with a small smile. He assured her, 'Never fear, I'm no *bandido*!', switching on *Rodrigo y Gabriela* and stalking off towards the right-hand rooms.

To the sounds of his searching and whistling, Martine took out her Galaxy and scanned her messages until, to her surprise, she heard the splash of a shower. She stood up when Gavin came back. His aura of woodsmoke and cigarettes had left him with his clothes; his pallid rib-cage was littered with dark moles.

'Older women are interesting. Their minds.' His words shocked her with adrenalin. 'You're going red!' He held out a long, almost hairless arm. 'And now I'd like to kiss you.'

Martine panicked: *I couldn't expose my body to a stranger now, even if I wanted to.* Water was snailing down Gavin's neck and he was grinning, his extended fingers rigid. He glanced at the knife, still close by on the table. Backing up, Martine fumbled her Galaxy, which fell. She had to stoop to retrieve it.

'No night on the town then,' she muttered, then rebalanced, struggled with the doorhandle and stumbled into the dark.

26 Taking the ball

Christmas 2010

One day that November, her mother called her. 'Tum-ti-tum. Now I don't want you to worry...'

All over England, Martine thought, *parents are reassuring their instantly worried children.*

The weeks went by, and she and Jonas and her mother met and debated with the specialists what best to do for an eighty-four-year-old woman with clogging arteries. Although she was otherwise fit, the answer wasn't easy at her age.

Martine's final earthbound sphere fell away behind her. In Sri Lanka, General Fonseka was jailed on corruption charges, and Mahinda Rajapaksa became Sri Lankan President, unopposed. Two hundred thousand were released from detention camps and the war was purportedly over, although thousands of rebels were still held. Martine's mother needed angioplasty, it turned out.

It was a snowy Christmas Eve, 2010. Mrs Haslett had had a stent implant at St Thomas's, which was close to Brandon Towers and had good facilities, Martine had insisted. Her mother was staying at her flat in the best bedroom for rest and recuperation with an air of injured bafflement. She'd brought a tapestry with her, but wouldn't settle to it. Every day she shuffled in blankets towards the living room window, where she gazed out through the netting on the balcony. She tended to fix on the youths far below among the salt pillars of the tower blocks making snow monsters and bike wheel stencils on any squares of virgin white, with a particular expression on her face.

Jonas was house- and dog-sitting at Harrow Weald, the snow so heavy now that travelling was difficult. Pippi and Gretel had descended the day before, salving his pique at his isolation. They were having their main festivities that night, according to

Astrid's native Nordic traditions, so Martine and her mother would do the same, Skyping in order to open their presents together.

Mother and daughter were chafing at each other. While Martine had been last-minute shopping, Ali had called. On her return, Martine had found her sitting with her mother, the two women hunched hugging mugs of tea in a conspiracy of murmuring and frowns. She wanted her mother to herself: suddenly, their time together seemed to be contracting.

Ali smiled up at her. 'I was recounting Conrad's fit.'

Conrad had had an episode of transient global amnesia, a rare, temporary state in which, for twenty-four hours, he was violently sick, recognised no one, didn't know who or where he was. Since then he and Ali had been reborn. Conrad had become an exercise fiend and, with their daughter steadily employed and living with her boyfriend, they were selling up for a narrowboat in Shropshire. Martine still couldn't process that they were leaving London.

She said, 'Glad to see you've kept Mum entertained.'

'We were both saying how brilliant St Thomas's has been.'

Martine hefted the bags hanging from her hands. 'Sorry, Ali, but Christmas Eve and there's a lot to do.'

Ali took Martine's cue, but 'There was no need for that,' Mum said when Ali had gone.

'Sorry sorry sorry,' Martine said.

Ever since Spain Martine had struggled with a sense of dwindling, of being squashed into a finite timespan. When on her own, she often fell to cataloguing the essentials of her existence: they included Ali, and especially Mum. A list that didn't take long, it was a foam that traced where waves had stretched on sand. For Conrad, since his episode, most events and people must also have receded. *No wonder Mum stands at the window*, she thought. *She probably feels the same.*

Once Martine had put the pheasant in to roast, she returned to her mother with ginger ale and cheese straws and a Burgundy for herself, illumined the tree lights and started *Carols from King's* on the player, ducking between the swags of cards. The older woman's balding pate strained at the view above her tortoise back in its trailing mohair blankets, humming tunelessly. Martine whistled tunelessly along.

Her mother said, 'Don't mock.' She changed tack. 'Hum-hum. I know, you know,' she said.

Martine fretted, 'Sit down, for Pete's sake.'

'I would if there were any decent chairs to sit on.'

'Know what?'

'Do I have to spell it out?'

If her mother had been working up to their mutual fear of parting, Martine saw that she had suddenly backed down. Eyes on a flying bird, her thoughts seemed to flit somewhere else – maybe, or so Martine dreaded, to her growing knowledge through the years of Martine's sense of utter bereavement.

'I wish I had more cushions,' Martine apologised, suddenly in a flap.

'I know that you...' Her mother tailed off, distracted by a plastic bag, flapping below in slush. 'Hum-ho. I think you know about my little... treats to myself?' This felt like a detour into a new topic, another taboo topic entirely. The older woman demonstrated with a small beribboned package in her hand. 'Although this isn't one really. Ali brought it for you, but she was chatting about me and Conrad and put it back in her bag. I just...', she searched for the phrase, 'liberated it.'

Martine said gruffly, 'What you do is up to you.' The present was a silver friendship bracelet. 'Hmph,' she said, irrationally ungrateful, channelling her confusions onto Ali.

Supper disappointed Martine, her mother barely picking at the brandied fruit pavlova. Afterwards, she connected her laptop to her TV, the older woman accepted a chair, there was a bubble burp from the screen and Jonas, Pippi and Gretel tilted into view.

'Wish you were here,' the girls chorused, the twenty-two-year-old Gretel in a saccharin tone, the older Pippi in a bored one.

Jonas looked tired and grizzled. 'Hey. This is our winter grotto.'

'Mum's hall cupboard.' Martine glanced at her mother expecting outrage at this, but she was just a bit bewildered.

In the fake snow scene in the emptied cupboard, Jonas, on a stool, was crushed by Gretel at his side, while Pippi had folded herself onto the floor in front.

Jonas's eyes toured his concept. 'Twigs 'n stuff from the garden. The tree...'

'If that's Mum's tree from the loft, you seem to have bent it.'

'We found the spray-on icicles. You're OK with all this, right?'

Jonas skewed the webcam. Christmas lights in the homemade grotto threw garish colours onto the white ground of polystyrene chippings surrounding Pippi and two worn toys, a badger and a squirrel, kept by Mum as memories of the girls.

'Those things are Mum's,' said Martine.

'Tum-ti-tum. My lights. Oh! And my robins.' Mum chuckled, unperturbed.

Jonas began picking gifts from his forest, sparking the girls into interest. Pippi's boyfriend and Astrid appeared in the corner of the screen. Astrid had come to Harrow for supper. She waved and spoke festive wishes, moving a dishtowel over a plate. Her hands were mehndied, matching her red-dyed hair. With the unexplained chin scar acquired a few years back, she looked worn and strange, Martine decided.

Pippi's chapped mouth stretched at Martine's voucher for accessories, but her sunken eyes were unsmiling, the aftermath of her drug years. 'Thanks, Martine.'

'Not yet!' Martine's mother stopped her reaching for an envelope in their tree, instead persuading her to open a framed photomontage of the nieces.

'Thank you, girls.' In her tiny flat, she wondered where to

hang it.

The doting grandmother had already bought Pippi new dance shoes and tickets to a show. Gretel, recently made redundant from an office job for the London Ambulance Service, had already got a keyboard for her busking. Their presents were long opened and forgotten.

In Harrow, Gretel opened the same voucher as Pippi, Jonas one for a gourmet weekend, both of them from Martine; in Kennington, her mother was reading the invitation from Jonas to an outing of her choice.

'Thanks, love. The smaller the gifts these days, somehow the greater the value.'

'I'm going now, Dad, OK?' Gretel shifted, hugging her hourglass figure, which she considered fat.

But she'd forgotten the snow, and Jonas had to remind her.

'Anyways, you've gotta stay. For the... you-know,' he said.

Then, from another envelope, he drew out flying lessons.

'You can start all over again,' his adopted mother said.

Jonas's grin looked unconvinced.

Martine's mother opened trial membership of Stanmore Golf Club with six lessons thrown in, Martine's prayer for a good future. She grumbled something.

Martine scolded, 'It could have been bowling.'

There was a package wrapped in red tissue in the Kennington tree. Inside the paper, Martine discovered a wad of designs sketched out by Jonas and Bill Kidmay: to ease book storage in her flat, they were building her a kind of Canterbury. Pleasure filled her.

Her mother finally passed her the long-delayed gold envelope. Jonas leaned forward, and Gretel shifted in the grotto doorway, letting Astrid in onscreen. Martine slid out a piece of paper. It was a travel-agency voucher for an air ticket to Sri Lanka.

She shook her head. 'That was then,' she murmured. Her

mother reached out and squeezed her hand. 'And this is now. I'm not going, no way.'

Mohan's phantom whispered at her, '*I knew that you would come for me one day.*'

Suddenly he was propelling her through some exosphere. There was a roaring in her ears, and the sound of the others' protests filled her head.

27 Line and length

(Common advice followed, whether wisely or not, by a bowling beginner)

December 2010–April 2012

On Christmas Eve the moon was waning, near perfect, yet not quite. After the present giving Martine's mother didn't sleep. Her daughter heard her: stifled sounds she didn't want to identify. She thought, *I ought to go to her.*

She wrestled. *How can I holiday in Kandy with Mum the way she is?* The voucher for the ticket proposed a flight around Easter 2012, the school holidays if Martine still hadn't retired. It was well ahead, so she could check out Mohan's location in advance of the flight if she wanted and make arrangements if she wanted, and do away with all excuses. Her mother had researched this, thought things through.

If I went, Martine told herself, *the place wouldn't be as I imagine. Not all ferns, cascades and dragonflies.* How could she look for Mohan? Should she, even? He'd be thirty-four – oddly, like her when their letters first started, the adolescent she still dreamed of long since gone. If she found him, to what purpose? And if she didn't? Martine chided herself, *I shouldn't have been obsessing about Sri Lanka, dreaming and over-dreaming in my sleep. Convincing myself that I'd built up armour through the years when it's been the very opposite: when all my protections have just been drifting off.*

In the morning she found Mum's tapestry, finished, outside the door of her bedroom. Not the acorns and blackbird that had been pre-printed on the canvas, but one word, 'Please.' But she was already in freefall, had made the decision to go. And of course it would have to be a search, not just a holiday.

She found a use for Gavin Godfell.

She rang him, mentioned the Costa Brava and said, 'You won't remember me.'

'Ah yes,' he remembered unwillingly. 'Marianne.'

She hesitated. *Could my wish to see Mohan be the dominant's sense of entitlement to the weak? Much like Gavin's last summer to me?* She dispelled her doubts. 'Actually, it's Martine.'

She went on to explain. She related the years of writing to Mohan, calmly, neutrally, and how Gavin's letter from InterRelate broke them up. He had no recollection, he said.

At first his line was 'Of course that would have been a decision imposed on me,' but then he became effusive, apologetic, clearly thankful that she hadn't mentioned their Spanish night.

At last Martine said, 'The Sri Lankan troubles are over. I'm going there. I want to know where Mohan is.'

He said warily, 'I don't keep up with things like that, with colleagues from that time.'

'But InterRelate still exists. I see it's Small World now. You can get in touch, ask them to help.'

'It would take a heap of work…'

'You can persuade someone, a charming bloke like you.'

Their Spanish night leered at him without her saying more. 'I'll see what I can do.'

Martine next rang up on 18 March 2011, giving a false name to the receptionist, just to make sure he'd answer.

Gavin said, 'Oh. You.'

'So what have you found out?'

'It's difficult,' he stalled.

Martine said, 'I had a mobile if you remember. Actually, I took pictures.'

And she could have photographed the knife pointed at her, possibly in threat, the pebbledash of moles, the presumptuous hand thrust out. Remembering his dishonesty to some girlfriend on the phone, her conscience easily excused her.

The following Monday Godfell phoned her. 'They're looking.

Now back off.'

In September Mum was well, buoyed up by talk of Martine's trip.

'They're busy,' Gavin sulked on the phone.

Martine pressed, 'Give me your Small World contact.'

'You won't tell them…'

'Give me the contact,' Martine ordered.

Sandra Gearing at Small World was keen to help.

'I assure you, we are looking. Since you're a friend of Gavin's,' she glossed. 'We don't have an office there these days, but we've kept some links.'

The air tickets were booked now: 'For next April,' Martine said.

'And you do know that we won't let you go alone, that we'd have to get someone to take you to him?' Sandra Gearing checked. 'As long as you're happy with that?'

Late one afternoon, mid-January 2012, Astrid dropped by, her red roots sprouting out grey.

'Jonas is in a bad case.'

Martine said, 'I see the girls, but never you.'

'I'm rather busy with my spirit travellings.' Astrid blinked. 'Can you help him?'

'I see him pretty often. Living with Mum and seeing the girls seem to help him.'

'Do you know that he sleeps often on my floor?'

Martine was taken aback. 'Does Mum know? Are you two…?'

Astrid shook her head. 'He tells her he is seeing friends. As you know, he doesn't have many.'

Martine gave herself a talking-to: *The promise of a view of Mohan out of my carriage window has blinded me that Jonas's journey is different.*

'Will you take Jonas with you to Sri Lanka?'

Martine recognised, *Part of me would like that.* It was soon after this that Jonas entered her dreams of Kandy, always looking for Mohan with her.

That night was Dr Sketchy's drinking and drawing night at the Royal Vauxhall Tavern. In the main arena space flanked by bars, the Dick Duet sang, a band of near-nude Vikings pole-danced and life models struck tattooed-nipple-and-buttock poses for the left-handed artist competitions. Pearl threw off her usual cartoon masterpieces, but Martine and Bernard drank more than they drew.

Martine was struggling with the noise and tumult, and Pearl was twitchy. 'He's stuck to me again. I know he is. Hangin' about somewhere outside.' A man with a beer belly and white goatee, whom Pearl nicknamed the Sticker, wouldn't let her be, but Pearl had issues, making him even more sinister than that. 'It feels like he's a punishment for the boy I used to be.'

They left earlier than they would have some years back, Pearl starting at shadows.

'Come back to the Towers,' Martine urged her.

Pearl refused. 'It's me. I shat on nature.'

Martine sighed inwardly, *Pearl is still a weather house, the man and the woman alternately popping out.*

Bernard insisted, 'See you onto the tube.'

Passing through the arches of Vauxhall railway, they arrived at the bus station and the tube mouth where the photo-voltaic shelter reared two-pronged into the night. They delivered Pearl to the train then climbed back to the surface. The late-night traffic clogged and roared. The moon's last quarter lit Martine and Bernard and the wide, light-dappled roadways, but Martine was preoccupied by Pearl.

'I'll walk home,' she said, wishing that a stroll could solve Pearl's problems. She grimaced, 'She used to be indecisive and now she's not so sure.'

Bernard put the back of his elegant hand to his forehead in a mock-weary gesture. 'We all live with uncertainty of some sort.

Her own worst enemy. Always has been.'

'What to do though?'

'There was a time you'd have had a plan.'

Martine smiled. 'There was a time you wouldn't have said "There was a time."'

Martine wasn't sure why Bernard was still talking in his distinctive throaty drawl, lowering that phallic nose to her, unless he expected to come home with her himself. Her pulse rose slightly.

She sighed, 'I miss your old queen.'

She thought, *And as much the man joined to her*. He looked at her a certain way, she chose to think, but she felt no Dame Tattlemouse chemistry.

He pouted. 'You could take her to Sri Lanka.' Martine considered this second nomination on the same day. 'Places to go... You'll be all right to toddle home?'

They clasped each other and pressed their cheeks together, Bernard smelling of hair tonic and beer, 'Mwah, Mwah,' camping it up. He held Martine away from him.

'Girl,' he winked, 'you haven't lost your sparkle. And you still smell fine.'

Sri Lanka was approaching. Sometimes for Martine, the plan was a sonorous rumble over sleepers towards a destination portentous beyond belief; sometimes, simply a trip to a place she'd like to see with the chance of meeting someone she once wrote to.

In February 2012 she still hadn't decided whether to ask Jonas or Pearl to come with her; she couldn't subsidise both. Then Gretel texted, asking if they could meet. Martine suggested Kew Gardens. It would kill two birds with one proverbial stone, because her recent internet wanderings had uncovered, to her shock, that Dr Freddy Garraway had long ago left Kew's Tropical Nursery and was working, as she'd liked to imagine when they were together, in the exotic field: the Indonesian islands, to be precise. At last she could go to Kew again, pass through the place where she and Freddy had done more things than meet. The experience might purge her, once and for all, of that gut-wrenching ending. Also, Gretel now worked occasionally digging, laying paviours and sometimes even planting for a garden designer, showing signs that she enjoyed it, so Kew might be an education for her.

The pair made their way, talking of nothing and something, from the winter displays at Victoria Gate through the woodland area and past the Temple of Aeolus, stopping at the dun surfaces of the rock garden nicked with *Galanthus nivalis*, over five thousand snowdrops.

They ended up under the peaks of the Princess of Wales Conservatory, exploring its tropical regions, the Asian orchids. In the centre, the giant water lily floated on the surface of the raised aquaria. Martine's mind wandered to an island village far away where ponds must frame the starred petals of lilies. Gretel picked at her jumper layers and stared at the fish through the viewing windows. Martine roused herself, searching for poison-dart tree frogs and baby water dragons, half-considering one as a pet.

Gretel talked about work. 'I might be digging a pond soon.'

'The lily used to be in the Water Lily House,' Martine explained, 'hence the name. But it didn't like the old pad.' Shooting Gretel her angled look, Gretel duly groaned. They consulted her leaflet. 'Oh. The Lily House is closed. Which doesn't matter, except that there are ferns.'

And memories with Freddy there, she thought. *But what the hey: those times have gone.*

'Different plants get on together,' Gretel said. She was staring at a pepper vine winding round a tree. 'Um. Same with people, you could say.'

'I had ferns on my old roof terrace if you remember,' said Martine. 'There was one, *Ceratopteris*, fleshy stipes and stipitate

282

fronds, feathery to you. The literature had it as exclusively aquatic. But it survived in soil for me. Maybe because most others were growing happily, who knows. It certainly wasn't because of me. It's an inexact science, gardening.'

Gretel said, 'Um. You're not here.'

'You were saying...'

'Um. That people can get on in different ways.'

They'd arrived at a banana tree with a pineapple plant spraying leaves beneath. Sensors had triggered mist into the warmth, a heady, fertile atmosphere that previewed to Martine the Sri Lankan climes she was impatient for. She saw this now as the third reason she'd come.

Gretel continued, 'Men and women. Um...'

'How about a drink? This place is making me thirsty.'

'Look,' Gretel burst out. 'There's a boy.'

'Oh?' said Martine, finally taking note.

'We don't... do anything.' Gretel kicked a tree.

Martine moved them hastily towards the exit. 'Maybe he's shy. Maybe he doesn't know...'

'It can't be just me. People can't all, can they. Dad and Pearl can't, surely. I just don't like it.'

Martine asked, 'Have you talked to Astrid?'

Gretel had, but consulting her mother hadn't been enough. Martine invented a man from long ago who'd never been physical, an aunt's love as a lie, while Gretel listened, head down, winding a sweater thread round her finger.

Then Martine repeated more or less what Astrid had said. 'We're all at different places on the sexual spectrum. It's rare for someone to be precisely on your wavelength.'

It was only when they reached Kew station that she registered suddenly, 'What do you mean, Jonas and Pearl?'

And Gretel told her. Most Sundays, Astrid helped on a Brick Lane stall – tasselled lampshades, dreamcatchers, oriental throws – in exchange for a corner to sell her shamanic wares.

Medicine drums, rattles filled with turquoise, jewellery, and the totems she made for fire, earth and air. In the case of water, she adapted plumbing parts.

One Sunday, apparently Bernard with Fleur and a new girlfriend had passed the stall, half-looking for a gift to make the troubled Pearl laugh. Astrid recognised him vaguely. Between them they'd sorted out why, then got onto Martine and her coming journey.

'I've told her she could take Pearl,' Bernard had said.

Astrid countered that she'd suggested Jonas. Unexpected rivals, they laughed politely.

Astrid asked, 'Why does Pearl need to be going?'

Bernard said, 'I'll bring her here next Sunday, doll. You'll see.'

And he had. But as it happened, Jonas, Pippi and Gretel had dropped by the stall as well. Pearl and Jonas had met a few times – and on Labour's election night, slightly more than met. There that Sunday, in Brick Lane, they started talking again, and discovered they'd got drawing in common, and then they were flirting, and now... Gretel shrugged, implying the upshot. Martine absorbed the news, not knowing what to say.

A few weeks after Kew she saw Jonas and Pearl together for the first time. She decided that she was happy for them; moreover now, she judged, neither would need her journey. She'd go to Kandy alone.

With a month to go, Sandra Gearing rang. 'Can you give me the boy's name again? And his parents'?'

So still there was no firm news of Mohan. For the first time Martine began scanning the internet, Facebook and Twitter for signs of him herself, but found no Liyanage family and no thirty-something man who sounded right. She had a ringing in her ears, and sometimes found it hard to breathe when the lifts were broken and she had to climb her stairs. She didn't go to the doctor, who would have diagnosed high blood pressure. She was still working, still hadn't retired, kept on giving herself to her students.

In the school labs she kept her Galaxy on, awaiting Small World news.

'Naughty naughty. Rules on mobiles, Miss.'

Out of work there was a muted drumroll from friends and family: tactful visits, cautious emails, texts and phone calls.

The usual gist was, 'Any sign of Mohan?'

'Stand by,' ran the gist of her replies.

Mum emailed, 'You will tell me? Can I help?'

'You can help me by being patient.'

Eventually, diplomatically, the drumroll faded out. 30 March was the last day of term. On Thursday the 29th, Martine recontacted Small World.

Sandra Gearing said, 'When is it you're going again?'

'Day after tomorrow. This Saturday.'

On the Friday Sandra said, 'Give me the time you leave for the airport.'

If Martine had had more notice of Small World's lack of competence, she could have done more internet searching herself. But it was Saturday, and she was on a plane now. She had notes on her laptop, and Mohan's letters with her. If she needed them, she prayed, there had to be researchers on the ground.

28 Country: the facts

(Country: Old name for the outfield; if a ball skies into this outlying area, fielders may have longer to make a catch but only by travelling further)

April 2012

Sunday 1 April. Martine took in Colombo as fragments: in the airport corridor, the dreamy honeymoon poster luring couples on; the passport queue marked 'Foreigners', for her and dreamers like her; the soupy night outside, where moonlight flooded over her; her first tuk-tuk, weaving through the honking traffic along boulevards that repeatedly flashed a folded ribbon sign and the name Dialog, the island's major telecoms company. The roads were smoother than expected. Mohan was in Kandy and not here though, she was sure.

She wasn't booked into a global chain hotel: to her that wouldn't have been Sri Lanka. Anyway, in big hotels you couldn't keep your door ajar. Her little Colombo guesthouse specialised in prospectors for adoption. The owner, dapper and friendly, ferried them by car to various convents. Martine thought of Mohan's Pieter. She met an Italian couple, young and tired and smiling, who were near the end of their adoption journey. In their case she refused to see either irony or hope. A recent couple who'd gone to Kandy had left an umbrella behind, and the owner asked if she'd return it when she got there.

In the morning she set off from Colombo station, among her luggage her laptop and a locally bought mobile. Lemon sepia tinted the platform offices with their clerks piling papers in slow motion behind glazed bars. The train, terracotta striped, reminded her of 1950s letterhead. People boarded round her, staring. She slid onto a cracked seat, shoving the window down, drinking chilled bottled water to cool off. Wafts of curried snacks, the foreign musk of others' sweat.

She checked any man who passed her against the photos that

she'd scanned onto her laptop, just in case. She sat across from a pair of older men, their whites of eyes unblinkingly on her.

'*Ayubowan,*' she smiled.

The train jerked and shook itself forward to periodic crashing sounds like jumping stacks of metal trays.

On her laptop, she pored over the facts that she'd amassed: Mohan's family, his schooling, his life, his village; the geography and geology and climatic zones of Kandy, the festivals, the farming. *Facts will check me*, she told herself; *they'll rein in my expectations, keep things real. I'll only find Mohan with facts.*

But she couldn't confine herself to facts. The scenes outside her window seduced her. The bunting of full washing lines in front of shanty shacks. Women sheet-scrubbing on rocks in red-brown streams. Cascades of bougainvillea. Maize and bell peppers butting the fences of cramped gardens. Children's games in a tangle of mud lanes. A railway worker, a sprat dangling his ragged legs out of the wound-back tin of a train carriage, his home. She rebuked herself for seeing beauty in poverty.

Among one travelling family, a little boy squirmed and tossed his sister's plait. The sister huffed, glaring through pebble glasses. The mother nodded happily, holding him still for Martine's approval. Remembering the early Mohan, Martine turned away.

Low plains of recently cropped paddy. The odd white punctuation stroke, a heron – crane to the Lankans – standing in citrus sun. The train climbed up through forest. Sheer drops to jungle, and short blackouts through rock tunnels. Her pulse began to elevate. Rainforest filed by the window, a botanical frieze. A group of youths – a similar age to the Mohan she was always trying to find in her dream – broke into song, drumming the carriage wall with the flats of their hands, voices rising and falling, other passengers softly clapping out the beat.

The boy escaped from his mother, fixing Martine with big brown eyes.

'*Ayubowan*,' she winked, but then was craning for her first sight of the mountains.

Their outlines blue, like smoke. There was an outcrop like a tombstone, Bible Rock to the colonials, and another like an arrowhead, where Mohan's hero Saradiel lived. She thought, *They look like stage flats, as if there's nothing solid in between;* palm trees protruded from the forested distance like pop-ups in a book. The boy's gaze trickled away. Among the trees tumbled shacks like cardboard cartons, out of reach.

In Martine's eyes, the train ride and the landscape stood for Mohan. It was as if he had a hand in how she saw things, as if he was revealing his life in stages on that journey: childhood, youth and the male in full maturity; shacks, paddy, forest unrolling for her like murals, mountains lining up. As if, eventually, he'd be unpeeling everything for her, one skin at a time.

In Kandy, at the busy little station, her sweat was a breaking tide, first a hot slick wave then tepid. The light burned through bronze dust. She took another tuk-tuk. The driver in his Watermen T-shirt jabbering into his mobile drove a little yellow house: rag rug, water bottles, curlicued chrome fittings, small cupboards with chrome handles, a pink troll and family photos on the dashboard, Sinhala warbling from two speakers. The air was the fragrance of sandalwood, the odour of drains, a talcum-powder sweetness from somewhere, the lush smell of vegetable growth, the saliva-triggering draw of toasted spices. The clay dust and exhaust smoke on the main town roads transformed the lemon yellow light pouring down from the hillsides into a brassy sepia screen, like wire mesh. Reality was potent, alcoholic, beside her soft-drink dreams.

In broken English, on the lake road, the driver shouted her a lesson on tuk-tuk driving. She grinned at the horn-blowing traffic stand-offs. She didn't fret for the tube, for the passenger's easy conviction of achieving her destination. Here the buses and tuk-tuks jostled and huddled, stopped and started, got gridlocked. She was so mesmerised she didn't get round to telling the driver what she was doing there.

Her destination was a mistake, she suspected, shrinking at the standard hotel welcome as she entered the dim lobby: dusky faces dipping over dusky steepled hands, papaya crush cocktails and an '*Ayubowan*: Long life' from the hostess in her turquoise local saree for the tourists. An obliging tunic-ed bell boy with a toothpaste smile would probably brush on her door at night, pointing out that 'Madam, this is safer closed.'

From a wrought iron table beside the hotel lawn she could see a border of vivid oleanders and the tops of trees, hedging off whatever lay beyond. She identified the lawn's dishevelled, strap-leaved grass as *Zoysia matrella poaceae*: in a way she'd prepared a lot, for many years, for this journey.

A boy brought sweet black tea.

Martine said, 'Will there be rain?'

The boy said, 'The sky is not so heavy. In your honour, there may be no rains today.'

Martine blurted, 'Sorry. I can't stay here.'

She didn't want James Galway fluting in the lift, frangipani laid by a dusky hand on the turned-back bedsheet, porridge and bacon on the groaning breakfast buffet: vestiges of a bygone, colonised deference.

The boy wagged his smiling head. 'OK, OK. I will bring the manager.'

Martine waited for the manager, and looked. Apartment balconies overhung the view to her left, cluttered with bicycles and buckets. A painted *huniyam yakka* mask, the Black Prince of Sorcery with his bug eyes, distended nostrils and cobras rearing from his brow, traditionally for *thovil*, the expulsion of an illness, hung on an outside wall. A shaking of branches, and Mohan's English teacher popped through them, a toque macaque with that distinctive fan of head hair, its expression fixed and comic. The fist twitched, under the lifted chin. It almost felt like a message from Mohan.

The crickets were ever-present, the white noise of their seething. Above the town the light was golden, limpid. Trees sprang dense from the hillsides down below. The landscape defied Martine's London life: that was engineering, the coordination of routines, of journeys by tube and car, entrances to and exits from shops and bars and offices and restaurants, rises and falls on escalators and in lifts. That was in her mind: this was in her pores.

She looked north and east, to the hills. She thought, *He's somewhere over there.* She pictured ferns by a mountain stream, and a dragonfly, like a splash of oil, bouncing against a bullrush. With the right help she'd get to Mohan. She had a self-revelation: she was like the scalloped spreadwing, her wings unpacking, gluey in the light, a couple of her limbs at most still in the holed boat of the nymph with its broken oars of legs that she was unfurling from.

Her gaze swept round again. High on a forested hillside a Buddha sat cross-legged, white as chalk. As the manager bustled towards her, in a long, smooth stroke the light withdrew from the sky, deepening like tea dregs.

'Madam, sorry, sorry. Very busy.'

City lights began to cluster below. The stars pricked on. A dog's bark echoed somewhere in a hoarse, foreign way. A yellow glow haloed the Buddha, white lights picking out one side.

'The Buddha says that all life is suffering,' Martine joked ineptly, quoting Mohan from long ago, 'and I'm afraid I must make you suffer by moving out.'

She transferred to a Kandy homestay. Up a winding unmade lane, it was a faded, crumbling house dangling cables of old cobweb from the ceiling, with bright gnomes and plastic windmills in the flower-filled garden and the portrait of some stern Victorian commander on the stairs. The doll-like owner, Hilda, spoke timid English and kept an evasive but smiley houseboy. Martine slept off her jet lag.

The next day, late, having showered in the antique bathroom, she went down. The kitchen was wooden drainers stacked with crockery and two old butler's sinks. Hilda greeted her, clearing spaces among the cooking pans on the long kitchen table. Two visitors already sat there, sipping milky tea from mismatched English porcelain. Hilda rebuffed Martine in shrugs when she went to help her with the piles of washing up.

Hilda's friends were a local couple who'd dropped by, she in an ornate, Indian-style saree and blouse, he in an expensive light-weight suit. She looked older; he had a fleshy, lived-in face.

The wife asked in Sinhala, 'Why are you in Sri Lanka? *Ayi?* Why? Are you a tourist?'

Martine attended to Hilda as she painfully translated.

Tourism was prevalent in Kandy, Martine had already seen. *Self-prostitution,* she thought. She found this hard to accept, not quite compatible with her expectations. The woman visitor's autocratic air seemed to link her to the medallioned officer on the stairs. A phrase came back to Martine, suited to the tourism and the woman: the imperialism of need. She took the letters and pictures from her bag, but finding nowhere to lay them, put them back.

'I'm here to see Kandy. Mostly to find someone. He's a Lankan, Sinhalese.'

Hilda interpreted, swapping Martine's teacup with a mango splayed in a floret.

The wife didn't react. 'We came back here to stop him working.' She put out a hand to stop her husband lighting a cigarette. 'And because I was homesick.'

The man said mildly in accented English, 'I just retired a little early.'

The woman studied Martine. 'You're a scientist like Vijitha?'

She indicated her husband.

'You can tell,' said Martine.

The woman turned to him. 'You say I always know.'

Vijitha kept to English. 'Mmm. It would be better for the world, perhaps, if more people remembered the word "science" meant something less definite than knowledge. I wonder if you agree.'

He looked at Martine kindly. He, his wife and his comment posted themselves almost at once into her dreams.

She asked, 'What was your field?'

'Light out of true. Gravitational lenses, specifically. I still study them, in my spare moments.'

'We were in Baltimore. And before that, Greenbelt,' the woman persisted in Sinhala. 'Vijitha worked for NASA.'

'I may need a researcher,' said Martine. 'Do you by any chance know someone?'

With a curling lip the woman said something, she could tell a knockback, although Hilda didn't interpret, merely exchanging Martine's fruit rind for an egg hopper.

Vijitha softened his wife's rejection. 'The Sri Lankan Tourism Promotion Bureau have a desk in the KCC. A mall in town. They have guides.'

'I want another cup of tea,' his wife signalled clearly to the room.

Martine set out on foot, carrying the umbrella. The shimmering sound of crickets, the cawing of a bird. *Enter on a computer the number of cricket chirps on average over five seconds and select a season: a programme calculates the ambient temperature. A cricket fact, girl.* She pulled her bad-joke face.

Down the lane, she stopped. The hills were steeply wooded folds pinned by the gilt brooch of the temple far below her, its dual kinked roof still hiding the lake from view. The hairpin of a transmission tower scratched the skyline, red and white. She knew that landline communication had largely bypassed this challenging, hilly country. People linked through the ether using mobiles and satellites, and the roads had been transformed in the last decade. More Sri Lankan facts. The white hulk of the Buddha gleamed across the valleys. She passed a hotel drive guarded by an army of vermillion, canna lilies on black stems, smiling a no at the line of tuk-tuk drivers.

The roads below were dense with traffic. A uniformed policeman was controlling the trucks and tuk-tuks with incomprehensible flicks of his stiff gloves. She crossed to the lake, and the matter-of-fact in her receded. It was as if, with the fine plume of the lake's water jet, Mohan himself was obscuring the ornamental garden of an island, and as if, using the island, he was screening the Queen's Bath House behind it, standing on white pillars on the water. Beyond the white block of the Bath House, only the roofs of the Temple were visible, the gold apex of the most sacred at their centre. Somehow, Mohan's dance of several veils.

Locals passed Martine, scanning her from under the shelter of umbrellas. Any could be a thirty-four-year-old Mohan, or a relative.

She followed the Cloud Wall round the lake, a concrete stencil of pierced white flames. Looking as she now did, the Temple complex opened up: the statues and planted paths of the garden, the wooden pillars of the ancient audience hall, the terracotta and grey-tiled roofs surrounding the Temple, its roof a beak of gold. She skirted the railings. At the Queen's Bath House she imagined a swim in the waters underneath, illicit, one moonlit night maybe. On the shoreline, a father bent to his son. The boy offered a plastic bag to the ripples, trying to scoop the crowding fishes.

She left them for the streets, climbing the escalator inside the KCC.

At the Tourism Bureau counter she explained her mission to a bright-eyed woman who waited for her to finish, nodding patiently, then said, 'Perhaps you have a letter of reference, from, ah, some professional. Back in the UK.'

'I'm a teacher myself.'

'Do you have a letter to explain this, and why you're here?'

Martine hadn't expected to need letters, introductions. 'Sorry, no.'

'In that case, it is too short notice for a researcher or guide.'

Hiring a Bureau driver would feel to Martine like patronage, but she swallowed her scruples and asked.

'Again that will be difficult.'

'Can you help with information, at least? Ways to the family that I could try myself?'

'The telephone directories are not so helpful I'm afraid. Most people here use mobiles. But the *kacheri*, the District Secretariats, hold electoral lists. And the Registrars' offices keep births, marriages and deaths. Although Liyanage: that is such a common name.'

Martine said, 'A map would help, one that shows the roads from here into the Mist-Laden side of the Mountains.'

For a moment she felt the irony of the location she clung onto: she'd always assumed that a better life for Mohan would mean a life made somewhere else.

The women struggled together over Google Earth on Martine's laptop, but the assistant said, 'We are a little behind here. Not all the little villages are even on GPS.' She offered her a paper map, 'Although again here,' she said, 'one or two places may be missing.' She checked, 'You say he came from the Mist-Laden Mountains to school in Kandy? Then the buses go only along here.' She traced a route from Kandy through towns called Matale and Raththota. Rising from those, just one, crinkled road. 'This is tarmacked now. But you need a sensible driver, isn't it.'

Martine thanked her and made to leave. The woman added, 'One small idea. You say the family was drumming in the Esala Perahera. It is not the time of year for it of course, but...' She mentioned the Media Centre, beside the audience hall of the Temple. 'Sometimes they arrange filming of such performers. You might try.'

Martine found Pizza Hut on the street corner next to the Temple entrance. She scaled the stairs. Under a plasma TV showing *Tom and Jerry*, a female pianist plinky-plunked a piano. In memory of Phil, Martine sent a thought out somewhere. Teenage waiters ogled the screen, unwillingly called away by pizza appearances or the need to whizz up smoothies and now, Martine's request to see the manager.

A man with a grey moustache and a tonsure of thin hair appeared and bustled towards her. 'My wife's umbrella. How kind, so kind.'

The woman at the piano got up and came towards them. '*Bohoma sthuthiyi.*'

Many thanks. She took the umbrella. Slim and graceful, she was decades younger than the man.

'Can we thank you with a pizza?' the manager asked, rubbing his hands. Martine declined. 'Well, can we offer you something, anything, else?'

She hesitated. 'I'm looking for someone who wrote to me. Beyond Matale and Raththota, in the Dumbara Kanduvetiya. I need someone English speaking to help me, maybe a driver. Someone who knows Kandy really well.'

The manager translated to his wife, and they murmured.

'My wife's cousin used to be a guide. He has been sick, but he is almost better. He has a van, good for the mountains. I will ring him.'

The man turned to his mobile, and within minutes he was leading Martine elsewhere.

In the alleyways off Yatinuwara Street crowded chattering traders at open shops and stalls, a knife grinder, an old woman mending umbrellas. Doorways spilled out goods, pouches filled with pirated DVDs, sacks of plastic toys and gadgets in fluorescent colours.

The manager led Martine up dark, steep stairs into the hot compelling stink of chicken biryani. Betel red walls, light filtering in from the grimy window, dishes chalked on a blackboard. The sign outside had said the Grand Imperial Eating House. Lunchtime diners, all men, alone, studied the *Dinamina* or the *Lanka Deepa* at cracked formica tables, shoehorning rice and curry into their mouths. Most glanced at Martine and then greeted her escort. The house manager hurried forward, grinning them towards a table. The Pizza Hut man refused it, addressing him in Sinhala.

There was a whine and a shriek, then shouts, and diners scraping back their chairs and shoving past Martine, towards the back of the room. At the basin for rinsing hands they circled a man, wet hair pouring over his face. With a hiss, water fired from the base of the tap.

The house manager stooped and turned the stopcock. He and the dripping diner traced the fault to a crack. The manager swore. Martine stood and watched from the blank between the mostly emptied tables and the dust-filled light from the window. In gestures, everyone seemed to agree a spanner was wanted. The boss skidded off. He returned with a cloth and a sink wrench. He ducked under the basin.

He struggled to loosen the tap nut. The quiet of effort fell. Martine's pizza friend tugged the man's shoulder. He tried too but had no luck, so each man tried in turn. The manager pulled the last man out and elbowed his way back under and strained and twisted and at last got the nut off and released the pipe under the sink. The tap fell into his palm.

With one man gone for a new fitting, the men lounged around waiting, lobbing cashews into their mouths, pantomiming about plumbing and patting each other uncomfortably, smiles sliding out. The manager brought Martine a plate of biryani. She sat down feeling helpless. One man with a frizz of hair spectating from a corner, uninvolved, brought her his own dish, and showed her how to eat it with her hand.

The runner remounted the stairs with a tap. Swiftly the manager dropped it in, secured the nut and reattached the pipe. The group deflated, still chuckling, their words fast giving out. The word *foreigner* was in Martine's head, as it had been since the sign at the airport. Masculinity was exotic and intriguing, a country far beyond her, as it had always been.

The boss gestured her to the newly functioning basin, passing her a towel. Then her Pizza Hut escort led her to the man who'd shown her how to eat, introducing him as Santha, his wife's cousin. A burly man near Martine in age, with a leonine head and paws of hands. With downcast eyes and muttered questions he listened to his relative, folding his newspaper slowly, over and over; from the chat, he seemed unwilling to take her on.

She explained her quest in English. He still didn't respond. She produced the letters and the drawings.

He squinted at them, turning them, then said at last, '*Hari, hari,*' OK, OK, swaying his head slowly, his lower lip jutting. He switched to English. 'Two hundred dollars for your two weeks here. Extra for diesel and *bata.*' He growled, 'I will do the best. We may find him or not, *ne*? Not my problem.'

'Santha is good,' the Pizza Hut manager assured her.

Martine thought, *I don't like him. But what other help do I have?*

And from then on, Santha also entered her dreams.

29 Run-up

Martine followed directions from the woman in the mall that took her up a quiet road around the back of the Temple, but the guards put up gloved hands. From what she could make out, she couldn't get to the Media Centre without some kind of pass. For the moment, she abandoned her attempt.

The next day, Santha collected her in his van. She ignored the open back door and climbed in beside him, a statement met with inquiring, pink-tinged eyes.

'I don't want to act the old colonial. Imagine I'm just asking you to help me.'

'For dollars.'

A hot odour floated round him, mown grass or rain-drenched leaves.

'Our history here makes me uncomfortable.'

'Everyone oppresses everyone, or tries to.'

'You mean in the civil war.'

'Not only in the war, *ne*?'

She showed him the route on her map, the only school-bus route through the right side of the mountains, according to the Tourism Bureau. 'Through Matale and Raththota.' Santha confirmed this from his local knowledge. She added, 'Mohan told me he was 40 kilometres from Kandy.'

Out of town on the A9, they touched and re-touched the wide current of the Mahaweli, at one point passing its sign carved into stone: a cobra with five thick necks, like a fountain. *Water is truth,* thought Martine, *if sometimes different from fact,* not really knowing what her thought meant. She glimpsed women bathers on a sandbank, separate from the men. If she'd had more time, she might have swum herself.

Through red-dusted yards of building materials and outlets for vehicle body parts behind their chain-link fences, the van bisected the wide streets of Matale with its batik workshops, passing Matale bus station and forking on and right, east and north-east. People everywhere. She stopped looking at faces and hoping: there were too many.

The roadside shops of several villages jerked by. Then they were in Raththota, an industrial village aspiring to be a town. The engine still turning, Martine's heart chuntered with it.

Santha flashed his bloodshot eyes at her, pointing to the dashboard and the dusty town outside. '*Here* is 40 kilometres.'

She got out and stretched her legs and gulped down bottled water, looking round at the little place. She thought, *Ugly*. Many buildings were partial, scaffolded with bamboo.

'It's got to be nearer the mountains,' she said.

She remounted eagerly. On the far side of Raththota, the one undulating road on the map began to narrow and climb.

Santha growled, driving slowly as if unwilling. 'Few buses between here and the mountains, *ne?*'

Martine insisted, 'But some.'

Santha countered, 'Two bus changes for the boy if he lived beyond here. Few buses out so far. Not practical for a Kandy school. It would not be allowed.'

'He talked of the mountains.'

'We all talk of the mountains.'

Martine said, 'Nevertheless.'

They wound up and round. Off the road, Martine eyed unmade lanes and tracks, simple houses squatting down behind the trees: wattle and daub or timber, sometimes brick. Did they count as villages?

According to Santha, 'Yes. But there's no paddy, which your family must have.'

On a hairpin, they bypassed an open-fronted shop with a table, chairs, an awning and a part-stocked chiller cabinet. A cool spot, the Lankans called them. Martine twisted her head and craned in all directions. She was sure she'd know the village when they saw it.

The land rose, lush green growth enfolding the snake of the road. They slipped through a scattering of shacks set in plots of vegetables and paddy, a village called Pelawatta, meaning Young Shoots.

'We're not near enough to the mountains,' Martine said over the engine.

'51 kilometres. This is the mountains,' Santha snapped.

Martine couldn't accept this. She consulted her laptop notes. At the top, Mohan had told her, were the 'scrubby summits' and the 'cloudforests', the montane region, with 'ferns, mosses and waterfalls in the high hills'; below, the tea plantations 'not far up'; below that, the 'lower montane and tropical regions', with 'our village and other villages and the paddy and many tropical plants'.

They passed through another small settlement.

Santha punctuated, '57 kilometres.'

Now I'm getting upset, Martine noticed. *Why am I so upset?*

They arrived in a towering forest, coniferous, dropping away to the left, and Santha stopped to urinate. The crickets scraped, and there was the burble of some bird. The scent of pine was vaporised in fresher, thinner air.

Santha grunted, 'The plantation is a foreign project of the 1970s. Timber for building.'

In the mattress of brown needles beneath the trees, nothing grew. Martine accepted, *It's an object lesson about foreign colonisation.* She was thirsty. For some reason, they had both run out of water.

Santha warned, 'Soon we'll be in the tea plantations. British history. Not for you, *ne?*' He reminded her, 'The boy said, "the tea plantations *not far up*". So when we reach them, that's too far.'

Martine shook her head. 'Don't stop.'

She had to test the facts to their conclusion.

Soon a basic terraced eating place appeared, the Riverstone

Holiday Inn.

Martine said, 'Please stop.'

Its rustic balustrade dropped sheerly before overlapping planes of blue and bluer mountains. Waterfalls slashed them, glinting in the distance.

Leaning beside her, Santha spat over the drop. She desired the waterfalls.

'40 kilometres could be poetic licence,' she entreated.

Santha heeled the rust-red soil, smiling down at his sandal.

He told her brusquely, '61 kilometres. For poetic licence too much, *ne*?'

At Martine's insistence the van ground on towards strange, cone-shaped hills. Beyond them she saw a red cleft flinging out a tall, white cascade. Now the hills surrounded them. A cool, moist haze perfumed with sandalwood enveloped them. Bushes clipped like cut-outs in green cork spiralled the cones in geometric lines, alternating with the orange stripes of soil, like easy mazes in a children's book. Dark women bent as if decoding them then straightened, flinging something onto their backs. Tea. The red-splashed parasols of flame trees rose here and there, shading the crop with leafy spokes. Pickers' houses in bright pastels nestled together, like enamels. *The ornamental gardening of the British imperialists,* registered Martine.

'Keep driving. Please.'

They passed a sign marking the beginning of the Knuckles Range Conservation Zone, with rules for walkers, campers and day-trippers planning barbecues. Plastic rubbish at the roadside. Wind hurtled through the landmark of a view with a TV mast up high. Tourism and technology, even here. Then over a ridge and below them lay the dry zone: bleached slopes and flats, old paddy.

'That's the end of Mohan's side of the mountains,' Martine admitted, and something in her stopped. 'OK, turn round.'

Santha revved noisily as if to underline a point and, in a

practised three-point turn, started them back the way they'd come. Martine told herself that the villages below the cloud-forests weren't so far from them, just a fingernail ride down a guitar string. It just meant halting in various places, feeling for the right note.

The first hamlet they returned to did have lily ponds. Shacks sloped down to either side of the road. Log stores, scrawny chickens running, gardens shooting up with vegetables and fruit and staring, weatherbeaten faces. The asterisks of the water lilies glowed on the sparkling water, like a children's book plate illustration.

'Mohan wrote of water lilies!' Martine said.

Santha grunted, 'The water is for survival.'

As are some of my other images, she upbraided herself: *children fishing, setting traps, scrambling among the ferns and moss for wood. Still, a romantic gloss always prevails.*

Santha idled the van through the few gardens by the roadside.

'There's no temple near, no Post Office or primary school,' he pointed out.

Martine had shown him all those references from Mohan. She wanted to wrench off the gearstick, jam it in his mouth.

By the next village down, the air was more humid, the growth more tropical and verdant. Santha meandered the van about. Along a lane there was a gilt Buddha in Perspex: Mohan's village had had a shrine. Martine spotted a stone tank for the rains, which, again with poetic licence, could be the well he'd mentioned. A paddy terrace sped up Martine's heart. There was a wayside shop that she supposed could be a Post Office.

'It's not,' barked Santha. 'And it's too far here even to walk down to a bus.'

Martine wanted to puncture him with a sharp object. They descended, the ferns and mosses and waterfalls left behind.

They pitched into Pelawatta again, the village called Young

Shoots. The first thing Martine saw was a small white structure with a dirt-streaked, cross-legged Buddha in front of it, off to the right of the road. The feet clothed in flowers and necklaces and brass ornaments. To the left of the road, a stream tumbled over boulders and, on a patch of grass, a tank stood that could take up water from the water table and call itself a well. Opposite, a small cuboid building.

'Community hall,' sniffed Santha as they passed.

'I'd like to get out,' said Martine.

There were the crickets still, and yapping dogs somewhere, and, from inside a hut, people laughing, and the caw of birds in the treetops.

Martine walked down the twisted road, Santha following. Clusters of shacks with verandas. Among the carefully tended vegetables and spice bushes, most gardens had a latrine shed. The stream passed under the road, threading through shallow terraces of paddy in which two men stood talking. She forged down a track while Santha waited, unconvinced. Among more dwellings, a tiny primary school lay out of sight of the road. Its peeling facade had unglazed blanks for windows, and there were bright blue swings in the playground.

Martine doubled back to the road. Along the verges, pepper vines embraced tall trees. She was no longer sweating. Or, it seemed to her, breathing. Cocoa pods hung down. There were erica-nut palms, clove trees, jak-fruit trees, breadfruit trees with baseball mitt-like leaves.

First, in a fenced houseyard at the roadside she saw the sulphur yellow flowers of a flame tree, *Peltophorum pterocarpum*. Like flags to arrest her attention. There was also a king coconut with drinks crates stacked beneath it and a tyre swing slung from a jak tree. In the middle of the red ground, a pitched straw roof covered a log store; in one corner stood a latrine. To the side was a huddle of buildings – no, building. Two parts of the house were wattle and daub, at right-angles to each other; there was a breezeblock annexe. Each dwelling had a veranda.

She recited under her breath, '"Senior father and junior father and the mothers and five cousins are living by our house not our house but on the side."'

It fitted. It fitted. Beyond the yard, rows of gourds, melons, carrots, beans, chillis and aubergines, a ginger plot and a turmeric plot, glittered in the sun. An irregular-shaped paddy field with channels cut across it, a red cow grazing the surface, tilted to the distant stream.

'He called the cow Bluey,' Martine said. 'It was red.'

'They're all red here,' said Santha.

At the tree-lined perimeter a dog erupted, barking. Martine didn't jump. Another joined it. She thought she heard another somewhere close.

'"We have three good brown dogs,"' she recalled without needing her laptop from the van.

Santha made a noise, pointing to a higher place on the road. She hurried back. A modest handpainted sign on a wall. Under a wooden archway, they took steps down. There was an unmistakable red posting box and a window for transactions, but it and the little lobby were empty. Somewhere out back, she heard the snuffles of a baby.

Martine quoted, '"Today the bus went past us then two houses on the snake road then the Post Office."'

'Past us?' queried Santha.

There was the putt-putt, whirr of a tractor in a field, and someone on a bicycle scribbled by.

'I will shout, *ne?*' Santha said at the counter.

Martine was torn as to who and how to ask. She ran down the road to the house with its three connected dwellings. She touched the treetrunks with her palms, knelt and pressed her face to the chain-link fence. She thought she saw something – *The beginning of my birthdate?* – carved into the breadfruit tree.

She called, 'Mohan!'

Humidity blotted up her voice. There was a cricket bat against the log store. Now she was sure. She began to imagine other clues, disregarding the forward march of time, disregarding all those years elapsed. *Cricket stumps: weren't there were some abandoned by the well back there? And a plastic hoop-and-post game scattered in the playground at the school?*

From a lane overhung by trees an elderly man with his sarong hitched into his waistband slowly made his way towards them, a bundle of straw on his back.

'*Ayubowan,*' Martine said as he drew level.

The man halted with a wariness in his eyes. Santha suggested he walked away and had a word with him. Martine reluctantly agreed.

They talked for a while, then Santha's gestures got emphatic, and the man was shouting hoarsely and poking him in the chest with a bony finger. Then they were both laughing, and Santha shrugged and came away.

He blinked as he reached Martine, 'I am sorry. There is no one in this village called Liyanage. I gave the names, the occupations, the ages, the mother who, sadly, died. No family as you describe them has lived here in recent times, *ne*?' Foreseeing Martine's doubts he added, 'He is an old man, but without problems of the mind, because I tested this tactfully. And he has been here all his life. I do not see that he would lie because, forgive me, I did offer him money.' For the first time, he frowned as if with concern for her. 'We can ask some other people here, but...'

A version of something Martine's mother had said came back to her.

'About Mohan. You were just looking in the wrong place.'

30 The field

(Field: The oval or circular area of play in cricket, consisting of infield and outfield around the rectangular pitch)

April 2012

Santha checked with the two farmers in the paddy, and the mother of the baby who eventually emerged, surprised to see anyone, at the Post Office. The old man seemed to be right: no Mohan Liyanage, or his family, had in living memory dwelt there.

On their return towards town, Santha parked at Matale District Secretariat, the low building surrounded by palm forest that held the electoral lists. As a local he was more likely to have success, so Martine lurked in the office lobby. She watched him being charming or overbearing as required, unexpectedly assiduous.

An official eventually brought thick files, and Martine saw the men discuss them for a while, but when he walked her back to the van Santha said, still in his animated state, 'Many Liyanages.' He expanded, 'It would take long to find the family from the names. Perhaps with an appointment, in a few weeks...'

They also called at the tall, pink, modern Matale Registry of Births, Marriages and Deaths.

Re-entering the van, Santha repeated, flashing his white-toothed smile, 'Many Liyanages.'

Martine couldn't think about defeat.

On the journey back to town Santha lapsed into thoughtful and morose.

Martine broke the silence. 'Where shall we try next?'

'He couldn't live beyond Raththota,' he said at last.

The following day Martine went back to the Tourism Bureau in the KCC, to be helped this time by a dithering girl with a coral manicure.

'Could I trace Mohan through his schooling?'

'Oh, well, I... It is the school holidays. You could have visited the Ministry of Education, if you had only written in advance. Some people could not trust you otherwise.' The girl hesitated. 'We sometimes have problems. People could become, ah, unfriendly or take advantage over you. And on your side...' She coloured darker. 'Oh, how can I say? A few foreign ladies come looking for boys of a younger age, isn't it. "Beach boys", so we say.'

Martine thought of Damion, Garey, Kumar, Ravi, Johnnie and other memorable boys at school, of the fine line she'd never crossed.

'Mohan's friend once met a boy, Pieter, at the British Council. Could there be a membership register?' The girl didn't know, but scribbled out the British Council address. Martine persisted, 'And Victoria's Secret? Where his sister used to work.'

The girl perked up. 'Ah! Now this... It's on Pallekele Industrial Estate.' She marked it 'V.S.' on Martine's map.

'Also,' said Martine. 'Small World, the charity. It doesn't have a phone number here, I suppose?'

It didn't, just as Sandra Gearing in London had told her; and Sandra hadn't armed her with any aid contacts on the ground. Martine had emailed, but the woman hadn't replied.

Martine texted or emailed her mother and Jonas at intervals. They were concerned for her, but fine. The days passed without a word from Sandra Gearing.

Next, Martine and Santha tried the British Council in the middle of Kandy. Stepping out of the lift on the third floor, they were among the shelves of a modern library. Santha approached the desk clerk, introducing Martine as a British teacher. The young woman disappeared to find her boss, who gave Martine his sole, birdlike attention.

Martine said, 'I'm trying to find someone local. He had a

friend called Cruz who came here, at least once. And Cruz saw a boy called Pieter here, Sinhalese, adopted. Have you got records we could see? Of membership? Or attendance?'

The man smiled at her. 'What year please?'

Martine showed the letter. '1988.'

His face shaded. 'A long time. We were in a different building then. And I was not yet working.' He shook Martine's hand. 'Sorry, we could not have papers from so long.'

As an antidote to what appeared the Council's bland cross-cultural condescension, Martine persuaded Santha to a trip to the public library, although he warned, 'No good, *ne*?'

On the ground floor, locals were reading newspapers, staff mounting cuttings at wooden tables and students absorbing tomes in panelled booths. Upstairs were texts behind glass, some written in the ancient way on palm leaves, many about the origins of Sri Lanka. Book-dazed women librarians stared.

Martine approached a woman of flitting movements in a blouse printed with butterflies. 'I'm looking for records of a family, of someone who was a boy in the 80s.'

The woman said, 'Very sorry. We have no records like that here. Please, however, take my card.'

Thilangani, her name was, her card embossed with astrological symbols. European science dismissed astrology. As much as astronomy, it was a lunar domain. But it never occurred to Martine to look for Mohan through astrology, through Thilangani; instead, Thilangani transferred herself, an exclaiming female butterfly, to Martine's nightly hallucinations featuring the Esala Perahera and the Queen's Hotel.

From the beginning, to Santha's disapproval, Martine wouldn't eat at tourist hotels, the Pizza Hut or KFC. Instead they used the eating houses of the Kandy alleys or pulled into roadside cool spots. The two sat opposite munching curries, glugging bottled drinks, sifting through the letters and her laptop notes.

She couldn't make Santha out. Whenever they discussed a possible avenue for the search his face brightened and he looked pumped up, his swollen lip jutting like a child's; when they reached a sticking point, he got taciturn, the shadows darkening like bruises under his eyes. He took pills daily. His illness might be depression, she supposed. Once or twice, she thought he was going to cry.

They were together from breakfast till late evening.

Over a bitter gourd curry one day she said, 'You're a moody sod.'

From out of his money belt he flung her a photo of himself drawing a woman towards the lens of the camera. Two people laughing by a fountain. Martine guessed that in some sense he'd lost her, but something about his manner stopped her from probing.

Often at Hilda's kitchen table, Martine found Vijitha the astronomer and his wife, the woman still stubbornly speaking Sinhala, Vijitha indulging her instructions to adjust her chair or polish her glasses or spoon more curds and treacle into her dish. He seemed to enjoy being tyrannised. Unwillingly, Martine rehearsed Charlie's phrase again: the imperialism of need.

'You're most welcome to visit our home,' he told Martine. 'I've built an observatory. I can show you what I've been studying.'

Hilda translated, tactfully, when his wife said, finger wagging, 'It would be better if Vijitha taught you some Sinhala.'

One evening of another frustrating day, Martine took up Vijitha's offer. In the tuk-tuk, unusual in bright violet, she had her head in her laptop notes. The house was modern, picture-windowed, open plan. Lights sparkled from the lake and town below. The moon was almost full. She saw it over the black stencil of the hills. She was suddenly conscious of it again, after all those years, imagining it awaiting her through Vijitha's telescope.

The wife issued Vijitha with a command in clipped Sinhala, Martine making out 'Jack Daniels.'

They drank and made lopsided chit-chat, Martine and Vijitha in English, his wife in her chosen language, which he translated. Vijitha was eager to show off his observatory, but the wife delayed him and Martine. 'These are for you.'

Grandly, she flourished a collection of handwritten recipes and a book of folktales with a picture of some bearded sage on the cover – Mahadenamutta, a comic fool from Sri Lankan culture. The recipes were on a hundred different papers in many different hands, all in Sinhala. The gifts seemed more than generous: a wild imposition, almost.

Martine said, '*Bohoma stuthiyi,*' thanks so much, 'but these must be precious to you. And I won't be able to read them.'

The wife snorted and said something, and Vijitha unashamedly translated, 'More precious than your Shakespeare and your Dickens.' He smiled indulgently as she continued. 'These embody our history, our traditions. Passing things on. Oracy, storytelling. My wife says that for us, word of mouth is first and foremost.'

Martine imagined some grandfather figure handing down the Mahadenamutta tales to the Liyanage children by firelight, not on paper but in words and gestures, Mohan restless and giggling. She pulled herself up, confused: *But I hoped for a richer literacy for him.*

Vijitha wondered mildly, 'Literature isn't a competition, is it?'

Martine observed silently, *Even while making her point, the wife was handing me the spoken written down.* But it wouldn't be fair to argue the universal truths of great literature with someone who to her seemed rude and stupid.

Down the garden, under the dome of his observatory, Vijitha showed her Saturn, the moon's near neighbour, that night almost as close as it could be. He explained gravitational lenses, how a powerful galaxy could bend other light towards earth, out of its natural path. His obsession with deflection at once stepped into her dreams.

She also saluted the moon, privately, through his telescope. Vijitha saw her interest.

He said, 'Out in the countryside on the island, away from light, the moon casts shadows.'

Suddenly she wanted to see moon shadows. For so long now, she'd overlooked the moon.

Martine wore Santha into conceding that, even in the holidays, some staff might be in schools. Mohan's scholarship and other clues meant that he must have gone to a national school, they decided. They could try talking their way in. They could ask to see old registers; they could narrow down Mohan's past school by demanding which took part, as Mohan's letters had reported, in a cricket fixture called the Battle of the Brave.

Martine came as far as the gates of the first school. From his shelter the old eyes of the caretaker, arms like twigs, scrutinised Santha as he disappeared towards the offices, then kept watch on Martine as she pressed her face to the fence on the drive. Buildings like lowrise flats with walkway balconies hugged the slopes. They had peeling paintwork, multi-coloured. A vast glazed Buddha dominated the playground. She imagined termtime, a dim seethe of activity behind the classroom grilles, and when a bell rang, boys in bright blue shorts or long white trousers spurting down the paths, idling by latrines and in the gardens.

Santha emerged. 'No old registers. And the deputy headmaster says that there is no Battle of the Brave, not anywhere in Kandy.'

Martine couldn't believe it. Was Mohan guilty of fantasy, even though he said he wasn't?

At the next few schools, staff became aware of her, and the dubious phrase 'beach boys' hung in the air, and Santha's efforts didn't go well. Visiting schools after that, he convinced her to wait out of sight, in a café or a cool spot. He dropped his account of Martine's search in favour of fictions of estranged families, longlost friends or cousins, a quest for himself, not her. But the teachers stayed unhelpful and suspicious.

He walked Martine through the subway to the market. She pretended interest in the blunt brown wood apples, the missile heads of plantain buds, offal-dark, and the heaped-up rice in many shades, while he plugged the traders for any farming contacts they might have, as he put it, 'from beyond Raththota'. Some wouldn't answer and some laughed, finding something funny that he couldn't explain to Martine.

While they were out, in a fever to achieve something, she bought a *thovil* mask and several carvings, some bolts of local fabric, two batik hangings and a bark bookmark that, the stallholder claimed, had been crushed by the paw of a leopard.

Back at Hilda's, Martine plugged on. 'The next lead is Victoria's Secret. Upeksha works there.'

'*Used* to work there, *ne*?' Santha stressed.

His discouraged mood was back, a glint of judgement in his eye.

Martine had bought an ovoid fruit that she now knew instantly as a breadfruit. It would soon be Easter back in England. She still shuddered inwardly, *All those eggs*. The yellow-green, barnacled body oozed sap onto the waxed tablecloth.

Hilda flitted about with cutlery and crockery, producing a chunk of the creaming fruit set on a sprigged Worcestershire plate.

She apologised. 'It's very ripe.'

The chunk smelled sickly-sweet, and Martine couldn't eat it.

'Victoria's Secret,' Martine probed. 'You know something about it.'

Hilda answered, 'It's on Pallekele Industrial Estate. The girls work hard.' It was early evening. 'They will leave work around seven to eight o'clock.'

More expansive than usual, she told her what she'd heard of the enticing wages, and the state-of-the-art machines used to sew the lingerie.

Martine urged, 'Let's go,' but Santha shook his head in his despondent way.

'Wasting time. Email the VS in their office, America or London.'

'I did that the other night,' said Martine. 'But there are e-forms to fill in. People will need to check them, and probably ask for more. It'll all take too long.'

He shook his head again. 'You still haven't been to the Temple. Or the Botanical Gardens. Or seen the dancing at the Cultural Centre.'

Martine thought, *I'm not interested in the travel-brochure interiors of Kandy.*

She said, 'I might go to the Gardens,' although she felt they were an unlikely route to Mohan. She still saw him somewhere in the wild, waiting and beckoning. She scolded, 'Don't treat me like a tourist.'

Santha drove her to Victoria's Secret. The industrial park certainly wasn't for tourists: a child's playmat of tarmac road and corrugated iron and concrete structures under orange lamps, like any trading estate. It said nothing to Martine of Mohan's landscape. They found the particular unit, its sign flaring under a white security light.

She imagined how Charlie would have scoffed, 'Cultural imperialism!', and she'd have said, 'But if that's what they want...' and he'd have countered, 'We overwhelm these people into wanting what we want...' *Us and them, the great divide,* she thought. Despite her best intentions, she felt the gap herself. And she'd have had to agree with Charlie about the architectural sameness, the locals' seduction by the technology, which would have been imported, the effect of global brands. A kind of levelling, but the ugly kind, the wrong kind. She thought, *You've probably got to lose beauty to know it.*

Santha's eyes glittered at the line of female silhouettes now filtering from the unit. *Maybe reminding him of the woman he's lost,* she speculated. She mused, *Beauty is there in what we see's not there for us. Or is that love?*

She strode ahead of Santha to the light pooling the exit. Spotting them, a thickset man stepped in front of the women, cutting them off with a halting gesture. A belligerent-looking older woman grasped him. Both had bunches of keys.

Martine set off in English, rambling slightly, about a worker, a girl from the countryside who... 'Upeksha Liyanage,' she finally got out.

She read the letter references from her laptop. '...her face is Fair'N'Beautiful. She has a ring with a golden stone.'... 'She has many sarees and jeans.'

How little they are to go on, she thought, feeling ridiculous.

The workers in skirts and jeans, sporting necklaces and earrings, were wandering away.

Some headed for scooters where a cluster of men was waiting.

One girl stayed, stumbling into English. 'How is she? We miss her stories.'

Santha's eyes were suddenly flashing. 'Stories?'

Another seamstress laughed and bit her lip. All at once Martine was burning, sweating fountains.

She contradicted the first girl, 'No, I mean I'm *looking* for...'

Their supervisor intervened. 'Upeksha... Liyanage? ... doesn't work here, I'm afraid.'

'But she used to?'

'She never came back,' said the first girl.

'No girl with that name has ever worked here,' the woman keyholder snapped.

The man made a helpless gesture with his hands. 'Could I

take your details?'

The woman stared at him meaningfully. 'She isn't here,' she said firmly. She turned to Santha. '*Kanatuii*, sorry. Our ladies must get home.'

As Santha walked Martine to the van, he said, 'If Anupama could tell stories, who could not?'

31 Falling from the bridge

April 2012

At the end of that week of failures it was Easter weekend back in England, another reason for Sandra Gearing not to answer Martine's emails. Santha had been busy using an acquaintance at the Media Centre, but reported back to Martine that they refused to give contact details of Esala Perahera performers, to him or anyone else.

Martine hadn't given the Bakehouse on Dalada Street, as she thought some Kandyan imitation of a French patisserie, a second glance. But that Saturday Santha and her new astronomer friend Vijitha reminded her that things aren't always what they seem. They led her past glass counters of pastries over the faux marble floor and upstairs, through a western-style bar. There was a crowded room at the back. Someone brought them chairs. They sat packed in, Martine trying to ease her suddenly aching spine. It was noisy with people shouting. There were more voices yattering through loudspeakers. Martine still felt especially hot. She mentally catalogued her dead ends, counting and discounting them, vowing new researches – tomorrow, if not today.

She stopped and tried to tune in to the amplified soundtrack. '...the second and final Test between Sri Lanka and England at the P Sara Oval in Colombo... Sri Lanka took the first Test. In the first innings of the second... 275, largely thanks to Jayawardene... England, with Pietersen in dangerous form, were 460 all out.... Sri Lanka are 218 for 6, 33 runs in the lead, but with only 4 wickets, a little perilous my friends...'

The voice of Mohan joined her. '*One side is the elephants, rabbits and rats and other hungry animals, the pests and the diseases. The other side is the govigayas like us... All must eat.*'

All ears took in the CSN TV commentary; hundreds of eyes followed two teams in white moving across a green sward on a screen high on the wall. The other walls were covered in cartoons, signatures, messages in biro and felt tip. Sports lovers' graffiti. There was a kite of the Australian flag pinned high, with the legend 'Wavey Navy'. A Barmy Army pinboard, thick with drinking and dancing photos.

Vijitha brought them wine and beer. 'This is your sport?'

Martine said, 'Spectating. Never played. But right now...'

'We should be out there looking, *ne*?' Santha finished for her. She gulped her wine. 'He's somewhere.'

A flush engulfed her. *I can't be drunk already*, she thought.

'Pay me nothing for today.' Santha studied her, shaking his leonine head. He asked with aggression, 'Why are you really looking?'

Martine suddenly felt too weary to excavate her reasons.

'...and Mathews! ... Oh! Dropped!' boomed from the speakers, amid a roar from the room.

'Are you all right?' said Santha. 'You are dark red, *ne*?'

Martine said, 'At this rate, we won't find him.'

'Swann bowls to Jayawardene, there's a most spiteful turn on that ball, it hits him on the gloves, to Cook! My friends. The captain is gone.' ... Martine tried to focus. 'Now Prasanna must... It's another sweeping right-hander from Swann... It's around his legs, oh no... Another wicket down.'

Out of nowhere, Santha was taking her elbow, making their apologies to Vijitha.

He sounded angry. 'Come.'

They got to the van, and he bundled her in, and then he was taking her up and out of Kandy, into the hills. She pieced together that much, and was grateful. She had an impression of crossing a river and re-crossing. She heard Santha pointing out a blink of the Victoria Dam she remembered mention of in the letters and later, a vast waterfall that briefly made her feel better. The astonishing smoothness of the road. She felt drugged, unnaturally tired.

The van took a near U-turn to the left. The surface of the narrow track jolted her back to full consciousness, grinding and twisting them upwards. Melon light crushed its way through broken leaf jigsaws at the windows. At last there were waterfalls gushing by. She ignored scraps of tea plantations, weedy and incongruous. They lurched over uncountable bridges, passing the gurgle of streams. Sometimes a shack or two, washing drying on the turf between them, interrupted Martine's bleary illusion of an untouched world.

She felt drunk, and more than usually hot. She polished off a bottle of chilled water.

'Where are we going?'

Santha grunted, 'It's as if the Portuguese went to Kotte.'

A zigzag ride; a roundabout route. He'd used this locals' grumble before. He seemed to resent the journey, as if he hadn't thought of it himself.

She repeated hazily, 'Where are we going?'

Santha grunted, 'Where you want to be. Not there, *ne*?' He shook a fist of dismissal at the so-called Deanstone Information Centre, a compact building advertising rooms for trekkers.

A wizened woman plucking at her front hedge. Sun-dried others swimming out of forest with bundles of firewood. The ferns that Martine had somehow needed, at last, at last, sprouting among the boulders of the waterfalls. Shimmering lily ponds. Vegetables in rows. Cloths over picket fences. And even there, in the Shangri-la wilderness, the odd latrine.

Hours seemed to pass.

'The Knuckles side of the mountains,' Santha muttered.

Martine didn't want the Knuckles side of the mountains, hanging onto the places they'd just been through.

They reached a spot between the lush and forested slopes where the track looked like a bridge with buckling bends at either end, the land falling or rising sharply on all sides. Santha parked on a verge, and Martine toppled out. A black and white butterfly flipped past. The layered hiss of crickets, and water falling somewhere. The ranges around them vivid green.

'Mohan Mohan Mohan,' Santha said.

He stretched out his arms and walked away from her, towards a ruined building, a sort of dead end at the abrupt track bend.

There was sharp pain behind Martine's eyes. 'Where?'

She followed, and he stopped, snapping, 'Not with me. With you.'

She didn't understand. There was a species of pink orchid in the grass, and outgrowths of dishevelled orange daisies. She knew she should have known the Latin names, but couldn't at once call them to mind. Around her flocked noiseless dragonflies with bodies of burnt orange. They came in swarms, sun metallising their amber wings. She thought, *Mohan would know what kind they are*; then the species name came back to her from some time during her fact-finding daydreams: *Asian groundlings*.

She was so hot it made her ache. She doubled up for a moment. When she straightened, she couldn't see Santha. The ruin, on the far bend, looked landed from outer space. Concrete, 1960s. Roofless, with unfilled windows and doors. She tottered over the road bridge and stepped inside, into a corridor with sky, and empty oblongs giving onto the view. The view was dizzying, vertiginous.

Santha appeared. 'One of your surveyors found this place.' He smiled. 'Yet it's still not on GPS.'

His arms were folded. There were torn political posters high on the wall behind him.

Her brain was fuddled. 'The house?'

In a corner of derelict floor stood a battered chair, an egg-yolk yellow pod on a stand. Gratefully she dropped into it, longing to sleep for weeks.

'Corbets Gap. Named after Corbet, one of your British.'

Martine said, 'I don't see why we're here.'

'You talk about the boy, then you talk about water and the

mountains.' Santha sounded mournful. 'You don't enjoy yourself in Kandy, see the sights.' He paused. 'Maybe here is what you want. Or may find.'

There was a stabbing behind Martine's blurred vision. 'What does that mean?'

'I did,' he said. 'I thought I wanted my wife and that she wanted me.'

Martine tried to follow his logic. 'The woman in the picture?'

He shook his head. 'That's her sister.'

'What happened?'

'I married young. We didn't know each other. I imagined my wife like Sita, the Hindu goddess, *ne*? Fertile. Fertile with ideas, not just for children. I thought she was good for me. She thought I was a husband who had run off with the anklet of a princess.'

'I don't know what...'

'I mean, she hoped I was a somewhat bad man, like a film, a rebel. And richer.'

'Mohan has nothing to do with Corbets Gap,' Martine said.

Santha continued, 'What she liked was to shop and stay at home, reading *Ghazal in the Moonlight*.'

Martine glimmered with understanding. 'You mean you were both disappointed.'

'My wife talked about her sadness to my cousin who plays the piano in Pizza Hut. At last my cousin's husband told me this.'

'And her sister?'

'My wife and I used to go walking with friends taking photographs of the country, *ne*? Her sister sometimes came, and once when we came here, she was with us. We talked, and she said she knew something was unhappy, and suddenly I wished for her. I found out what I wanted.'

'Did you...?'

'My wife left me. But this sister was married. It was not honourable to go with her.' Santha shrugged. 'I still like this place for helping me to see.'

321

'Like' seemed not enough for Santha's story. Martine pivoted the yellow seat away from him. She felt fiery and exhausted. She scrabbled at her blouse, then her bra, and at once it fell into her lap without Santha seeing, without her knowing what she was doing.

'With the few buses, and the roads, he must live in Raththota, or even closer to Kandy,' Santha said.

Martine said, 'But at the low level of Raththota there's no paddy.'

'There is another idea,' Santha said, more gently. 'A charity might invent letters. They might not be real.'

Martine's brain dipped and dived, rebuffing that too.

She said thirstily, 'There are the photos, the drawings, his news, his mother dying, his father's problems, all that. No one would go to those lengths.'

She felt Santha coming closer. 'It made you interested. It kept you giving money. They could make up the story and send the same to many people abroad, *ne*?'

She smelt Santha right behind her, again that odour of something growing, something crushed, a confusion of saplike vigour and the landscape. 'I thought you believed the letters.'

'Well, then he lived in Raththota,' Santha said with determination. 'Or one of the little settlements that are now part of Raththota.'

'That ugly town with no paddy.'

Their argument was going round in circles.

'He won't live anywhere else.'

The chair was turning, dizzying Martine. Santha was turning it. She registered the turmeric-bright daisy, held out as if to stroke her, before his frown and the pink eyes flaring down at her undress.

He backed away. 'Are you...? You are ill, *ne*?'

She felt as if fire engines should come. Rivulets coursed between her little, flaccid breasts. She thought, *No more mechanical, London life. No tubes and trains and escalators and lifts, doors closing, boats, planes, crowds shifting in interiors. Here's the opposite, my opposite. No more containment. All interiors blown open or away. Stillness. Waterfalls and ferns nearby; here, crickets and dragonflies. Only a cool, moist vapour is missing here from the exotic landscape I wanted.* Understanding surfaced for a moment. *Is it this that I've been seeking, more than Mohan?* Then it slipped away. As she tipped sideways, lost what was happening, she skewed what Santha had said, made of it the best she could.

'He won't live anywhere else': *But that can't be Raththota,* thought Martine. *Mohan isn't anywhere but at this spot, just here.*

32 No man's land

(No man's land: An area of the pitch where there are no fielders, and where the ball travels, often when mistimed)

April-December 2012

Things happened slowly and quickly, as so many crises do. Santha got Martine to a local hospital. Martine had dengue fever.

'It's nothing but wait, isn't it. You'll either die or recover fully,' the doctor said evenly, prescribing pills, and left.

She lay in bed there, then at Hilda's, with Santha a constant visitor.

Later she'd remember little. Sleeping, jugs of lime juice. And the dreams. The colour turquoise everywhere. Standing in the dock with a partner she didn't know for the crime of having twins, under threat of execution. The moon, throwing a mountain silhouette over her bed. When feverishly awake she tried to prime herself with images, possibilities that could finish off the dream at the Queen's Hotel. She couldn't, as if the doctor had prescribed against it. Sleep rubbed out any sense of failure. When she began to think straight, she craved baked beans on toast in Brandon Towers.

She slept on the plane ride home, nudging open the door of her flat with an arm that weighed like lead.

One of her answerphone messages dated from just after her outward flight. 'Martine, this is Sandra Gearing. I tried your mobile but no joy and I think I must have your email slightly wrong and, sorry, you told me, but I can't remember exactly when you're going. We've found Mohan. He's looking forward to meeting you. Please, give Gay in my office a ring. I'm away on a long holiday over Easter. The number's…'

Martine couldn't help recalling her adoption efforts, because this was more bungled bureaucracy. And the mix-up was thin and feeble, without the drama befitting what had been at stake. Dismay was like drunkenness, she discovered: there was a stage where you couldn't feel any more dismayed. She'd peaked on fury, horror, frustration, misery. She trailed a bin liner from the kitchen into the second bedroom. She emptied the soft toy pigs and china pigs and the pig badges and flying pig mobiles and snowshakers from the two desk drawers that, over the years, these gifts had expanded into. She looked at the mountain of them, couldn't put them in the bag. She crawled off to bed dry-eyed. From there, she rang her headteacher and resigned.

The next day she phoned Sandra Gearing, but she wasn't yet back from holiday.

Her colleague Gay was discreetly apologetic. 'If there was any miscommunication, we're sorry. But Sandra was looking for Mohan in addition to an extremely heavy workload. These things happen.'

'But do they though? But do they?'

Martine pictured a man in his mid-thirties, his face fluttering like a tobacco leaf, not handsome but with something winning about him, yoyoing from a chair outside a small, painted house, glancing repeatedly at a watch. Maybe a wife and children, washing on the line, a vegetable patch, a log store, special-occasion curry and milk rice rolling their smells out from a dark interior where there was stowed a bundle of letters.

'Can you give me a contact address *now*, so that I can write and apologise?'

'Sorry. We don't give out personal data. But of course we'll send on something, if it's suitable.'

Martine had to assure Mohan that her no-show wasn't her fault. 'I want to say what happened.'

The woman wouldn't budge. 'We'll forward it, as long as it's OK.'

So the office would censor a message that even hinted at Small World's failure.

Before Martine had written, an email arrived, composed in perfect English.

'To: **info@smallworld.org.uk**
Sent: 16 April 2012 00:45
FW: From: Mohan Liyanage
Subject: Martine not here please send
There should be more greetings. Because this time, it doesn't work to call you 'Dear'. So I call you Martine. Till now I've never once called you Martine: just Martine, I mean to say. Both points are significant. Please notice.

'I could ask why you have done this – or not done this.

'I could start, as I used to, "My question is..."

'But I already guess the answer. You have done so many things I'll never do you probably think you can do or not do anything. The neglect of me, a child to you, will always seem as little as a child.

'Picture a simple threshold. To either side, a water bowl; Sri Lankan lilies of the water, white with yellow centres, floating in them, waiting for our meeting. Still floating now? No one cares. I don't see them; you don't see them; neither of us is there.

'Your letters made strange sense sometimes, but now I think they may not have sent right meaning. The words you sent, aiming to be honest, perhaps were corrupted, dishonest all along. They may have abandoned me long since. In which case, this goodbye is overdue.

'I could be wrong. Light works in such a way that our sky looks blue and our breadfruit, bright green although they are not. My sister taught me that long since. So maybe it was not that you deceived me. Maybe it was in translation that your meaning was spilt, as if one person were passing an overfull bucket of water to another, and they onto me, another, so that precious drops fell.

'On my side, I was truthful; I think I was. Then again, perhaps I was not. Perhaps I pretended that you were something to me that you weren't, and from that falsehood, dreams began that shouldn't ever have started. Perhaps I'm angry with myself.

Anger at yourself is hard to bear.

'Anyway, either you lost me or I lost you – or both; more than our bodies, more than the outsides of what we are: somewhere inside us, our substance leached away.

'This final time I strive to spill no drops. I say, how dare you neglect me, fail me, lose me? Just when I thought I'd got you, why weren't you there – not least to help me with the fact that you weren't there?

'I wasn't safe with you at all.

'My world you'll never know now: for you it won't exist. My family is well. My sisters are well. My brother is well.

'I'll live on without you. And that's fine.'

Martine went back to bed and stayed there. The letters were in her bedroom, just tipped out of her luggage. She delved for the cricket photo, the latest one of Mohan. She tried to convince herself, *I did meet him, in letters and photos. Maybe even in the flesh: some glimpsed railway worker; that stallholder who sold me the leopard's bark; one of the smiling staff at the Kandyan hotel; the driver of a tuk-tuk. Then there was the invisible Mohan of that strange journey with Santha.* But the thought of near misses didn't help, and she lapsed into her disillusioned self.

Martine's mother's angina was back, but she and the doctors were doubtful about a second operation. Jonas, at Harrow Weald, was trying to stop Mum doing too much. Speaking to them by phone, Martine tried to rub her Sri Lankan disappointment from her voice. She knew she couldn't keep it up in person, so didn't visit.

Days passed. She had to resolve things with Mohan, in some sense have the last word.

She laboured over an email, striving, as Small World wanted, to put aside blame. 'I was just about to write to you… Please, give me a chance to speak… I did look for you when I got there….'

She sent it on to Small World.

An answer arrived, this time in Sinhala, with an English translation.

'To: **gay.reed@smallworld.org.uk**
Sent: 24 April 2012 08:45
FW: From: Mohan Liyanage
Subject: Please send to Miss Martine
Dear Miss Martine
Thanks for yr email.
'I C. What a pity it did not work.
'Did U take a plane or did U run away and take a boat then a bus then a tuk-tuk?! Did U bring me a big present?! (LOL)
'I hope U R well.
'Perhaps another time??!! L8r allig8r.
Mohan'

The first email was the message that Martine judged that she deserved. It punished her, so it must be true. *The second,* she decided, *is too cruel, even for me. It mustn't be Mohan; it surely can't be.*

Its effect on her gave her a dread of more unpleasantness, from Mohan or anyone else. She began to doubt some things, then many things, then everything. *How convenient,* she anguished, *that they only found Mohan once I'd got back to London – maybe because he doesn't exist at all.* She stacked the letters round her on the hot pillows and re-read them, poring over each piece of Mohan's news and local detail, checking for consistency and plausibility, veering from reassurance to outraged disbelief.

The words of Vijitha's wife now taunted her. 'For us, word of mouth is first and foremost.'

Perhaps she should have agreed: any written word was flawed. Ironically, a view shared by the email she preferred, the one of the two she was more inclined to believe in.

In Martine's mind, her sleeping dreams of working in Sri

Lanka and the Esala Perahera seen from a hotel window began to blur with what had actually happened in Sri Lanka. Now, when she dreamed about night-time processions, or a breadfruit overripening, or a dragonfly, she couldn't distinguish which came from before her trip, which after, which from her net surfing, and which from events. She wondered now, *How much were Mohan's character, his desires, and how much my projections? Who has this boy-man, all these long years, been?*

Somewhere deep, Martine began to comprehend that shame and disappointment had confused in her an email fact with an email fiction. That Mohan's first email was a figment of her distraught imagination, and never came to her. Tyrants, colonisers, obsessive lovers, domineering parents, correspondents of all kinds can be at their most creative when they feel rebuked or guilty. Martine had conjured the email up: its blame and sheer panache came from her mind's lurking side, her poetry. It wasn't even in her inbox, if she'd checked; slowly it receded into a fable in her mind.

The real one, with its 'L8r allig8r', wouldn't recede. She didn't re-read it, in fact ignored all emails and screened phone calls, heart banging when she heard her landline's strains of *Für Elise*. And yet she was unable to delete the email, let it go. It offered hope that Mohan might exist. One day she made a sub-folder and slipped it in like a cutting into a pot, as if it might one day propagate into something she could face. The letters she meanwhile heaped into the big grey cardboard box where they have ever since stayed. She didn't notice for a while, but Mohan's whispers in her ear had also died.

Days passed. Spring rain and winds whipped the clumps of trees far below her tower, lashing her neighbours with their shopping bags and the teenage gangs indoors. Insomnia, nightmares. She couldn't go back to Sri Lanka again: she was all out of stamina, even enough to feel disappointed. And her friends were here, and her mother was ill, and... Turning her head on the pillow one way she saw the shelved niche with her books, the Lankan recipes, and Mahadenamutta, the comic fool; turning the other, she found in her mind's eye her mother, starey-eyed, unvisited by her daughter, Mohan's recrimination in another form.

Martine had restlessness like an illness, intermittent but intense. In the hyperactive spells, she set about her retirement paperwork or did deep cleaning in the flat. One day she went back to her guest bedroom, stuffed the rubbish bag with the pigs and hauled it to a bin on the estate. In periods of deadness, she watched sport on TV, any kind where people lobbed with force, twisted and shoved, broke into a run over a demarcated landscape, disciplined their violence. Standing close to the set, wanting and yet not wanting to join in. Or she lay in bed and ran through her mental index: Damion, Garey, Kumar, Ravi, Johnnie, Kieran, Bobby, Tate, Mohan. She still had an ache for children like them, all boys.

Her historic claustrophobia worsened, even with the door cracked open. Through sleepless eyes, she glared at her furniture. It suddenly seemed angular and unconsoling, circumscribing and oversized. She hefted chairs and tables and desks and dressing tables and the TV and her bookcases and the Canterbury around her bedrooms and sitting room. She stacked them against the walls as if the corners, like chimneys, would draw them up as smoke. Some offending pieces she exiled to the balcony. She laboured through a day, a night and most of another day. She decided to sell some items, but couldn't work out which. For the moment, she replaced them where they'd been.

One stormy morning she turned out her clothes and jewellery. She remembered her armlet, unworn for years except in Sri Lankan fantasy. She couldn't find the pale-green padded box. She turned the flat over again. It was in an empty Tampax carton in the shower room. When she found it, she stood listening to the thunder and put it back.

Phone calls with Harrow Weald were hard. With her bridges burnt – love, work, Mohan – Martine talked to her ailing mother with edited honesty.

'How are you?'

'Fine.'

'But how are *you*?'

'Things could be worse.'

Her mother knew what hadn't happened in Sri Lanka, and Martine saw the end of her parent coming, but how could they admit how bad things were? Communication was a pontoon swinging over concealment and shifting ground on either side.

Late one morning, when Martine was chasing sleep, there was a pounding on her door. Jonas pushed into her lobby, peeling off a dripping raincoat, fleece and sweater. Pills alone didn't work, so she was trying to stupefy herself by keeping the heating on high.

'*Mom is sick*! Deal!' He glared.

There was a mottled bloom to his face, as if changing between happy and sad so often had confused it. Although he was living at Harrow Weald, he and Pearl were still together.

Martine was flustered. 'How's Pearl?'

Pearl was just as screwed up, these days about what she was doing to Jonas, whether she was now screwing him up.

'You mean how's Mom? She's in the car.'

Martine started. 'You can't leave her out there.'

She flung on a bathrobe and swept with Jonas into the lift, not seeing that he'd shut her door behind her.

Rain was drilling at the roads of the estate. In the back of the car, its engine idling, a swathed figure leaned towards her. Head down against the weather, Martine struggled with the door. She tried to help her out, but was gripped by a fist and yanked inside. In the driving seat, Jonas was already starting off. Struggling to climb out again, she found the grip didn't feel like her mother's.

'What d'you think you're playin' at, Mar?' Pearl accused.

It was Pearl who reached across her and slammed the door.

As they accelerated away, Pearl, tight-lipped, unwrapped from her disguise. Jonas kissed Pearl and dropped her off on the north side of the river, and the journey continued in near-silence. Martine slept much of the way from a kind of relief, responsibility snatched from her. By the time she and Jonas had got to Harrow Weald, she was indifferent to her kidnap.

Entering the house in sodden slippers, she found it changed. Its associations with too much human shuttling had gone. Her mother was as stationary as Jonas could persuade her to be; room shuttling had become the role of the furniture. To stop her climbing the stairs, he'd tried it in various configurations. The dining room was for now the old woman's bedroom, the table and chairs and sideboard, by Bill Kidmay's graces, in store. So that Jonas could work part-time and devote himself to the patient, the latest mutt was at a neighbour's, along with all its things.

Martine's mother was seated in the living room, not as brave-faced as Martine had hoped. The angina bouts had become recurrent, now striking even at rest.

'Darling. Sorry.' The woman threw her a pleading look.

They hugged and stayed in hold.

Martine said, 'It should be me saying that.'

When they disengaged, tears stained her mother's face.

'Even if they'd give me one, I couldn't face another op.'

'Then don't have one,' Martine said, and a piece of her fell away.

She took in this narrowed world. An automated recliner of Bill Kidmay's with a footrest seemed to swallow her mother, an alien craft among the feminine clutter. Once a day she took a turn with Bill Kidmay round the garden among the few scorched-looking rosebuds; twice a week he brought the dog to see her. A low cupboard by the recliner stored her mother's laptop, pill bottles, crossword-puzzle books and the blackbird on the acorn bough, unpicked of 'Please', reworked and nearly done. On the cupboard top, a jug of water and a saucer with crushed pill traces. The TV remote, the phone and a handful of tissues. And on her lap, the Playstation console that had become her addiction: *Apache Air Attack, Skydrift, Birds of Steel*. As they talked now, some futuristic aircraft left unmanned between the walls of the Grand Canyon suddenly erupted into flame on the TV screen. Everywhere, Martine could see defeat.

She and Jonas arranged a rota: on alternate weeks Martine moved in to Harrow, which gave him more time for Pearl and work. Martine fought down the panic for her mother, still couldn't sleep.

One day she found Mum with a book. 'Bill got it in a second-hand bookshop.'

The London Underground 1945-Now: A Post-War History. 'Now' was 1974. Shrivelled fingers reached for the bookmarked page and Verdon Haslett stared out, the back of his hand propping his chin, before a photo on his wall of one of his tube trains: Class 487 stock, English Electric.

Martine's mother thrust her the volume. 'I thought you'd like it.'

'Not now.'

'What would you like then?'

'You to feel better,' said Martine, withholding the strain from her voice.

But the woman seemed desperate to give her something, jabbing, in turn, at every knickknack crowding round her. The glass fish and Venetian bowls, the miniature gardens of cacti, vases of silk flowers, the porcelain plates on their hangers on the walls. Martine shook her head.

'There!' Her mother rose quickly and had to sit down.

She was insistent. Martine fetched the ornament she meant. A porcelain woman with a child of unspecific gender with tousled hair, the female in the long skirt of some idealised century bending to the child over a book. Grey and the palest violet, like an elongated ghost. Cheap and populist, mass produced. Martine murmured, pretending appreciation.

Mum claimed the woman looked like a teacher. 'So she could be you.'

'I don't think so.' Martine felt, *A mother.*

Ever since she'd had the thing, her mother must have seen it as the pair of them together. Now, with a full stop looming, she'd adopted a different view.

Martine carried it home. Too sentimental even for her mother, surely: it couldn't have been something that she'd bought. Martine wondered where she'd filched it from. On the internet, she found it in a range named 'A Woman's Calling', subtitled 'Teacher', but to her its motherly look overrode all else.

She never displayed the figure. She did borrow the train book later, making a print of her father for the lobby.

In October 2012, when Jonas was out shopping, Mum had a stroke while walking in the garden with Bill Kidmay. By November, the hospital had released her.

One morning on Martine's watch, her mother found she couldn't get up. From the French windows of the dining room-cum-bedroom, rosebuds and lawn lay iced in frost.

She could barely move; yet 'Love you,' she told Martine.

And with miraculous effort, turned away. At her bedside, Martine didn't move.

Through the arrangements, the funeral and afterwards, Martine fumed about Jonas. He gave her the impression he felt released; his talk had turned to America, to moving there with Pearl, as if, towards the end, he'd only been hampered by her mother.

In a flat and bleak December, Martine spent days digging through the silt of her neglected emails. In among them glinted a suggestion from her mother, dated way before she'd died.

'To: **MartineHaslett@hotmail.com**
Sent: 4 October 2012 18:42
From: **Bobbie@Haslettfamily.co.uk**
Subject: Bill's niece
Darling
Bill comes to see me often, as you know. (Lately I've found him a bit clingy, just between ourselves. They talk about letting go, but to me it doesn't feel like that, a giving in. More as if I'm reaching out somewhere more interesting, dying (!) to be adventurous in a way that Bill doesn't seem to understand.)

'Anyway Alice, your old schoolfriend, is in Australia these days, you remember. He tells me her news and I pass it on to you. But she has cousins. His eldest niece is helping with the fallout from the Haiti earthquake, another one struggling as a single mother. But he brought the middle one, Jocelyn, to see me the other day. Chatty, a bit tart.

'She runs an agency for schools with international experience programmes. It connects them with hosts willing to take care of the children during their exeats and holidays. Looking after a foreign student: couldn't that be something you might do? The address is guardians@theschoolgate.co.uk. Her surname's Teague.

'I won't mention this again. In the end, it's up to you.

All love as ever, Mum X'

Martine's mother had left her something beyond a figurine. Not the idealistic path of one niece or the rough way of the other's, but – although it's taken her all this time to admit it – a modest, more manageable way.

33 Changing ends

07:29 in the morning, and Martine's visitor arrives today, and she must get up, but her dream of the Queen's Hotel is still wrenching out of her like badly perforated paper. Today of all days, she doesn't have time to mope.

She climbs out of bed, negotiates the maternal obstacles on her floor, slings on a dressing gown. She humidifies Sancho's cage, feeds him his water jet and crickets, knocks the breadcrumbs from the breadboard through the netting at the pigeons. Then she feeds herself and drinks strong coffee till her pulse booms. She honestly can't identify her state.

Matt the painter appears at eightish to help her reassemble the spare room. They take each end of heavy objects, mistiming the lifts, teasing each other. The configuration ends up as it had to, single bed, chest of drawers, bedside table, narrow desk under small window that no one can look out of unless they stand on the wooden chair and climb from that onto the desk. The paint fumes have abated, but despite the green, it's no Enchanted Eden. Martine thinks, *Enough already. Stop wanting things so perfect.*

The Amelia Earhart scarf of her mother's, now in its frame, she also needed help with. She's already offered it up to the lobby wall, facing that office shot of her father, doubting herself about it: *How can I put Mum's picture close to his? As if they're still in opposition.* Earlier she foresaw the hammer's downforce, her horny nails scraping for tacks in the tray, the empty sound of knocking, the faffing about with twine on the back of the heavy frame, trying to level the picture, and couldn't even begin.

Now Matt coaches her through it. 'Oop-la! 't's right. Down a bit. Left a bit. Right a bit. Up a bit. Bish bosh. Looks good.'

'You've been a basinful of brilliant.' Martine pays him more than they agreed and braces herself against the pang now that he's leaving her, his tic and more, probably, shying him away from kissing her, in her night things, on one cheek.

Another boy that she may not hear from again. When he's gone she notices beyond the glass a lipstick smear on the scarf. Her black eyes squint through her varifocals. The tint is her mother's colour, not hers. She needs it closer than behind glass.

An ineffectual winter's day, cold, grey, a bit damp and lifeless. She scours the local shops for a scented plant, buys enough food for breakfast for two till Sunday and comes back to research events for the weekend, things her guest might enjoy.

She reads her texts and emails. Jocelyn Teague has had to forward her the directions to the school again because Martine seems, as if deliberately, to have lost them. From her laptop, she sends them to her printer by the breadbin.

Jonas has messaged, 'Go, Martine.'

Bernard says, 'Good luck girl.'

Claire says, 'Dogs send their very best wishes,' tongue in cheek.

Pearl snarls, 'Ooh-er, panic, gather round. What is it with you women?', a sarcastic 'No thanks' to Martine's anxious soup supper invitation the night before.

'*You* women,' Martine notes. She remembers Pearl's old text, two weeks since: 'Mar, remember what the feminine side did to *me*,' Pearl distancing herself from the very gender she has chosen. Something in Martine shifts, rising up to defend the sisterhood, but she can't antagonise the already unstable Pearl. Pearl will fly with Jonas to the States soon. Martine takes a moment to worry for them.

She showers, walks through a cloud of Eau Fraiche, then dresses in the floral smock over leggings that have been hanging pressed in her wardrobe for three days: a maternal look, she hopes. Recalling her mother's style gave her no help in that direction. Photos of Mum marching for Women's Lib in the 60s, and, with Martine, for nuclear disarmament in the 70s show her unvaryingly in plain skirts and dresses – keeping on her bra. It was soon after Jonas arrived, she remembers, that the older woman took to wearing trousers.

Last, a little makeup, fingers through her mutinous hair. Martine gives the kitchen a final sweep with the dustpan. She groans to her feet, and an adage patches together in her head, *A new broom gathers old moss*, welding the past and the hoped-for future.

In the grey day, she descends at Kennington to the Northern line. Against the smutty draught she wraps her scarf, pulls her cap over her eyes. Beyond the platform rats dodge the rails, recalling a sparrow under a train that she once puzzled over. She boards her ride, which rattles her to Finchley Central, the passengers moving zombie-like on and off, while she remembers another day when the travelling throng smiled at her in her fruit dress as if her sense of occasion was plain. She doesn't like the tube so much these days, no longer sharing its thundering sense of the definite. Today she can't tell if she's tensed in anticipation or against more disappointment. A branch line takes her to Mill Hill East. She exits the station and searches for the bus stop.

The bus takes her on for nearly a mile to a stop near the gates, the end of the long school drive. A plaque on a lion's-head pillar names the far collection of grand buildings as Addis Hall, the school. On foot the gravel approach seems long, a deserted sports field to the left, rows of winter-grizzled vegetables to the right. Mercedes and four-by-fours swish past her into the world with their gesticulating charges in the back. She's a bit late. Picking up her pace, she tells herself, *Expect nothing*.

On the shallow steps of the main porch, teenagers cluster with their bags as if still hoping to be picked for a team. A woman in a suit, her hair scraped into a bun, stalks round them with a clipboard, keeping them corraled. Some boys and girls are fiddling with papers, possibly photos of their guardians-to-be. Martine feels at a disadvantage: she has no aid with her to recognise her match.

She slows and scans their faces, especially the dark ones. The stream of cars has dried up for a while. The children shriek with laughter, manhandling each other but especially one among them, snatching at a paper, prodding it and hooting, gesturing towards Martine. It could either be harmless teasing or something more aggressive.

From their pointing, she can tell that their target is her charge. 'You do not have a car?' the target's accented voice calls out, either desperate or insolent. 'But all this luggage!' it objects.

Martine doubletakes. *My first black mark: no luxury pickup.*

'We'll manage somehow. Lovely to meet you.' She smiles and takes the steps, trying to look unfazed.

Things happen fast, introductions, an exchange of details with the Housemistress and paperwork in the hall, the actual handover. Martine registers an elfin haircut, with random tufts dyed red. An angular, dark jawline. Black jeans trailing on the ground, and a T-shirt printed with a corset, its strings half-severed by bloodstained scissors. They're moving off now. She can't feel anything. This is her last chance to refuse her charge.

* * *

Anupama

In an experiment, Anupama has hung squares of differently coloured fabrics along the northern fence of her garden, each labelled with a number, date and time. She's had no texts from Mohan for the last five days. In their pattern of communication, she behaves and he still treats her like his mother.

She texts Upeksha. 'Could Kanchana most kindly sell my sarees?'

Upeksha's friend might help her start her fund, she's thinking. But it'll need to be a huge amount for this solution to her barrister training.

Eventually the phone winks back, 'Don't be foolish.'

'Oh, Auntie-Uncle Moon,' she exclaims, seeing the lines behind Upeksha's lines. Upeksha doesn't know about her English game plan yet, yet the woman's already fazed. According to her sister Upeksha, it's Anupama's job to make sure that they meet at festivals and celebrations, stay bound together; to advise when things go wrong; to be hospitable and generous to Upeksha's and Jayamal's children; but never ever to need family help herself. Long ago, Anupama championed Upeksha over that bother with her boss at Victoria's Secret, the man who nonetheless became Upeksha's husband. In the older sister's eyes, that set the seal on Anupama's maternal function. Forget that even today, Anupama still mourns a mother herself.

Anupama taps out, 'I am most happy in trousers. Sometimes skirts. Sarees for a few occasions merely.'

There's a long silence, then she reads, 'Sarees flatter you the most.'

'That is nonsense, Moon, you know,' Anupama huffs.

Despite having children, Upeksha has stayed petite and trim, but over the years the childless Anupama has swollen at the base like an unpicked gourd.

All their wedded life, Asiri has also preferred Anupama in sarees. He's lavished them on her like payments for being domesticated, intelligent, well read, devout, attentive to his mother and extra-responsive in copulation – although her cooking is a write-off. She wonders now if her harpings-on about a career, her notes of websites that he'd like, the books borrowed for him from the library, the starching and ironing of his shirts, her hand on the nape of his neck at every mealtime, have been such a different payment, such a different load, to him.

Ultraviolet breaks down the chemical bonds of each swatch in the garden differently: that much, Anupama has established. She's enjoying this activity: since revealing the truth to Asiri, she's bursting with curiosity and energy.

'However,' she confides to the absent moon, 'it is still hard to say which sarees will fade the fastest. All seem unpredictable except yellow and white. I think that I shall keep only those.' She says, 'Selling all but those two sarees may return me to myself. White will suit my devotions; yellow, as you know, Moon, symbolises liberation from extremes.'

She thinks, *The monks say that liberation, the middle way, is a most supreme effort, an effort to be only. Yet before that, I have to change. I have to change to return me to myself, in order only to be. I am absolutely determined not to fade.*

Anupama walks from the garden into her bedroom, is met by the rumpled bed and blushes: having absorbed her career plan B, Asiri made love to her last night with even more ardour and imagination than usual. Afterwards she heard him in the garden, pacing, clearing his throat. Anxiety always brings on his hypochondria. They're stuck in the skin of change, half in, half out, not knowing if they'll survive this. But she's undeterred. She peels off the telltale sheet for washing, goes to the garment closet and begins to heap a rainbow of her sarees on the bed.

Suddenly, Mohan gets in touch by text, demanding. 'What have you decided?'

* * *

The object

Martine's guest is finding it hard to share the load of luggage, harder to leave with a stranger in full view, struggling up the drive and onto a bus. Dead Moon Circus on the steps, jeering among themselves, not even saying goodbye. Adults never fully understand the adolescent's sense of power imbalance: no home, car, private bank account, or space of your own, truly yours, to retreat to. Of course you cling to the things that you do own.

In the well of the bus, standing guard over the bags and fencing gear apart from the seated woman hides all shyness for now. A furtive rosary with the neon bracelet, fingering each feather and each key: *sixte, quarte, octave, septime; marche, liement, en garde.*

The tube is dope, grungy in parts, and everyone limits their contact.

The woman says in a smiling, liquid voice, 'Call me Martine.'

Her English is understandable, a relief, and she doesn't insist on yabbering, which is cool: at a guess, she's nervous too. Impossible to look at her quite yet. Standing together, gripping the pole, their arms are close. On the flesh of her hand, which is like soggy parchment that's been squeezed, freckles have spread into discolourations in a way that can't be seen on old, dark skin.

The grimy towerblocks are sick, but her flat, seven high floors up, feels stifling. The woman is explaining something about the balcony.

'Meet Sancho.' She indicates a cage in the kitchen, a green-grey lizard or something.

Cruel, to keep a creature prisoner like that. She begins to lug the bags through somewhere else. The important thing is to set up the bedroom, appropriate that space.

34 Breaking in new balls

From the guest room, drawers slide and bang.

Martine's foreign visitor is arguing, either on the iPhone or Skypeing on the iPad seen among the luggage.

'No! I'm not,' she makes out in that foreign language. 'Not interested.'

She discreetly moves away, re-passing the living room, the TV on as homely burble. In the kitchen she squeezes past the cage, opens the oven door and dances a finger off the giving top of a muffin. She takes them out, chocolate and banana, smelling hot and sweet, and lays them on the worktop in the hope her guest will try them. For ease of language, she'd better call them cakes. Her joke fund supplies, *Definition of a muffin: a drag cupcake on its day off.*

Through the darkened window she sees a child's sky drawing, a froth of clouds and pinprick stars glimmering in the light pollution of the city. The moon's not there: she misses it. She's just watched the news. Today, over the Urals, its rock pieces streaming like tracer fire, a ten-ton meteor ruptured the sound barrier, crumpling walls, shattering glass and injuring more than a thousand Russians. This same evening, Asteroid 2012 DA14 buzzed over, half a football pitch in size, only seventeen thousand miles from earth. The astronomer in her is interested; the astrologer in her, casting this weekend as a turning point, feels that the moon would have added to her sense of portent.

She calls out 'Cakes!' in the lobby, getting a grunt in response.

In her bedroom, she leaves the door less open than usual and lies down. She feels wiped out, and yet she's only just begun this. She stares up at the wardrobe where the carton of letters lies. She tries to recall her mother's messages, also in the box, but resists reaching for them. *That would be to give in to the past, plus I'll have misremembered things, miss what isn't there.* The creeper pattern on the undrawn curtains looks like a map of dark and broken tracks she's only partly taken. She never thought she'd end up here, like this.

Lying at rest, she's aware of her guest blundering to the kitchen and back, trailing behind the steamy scent of muffin.

No called-out 'Thank you.'

Shy, probably, she excuses. After all, she too is lying there frightened.

* * *

Anupama

Mohan texts Anupama again while driving his tuk-tuk. 'I said, what have you decided?' He's pointedly on a budget, texting rather than calling because he's requesting money.

In the spirit of her and Asiri's decision about Mohan's plea, Anupama texts too. 'Where have you been?'

'Change 2 new phone.' His text is abbreviations, his Sinhala sloppy. He prods her, 'The carbonator doesn't cost much.'

He can't wait, impatient for her answer, just like when he was small with his 'What present will I get? What present will I get?' or, 'What date is it today? Will Miss Martine's letter come soon?'

He pricks Anupama again. 'The bottling and distribution will need a little more outlay.' Slick phrases: Jayamal's, probably.

Jayamal is not to be listened to, in Anupama's judgement. She still blames J for giving Mohan the idea, as a boy, of illegally mining sapphires. J fancies himself as one of the elephants, leopards and bears, a big shot. Since tatta died, having been most courageous with that elephant in the paddy that, with others, went on to wreck the village, J has done anything and everything not to support the family, not to farm with senior father and the cousins up at their new home. Now Jayamal has got Mohan all fired up about selling fizzy water with a hint of guava or mango.

For J, turtle poaching was merely the teenage warm-up. Lately she's seen axes and bandsaws in his van. He smirks that he 'loves the reservations', and once offered her a Buddha carved out of ebony, origin unknown, at a family discount price.

It was J who made Mohan feel that he had to compete with him, try his hand at business. When Mohan left school at sixteen, he circled Kandy lakeside with his homemade pestles and mortars and medicine bead necklaces and coconut shell monkeys that hooked in a chain together.

'Retro ethnic', Jayamal called them.

But he didn't earn enough for a stall, or even a barrow. Then there was the job in a tourist shop. It soon emerged that written English was all that Mohan excelled in: he couldn't speak it comprehensibly, or even read it well. It should have been Mohan's teacher who was tusked by that elephant.

Then a friend of a friend loaned Mohan a tuk-tuk, and he transported an American couple around on a honeymoon tour to Galaha, all of his own devising. Luckily, they didn't talk much. Borrowing the tuk-tuk, driving it without a licence, was illegal, of course. The couple were so ecstatic with each other and blasé with their money that before they left for Houston, they funded him for a tuk-tuk of his choice.

'What's your answer?' Mohan texts, still waiting on her financial verdict. 'Cd B there in 40 mins.'

The 40 mins is a joke. With Mohan, every time count is 40 mins.

Anupama agrees. 'Come to supper.' She delays what he wants to know. 'How is yr noisy eggplant?'

The purple tuk-tuk, purple being his favourite colour, the numberplate including 40, his favourite number. Anupama lays down the phone beside a propped-up A-level textbook opened at the orbits of the earth and sun and moon, and begins assembling the ingredients for a curry.

She asks the paper moon – which is, after all, the real moon in book form – why 40? Unable to remember. 'Was it because of that

TV show he kept telling us of, long ago? *Kermit en Ali Baba en de 40 rovers*, showing off his Dutch accent? He said the show was funny, although I do not think he saw it. Or perhaps it was because of the model number of an aircraft that he liked.'

With a sudden violent memory Anupama's mouth drops open, causing her to hurl the beetroots into her bowl of water. 'Oh! He insisted also that I told Miss Martine that our village, now most sadly destroyed, was 40 kilometres from Kandy, when it was 53. Oh, how I missed it when the family left. Off the snakely road, up our dirt track, hidden by trees.' In her mind she retraces the long walk down to Raththota, onto the buses towards school. 'Yes, Auntie-Uncle,' she rehearses, 'he was most youthful then. He most definitely asked me to say 40.' She shakes her head in disbelief. 'So perhaps his was the first untruth in the letters, not any one of mine at all.'

Mohan texts back tetchily, 'I always thank U 4 the tuk-tuk.'

Anupama and Asiri paid for his tuk-tuk lessons and the bribe to get his test. His job suits him, Anupama believes. At least he's his own master, and tuk-tuk driving doesn't demand conversation, in English or any other foreign language: maps and place-names are enough to connect Mohan with his passengers, usually on a Blackberry or mobile.

'Little man,' Anupama taps out on her phone – thirty-four: she can hardly believe it sometimes – 'you are Kandy's most famous driver with our only purple tuk-tuk.'

It's an automatic reflex to soothe him. But her recent revelation is making her eyes flash now, and her mortar grinds the spices hard and fine.

'Was that yes 2 supper?' she texts him.

He lives with J and his family on the other side of Kandy, but J's wife doesn't really like him being there. Still not married, he whisks through a blur of girlfriends; she and Upeksha feed him often, sometimes wondering if their fussing has spoiled him for someone else.

'Yr deicison is?' Mohan misspells.

'I'll tell u if u come 4 supper.'

Mohan answers, 'As long as it is not yr pol sambol.'

* * *

The object

The object uses the woman's wi-fi code. It's been cool getting back in touch with everyone, despite the news at home and the row with Dietrich. The bedroom's tiny but not yellow.

The woman raps on the door. 'Food in fifteen.'

From his dog-and-llama mansion, Dietrich has asked by Skype to be 'special-more-than-friends'.

The answer was, 'I'm not, I mean... Not interested.'

Best friend Luna has a boyfriend; at Addis Hall many of Dead Moon Circus, let alone the English students, are paired up. It was scary being asked. It's because it's the unknown, the coming business of boyfriends and girlfriends.

Back home, Creepy is in disgrace. Apparently she thought that she saw BS Shit at the bus station and they told the police, and now she thinks she didn't, and the family has gone mental.

BF Luna asks on Skype, 'How goes it at this woman's?'

The honest answer is, 'Not totally crap.'

The woman calls 'Suppertime!' then can be heard announcing to her reptile, '*Necesito comida*, Sancho.' I need food.

The woman gestures to a chair in the crowding kitchen and gives the spaghetti one last stir, whacking the slatted spoon on the pot side. Luckily the gross chameleon goes still; you can still smell it though, animal and foreign.

'They said you weren't vegetarian or anything. Meatballs in tomato sauce. Is that OK?'

'Thank you.'

The woman says, 'Food is a kind of nutritional textspeak now. When you're abroad, away from home, I mean. We all understand hamburgers and pizzas and hot dogs and Chinese takeaways, don't we? Maybe it makes things easier. Less... stressful.'

She sits opposite, the table so small that their knees knock. She'll never have been pretty, and the hair is a bit mad. Not everything she says is comprehensible because now she's talking way too fast. Luckily she hasn't yet said 'you lot' or 'young people'. The glass table rises up, banging the elbow by surprise as the hand tries to lower the fork to scoop up pasta.

'You must know about my half-brother and my nieces. He's about to go to America. I've got photos. I'll show you if you like.'

It needs concentration to avoid slurping, and a moustachio of red sauce.

'There's a framed scarf in the lobby. My mother's. She loved flying.'

The verbal drone is getting annoying. Why can't people do silence?

'You do not have to talk so much. I'm not here for my English.'

That shuts her up for a minute; an ashamed feeling descends.

'My parents divorced,' the woman shares.

'Mine did not. My family is very nice.' Not a wholly honest opinion, but you have to defend your own.

'So's mine,' the woman says.

The tidal feeling comes, colour rushing up the neck.

'They want the best for me,' sticking out a sock-clad foot, noticing that there a few small holes.

The woman says, 'Most adults would say that they want the best for their children.'

Out of loyalty the guest won't mention the suffocating child protection at home, but can't help agreeing in general terms. 'My parents say many things like this. The things are rather boring and they do not think what they mean.'

'So you don't think they'd support you? If you did something they hadn't expected, for instance?' Now the woman is being nosy.

'My parents are not at trial here are they?'

The woman offers more meatballs, and spoons on yet more sauce. For a while they eat in silence, but the desire to agree won't stay in.

'Sometimes it would be nice to do something my parents would not like. I am trying to be not boring like they are, after all.' A grin can't help but spread, probably showing that chipped tooth.

The woman says, 'I doubt you're that. What did you have in mind?'

It all comes spilling out then. 'I do not want to find someone *special* and a *regular* job and a *nice* house and settle down and make children. I want to do many things. Especially to travel. Also to be an actor. The other things will come when I am ready.'

The woman swallows something, maybe an objection. 'I saw *Romeo and Juliet* recently.' She looks a bit lost, as if she doesn't know why she said that. 'My nieces both want to be performers, one a musician, the other one a dancer. Method or classical?'

An admission is needed. 'I do not know all of your words.'

'Which do you prefer, getting into a role by being yourself or by being someone else?'

So many questions. The woman can't seem to stop.

'To be or not to be,' the visitor laughs nervously.

'To be or to do, to create, to change yourself, I suppose I'm asking.'

The visitor frowns, throwing back a can of Coke. 'Why are you doing this?'

The woman drains her wine, returns her glass to the table. 'Did you know that some of what you say to me sounds rude?'

Powerlessness starts boiling up: not at her necessarily. 'Why do you want to look after me? Why are you doing that?'

'Sometimes you feel you have to give something, do something.'

'I am not for charity.'

'Good, because I'm not a charity. Anyway, no giving is one-way. For example, conversation is giving on both sides. And you sound rude.'

The guest clatters down the fork and shrieks the chair backwards and slides off in stockinged feet on the linoed floor, skirting the pathetic creature's cage, out of the tiny kitchen and away. In embarrassment for the usual anger and frustration, more than anything.

35 Following through

(Following through: Bowler's actions to stabilise the body after the ball has been released)

Friday 15–Saturday 16 February 2013

Martine stands in the kitchen for a moment. She thinks, *Well that was a triumph. And I was going to be so laid-back.* Eventually she washes up. Unopened ice cream goes back in the fridge.

Now there are bathroom sounds, water sluicing and tooth-brushing, indications of getting ready for bed. She'd hoped to use humour and hasn't. *Tomorrow, maybe,* she thinks: tonight she just feels spent. She feeds Sancho more crickets, runs herself a glass of water, switches off the TV, extinguishes lights behind her.

No Sri Lankan dream arrives, of course: not even the start.

Later, in bed, she gasps, swimming back into consciousness. A hollow echo from the bathroom, something like a growl. She studies her watch. It's 06:01 and dark, but then, she's drawn the curtains, she remembers. *No more Mum,* she also remembers with a lurch, as she always does first thing.

An echoing cough from the bathroom, a sharp grunt, then a whoosh into porcelain, an expulsion. The noise propels Martine out of bed. She goes dizzy, sits on the edge. She pushes through golf clubs and suitcases. According to the mirror, her fringe is still as clueless for direction. She staggers towards the bathroom, heart cantering, thinking, *That's my food being thrown back at me.*

Bending to the door she gabbles, 'What can I do?'

Her guest goes silent. She can normally deal with attitude – she's encountered plenty in her line of work – but last night she found it hard. *Maybe I started it,* she thinks. *Giving off some signal about my hang-ups as a host.*

She's reminded, *A pile of vomit walks into the worst restaurant in town and says, 'This is the place I get most sentimental about.'*

'Hello?' she asks, staring down at her coarse fingers pressing the door.

The voice is gruff. 'It's nothing important. I don't want a bother.'

'Nothing important': the phrase has personal significance, she can't locate where from.

Her charge mumbles, 'Your country has mad cows.'

Anxious about the meatballs, then. *Not letting on till now might be a sign of consideration for my feelings,* she notes, *which would be something.*

'The only mad cow around here is me,' she replies. She adds, 'That was years ago.'

Into the echo chamber of the toilet, the visitor begins gagging again. Martine has no idea if this is more than foreigner's paranoia: food poisoning, some real illness, eating disorder? Abruptly she thinks, *I'm responsible for this sixteen-year-old.*

She asks, 'What would you like me to do?'

Loud spitting, but no answer.

Martine ponders the gender of the creature behind the door. *With a female, at least in theory you can rush in and hold the brow and stroke the spasming back and make soothing noises. With a male, on the other hand, you can't do any such thing.* She wonders if that's fair.

'Can I come in?' she calls.

No answer.

'What can I do?'

'F... Go away, to be honest.'

'To be honest': again the phrase triggers something personal, something past.

Martine shakes the sensation off. She springs up, retrieving a notepad and pen from her bedroom, and hurries back to the bathroom. *You gabbled at supper,* she tells herself. *Just listen,* she tells herself; *wait.* She writes a question mark and an exclamation mark on the top sheet of the notepad, tears it off and slides it under the door.

After twenty-five thudding heartbeats the note peeps up at

her turned over, with a message in her own eyeliner. 'I AM NOT A CHILD.'

From beyond the door, in the stink of sick, Martine smells fear. *I'm not an adult either*, she silently admits. She wishes this insight would stay with her, after all it's ludicrously simple, and she's had it many times before. *The struggle isn't learning to be a parent, or resisting being parented: for everyone, it's the pressure of growing up. We're all still growing up.*

The gagging loses conviction. A piece of toilet paper appears, on it a crude drawing, a cow on its hind legs with a plate of meatballs in its hoof and arrows of dizziness circling its head. *No artist then*, she thinks; then, *Playfulness equals progress*, she can hope.

She posts back a further message: 'Tell me what you want.'

A pause, then another sketch slides out, possibly a jugful of iced water.

She hurries off, fetching a jug, a glass, two crackers on a plate, a dampened cloth and a box of tissues. She lays them on the carpet. There's a sniff and rustling, sounds of gathering together.

'I'll leave the things just here.'

She gropes along the unlit lobby culminating in the small cube of her bedroom. She finds herself by her four-poster, the metal columns white and cold. She pushes past the golf clubs and crawls under the duvet.

* * *

Asiri is out at work. While the beetroot curry is bubbling, Anupama studies. It's only a day since Asiri finally got the message about their future, but he's already vanished his cuckoo clocks from the kitchen, as if they're a reminder that their time together may be fleeting. At last she can spread her textbooks far and wide on the table.

She keeps the orbit chapter open for the illusion of the absent moon's support, even though she finds the sciences A level relatively easy. It's the English that she's now struggling with. She crosses out the English word 'faeces'. In English, 'flowers' is a totally different word. Then she huffs to a standstill.

She tells the earth-moon diagram, 'I cannot concentrate now I have remembered Mohan's lie to Miss Martine about the distance of our old village.'

She breathes in and out, long and deep, focusing on the little stone Buddha on the unmoonlit windowsill.

She tells Asiri by text, 'Mohan is coming about his fizzy drinks plan.'

Asiri replies at once, 'Please B firm. What will U say?'

'Trust me,' Anupama answers.

She picks up her phone and rings Mohan, this time to talk.

'What?' he asks. She can hear the trapped wasp buzz of the Bajaj, and chattering Japanese passengers. 'Are you going to tell me your answer?'

'You know how you most like the number 40?'

Mohan sniggers. 'It wouldn't be funny if that was how much you and Asiri...'

'You told me to write to Miss Martine that we lived 40 kilometres from Kandy.'

'Did I? When? What's *she* got to do with anything?'

Anupama sees that he doesn't recall, and understands, abruptly, that a scolding wouldn't mean anything to him. As for his tone about Miss Martine: she sucks her cheeks.

She recounts grimly to the printed moon, 'You will remember that only about a year ago, there was much for my album of facts. We heard that Miss Martine would visit. I had written her all those letters long ago, forming a bond she probably did not know. Now I could meet her. I had my hair cut, and Upeksha's friend taught me how to improve my makeup. I bought a skirt and blouse with a paisley design. I waited for her, longing to talk about England and injustice, and how we had both changed. We would have a stimulating conversation, even though I suppose I would have had to confess about my part in the letters.'

'Hello? Hello?' Mohan's voice fires off over the background traffic. 'Are you telling me something or not?'

For once, Anupama ignores him. 'Mohan had a plan to hang a balloon over the gate at J's, where he is living, and take Miss Martine to Pizza Hut. I wanted to float water lilies in bowls outside this house, welcoming her here, but never mind: at least he said I could meet her. Then her email came explaining that she had been and gone, apologising most graciously.'

At last Anupama turns to the phone and Mohan. 'Last year, when Miss Martine did not come, what did you mean in your email to her saying "Perhaps another time? Crocodile" or something? You asked the translator to say it in English.' The bitterness of lemons sours her voice. 'You said it was funny. On your phone you showed me.'

She remembers, 'Handanandāmāmā, that email upset me utterly for Miss Martine, and of course for myself, but also because Mohan was concealing how he felt. That she did not come could have disappointed him utterly, it might not have mattered to him, or something in between. I could not tell; he was not going to tell me.'

'Can't hear you. Dropping these passengers off,' Mohan shouts. 'Give me 40 – um, ten mins.'

And the call is at an end.

'First he makes me lie in the letters, my very first lie of all,' Anupama wags the dead þhone at the 2D moon, 'then, over the years, he withdraws from me.'

There's a sizzling and a burning smell from the curry. She leaps and crosses the kitchen, flapping a towel at the smoke. The cause of her real distress will be here soon.

* * *

The object

The nausea's gone in the morning, a relief. The light through the little apartment window is grey, like the pearly tiles in the woman's bathroom, where hopefully – how embarrassing – the sour reek may have faded. There's the sound of the woman showering.

On with underwear, and today, as a top layer, the bright green should be OK. It's cool, having this peaceful time. A smoke or two, some reading, until a plastic object on the ceiling begins a *Psycho* shriek, and the woman's tapping on the door and shouting. Swinging it wide, it hits the woman's knuckles, and there she is gawping in, wearing black leggings and a tunic appliquéd with circles of black and white.

'For crying out loud.' She pushes into the green sanctuary.

'Who is crying?' the object asks. Her English is bewildering.

Cigarette smoke is rolling out between them. They blink at each other. The woman's outfit looks as if she's given up pretending something: as if, unlike yesterday's, it says who she really is.

A clasp of the elbow, warm and dry, then the woman pounces on the badminton racket, jabbing its handle at the off spot on the ceiling. 'I asked you to smoke on the balcony!'

'You said something different!'

They shout over the alarm.

'I said if you had to smoke, I'd rather you smoked on the balcony!'

Righteous indignation wells up. 'Yes. Now you are perfectly honest! Does that not mean I can also smoke in here?'

The woman looks thrown. 'I see. My grammar foxed you!' She snatches away the latest cigarette and grinds it out on the lip of the water jug.

It's a swift action for the object to unsheath the fencing foil and poke it at the device, words rising unexpectedly. 'You don't like me. You stay away from me too much.'

'So do you!' the woman shouts.

She grabs the ruler on the desk, trying to halt the noise with that.

'You are like an animal in a hole!' The guest glances at her clothes. 'Black and white!'

'A badger!' cries the woman.

'A batcher?'

The woman hurries out and returns with a golf club, but by then the squeals have stopped.

They look at each other in the quiet.

'I like this...' The object has changed the subject to the woman's tunic, with its circles of black and white.

'And this is very... unusual,' the woman reciprocates, her fingers hovering proud of the slippery green nylon then whisking round to tuck in the label, which must be sticking up at the back.

'Thank you.' The object accepts the compliment happily.

There's a stillness, then the woman tries an *en garde* pose with the golf club.

'Your behind foot should be at right-angles to the front one. Go down more. Like this.' Hips in parallel beside her give an easy demonstration with the foil.

It's a laugh to see her knees and *biceps femoris* strain, trying to squat more deeply. She lunges, but the tip of the club shaft falls away from her, striking the ashtray of folded paper off the bedside table, spraying ash and stubs on the carpet.

'Whoops.' She drops the club.

They bend and scoop up the mess with the makeshift ashtray.

When the woman straightens, now the smoke is clearing, you can see her glancing round, noticing how organised, reorganised, the room is. Along the back of the desk, your row of graphic novels. iPad and iPhone are squared up beside a line of your homework pages, pens and a protractor. Her pot of bright blue hyacinths looked nicer off the narrow windowsill and on the bedside table beside the travel clock and framed family photo, scenting the room with early spring despite the smoke. The bed's neatly made, of course, with drying towels and your newly washed underwear perfectly folded over the rail in front of the heater. The emptied luggage is flattened, its contents stowed. Even the makeshift ashtray seems to surprise her.

'I have told you. I am grown up.'

The woman cocks her head at the words, mussing her hair. She picks up the golf club, her guest re-sheaths the foil.

'Breakfast?' the woman asks.

36 Women's cricket

'One animal is trying to get in and one is trying to get out,' the sixteen-year-old points out to Martine, waving towards Sancho's barricaded stare and a battering sound from the balcony.

Martine has loaded her few kitchen surfaces with juices, fruit, ham, cheeses, salami, croissants, breads, jams, cereals. There are eggs, bacon, tomatoes and mushrooms on standby near the hob. She's run out of places to put things, gone a bit over the top.

'Have you got any more to wash?' she asks.

The motherliness of her own question strikes her pleasingly as she leans sideways, looking through the window to see what her guest was waving at. A pigeon's scrabbling, claw caught in the netting of the balcony. Its beak opens without sound. Feathers fly. Over the years, bird droppings have puttied feather skeletons to the wires. She fumbles, unlocking the balcony door.

'It isn't caught. When it sees you it will go free!' shouts her visitor.

The door squeaks, and sure enough the pigeon takes off, panicking.

The foreign guest observes, grinning, 'We're not animals hiding in our nests at the moment. The batcher and the...' Martine watches the mental run-through of English beast names. 'Lizard.' The adolescent torso is swathed in bright green nylon.

'Badger,' corrects Martine. 'But badgers live in setts. And lizards live in holes, on the whole.'

'Is that funny?'

Martine thinks, crestfallen, *Humour doesn't always translate.* Still, she nearly adds, 'And you've still got your holey sock on.'

The foreign creature runs eyes over the breakfast choices. 'I want to eat in that other room.'

Martine has decided that the rudeness is mostly bluster. 'Sure.'

'What's English for where all animals must live? And what they must eat.'

Loading two trays, Martine offers, 'Cage. Pen. Habitat? Diet?'

Smoke-brown fingers run along Sancho's bars, a clangy musical scale. 'You shouldn't keep him. It's not fair to an animal's nature.'

'I know that now,' Martine says, handing over a tray.

'You know everything,' grumbles her visitor.

Martine, tray in hand, backs against the door of the living room, pushing it open with the sole of her Ugg boot.

'You can sew my sock,' the voice behind her says, following her with a musty scent, reminiscent of old cupboard spices. 'My Mum tells me always to save money.'

'I can't sew.' Martine suddenly regrets that her mother never taught her. 'Can't you?'

'So,' says the visitor, 'you don't know everything.'

They pick at their breakfast, upright on the rigid tubular chairs.

'What's this, on the wall?'

'My more everyday face.' It's the *thovil* mask Martine once bought, with its painted cobras.

Martine's ward doesn't smile, just covertly tongues out the salami. And the collection of keys and feathers is still dangling from that wrist. Martine wonders if they have significance. Close-set eyes point at the TV, at Martine and back again, but Martine doesn't flick it on. They continue wandering among the batik hangings and carved mirrors. Although Martine returned with all those artefacts last spring, it's taken her a whole long year to hang them.

'You've travelled far. I also want to.'

'You said. Although you might find…' Martine stops herself from lecturing. 'Where would you like to go later? Shopping? A movie? Do something sporty? Swimming?'

'You have plans for us?'

Martine can hear resistance.

'You don't want to go out,' she says, unable to hide her disappointment.

'This is our nest.'

'We should get some air. I know I need some.'

'There are many things here.' A dark arm sweeps round taking in the wall coverings, the furniture, the TV, Martine's own laptop in the corner. 'I want to stay.'

Martine imagines silence rearing up at them through all her surface bustle. She thinks, *What will we talk about?* She tells herself, *It's only like a one-to-one with a student.*

The landline rings.

'Two weeks and counting.' Jonas mentions America, Martine knows, because he can't think how to ask about Martine's visitor.

'Bad timing. Having breakfast,' she responds.

'Guy or gal?'

'Oh, Jonas.' She's told him the answer to this one: she can't believe he's forgotten. 'Could you ring later?'

She restores the phone to its stand. There's not much later left. For the umpteenth time she rehearses, *When Dad died, Jonas didn't go to the States; so why leave now?*

After they've cleared away, 'Let's game,' Martine's visitor suggests, descending cross-legged in one smooth movement onto the floor cushions.

'No equipment,' says Martine, lowering herself stiffly alongside.

Her guest proposes an anime called *Sailor Moon*. 'I get it on my iPad.'

Martine counters boldly, 'Or we could talk to each other.'

She gazes at the teenager who has recently uttered phrases – 'perfectly honest', 'nothing important', 'I am grown up' – that still resonate from somewhere.

'The television is there. We can see a film.'

'Let's talk,' Martine persists.

'Actors learn from films and stories. They help me.'

Martine stays adamant before the coffee-bean eyes under the scowling eyebrows, paler palms upturned in the lap, lost without the normal diversions, iPad, earphones, anything.

'I sometimes think life is all stories. I could tell you one.' She considers how much. 'About the longest journey.'

The visitor's dry lips purse in a possible sign of interest, but then Martine remembers, *You can't tell anyone anything: people have to make their own mistakes*, and knows that there's no point in telling her whole Sri Lankan tale.

She can only bring herself to say, 'A woman knew... let's say a foreigner. They lost touch. A lot later, she was offered a meeting with... another kind of foreigner. But she didn't know if she could do it, go through all that travelling again.'

'Where must she travel to?'

'Addis Hall.' An unwilling laugh explodes from her guest, exposing that chipped tooth. 'You'd stayed with another guardian the holiday before, but she'd got a family crisis. You didn't look happy to see me.'

'Your story is a bit crap,' the guest says, and Martine can't help grinning. 'Why was that your longest journey? It wasn't far.'

'Because the journey to my first foreigner led to you.'

'It's not a very straight way.'

'That's true,' agrees Martine.

* * *

Anupama

It's the day after burning the beetroot curry – although that could be many days. Anupama is washing up only now, her hands in bubbles. She and Asiri are in a hectic limbo. He came in late last night and ploughed her deeply once more.

'What did you tell your brother, and what did he say?' he says, chin on her shoulder, asking yet again about Mohan's madcap project.

He's begun to micro-manage her, clenching against uncertainty, and Anupama wails mutely, 'Auntie-Uncle, I want to reassure him about the future, but I cannot.'

'I said, "I am sorry, little man,"' she repeats, 'and he gave a shrug and laughed that my food was horrible as usual.'

Asiri checks, 'And that was all?'

'No, Auntie-Uncle, that was not all,' Anupama laments silently, staring at her arms deep in bubbles. 'Although, yes, I have caused the bubbles of Mohan's fizzy water to disappear. However,' she sighs, 'it was Miss Martine who taught me that evaporation is one of the changes when surface tension breaks. Even in scientific terms, evaporation is the acquisition of a new state merely, so I suppose the inspiration of bottled water may remain with Mohan, in fantasy or somewhere.'

The bubble image holds her. Yesterday at the top of the escalator in the KCC, she bought a new charger for her mobile, then passed a display of photographs in the nearby glass-walled gallery. Portraits of people eyeing bubbles, apparently of mercury. The people were in white coats.

The show looked scientific, so she stopped and read the explanation printed large at the entrance. 'People are spheres floating in the air. The air is a mirrored surface. We reflect each other and our world. The Buddhist life, like the photographer's, is self-observation and connection.'

The photos aimed to be both scientific and spiritual, molecules but meditation.

'They made me most irritated,' she tells the moon in her head.

Asiri runs a knuckle up her spine from the base, making her tingle. She thinks, *Life is all disruption and agitation, and science the study of that agitation. Buddhism may be its tolerance, but the photos seemed absolutely to deny any disturbance, made everything look too peaceful. I waited to dispute with the woman photographer, but an admiring group surrounded her, so I gave up.*

Last night she had it out with Mohan about the 40 kilometres, and he remembered nothing. This made her most annoyed. So then she tackled him again about his offhand way in his email to Miss Martine last spring – his offhand way with her, his sister, also, in sharing nothing of his feelings about the Englishwoman's failure to appear. He listened to her accusations but just looked blank. Then she told him that she might have to go to England.

All he said was, 'Lucky you,' and after a pause, 'Actually, I've got a mate who could do with a contact there. He can't get a visa,' and winked, as if he was J.

So she said most angrily, 'If I go, I might find Miss Martine,' and he looked at her without expression and said, 'My question is why.'

Agitation on her side, tolerance – or indifference – on Mohan's.

'So no,' she confides to the moon but not Asiri, 'that was not all.'

'The worst is, I knew that Mohan was right,' Anupama concludes to her lunar confidante. Asiri is snaking an arm about her waist, and she stiffens. 'Miss Martine would not be interested in me. A lot of time has passed since we wrote the letters.' She shakes her head, examining a charred saucepan. 'Anyway, my anger suddenly left me, because, after all, it was I who agreed to write Mohan's lie of 40 kilometres. Also our separateness must have started partly because of my deceit in the letters. Furthermore, if I can separate from Asiri, I cannot complain that Mohan separates something of himself from me.' Asiri's muscular arm leaves her and slides past her, picking up plates for drying. She smiles sadly to herself. 'I have always found it hard to allow Mohan the right to self-determination, I suppose. Good barristers must lie as well as tell the truth, so the work should suit me, a master of self-deception and lies.'

The doorbell jangles.

'It is very early,' she exclaims to Asiri.

She leaves the kitchen and walks to the door on to the street. A yellow tuk-tuk is standing there, and leaning on it two friends of Mohan's, one of them chewing betel.

He grins with purple teeth, 'Is Mohan here?'

Mohan's more popular than his brother, despite J's talk of big boys' play with the elephants, leopards and bears.

Anupama wipes her hands on her apron. 'The last time I saw him was last night, very sorry.'

They chat for a while, then she re-enters the house under the star windchimes that revolve slowly in the heat over the door.

The tin oval among the tin stars could be the moon, at a pinch; it follows her mind's eye, remembering. 'Little man was going down the step and towards his tuk-tuk. Although he is quite tall, his strutting walk reminded me of when he was younger, of how, despite that strut, he used to turn round and look at me most wistfully.' She reflects, 'It is most strange how, from the back, you can see some aspect of someone from long ago, yet nothing of them now.'

* * *

Kern

The woman's half-brother – Jonas, was it? – is on the phone again.

'Yes, Moroccan,' the woman – Martine – says, rolling her eyes conspiratorially at Kern. They come to rest on her long green nylon dress, the tabard top frilled at the edges. 'Moroccan family. Lives in Düsseldorf.'

The woman's fist does a cranking-handle gesture.

Kern feeds her information mock-loudly, for the half-brother's benefit. 'My father is a mining executive, my mother is a nurse. I have two sisters and,' she adds smoothly, 'a brother. We are all very clever.'

The woman, Martine, grins and nods. 'Yep. He's got that.' She playacts stupid, angling the mouthpiece. 'Name, dear?'

'Kern!'

Martine holds the phone away so Kern can register the response.

Kern hears sounds of incomprehension and volunteers, raising her chin, 'It means "seed".'

Martine repeats, 'She's telling you it means "seed".'

'In Germany it's a name more for the boys,' Kern says.

The half-brother hears that, and says something back.

The gaze of the woman, this Martine, scuttles to the ceiling. 'Well, Guardians' gender rules is gender rules. But you did know...'

The man says something, an apology?

'Never mind,' says Martine.

While he says more, Kern scans the interesting room again, noticing something under the corner of the TV.

Martine replies, 'You know me so well.' The next words are obscure. 'Your life is up to you...' She pauses. 'I don't.' She adds softly, 'No, that's fine. I'll miss you, but I'll be fine.' Kern tilts her head. Martine is thinking, studying Kern carefully. She grins at Kern. 'I must go.'

At the call end Kern gets up, holding the digital print-outs she's just found. 'What are these?'

'Pictures of my Mum's, in store for now; mostly prints, a few paintings. I'm deciding how to sell them.'

Martine takes and flicks through the documents, looking dazed.

Knowing that the half-brother is leaving soon, Kern risks an intuition. 'It sounds like you are free of him but not happy about it.' She suddenly wants to help. 'Last night I told a boy I have met at school, well, no, friends is enough. He did not like it, but...' She pronounces, 'I think it is good not to need anyone,' surprised to be sharing that much.

Martine goes quiet. 'Need,' she stresses, repeating. Kern

watches her resurface from a thought, then the woman asks, 'Where do *you* think the pictures should go? Also there are framed photos, lots, of the family. And a box of ornaments and stuff.'

Kern looks round. 'Have not so many things.'

Martine flinches. 'I tried that back last spring.'

Kern is heaving chairs, enjoying it. 'This is a nice old chair. Put it by the window. It will have the light. Take away the chairs with metal. They are hard.'

Martine says, 'Louis the 14th.'

Kern mentally translates. 'Not really?'

'I bought them from a man called Louis on the 14th.'

Kern thinks this is unlikely.

She studies the floor cushions. 'These are for young people, not you. Have just two comfortable chairs here, for you and someone, or two friends.'

She arranges everything like a stage set, the actor in her coming out.

Martine reels off meaningless names: 'Claire, Bex, Leanne… Ali, when she's in town… Bernard, Fleur… Marks 1 and 2… Matthias. Pippi and Gretel. I suppose you're right,' she says. She murmurs something about 'an ever more female balance.' She sighs, helping to stack the tubular chairs in the lobby. Of the banned cushions, covered in Asian fabrics, she suggests, 'You could take some back to school.'

Kern thinks this unwise, if not forbidden, but continues, 'No one can look in, except when they are visitors on the balcony. You don't need curtains. Take them off for the light and space. The views will be clearer.'

Martine smiles a complaint. 'Who's in charge here?' Eventually she concedes, 'Apart from my jungle curtains in the bedroom.'

Suddenly she takes against the batiks, and the serpent mask too. They work in silence, stripping the walls. Then, pressing against the window, they stare out at the balcony.

'The wiring fence is like a prison,' Kern says. 'And it doesn't stop the birds. If you take it off, you could put a chair outside. There will be sun on you.'

'And moon,' Martine the woman says, oddly.

Kern says, 'Or grow something.'

Martine mumbles, 'Potatoes in a trough, maybe, or herbs.' For no reason, she adds, 'Not ferns and mosses.'

She begins to flurry about. 'I've always wanted to do this.' She grabs a marker from a pot on the TV table and, holding the digital print of a seascape up to the scuffed wall, pens a crude pair of curtains round it. 'Graffiti,' she smiles.

She holds it there with the heels of her hands, studies it close up. Kern looks at it too. In the picture the moon shimmers. Is that a walker on the beach?

'I think I like it,' says Martine.

Kern finds Sellotape, more pens.

She pronounces, 'Pictures are good in groups,' but Martine is adamant. 'I like them spaced. Like windows on a train, look. Or portholes.'

They're nearly all landscapes. Martine selects the ones she likes.

They tape the pages to the walls, let them hang. Houses clustered on a hill. An archway onto a crowded street. A busy square seen from a balcony. Riders on horseback trying to cross a river in spate. Kern feels something developing with Martine as they scribble shutters and curtains with their tongue tips in their cheeks.

Afterwards, they wash their felt-tipped hands in the kitchen.

Kern asks, 'A garage sale isn't for garages?'

Martine grins, her soapy fingers fumbling for the tap. Kern sees that she looks better when she smiles.

The girl says, 'I saw a poster in the lift. A garage sale is here tomorrow.'

37 Match fixing

In bed that night, Martine drops like a stone into the old Sri Lankan dream, and it continues where it usually stops.

Lakshman re-passes Martine at the Queen's Hotel, retaking his seat. Soon he rises again, calling from the doorway for a waiter. But that mustn't distract Martine from the dream, from her position at the hotel window. She stares down at the crowded, glittering street, the fizzing smoke, the trooping performers, especially the drummers, still glancing at the photos in her hand.

Someone calls out from the crowd, 'Jayamal!'

A drummer with a drooping lip whips up his head. He nods and grins and, still beating, strays from his path towards the voice, starting an animated conversation in Sinhala.

Martine thinks her heart has stopped, whether in her dream or outside it. She grips the hotel balcony rail. Her eyes rake the throng below. Several men and boys are shouting to the youth called Jayamal; his responses, in a gruff voice, boomerang back. Jayamal, Mohan's brother. Mohan's there among the boys, she's now convinced. *But where?* she thinks. *But where?*

She searches the heads, windfalls thick over grass, mostly in shade. The moon isn't sick and pale, as Shakespeare's *Romeo and Juliet* would have it. Close to the boys who shouted, almost under the shadow of the balcony, it spills light onto an upturned face. The face stares at her. The widow's peak is prominent, framing the features, the slant eyebrows are filled out and nearly meet. The eyes are big and glistening, reflections in a raindrop. For a fraction of a second she's torn between calling 'Jayamal!', the one she's certain of, and mouthing 'Mohan!', the one she really hopes for, then a hand from beneath the overhang reaches out to the second face, the special face, and without warning, it's no longer there.

'Did you see someone?' Jonas asks, at once on high alert in the window.

'It's the Gajanayake Nilame now, of course,' sniffs Vijitha's lately unmasked wife without turning, without sensing anything different about Martine.

Martine sits back on her specially placed chair. She hunches, and her head drops into her hands.

'Fuck,' she says. 'Fuck fuck.'

She presses her temples. Her friends are on their feet now, flocking round her.

She pushes up through them babbling, 'He's downstairs. I've got to get downstairs.'

Arms grab her, pull her back. Adrenalin surges inside her. She struggles.

'Wait a minute,' Gerald says, 'and have a drink.'

'I think a drink is coming,' Lakshman says.

A waiter shows her a tray. She pushes it away. The men still have her by the arms. They're smiling. Everyone's smiling except Jonas, who's beside her.

'Get off of her,' he says.

Lakshman is speaking to Martine. 'This is one drink you may want.'

Glances pass between him and Gerald. Somehow he makes her take a seat at the table. She's aware that all at once, in the room, there are men in *thuppottiya* skirts, turbaned, their oiled chests shining. One's a drummer; two are. The waiter takes a tall glass from the tray. It wavers in her eyeline, smeary at the rim and bubbling with tonic, packed with lime. Fingers hold it. The other hand arrives and cups it too, as if it's a flower and she's supposed to admire it. The glass descends.

The waiter isn't in a waiter's jacket; instead dark, naked cabled arms rise above her. In the left forearm, a small bone twitches. She follows this to a vein, then the vein up to the face. The face, in the street glossed over by moonshine, she now sees to be acned around the nose and mouth. He's almost, if not quite, as she imagined. She blames the moon for any difference, for misleading her a bit too far into poetry. He's wearing a T-shirt, the T-shirt printed with a shield. She thinks, *The boy looks terrified.*

She says '*Ayubowan*', unsure if the sound comes out.

'Dear hello. Madam Lady. Martine Haslett,' stumbles Mohan in poor English, his voice bell-like.

Within the shield there's a lion brandishing a sword, the national cricket crest. The T-shirt's brilliant white. *This isn't right,* she dreams. *This isn't right. Mohan should be as fluent speaking English as on the page, shouldn't be saying 'Dear hello' and 'Madam Lady' and 'Martine Haslett' but 'I'm glad you have come at last, I always knew you'd come,' something articulate.* He's meant to be her counterpart, her best opposite.

She wakes up. She sees the dream is solved, but not resolved.

Head on the pillow, she has a sudden memory. When her mother first got her to meet Jonas, she walked into that cluttered Harrow front room and found two men sitting. A compact, athletic-looking, burnished young man rose, laughing and talking brilliantly. Despite having seen photos, something in her wanted her half-brother to be him, not the untidy, twitching large stranger who eventually mustered a faint 'Hi.' Her choice turned out to be some African-American neighbour, invited in to help put Jonas at ease.

She feels hollow. She expects corny jokes but none come. In the dream, she sees, she's always thirsted for water but never eaten. Somehow she knows that the dream will never return. And that even that wasn't perfect. She hopes nonetheless that its resolution, which has come nearest to her rugged side, will be archived deep inside her now that she knows it, just as her mother courses through her, cool and clear. Alongside of course must run the other ending, the real one, the journey to Sri Lanka, unfulfilled. She sees she'll always have to ride the cusp between them.

* * *

Sunday 16 February 2013

Whenever Martine sits on a train, she remembers that it's not just the landscape moving, that she's not motionless either, though it's an illusion others succumb to. Whenever she sees the moon, seemingly immobile, she never forgets that it's turning. She's a scientist. She's always felt the world revolving, pushed with it and against it.

All that urgency, all that resistance, she now feels must stop. This morning, she sees the usefulness of the moon's invisibility the last few nights. Maybe it's a message that it's her new phase too: her future's up to her.

The girl Kern is in her bedroom, singing more and more wildly to some foreign song, by now nearly unbothered, so it seems, whether Martine hears her. Martine raises the water jet to Sancho. *Maybe,* she thinks, *Kern's foreignness is the answer. Maybe all I want is the exotic, some kind of opposition.* She has a flashback to Kern's bedroom: among the lineup of iPad and iPhone and homework pages on the desk, an essay headed 'Communication and Culture: Otherness module'. *My preoccupation with maleness,* she thinks, *condensed and packaged into a module.*

She thinks of Kern, that she's quite a character, wonders now what her fuss was all about before the girl came.

She makes a clear decision. *Today we'll leave Sancho in his cage to go to the garage sale. We'll reach the lock-ups near the Towers and beg the end of a trestle table and try to punt Mum's knickknacks, the golf clubs, the unwanted chairs, that boxful of Mum's thefts. I'll smile at Kern and watch her, and a few estate boys will circle heedlessly round us. I might pocket a pair of goggles or a Hawkeye model or a compass or something in exchange for Mum's hideous Woman's Calling figurine, by sleight of hand, without money being exchanged, without Kern noticing. An illicit trade. An unspoken act, in memory of Mum.*

Acknowledgements

To Laurie Akehurst, London Transport Museum; Rohanna Burrow, Events Executive, the KiaOval; Jane Bidder (Sophie King and Janey Fraser); Rebecca Cotterell (photograph of hand holding photograph, cover); Chitrupa de Fonseka of the Garden Guest House, Colombo; Edward de Mel, Deputy Residential Project Manager (Agriculture) for the Mahaweli Authority; Jody Day, founder of Gateway Women; Angela Dowman, retired Administrator from the Institute of Developing Studies, University of Sussex; Buddhini Ekanayake of Watermelon Creatives, Colombo; Rosie Eva (moon image, cover); Simon Ffrench; Lizbeth Gale and Tracy Wells, Herbarium, Library, Art and Archives Directorate, Royal Botanic Gardens, Kew; Lakshman Gallage, owner-Manager, the Imperial Hotel, Stroud; Anura Ilangasinghe, Foreign Media Coordinator and Network Officer, Media Bureau, Kandy; Hilary Johnson, literary consultant; Dan Lewis of Five-Fifty (cover imagery); Clare McKeown-Davies; Nalin Munasinghe of the FAO IPM project, Plant Protection Service, Peradeniya, Kandy; Nuno Orsi; Prabash Ranasinghe, the Imperial Hotel, Stroud; Asiri Samaraweera, National Guide with the Sri Lankan Tourism Bureau; Hector Senerath, retired National Expert of the FAO Programme for Community IPM in Asia, Plant Protection Service, Peradeniya, Kandy; Vijitha and Indrani Seneviratne; the staff of the Serene Garden Hotel, Kandy; Andrew Stevenson; Senani Weligamage, Research Officer for the IPM Vegetable Programme, Plant Protection Service, Peradeniya, Kandy; Denushka Milan Sameera Wederalalage (boy of the photograph, cover); and U.I.B. Wijesuriya, Chief Official in Charge of the Elephants of the Pattini Temple, Kandy: for your support, information and help, *bohoma stuthiyi*, a Sri Lankan tankful of thanks to you all.

At Roundfire we publish great stories. We lean towards the spiritual and thought-provoking. But whether it's literary or popular, a gentle tale or a pulsating thriller, the connecting theme in all Roundfire fiction titles is that once you pick them up you won't want to put them down.